COILS

What Reviewers Say About
Barbara Ann Wright's Work

The Pyradisté Adventures

"…a healthy dose of a very creative, yet believable, world into which the reader will step to find enjoyment and heart-thumping action. It's a fiendishly delightful tale."—*Lamda Literary*

"Barbara Ann Wright is a master when it comes to crafting a solid and entertaining fantasy novel. …The world of lesbian literature has a small handful of high-quality fantasy authors, and Barbara Ann Wright is well on her way to joining the likes of Jane Fletcher, Cate Culpepper, and Andi Marquette. …Lovers of the fantasy and futuristic genre will likely adore this novel, and adventurous romance fans should find plenty to sink their teeth into."—*The Rainbow Reader*

"*The Pyramid Waltz* has had me smiling for three days. …I also haven't actually read…a world that is entirely unfazed by homosexuality or female power before. I think I love it. I'm just delighted this book exists. …If you enjoyed *The Pyramid Waltz*, *For Want of a Fiend* is the perfect next step…you'd be embarking on a joyous, funny, sweet and madcap ride around very dark things lovingly told, with characters who will stay with you for months after."—*The Lesbrary*

"This book will keep you turning the page to find out the answers. …Fans of the fantasy genre will really enjoy this installment of the story. We can't wait for the next book."—*Curve Magazine*

Thrall: Beyond Gold and Glory

"…incidents and betrayals run rampant in this world, and Wright's style successfully kept me on my toes, navigating the shifting alliances… [Thrall] is a story of finding one's path where you would least expect it. It is full of bloodthirsty battles and witty repartee… which gave it a nice balanced focus…This was the first Barbara Ann Wright novel I've read, and I doubt it will be the last. Her dialogue was concise and natural, and she built a fantastical world that I easily imagined from one scene to the next. Lovers of Vikings, monsters and magic won't be disappointed by this one."—*Curve Magazine*

"The characters were likable, the issues complex, and the battles were exciting. I really enjoyed this book and I highly recommend it."—*All Our Worlds*

By the Author

The Pyradisté Adventures

The Pyramid Waltz

For Want of a Fiend

A Kingdom Lost

The Fiend Queen

Thrall: Beyond Gold and Glory

Paladins of the Storm Lord

Coils

COILS

by
Barbara Ann Wright

2016

COILS

ISBN 13: 978-1-62639-598-5

This Trade Paperback Original Is Published By
Bold Strokes Books, Inc.
P.O. Box 249
Valley Falls, NY 12185

First Edition: September 2016

Credits
Editor: Cindy Cresap
Production Design: Susan Ramundo
Cover Design By Sheri (graphicartist2020@hotmail.com)

Acknowledgments

As always, to Mom and Ross. You're just that great. A big thank you to Angela, Deb, Erin, Matt, Natsu, and Pattie for reading my work and making it better. Thanks to Cindy Cresap for the same. Thanks, David Slayton, for always being awesome and spending more money on my books than you should. And thanks to all my wonderful mythology teachers. I loved every minute.

Dedication

To Sarah Warburton, who loves old Greek stuff
as much as I do, maybe more

CHAPTER ONE

June's disappearance would have made more sense if her apartment had become a crime scene, with smashed furniture and yellow tape, definitive marks that *something* had happened. Instead, Cressida had to make do with one email, and as she stood in her aunt's tidy living room, she read it again on her phone, dissecting it, looking for anything that might make a woman disappear as handily as a magician's trick.

"Found something wonderful," it read. "Maybe impossible but still wonderful. See you soon. Love, Aunt June."

Wonderful could mean anything, but to June, who signed her emails like letters, it had to mean a relic of a bygone age. Impossible meant something that other experts had dismissed as myth, but if anyone could find the impossible, it was June, the woman who'd taught Cressida that studying classical literature had more to it than dusty old books.

But June's apartment wasn't Greece, Turkey, or Libya, all places June had once taken Cressida, wanting her to stumble on the secrets and tales just waiting to be discovered. And this wasn't a story told around a flickering campfire like those that had guaranteed Cressida would follow somewhat in her aunt's footsteps and seek out a doctorate in classical literature, so close to her aunt's doctorates in archaeology and classical studies. Cressida's parents had warned her that June would get her into trouble, that June's study bordered on belief, but this wasn't trouble. This was just…gone.

Four days and no news, unheard of for a woman who loved to share her discoveries and stayed in touch almost daily while she was jaunting. Cressida had tried June's contacts in Greece and various universities, but no one had a clue. Her apartment sat as if waiting for her. With all her bills set on auto-pay, it would wait until the money ran out.

With the email reciting itself in June's high-pitched, excitable voice, Cressida searched. She felt like a snoop, but if she went missing, she hoped someone would do the same to find her. The bedroom was tidy, the clothing utilitarian with only a few empty hangers and clear spaces in drawers. Her backpack was gone, no surprise when jaunting after the impossible. The police wouldn't open an investigation because she'd clearly left on her own.

June's study looked like *Archaeological Digest* with its framed photos of dig sites and artifacts fighting for space with artists' renderings of every goddess imaginable. Snaps of every relic June had ever authenticated were packed into thick scrapbooks.

Her laptop sat on the desk in between mountains of paper. Strange, she usually traveled with it, and Cressida wondered if its presence was a clue in itself. She flipped it open and turned it on as she had before, hoping that it would miraculously bypass the password screen this time. She'd already asked her parents for ideas, and they'd gone through every myth they knew.

Cressida rested her chin on one fist and wished she'd watched more crime shows or that she knew someone who hacked computers, but TV hackers usually only hacked the computers of the dead. Cressida shuddered and pushed that thought far away. A dead June was impossible; it would be like killing a tornado.

She turned to the stacks of paper, looking at those on top. Most were copies from university reference texts. Most were in Greek, and from what Cressida could make out, most were about the Underworld. June had highlighted a few lines about Hercules visiting the Underworld. She had the entire tale of Orpheus's attempt to rescue his wife, and she'd underlined passages in *The Odyssey.* She had articles on the gods and monsters who were said to dwell in the Underworld and the Titans who were imprisoned there. She must have been hard at work on her next article, but what could she discover about myths of the Underworld that hadn't already been written? On top of one paper June had written, "Eleusinian Mysteries," and underlined it three times.

Cressida frowned. The Mysteries were the secret rites of an ancient cult that worshiped Demeter, goddess of the harvest, and her daughter Persephone, queen of the Underworld. But the Eleusinian Mysteries had died out long ago, as extinct as the worship of the ancient gods. As secret rites, all that was left of them was rumor. Maybe June had found some new insight.

But if she had, she hadn't written it down anywhere for Cressida to find. She pulled June's email up on her phone again. "Love, June," it read, and June didn't even write "love" when she emailed her sister. Cressida had been included on some of the emails between her mother and her aunt; they'd been signed, "Best, June," or "Have a good one, June." They loved each other, but they weren't so close that they just up and said it.

Cressida looked to the password field on the laptop again. "Oh, Aunt June, tell me you didn't." Cressida typed her own name into the password field, and when the start screen loaded, she felt both elated and ashamed. It wasn't as bad as "1234," but it still made her cringe.

When she opened June's email and saw the flight confirmation, she punched the air. It was for London, not Greece like she'd thought. But before she could call June's friends in the UK, she noticed the flight was going the wrong way. London to Austin, a recent ticket for someone called Nero Georgiou.

Who named their child Nero? It was dated one day before June had sent her email to Cressida. She kept scrolling and found a reservation for the Doubletree near the university. Cressida picked back through June's papers until she found a sticky note with the words, "Nero 319," a clue that had meant nothing before.

"Got ya!" She pushed back in the chair, but whom had she gotten? A lover? Possibly. June found lovers at every port, of every sex, but she hadn't yet flown any to her. Maybe Nero was just that good in bed.

With forward momentum pushing her along, Cressida grabbed her purse, locked up, and nearly ran to her car. As quickly as the lights would let her go, she sped toward the university district and parked at the Doubletree. She passed through the lobby and strode toward the elevators as if she had a right to be there. June had always told her that the right look went a long way; a confident gait had gotten her into many exhibitions she hadn't been invited to.

Outside of 319, Cressida hesitated. What if June was in there, and the two of them had been lost in a haze of drunken sex? No, she still would have found time to call. And the sex couldn't be good enough to be called wonderful *and* impossible.

And if June was in there hacked to bloody pieces? Cressida's hand fell again. She looked down the hall, measuring the distance to the elevator and stairs. She looped her purse around her fist and hoped it would make a good enough weapon. She owed it to June to see this through. She hoped Nero was some visiting professor, maybe an expert on the Underworld, and that he'd have a simple explanation for June's disappearance all ready.

She knocked and lifted her purse, ready to wail on whoever answered the door in case the explanation was murderously complicated.

"Who is it?" Not June's voice, a man's, a bleary one by the sound of it.

Before she could answer, the door opened, and a young man in a half-tied robe blinked at her. She hesitated, purse still lifted. He pushed black hair out of his eyes, looked her over from head to toe, and smiled. "This must be my lucky day."

She gave him the same once-over. Skinny, very young, definitely not June's taste. "I wouldn't count on it."

He stood wide, gesturing for her to come in. "Did one of my friends get me a present for being such a good boy?" His accent pegged him as British with a hint of something else, possibly Greek. In his sty of a room, sheets were strewn everywhere, clothes on top of them. Room service trays perched on various surfaces. If the maids had been in since he'd taken up residence, they'd probably died of fright, and he'd stuffed them under the bed.

"You a dancer, sweetheart?" he asked.

Cressida strode past him, confident she could break him in half if necessary. "I'm looking for my aunt June."

"Never heard of her." But he turned away as he said it. He looked about nineteen. Not a visiting professor then, unless he was a genius.

"Are you Nero?"

"The one and only."

"Then I'm betting you know the woman who flew you over here."

He blinked at her hazily, and she noted the liquor bottles scattered here and there. A bra hung from one of the light sconces. Bright turquoise, it didn't look like June's style.

"I know lots of women, sweetheart. They come, they go."

Cressida took a menacing step toward him. "Tell me where my aunt is, or I'm calling the cops. You were the last one to see her. I'm sure they'd be interested in that."

"Look, sweetheart—"

"Cressida. One more sweetheart, and we find out just how good of a weapon this is." She lifted the purse.

His eyes widened, then he smiled again. "If you think I'm dangerous, why did you come alone?"

She snorted. She was taller than him by several inches, and though she'd never been in a fight, she thought he'd be a good first experience. She had rage in her corner, too, shouting at her to grab his skinny ass and dangle him out the window. "Are we calling the cops or what?"

He barked a laugh. "Better call them now if you want them in an hour. Traffic here is a bit—" He wandered close to the window, and his smile slipped. "Did you tell someone you were coming here?"

Thinking he really meant to try something, she readied the purse again. "Why?"

"You were followed. I told her to watch for that, and she should have told you the same." He began to hurry around the room, gathering his things. "She said you were smart," he mumbled. "In college and everything."

"A grad student, actually." She looked out the window and saw a man standing near the bushes, looking up at the hotel, at her, but he shouldn't have been able to see her through the window in daylight. He wore a turtleneck too warm for spring and was as bald as a cue. Another man joined him, twin in looks and dress, and when Cressida glanced toward the sidewalk, she saw another striding to join them.

Incredibly creepy triplets? She would have hoped their parents taught them to dress differently, but maybe they liked freaking people out.

"Do they have something to do with June?" she asked.

He'd pulled on jeans and a black tee while her back was turned. "I can't believe you didn't check to see if anyone followed you!" He threw more things into two bags: clothes, empty liquor bottles, half full ones, it didn't seem to matter.

"What the hell is going on?" She grabbed for him, but he twisted away.

"Just help me get out of here, and I'll tell you." He opened the chest of drawers and removed a carved wooden box from the lowest one, handling it with delicate reverence, nestling it into his clothes before zippering the bag closed.

"Tell me now! Do they know what happened to June?" She pointed toward the window.

"Yes, but they won't tell you. If they catch me, they'll kill me, and then you'll never know." He grinned, the little weasel. "So you better make sure I stay in one piece, College."

"So, let's stay here and call the police!"

"Hmm, better not. My things aren't exactly legal in the pharmacological department."

She pressed a hand to her pounding temples. "You're a drug dealer?"

He laughed. "If I was, I'd have better security than a student." He put on a bright smile. "A beautiful student, but still." She lifted the purse again, and he hurried on. "Call someone if you want. I'll be long gone, and you'll have no June, and until the police get here, you might be at the tender mercy of that thug."

Cressida looked out the window again. "Thugs."

"Right. So, you coming?"

She let her own evil smile show through. "Maybe you tell me where June is, or I'll go tell them where you are."

Nero froze before his lips curved into his own evil grin. "You're not cruel, College. I can tell. Besides—"

"Yeah, I get it. If I want to know, etc."

She lifted one of his bags, wondering what she was doing helping this asshole who might have landed her aunt in the hospital or worse.

But June didn't trust just anyone. She wasn't a fool. And Nero didn't seem like a clever con man, just a stubborn kid. Of course, Cressida had never met a true con man. She bet a good one would know how to fit in. He wouldn't be any good if people could spot him from the get-go.

The elevator dinged as they went into the hall. Nero switched direction seamlessly, heading for the stairs.

"Just how many times have you had to sneak out of hotels?" Cressida asked.

"Do you have a car?"

"Of course."

"Good. We can go to your place."

She almost said that there was no way she was taking a nutjob to her apartment, but at least he'd be in unfamiliar territory there. And her neighbors would hear it if she called for help. She thought of calling some of her fellow grad students, but there weren't many she was close to, none she'd really call friends.

I should have gotten out more.

Ugh, that was something her mom would have said. Besides, she didn't need friends watching her back when she had a baseball bat under the bed.

"This way." She led him down to the street and hurried outside. He looked over his shoulder the whole time, and she started to feel as nervous as him. When she took a peek across the parking lot, she caught sight of the turtleneck triplets hustling toward them.

Nero dove into her car when she unlocked it, his nerves feeding her own. "Go, go, go," he whispered.

"Shut up!" She missed the ignition and wondered if this was how people in a horror movie would feel if they could hear the audience screaming at them to start the damn car. The triplets were running, and she had to stop and watch them. Their footsteps fell in perfect sync, and she'd never seen anyone so fast. It was almost hypnotizing but calming enough that the key slipped into the ignition without fuss.

Nero leaned into her vision. "What is wrong with you, College? Go!"

Spell broken, she pulled out of the lot and sped away, nearly hitting three other cars and wondering idly if the turtleneck gang would catch up to her once she was stuck in traffic, but as she took a corner, she lost them from her rearview.

When they reached her building, Nero stayed on her toes, nodding to the day guard minding the desk. Cressida stopped, though, speaking loudly. "My guest will only be staying a few hours."

The day guard nodded slowly as if she was the crazy one, but now someone knew Nero was with her. On her floor, she stopped to say hello to a neighbor, and Nero laughed, waiting until they were alone in her apartment to say, "Making sure enough people see my face? What do you think I'm going to do, College?"

She waited as he dumped his stuff on the rug. "Talk."

He walked around her living room, looking out the window, fingers passing over the shelves stuffed with books, the television sitting on another pile of books that served as a low table. Piles of notebooks and paperbacks dotted the room like snowdrifts, fiction and nonfiction mingling wantonly, as June would have said. She'd always been tidier.

But she hadn't always been careful, especially when she was on the chase for a new relic or a fresh take on a myth. Cressida ducked into her bedroom, got the bat, and stepped back out. "I said, talk."

Nero put his hands up. "Whoa. What do you plan to do with that?"

"Beat the truth out of you if I have to."

Hands still up, he sat on the sofa and shifted a pile of books out of the way. "I inducted your aunt into the Eleusinian Mysteries, and she went to the Underworld."

Cressida waited for him to get serious, but he didn't smile, didn't try to play cute. "What?"

"I inducted—"

"Bullshit!"

"I'm the last hierophant."

She blinked at him, trying to conjure up images of hierophants: priests of ancient mystery cults, secret sects that worshiped the Greek gods *inside* their own religions. Hierophant identities had been carefully guarded secrets, but they'd died out with all the rest of it. "There hasn't been a hierophant for the Eleusinian Mysteries in a very long time."

"They were getting too well known, so we went underground, so to speak. Now there's only two of us at a time, the hierophant and an apprentice, just like the Sith."

"Great. Good to know you see yourself as having something in common with *Star Wars*. Confirms you're a nut." When he only stared, she sighed. "And you're the apprentice?"

He shrugged and stared at the carpet with a sad smile. "Not anymore. My predecessor died not long ago, and I have yet to choose an apprentice of my own. That's why..." He stared at her. "Look, I'm really sorry. I didn't know what it would mean, all right? I didn't know what I was doing. I couldn't believe I'd found someone who wasn't in the scene who still believed in the Mysteries, so when June told me what she wanted, I had to find out if I could do it."

"Had to find out if you could send someone to the Underworld?" And she hoped her skeptical tone said it all.

"Besides me, you need a gate," he said, "and you have to sneak in. You have to be familiar with the Mysteries first and go through the tale of Persephone and Demeter. You have to know their pain before you can even see the gate. You do recall the story of how Hercules traveled to the Underworld?"

Cressida waved at him to stop. In the myth, Hercules had been forced to perform the Eleusinian Mysteries. Connecting with Demeter and her struggle to find Persephone supposedly made a person able to see the gate to the Underworld, but that was just a story. The Mysteries had been real, but they were gone. It was all gone.

Cressida sat down on the opposite chair and wondered just how crazy he was, how crazy June would have to have been to listen to him. God, she must have been in some kind of crisis, or this guy would never have been able to convince her he could do what he claimed.

Or maybe he really believed it, and he killed June and thought of her as being in the Underworld instead of just dead. Cressida clutched the bat tighter.

He watched her hands as if he knew what she was thinking. "She's not dead."

"And you expect me to believe all this?"

He lifted his hands and dropped them. Then he snapped his fingers. "When she underwent the Mysteries, she communed with a sacred object. Some of her essence should still be on it." He dug in his bag and came up with the carved box again. With careful, practiced slowness, as if it might bite him, he opened the lid and brought forth a stalk of wheat.

Cressida breathed again. Sacred objects sometimes included a phallus, and she'd imagined Nero holding an enormous dildo. She definitely would have hit him in the head and thrown him out of her house then. But wheat was sacred to Demeter, definitely part of the Eleusinian Mysteries, and he wasn't holding it with gloves or anything, so it was probably safe.

He held it out. "Here."

"What am I supposed to do with that?"

"Just touch it."

And now, no matter what her rational mind said, she did not want to "just touch it."

"Why?"

"Because it's got some of your aunt's essence."

"And I'm supposed to be able to sense that?"

He rolled his eyes. "No, I drugged this bit of wheat with something so potent, you're going to fall unconscious even though I seem to be holding it with no difficulty."

Well, now that he said it... Still, she reached out hesitantly, but he didn't jerk it back or throw it at her. And it *was* just a stalk of wheat; she could see that plain as day. With one last aggravated sigh, she grabbed it.

The world fell away. Lights bloomed behind her eyes, and she saw flashes, heard voices, so many voices surrounding her; smells and sights flashed before her eyes, the faces of people, of creatures she'd never dreamed of, all babbling and screeching, and oh God, was that one flying?

It was over in a flash, and she nearly fell forward, gasping. She steadied herself, staring at Nero with her mouth open. "What the hell?" A nimbus of light floated behind him like a halo. The wheat had fallen to the floor.

"A glimpse of what your aunt is seeing now," he said. "Well, things she's seen."

"Wait, wait, wait," she said, still blinking away after images. His halo faded. "That isn't... You can't..." She took a deep breath. "The Eleusinian Mysteries? Where people reenact the kidnapping of Persephone and try to cheer up Demeter?"

He blinked at her. "I know what they are. I'm the—"

She threw her arms in the air. "You can't be a hierophant. There are no more hierophants. They died out with the Eleusinian Mysteries!"

"Or," he said, lifting a finger, "they went underground where they were always supposed to be because they were a secret that was getting way too public. You shouldn't even know about the Persephone-Demeter thing."

"Everyone knows about Persephone and Demeter! Hades kidnapped Persephone. Demeter was really sad about it. That's why we have winter!" Now she was shouting, but she didn't know how to stop. "No one worships them anymore!"

He gave her a scathing look. "No one you know, maybe."

"Myths! Legends!"

He waved. "Christianity. Judaism. Islam. Hinduism."

"Those are different!"

"Buddhism. Wiccans. Taoism."

That one made her trip. "I thought Taoism was more of a philosophy."

"They've all got their different philosophies, and as many of them would tell you, it's about faith."

She stood up and had to sit down again. She needed water. The kitchen was only a few feet away, but it was still too far. She slid down to sit on the carpet, keeping her hand away from the wheat, but flashes were still playing behind her eyes. She'd visited different churches with friends when she'd been little, but she'd never felt anything like...

Had it even been real? Couldn't have been. Couldn't. "Can I do it again?"

His eyebrow quirked. "Ready to believe, are we?"

"No, that's why I want to do it again. You know, scientific experimentation?"

He frowned. "I don't know if science would agree with you, but all right." He gestured to the wheat.

She grabbed hold. There, dress and costumes she recognized from pots and statuary and oh so many myths, stories that had been studied and rewritten and redone, powers that couldn't exist, legends that couldn't be true, and there was that flying thing again! She groped forward until she caught Nero's wrist and let the wheat fall to the floor.

"Gods, Mount Olympus? It can't be true. Is it the only real religion? Did people discover the true realm of the unknown, the only real gods, and then abandon them?"

"One thing at a time."

She squinted. "Maybe you're some kind of hypnotist."

"I'm pretty sure a person can't be hypnotized unless they want to be."

And she didn't want to be, but June would have leapt at the chance to believe in gods and goddesses and myths. "What happened to her?"

"She dug through tales and rumors, all around the world, until she found me. It took years, but she found the line of hierophants, one replacing another, the better to keep ourselves secret. No one is worthy of the Mysteries unless they can seek us out. We emailed back and forth for a long time, spoke a few times, and then she had me brought over so she could speak to me face-to-face."

"And the bald triplets?"

He bit his lip. "Would you believe me if I said that was Cerberus in his Earthly disguise?"

She shot to her feet, shaking. "No, no, no. Bull. It has to be."

"He guards the gates to the Underworld. He doesn't like that I sent someone there. It's a good sign, really. It means June got past him."

"Why?" Cressida said at last, and she felt the tears threatening. She pressed on her eyes to get them to stop. "Why would June want to go to the Underworld?"

He shook his head. "You should know as well as I do. I mean, we can't have had as many conversations as you must have had. She was looking for what she's always been looking for."

"Something real."

He nodded.

This time, she couldn't hold in a little sob. "I'm real."

"Hey." He seemed uncomfortable but didn't try to touch her. "She spoke about you all the time, College. Couldn't stop talking about you some days, when we video chatted. She didn't intend to stay in the Underworld. It was supposed to be a quick trip. She planned to have this conversation with you when she got back. She wanted to introduce us. Hell, I've never sent anyone to the Underworld. I wasn't even sure it would work." He shuffled his feet. "I…was just about to call you, actually, let you know something was up."

She thought of the liquor bottles and room service trays. "Oh really?"

"Yeah, sure." He smiled and looked guilty as if realizing they both knew that was a lie. "Don't panic. We're linked, she and I, since I helped her get there, and I would have felt it if she'd…died. I'm pretty sure."

She searched his face for a lie, but she hadn't known him that long, and someone who hid special Underworld powers from the rest of the world had to have a good poker face at least some of the time. "And you think I can contact her where you can't?"

"Contact. Sure. You can find her in person."

"You want me to go to the Underworld?"

"Dead simple. We go to this cave I found that has the right spiritual resonance, the same place she went, and then I'll perform the Mysteries." He wiped his lips. "I have to warn you. Your aunt found a way to sneak past Cerberus because he wasn't looking for anyone, but now he's on high alert. If he finds you, he finds me."

"If June found a way…"

"I think she had help. I sensed a presence."

"What kind of presence?" And why was it making her blood run cold? She told herself she still didn't really believe any of this was happening, but she'd had the visions, and it wasn't like any drug she'd ever heard of. And now they were talking about the dangers of Cerberus and an unknown presence.

"Well, based on what I've learned, living people are a hot commodity in the Underworld. If she's smart, she made some kind of deal to get her back where she belongs." He sighed and paced, rubbing his hands over his head. "To tell you the truth, College, I have huge doubts about helping you. I liked June. I don't want to think I sent her to something bad, and now I'm sending her niece to the same fate. It's why I didn't want to tell you in the first place."

"Fuck that!" Cressida said. "If she's in trouble, I want to help her."

He laughed. "If Cerberus is here on Earth when I part the veil between worlds, you should be able to slip past, but we need to do this before he catches up to us."

"But you'll be left here with him."

His head hung a moment. "Let me worry about that." He rubbed his hands together. "First, you need to pack. You can't eat anything in the Underworld, so you'll need your own supplies."

She paused on her way to the kitchen. "Did June have enough food for four days?"

He shrugged. "Her life force is still going strong. I don't think it would be doing that if she was now a permanent resident. Maybe time or hunger works differently there?" Another shrug. "The stories vary."

As she gathered some things, still not believing what she was getting herself into, he went over what he did know, telling her that people in the Underworld could do anything living people could do: eat, drink, talk, have sex. She paused at that one, giving him a look.

He shrugged. "They can't have children. That's about it."

"And what happens if they die in the Underworld?"

He shook his head. "All I know is the stories. But since you're still alive, College, if you die there, you're stuck. I don't know if you'll have to feed your blood to the shades in order to speak to them like in *The Odyssey*. Reports are…mixed where the Underworld is concerned. That eating or drinking thing is a definite, though. Eat any Underworld food, and you'll also get stuck."

"I got it. And the sex?"

He raised an eyebrow. "Are you planning on it?"

She thought to blurt out no, but if she was going to take this seriously, well, myth was full of lovely ladies. She shook the thought away. "No, I mean, this is a serious—"

He put a hand up. "Look, the simple question is, do we need to get some condoms or what?"

She glared at him. "For any fellow lesbians I happen to find?"

"So, latex gloves? Dental dams?"

She'd hoped to embarrass him, but now felt her own cheeks burning. "Shut up."

"Don't blame me if you come back with undead VD. I'm trying to keep things classy."

"How will I find my way back once I have June?"

"Well, I can give you the same thing I gave her." He took a vial of oil out of his bag. "This'll let me know you're still alive, and in theory, you should be able to follow it back." He dabbed a bit on his finger. "I need to touch your chest, over your heart; your forehead; and uh, over your womb." It was her turn to raise an eyebrow. He rolled his eyes. "So I can sense your lifeline, College."

He touched her forehead, and she pulled her shirt down enough for him to dab over her heart and pulled her pants low enough that he could touch over her uterus.

He looked up. "Now, it's just your labia, and we're done." When she leapt away, he laughed. She gave him a black look, and he shook his head. "Kidding."

"Would you shut up and finish this already?"

"All done on my end."

She scratched idly at the oil as she gathered some last minute things, stuffing them into an oversized backpack June had given her. "That stuff itches."

"It's not the oil; it's your lifeline." He put a finger up and plucked at the air as if playing an invisible guitar.

Cressida shuddered as the feeling shivered down her spine. "Stop that!"

"That, College, will help me know where you are."

"Okay, but you can't play me like a harp."

"Yes, I can. Hierophant privileges." He ignored her look and bustled around the room.

"If this will help me get back, why didn't it help June?"

"I don't know! All of this is theory. Do you want to go or not?"

"I don't have a choice." She cinched her pack and laid it on the ground. "Now what? We find your underground gate?"

His laughing look gave way to a more serious one. "Yep, and there we will perform the Mysteries."

Cressida took a deep breath. Despite what she'd felt from the wheat, and the way Nero could touch her lifeline, she still doubted what he said. Once they started the Mysteries, she knew everything would become clearer, that if she watched him, she might spot a rational explanation for everything that was happening.

At the moment, it was the best she could hope for, apart from finding June in whatever cave Nero had left her in. "Let's do it."

CHAPTER TWO

Cressida had been expecting one of the many tourist attracting caves in the Austin Hill Country, but Nero led her to an innocuous divot in the bottom of a hill that could only be called a cave if she squinted. They'd had to park on the side of the road and ease under a barbed wire fence, and the entire time Cressida had been looking for evidence of June—a dropped tissue, a booted footprint—but in between the gravel and the scrubby plants and cacti, she saw nothing.

Standing in the unimpressive cave, Cressida's confidence plummeted. What the hell was she doing here? Had she just driven herself to her own murder scene, just like June? Any minute now Nero would tell her that in order to complete the ritual, she'd have to dig a grave-like hole.

He set his bag down and rubbed his hands together. "You might want to take your backpack off. You're going to be a little stumbly."

And it would save him the trouble of wrestling it off her corpse. She dropped it to the ground and watched him so closely it made him chuckle.

"If you want to back out," he said, "now's the time."

June hadn't backed out. Wouldn't. And there didn't seem to be any sign of recent graves. "Where do we start?"

He opened the box and showed her a bottle of greenish brown sludge. "Here."

"That's..."

"Kykeon, the stuff that gets you high, yeah. Barley and pennyroyal mostly."

"Is that really necessary?"

"You want to get into the Underworld? No one goes sober."

And that was it. Nero was going to feed her sludge, rob her, and sell her to the creepy sweater triplets, just like he'd probably sold her aunt. But why bother with something so elaborate? To claim he didn't force her to do anything? And though June always wanted to buy into the myths, she wasn't stupid, far from it. She would have done her research on Nero before flying him over.

"Just get set up, and let me wrap my head around this," she said.

He shrugged and set to work assembling a makeshift altar. Cressida peeked into his bag. There were more to the Mysteries than drugs. Ancient Greeks reenacted the kidnapping of Persephone, the agony of Demeter at losing her daughter. They told dirty jokes to make Demeter smile; they worshiped sacred objects. Nero wouldn't have bothered to bring anything else if he was just going to drug her and kill her.

The box that held the sacred wheat was in there, as well as a basket and what looked like ceremonial robes. Nero donned them quickly, enough green fabric to nearly swallow him, as well as a heavy gold necklace and a crown. She couldn't hold in a laugh.

He gave her a dirty look. "Sacred ceremony, yeah?"

"Sorry." But she could barely hold it in.

"Want to start with the ritual cleansing?" He held up a bottle of water.

She eyed it and then him, hoping her expression conveyed that if he dumped that over her head, she would punch him.

He sighed. "She didn't want you to see the video, but I see you're not going to move forward without it."

"The what?"

"I filmed her induction. Quite hard to do while performing it, you know, but it was my first time and everything…" He sighed. "She didn't want you to see it. She knew she'd act a fool during the ceremony, but everyone does. Your aunt, though—"

"This whole time you had a video that would back you up, and you didn't say anything?"

"I promised that I wouldn't, that I'd only use it as a reference for myself, but I thought you were starting to believe me."

She held up a hand. "Just show me. I promise I won't mention it to my aunt."

He took out his phone. "I wanted to study it. See where I could improve my technique. First, swear a vow of secrecy."

She nodded. "I swear."

When June came to life on his phone screen, Cressida's heart thudded, and she felt a few wayward tears gather. She watched June and Nero enter the cave, watched the robes come out. June drank the kykeon and babbled about how myth was so unjust to women, about all the wrongs that should be righted, all the tales that should be rewritten.

For the most part, Cressida agreed, but they were just stories, reflective of the time they were written in, but June didn't seem to see them that way. She acted as if there was something she could do about it. "The least I can do," she slurred, "is hear the truth from their own lips."

At one point, she tried to cut herself, and Nero had wrestled a knife away from her as Cressida watched, wincing. Another time she tried to take her clothes off, but Nero had stopped her with, "That's enough of that, sweetheart. We don't want to greet Hades in our underpants, do we?"

When the Mysteries had concluded, June nearly passed out, but Nero helped her put on a backpack that was the twin of Cressida's then led her toward the back of the cave. The video did this shuddery shimmer, and she was gone.

There were ways to alter video. Everyone knew that, but Cressida didn't have the time or the means to look for them. She didn't even know where she'd start with such a thing.

Now she was just wasting time. If what she'd seen so far didn't prove that June had really taken a trip to the Underworld, nothing would. A true skeptic never stopped looking for the zipper, but June was a believer, so to find her, Cressida knew she was going to have to act like a believer, too.

And if nothing happened, well, then she'd know, and then Nero would regret ever being born.

"How do I find her?" Cressida asked.

He had the decency to look apologetic as he shrugged. "Ask around."

"Fantastic. Can't wait."

He lifted the water bottle high and whispered something before he dumped it over her head.

She resisted the urge to glare, and when he handed her the kykeon, she took a big drink. Her logical mind screamed at her, but the part of her that had listened wide-eyed to her aunt's stories around a campfire sent a silent prayer that she would see her aunt soon.

For a moment, she felt nothing, and she was about to ask when it would kick in, but Nero leaned far to the side, farther than anyone had a right to lean before he oozed slowly up the wall.

"Stop that," she tried to say, but her tongue wouldn't obey her.

"Right, now we re-create the kidnapping of Persephone," he said. "I'll play Demeter, and you're Persephone, so make sure you cry a lot because you've been kidnapped by Hades, and being separated from your mother and the other gods is severely bumming you out."

She wanted to say she felt a little silly, that she might need more prompting, but what came out was, "Okey dokey." She fell to her knees and lamented her fate while he cried for her, but to her surprise, Nero wasn't himself anymore but the goddess of the harvest and the land, wailing because she missed her daughter, and Cressida felt Persephone's anguish, Demeter's pain.

Someone was playing a drum? Nero shoved the wheat into her hands. She tottered along beside him slurring, "Fuck, yeah! Demeter is the shit, doing all the growing things and all the crops and stuff, and did Hades think of any of that? Noooo. He was just thinking with his dick! And he could have said, 'Hey, Persephone, you wanna go out sometime?' But he probably knew she would be all like, 'No, you're a fucking cockbag,' and that's why he kidnapped her! And now her mother is so sad because they were so close. Hey, that's my arm, give it back!"

Nero led her arm toward the engraved box, and it towed her along. Cressida laid the wheat down so Demeter would know that Cressida was on her side, that Cressida wept for her because her daughter was missing like June was missing.

Cressida threw herself down before the makeshift altar and wept, thinking on June and Persephone and how they'd both been carried off, but Persephone got to come back sometimes. June might never get to. "I'll rescue you!" she said, and she didn't know whether she was talking to Persephone or June.

Nero whispered in her ear in Greek.

"Speak up," she tried to say, but all that came out was a whistle. Then she realized the whistling inside her was actually around her, and goddamn she was powerful; she could make a whole cave whistle! Something tugged on her back. Nero had helped her put on her backpack, but it hovered a few feet overhead.

The air felt swirly, as if she was falling. "This is it!" she cried. There actually *was* an entrance to the Underworld in a shitty little non-cave in Austin, and the thought made her laugh and laugh until the swirly air seemed to focus on one point, and she was stumbling toward it and falling again.

Someone pulled her lifeline taut, and she gasped, her limbs flying out like a marionette's. She turned to yell at Nero, but her feet crunched into something.

The cave had gone dark as pitch except for a faint light coming from far away, down a tunnel that hadn't been there before. When had it gotten dark? Her head was clearing, the drug fading like water sliding off her skin. She fumbled for her flashlight, but when she flicked it on, she had to stifle a yelp. Mounds of skeletons lay strewn across a huge cavern, piles of yellow-white bone heaped like macabre dunes.

The entrance to the Underworld, the spot where Cerberus waited to strip the flesh from any mortal trying to sneak into the land of the dead.

❖

Medusa slipped deeper into the mud bath and tried to remember what it was like to get drunk. The alcohol of the dead relied too heavily on the taster, powered by memory and imagination. Labels instructed those who imbibed to recall spending an evening with friends and family or to summon the memory of relaxing moments in groves and meadows, as if everyone had spent their lives in a beer commercial.

But it was hard to remember a blackout drunk. That was part of the charm. Memory and inhibition pissed away in dribs and drabs until a person couldn't remember where her feet were and then couldn't recall what they were for, either. Medusa hadn't been a heavy drinker in life, but she still wanted the option from time to time.

After more than three millennia had passed in the mortal realm, a living person had visited the Underworld. It was an impossible amount of time to think about, let alone live, but time worked differently for the dead. Days were hard to separate—and weeks, months, years—but Medusa recognized that it had been a long time, too long.

New spirits trickled down occasionally, those who worshipped the old gods, but they were fewer and fewer, and a living person? Virtually forgotten. She'd felt the ripple in the air when the living woman had shown up; all those with more awareness had felt it, too, and she knew everyone would be scrambling to put long dormant plans into motion. A living person was too great an opportunity to ignore.

Medusa sank into the soothing mud until it covered her chin. She shifted, letting scales cover her body, her wings stretching to either side, and her hair lifting and transforming into writhing snakes before she settled into her human form again, letting her human hair drift on the mud's surface. She'd seen the living mortal. Her face was etched upon Medusa's memory as she stared at the Underworld in wide-eyed wonder, but Medusa hadn't been fast enough. Someone had swooped in and gathered her up first, and Medusa hadn't even seen who it was.

Her body tightened, fists clenching until she forced herself to relax again, to let the mud do its work. She had to think of a plan, a way to find the mortal before it was too late, and Perseus was reincarnated again.

A jolt like lightning passed through her, and for a second, she thought it was anger at the man who'd killed her and her sisters, but this was the same feeling that had made her hesitate before. Another living person had entered the Underworld.

"So soon?" she asked. But it didn't matter if it was a new one or if the other had left and now returned. She leapt from the tub and wrapped a robe around her muddy body. She dashed into the living room of her high-rise apartment and looked out over the jumble of the city, trying to see past the mishmash of concrete and glass buildings, some temples and traditional houses stuck amidst the press by diehards who refused to move with the times. Over it all hung the thick shade fog and the crisscrossing elevator cables that let the denizens move from one place to another.

"Stheno, Euryale!"

They glided into the room, almost specters now, nearly the same as the floating shades that made up the fog, all the people no longer remembered by anyone walking the Earth.

"Sister?" they asked, talking on top of one another, their closeness the only thing keeping them in form. Too many people had forgotten them, but it seemed some still remembered the old myths. Medusa often thanked the gods for liberal arts programs.

"Another mortal has come. Find her." Medusa dashed away, grabbing some jeans from the floor and pulling them on, mud and all. Her sisters crowded around the window, tapping into the fog of floating shades, searching, listening.

Medusa turned, looking for a shirt, but there wasn't one handy. She cinched the robe tighter and ran out of the apartment, sprinting toward her building's elevator. There wasn't time for anything else. Everyone would know, everyone who was remembered by someone who still lived would realize there was a mortal in their midst, and they'd be after him or her like a shot.

She hit the ground floor and ran into the street. She reached up, grabbed one of the floating shades, and tugged it along with her, using it as a conduit to speak with her sisters, their voices vibrating through the spiritual fog.

"Which way?"

They guided her through the streets, past the myriad elevators that traversed the city, traveling up or down or sideways, leading her toward Cerberus's tunnel.

❖

Cressida froze, waiting for the hot breath of Cerberus to wash over her back right before a set of huge jaws clamped over her head, shutting off air and light forever.

"Oh God," she groaned, then clapped a hand over her mouth. Her bladder shrank, and she clamped her knees together to keep from giving in to the sudden urge to wet her pants.

Nero's words swam into focus in her head. Cerberus was in the real world, looking for Nero, looking for her, but if he sensed that she'd crossed over, he'd be on his way quick. She ran for the light, skittering over skeletons and crunching bones under her sneakers. She wobbled, the sharp ends of femurs sticking into her legs but not penetrating her jeans. She tried to run in bounding hops until she tripped, and the sounds of clattering, skittering bones echoed off the walls.

A deep growl sounded far off behind her, as if the cave was warning her to be quiet, but her imagination supplied her with the three-headed dog she couldn't see. Cressida tried to swear through clenched teeth and fumbled her way forward, finally breaking into a clearing where she ran for all she was worth, her backpack pounding up and down, and her heart hammering in her chest. The growling had reached the bones, and huge feet knocked them aside like kindling.

An opening loomed ahead; bluish light poured out of a hole too small for Cerberus in his three-headed dog form, or at least she hoped so. She ran faster but heard him gaining, his paws rasping against stone, and she pictured all three jaws opening wide, slick with drool, red tongues lolling.

She didn't even see the drop. Suddenly weightless, she spun her arms, legs still running but with nothing to catch on. She struck a slope on her heel and skidded, fighting to keep her balance, knowing she was going to fall and unable to stop it. Bits of skin sloughed from her palms as she fell forward and lost the fight with momentum. She rolled for a few stomach wrenching turns before finally sliding to a halt.

Cressida put her arms over her head and breathed, wanting to be as small as possible when she was eaten. Maybe if he didn't chew, she could claw her way out from the inside.

Nope, that was too much. She uncurled enough to vomit, and it wasn't until she dry heaved over and over that she realized Cerberus hadn't caught her.

The hole above her was packed with three snouts jockeying for position as they sniffed and snarled. He couldn't fit. She barked a laugh, and the noses stopped as if listening. Cressida tried to keep another laugh in, but it wouldn't be silenced, and soon it had friends, more and more until she was laughing hysterically, and the snouts began barking, one after another poking out the hole in impotent fury.

Cressida pushed to her feet, her elatedness at remaining uneaten making her call, "Good boy!" The wall of a cavern shuddered as if Cerberus banged against it, and Cressida turned away, starting to run, but she staggered to a stop.

She'd expected rivers, caverns, maybe the odd lake of lava, but an alley stretched in front of her, slick dark bricks covered in graffiti that glowed in a meager streetlight. Maybe the Mysteries had gone wrong and instead of sending her to the Underworld, Nero had transported her to the magical land of Cleveland.

Cerberus guards Cleveland? It was enough to prompt another sputtering laugh, but she clamped down on it quickly. June was depending on her. This was no time to go insane. After a final look at Cerberus's snouts, she walked from the alley onto a street only wide enough for foot traffic. Neon signs flickered off glass paned buildings, and towering skyscrapers glowed like some kind of undersea creatures. There were billboards of moving lights, and long, snaking cables that crossed and crisscrossed the buildings, all of it covered in dingy fog that made it impossible to see whether this place had a sky or the roof of a cavern.

People hustled to and fro, going into and out of doors, gathering on platforms stuck to the sides of buildings as if waiting for a train, but an enormous elevator came down from one of the cables, and a bunch of people hurried in while others hustled out.

"Manticore," someone beside her said.

She turned slowly, as if any sudden movements would shake her from this dream, and when she saw what had spoken, her mouth stayed open. The creature stood as high as her shoulder, and her brain went on autopilot to confirm that it was indeed a manticore. It had the lion body, the human face, a twitching serpent for a tail, and this version had the wings of a bat that some legends included, and some did not.

"Yes?" she tried.

"Manticore." It shuffled closer, eyeing her up and down.

"Um, good?" This couldn't be real. She was hallucinating in a cave while some young twerp riffled her pockets.

The creature growled deep in its throat, and she stepped back. A small hand rested against the manticore's flank, and a short man stepped up beside it.

Satyr, Cressida's mind supplied: a man with a goat's lower body, furry chest, and ram's horns among his curly hair. "Pan?" she said.

He brayed a laugh. "Don't I wish! But thanks for the compliment!" He leered and then cleared his throat and put on a more businesslike expression, as if she only got a small taste of flirting for every compliment she paid. "Do you want to rent a manticore?"

"Rent?" She looked at it again, and it was still staring. "He's renting himself?"

"She, darling, and manticores don't rent themselves. All they really do is say, 'manticore' and then do the job assigned to them, mostly guarding valuables. So, what do you say?" He slapped the monster on the flank.

"Manticore," it said again.

She was about to say no thanks, but now that her brain was engaged, it was hard to turn off. "Why does it only say manticore?"

"What else would it say?"

"Well, if it guards things, why wouldn't it say, 'go away,' or 'be gone,' or 'get the hell out of here before I eat you'? What good does it do saying your own name like a Pokémon?"

He shook his head, and she found it curious that his first words weren't wondering about what a Pokémon was. "Well, so the person trying to sneak through your house or whatnot knows there's a manticore there. If he said get out, he could be anything!"

Her survival instincts tried to tell her to walk away, but the stubborn, logical part of her brain put them in a headlock. "But anyone could stand in a dark room and say manticore, and then they wouldn't have to pay you."

His mouth worked for a few moments, and he glanced around. "Look, are you trying to make trouble?"

"No! I'm—"

"If you're not looking for a manticore, why don't *you* get the hell out of here?"

And what was she doing standing around arguing with a satyr about manticores when she was in the freaking Underworld? Her stubborn brain finally shut up. "Um, right. Sorry to bother you."

He gave her another look up and down. "There's something strange about you."

"Right. I'm the strange one." She shifted away, remembering what Nero had told her about living people being a hot commodity.

The satyr moved closer, staring harder, and she hurried into a crowd, but the more she banged into people, the more weird looks she got, as if everyone was cluing in to some subtle hint that she missed. At last, she ended up in an alley, breathing hard, trying to shrink into the darkness to avoid anyone seeing her. Maybe she should have hired a manticore just to keep the curious at bay, but she had no idea what anyone here used as currency.

Here. The Underworld. It was almost enough to make her try throwing up again. She sneaked another peek into the street. Some feeling was rising in her, fighting past the shock and uncertainty. Glee fought past disbelief and even pushed anger aside. It was the Underworld. The *freaking Underworld*!

And she wouldn't find June if she was busy gawking. She straightened her backpack and glanced around, looking for someone who seemed trustworthy. Most people had their chins tucked in as they walked, not looking at anyone, just like in large cities around the world. She wondered if there was somewhere she could get a map.

She glanced over her shoulder, and a man walking behind her smiled. His brown hair was artfully tousled, his skin deeply tanned, making the white of his cable-knit sweater gleam. He looked like something out of a catalogue with his perfectly balanced, impossibly handsome face, especially when he winked with bright, turquoise eyes.

When he swaggered closer, she dropped back a bit, just to find out what a dead catalogue model might have to say. He laughed, sporting a smug look, but he couldn't know that she wasn't the least bit interested in his body, just curious enough to talk to someone who wasn't a monster salesman.

He slipped an arm around her shoulders as if that was his right. "Come along, darling."

She ducked out from under him. "Why should I?"

His face fell, his look so mystified that she laughed. "I don't understand," he said.

"That's my line. Just who do you think you are?"

He blinked. "Adonis."

She thought he might be joking but then remembered where she was. "No shit, really?"

His smile came back in all its confident glory. "Of course. Now…" He made as if to grab hold of her again, but she shook her head.

"Keep your hands to yourself."

Again, that look of utter confusion, as if wondering how she could be resisting him. "But…I'm…"

"What do you want? Let's start there."

"I want you to come with me."

"In order to…"

"To help me." He spoke so slowly, she wondered if he was trying to figure it out as well.

"If you need help, there are better ways to start than, 'Come on, darling.'"

He stopped cold and pulled back, his frown suspicious now. "What magic do you have?"

She had to laugh. "Whoever sent you should have done a little more research." She started walking again. There had to be someone else who could help her.

"Look, are you going to come with me or not?"

"Not."

"You're just like your aunt."

Cold fingers played up and down Cressida's spine, but she kept any emotion off her face, wanting to know what he knew. "My aunt gave you a hard time?"

"She's made certain things very difficult."

"And that's why she's now…"

"In the—" He eyed her and smiled. "Nice, but beautiful doesn't always mean stupid."

"Where is she?"

He pursed perfect lips. "What if I told you that you'd find her if you came with me?"

"What could I do for you that June couldn't?"

He eyed her up and down but with a calculating look. She thought he might turn on the smarm again, so she picked up the pace.

"We do need your help," he said.

"Who is we?"

"Narcissus and myself."

"Holy shit, Narcissus, too?" The man who'd gotten killed because he couldn't help flirting with himself and the man who had two goddesses fighting over him because he was so pretty? Their house had to have a *lot* of mirrors. She wondered how long it took either of them to get ready.

"Like you needed June's help?" she asked.

He walked in front of her, going backward. "Help us, and we'll help you get her back."

So they either had her and someone else had taken her, or they knew who'd had her from the beginning. At least her odds for being alive looked better and better, though the time it would take to find her seemed like a long road ahead. "From where?"

"Hecate's palace. You'll never get her on your own."

Cressida's heart sank. Hecate, goddess of magic, patroness of witches. Nero had never said there'd be actual deities in the Underworld. But June was the best at what she did. It was only fitting she'd find the *most* trouble. "Start at the beginning."

❖

Medusa slid to a stop as Adonis took the mortal woman under his arm. "Oh, for fuck's sake!" She clutched her muddy robe, tempted to go scaly in front of everyone. Bad enough that someone else had gotten to the mortal first, but fucking Adonis? Now the mortal would swoon and fall into his arms, and Medusa's chance for revenge would be gone faster than a bottle of moisturizer in Adonis and Narcissus's house.

It was a pity, too. She was quite pretty, young, with intelligent blue eyes and a mass of red curls. She was clearly prepared for a lengthy stay, if the enormous backpack was any indication. And she sparkled with life, a little shimmer that extended just past her enticing curves. When she ducked out of Adonis's embrace, Medusa choked on her own laugh and picked up speed to try to hear what they were saying.

He tried to charm her, and she thwarted him. Medusa wanted to whoop for joy, wanted to slide right between them and introduce herself, but Adonis mentioned the other mortal and how these two were connected. The young woman tried to play it cool, but Medusa could read the lines in her stiff neck, the slight tremble in her voice. She was worried for the other mortal, her aunt June.

Adonis played on that, claiming he could bring them together again, and she seemed as if she might believe him, but what choice did she have, alone as she was? People on the street were beginning to notice her, no doubt seeing that telltale shimmer. A harpy in a trench coat moved out from under the awning of an Ethiopian restaurant and followed them.

Medusa sped up until she was at the harpy's side, the harpy's long claws clacking on the pavement. The harpy glanced down with a woman's face and then did a double take, staring at Medusa's muddy robe, her bare feet.

"Hunting mortals, are we?" Medusa asked.

The harpy grinned with sharp teeth. "Yes! Long has it been since I've tasted real human flesh." Her voice screeched like discordant violin strings, and she smelled like the floor of a butcher shop.

Medusa winced and tried to cover it with what she hoped was a convincing smile. "I was just saying the other day that being dead wouldn't be so bad if we could eat one another."

"Yes, yes!" The harpy bobbed her head on its skinny neck, her lank hair barely moving. "Now is my chance, yes." She glared. "I saw her first."

"Absolutely! But you'll need some help with him, surely." She nodded toward Adonis. "A powerful spirit, fully aware. And the woman is a grown mortal. Big enough for two?"

The harpy tilted her head back and forth. "Yes, big enough. I see it. If you help with the man, yes."

"Perfect." Adonis and the woman had slowed. Medusa pulled on the harpy's arm. "Just duck in here a moment, dear, and I'll tell you my plan."

Power roiled through her as they stepped into an alley, and the harpy didn't have time to blink before its flesh shuddered and hardened, petrifying into stone. Medusa's power might not have been as strong as it was when she was alive, but it was enough to work on some no-name harpy. As she stepped back out, she told herself it was the harpy's own fault. She should have found out just whom she was talking to.

CHAPTER THREE

Hecate's palace had a metal fence around it like the one surrounding the White House. Cressida curled her hands around the bars and stared across a lush green lawn spotted with purple and yellow flowers. In the distance, the palace rose like Zeus's temple, gleaming white amidst the flashing lights of surrounding skyscrapers. It lived up to some of what Cressida had been expecting of the Underworld in general. Huge columns held up a high, peaked roof, and statuary dotted the yard. Braziers glittered around a large reflecting pool, and hints of gold shone from inside the palace's huge open doorway. Cressida squinted, but the fence was set too far away for her to really tell what lay inside. No one moved in or out, and she stood on tiptoe, trying to see past the shadows. It wasn't like looking at a relic or museum replica. The feel of it hummed in the air, as if it proclaimed itself a sacred place. Even without any people, the palace seemed vibrant and, for lack of a better term, alive.

"If we stay long enough, it will shift into something else," Adonis said.

She blinked away visions of the palace's interior, the wonders it would hold. "What?"

"Well, sometimes it becomes a high-rise or a medieval castle or a big pile of cotton candy or whatever she wants it to be. She is the goddess of magic, after all. The whole thing is nebulous."

Cressida's imagination popped like a soap bubble, and she let her hands fall to her sides. "That's a little disappointing."

He put on an exaggerated pout. "Aw, the goddess will be so sad to hear that."

She gave him a dark look. "What is with the Underworld anyway? Where are the theaters? The agoras? The tombs and stadiums? This is all just so…" She gestured at the modern architecture warring with the ancient and sometimes coming up somewhere in between, most with a decided lack of columns. "Anachronistic."

He snorted. "Well, excuse us for not being Greece-land. We keep abreast of culture. It filters down to us. We may be dead, but we're not blind, deaf, and dumb." He thought for a moment. "Well, except for the blind, deaf, and dumb."

"Then you should know we don't say dumb anymore."

He barked a laugh. "Sometimes, things change so fast up there we can't keep up."

"Fast," she said, thinking on the millennia that separated them. "Right."

"How else do you think we're communicating? We hear all the languages. Well, those of us who are aware hear them. If the shades know what's going on, they're not telling anyone."

"Shades?"

He gestured upward at the fog.

She glanced that way but saw nothing. "What?"

He sighed, jumped, and snagged a piece of fog. She took a step back. No one could grab fog, or maybe that was his undead superpower. She flicked through the myths she knew but couldn't find anything similar. When he brought the fog close to her face, she leaned in, watching the swirling shapes until she noticed they were staring back at her.

She jumped away. "It has a face!"

Adonis laughed so hard, he leaned forward on his knees. "Of course it does. It's a ghost, a shade."

"But you're all ghosts!"

He put his hands on his hips, and the shade wriggled in his grasp. "Excuse me? I'm a sentient dead person."

"Right. Sorry, don't know all the terms yet."

He shrugged. "You'll learn."

"So?" She gestured at the shade, still a little queasy at seeing it wiggle.

He let it go, and it drifted up to rejoin the rest. "Not everyone who died is able to live like those of us who are aware. Most of them just drift around. It's belief from people in the mortal world that sustains us. The more people who remember our names, the more substantial we are, though how often you mortals get things wrong is astounding."

"You were mortal, too, pal, or you wouldn't be dead."

"You know what I mean." He sighed. "I guess one day mortals won't remember any of us, and then we'll all become shades."

"Poor things." It was a bummer, and she wondered if the same fate awaited everyone who died, no matter where they wound up, if every person who'd ever lived but wasn't remembered was floating around in their own afterlife. It gave her a sinking feeling, as if the world was sliding out from under her feet, and she tried to banish the thought.

"It's weird," Adonis said. "Sometimes, one of the shades will come popping into awareness as his or her life is discovered by some scholar who'll publish a paper on the Internet and boom, instant sentience."

"Are they aware of anything?"

"They have a kind of joined consciousness. The rest of us use them to communicate with one another."

She stared, horrified, but he shrugged again. "This whole place is shaped by the collective consciousness of the people who live here, but we can't do everything we dream about. We're not telepathic. We have to use the tools we're given."

She stared at the modern town, the flashing lights. "So right now you're all stuck on ultra-modern?"

"I like it. We went through a French Revolution thing once. That was terrifying."

She nodded but ducked a little to stay out of a patch of billowing shade fog. "So, do you know Hecate?"

"Not personally. Narcissus and I know almost everyone else worth knowing here. We can't cross over to the Elysian Fields—

none of us can—and I suppose I could visit those writhing around in Tartarus, but who would want to?"

Cressida pictured both the Elysian Fields, rumored home to the heroes of Greek myth, and the fabled Tartarus, where Zeus cast those who'd committed heinous crimes against the gods. She wondered if either would look as she'd imagined them, if the Fields were green meadows or if Tartarus was a craggy, violent land covered in punishments. She went through the layers of the Underworld in her head. "So that just leaves the Fields of Punishment and the Meadows of Asphodel. Where are they?"

"You're standing in them. Well, the Fields of Punishment aren't really a thing, not anymore. All the really bad people and creatures are locked in Tartarus, and no one really remembers the people who were stuck in the Fields of Punishment anymore, so they just sort of merged into Asphodel."

She had so many questions, but she tried to shake them away, to keep her mind on the task at hand. "How do I get into Hecate's palace?"

"With lots of help." He gave her a dazzling smile. "The kind that only we can provide."

"And what do you want in return?"

"A very simple task. As a mortal, you can pass through the layers of the Underworld with ease. We need you to go to the Elysian Fields, snag some ambrosia, and bring it back. Nothing too hard."

"Ambrosia."

"Simple, easy peasy, darling."

"It's Cressida, thank you so much for asking. What do you need ambrosia for?"

He blinked and seemed a little appalled. She bet he prided himself on being suave, and forgetting to ask a lady's name was anything but. Maybe all the other women he hung around responded to darling, and it had never been an issue before. He recovered quickly and put his oily expression back on. "It's a delicacy, one we can't get here unless someone on the Elysian side brings over a batch, but lately, the charity has dried up."

"Wait a second, why aren't *you* in the Elysian Fields? What are you doing out here with the regular spirits in the Meadows of

Asphodel? I thought that was reserved for people who didn't do anything with their lives."

"The words are, 'didn't live up to their full potential,' and what do you know about it?"

It seemed a sore spot, and she knew she shouldn't pry, but she couldn't help herself. When would she ever get this opportunity again? "I mean, you weren't a normal man."

"Thank you."

"You weren't exactly a hero."

He glared.

"Well," she said quickly, "not the sword and sandals type, but you were beloved by the gods."

"Yes."

"Especially the goddesses."

"The gods, too. Bisexuality isn't something to be ashamed of."

She sputtered. "I know! So, why are you here?"

His head turned slightly to the side, mouth twisted downward. Maybe she wasn't supposed to ask. Maybe one's status in the Underworld was a touchy subject. When he didn't answer, she said, "I'm sorry. I shouldn't have asked."

He shrugged but didn't offer anything more.

"The people in the Elysian Fields won't try to stop me from taking ambrosia?"

"Why should they?" But he turned his head again as if trying to keep from saying something or looking her in the eye, and she knew nothing was going to be as simple as he thought.

And she didn't trust him, but what choice did she have except to listen. She didn't see a gate in the fence, didn't know how to get inside. She had to start trusting someone, even as she kept a close eye on him.

❖

Medusa stayed well back as Adonis and the mortal paused near Hecate's palace. Hecate chose to live near the middle of the Meadows of Asphodel, a point of pride for those who couldn't leave. Some said the goddess wanted to live among them because they were more down-to-earth than heroes prancing around talking about themselves all day. Hecate was rumored to think that the Elysian Fields were mostly full of Zeus's children and therefore insufferable by nature and always going on about their father.

When Adonis and the mortal lingered, Medusa wondered if he was taking her on a sightseeing tour of the Underworld. Medusa had expected him to lead the mortal straight to Narcissus, but by the set of her shoulders, she wasn't going to be led quietly. They were bargaining, and the only question was, for what?

The mortal spoke her name at last, Cressida, and Medusa sighed. It was a lovely name for a lovely girl, and Medusa wondered again if she should leap between them and try to hustle Cressida away, but Adonis was too aware to fall easily to her power, unlike the common harpy, and he and Narcissus had a whole gang. They might even have someone watching them at that moment, or watching Medusa watch them. She cursed the fact that she didn't have cronies of her own, but any she managed to collect always ended up pissing her off. None of them could help Stheno and Euryale anyway, so what was the point? Besides, there were rumors that Persephone still did favors for Adonis from time to time, seeing as how she was one of the reasons he died, and all the cronies in the world couldn't help fight the queen of the Underworld.

The way they were staring at Hecate's palace seemed to indicate they were going to pull another goddess into whatever scheme they were cooking up. Medusa curled her hand into a fist. That was just her luck. If Adonis was on some errand for Hecate, and Medusa interfered, she could quickly find herself floating with the shades. Cressida leaned into the fence, eager, it seemed, to get closer to Hecate's palace. Perhaps that was why she or the other mortal had come to the Underworld in the first place.

Rats. Once she went in there, she'd be out of reach. Medusa tied her robe even tighter, ready to sprint and grab Cressida, haul her off somewhere and explain later, but she and Adonis turned away from the palace, and Medusa's heart went back to a normal tempo. She followed them, trying to hear, but they chatted so softly, Cressida casting longing looks at the palace as they walked.

Interesting. If Cressida was a worshiper of Hecate, rumored as a source of feminine power, she might be more willing to help Medusa than she would Adonis, especially after Medusa pleaded for her help. Well, pleaded and lied. Medusa only needed her to commit one little murder, but she knew that people could be touchy about that sort of thing.

A plan was beginning to take shape in her mind. She reached out for a thread of shade fog and pulled it to her. "Stheno, Euryale, make contact with Medea. Time to put some events in motion."

Adonis led Cressida to one of the giant elevators, a behemoth that looked as if it could carry freight for the world's largest IKEA. Buttons ran like barnacles down its insides, across the walls and ceiling, numbers and letters and symbols more batshit than anything made by Willy Wonka. As they waited on a platform, she noticed that the elevators that crisscrossed the city went aboveground and below, moving in every direction.

After they boarded, Adonis blocked her in the corner and stood in front of her, shielding her from view. The deeper they got into crowds, the more odd looks she got, including some covetous glances she could have done without. The car zigged and zagged and shook, stopping over and over to let people in and out until Adonis finally moved out of the way, and Cressida saw the car was empty.

"What happened to everyone?"

"They weren't going where we are."

He gave her another of those winks that probably would have melted the heart of anyone who was into him, but after she rolled her eyes again, he shrugged.

"Habit," he said.

"I get it."

When the doors opened, the landscape looked like the set of an apocalypse movie. The streets were abandoned except for a few suspicious piles of clothing that might have protested upon prodding. The buildings were devoid of neon or any signage. Most had boarded up windows, and weeds grew in patches through the sidewalk.

"If this place is designed by the minds of those who live there, how does it go to shit like this?" she asked.

"This is what the residents think it should look like close to the border. Hopeless for those without hope. Stay close."

It looked like a desperate place, so Cressida supposed she shouldn't have been surprised to see a line of people stretched across a chain link fence, staring into a bright white light. They shuffled and moaned like zombies, sometimes banging on the fence, sometimes hanging from it and crying out.

"What are they?" Cressida asked.

"The desperate. Sometimes it's just the shades who collect here. Other times it's the relatives or lovers of those who live in the Fields. Maybe some of them think they should be in there. Some are just drawn to the light, and their very desire gives them a bit of form."

As they drew closer, she watched one shade drift out of the sky, gaining a faint solidity even as the fence turned him back. He clung on, his form a hazy blob without a face, only a flesh-colored smear with darker holes where his mouth and eyes should have been.

"Poor things." It made her want to tear up, but she told herself to stop being so soppy. "I guess there's nothing to be done for them."

"No." He looked up and down the fence. "Though you will have to get past them."

She eyed the hungry ghosts again, the zombies, the more solid ones rattling the fence. "They'll try to stop me?"

He mumbled something, and she realized he had no idea. Either it had been too long since a living person had attempted this, or no one ever had. "You do have a plan, yes?"

He led her close to a boarded up warehouse, and they kept to the side as they crept toward the fence. If she squinted, the fence blinked in and out of focus as if washed out by the light coming from the other side, though the zombies couldn't move through it.

"Is there a similar line of people on the other side?" Cressida asked.

"Begging to be let in here? You must be joking. Anyone in the Fields can come over anytime they like, though they rarely do."

"But what if their family is here? Their friends?"

His mouth set in a firm line. "They probably forget. Wouldn't be paradise if they were forever mooning over those they'd lost, would it?"

She frowned hard and was about to argue, but he rested a hand on her back.

"Get ready to run," he said.

"What are you going to do?"

"They're attracted to the blood of those more aware than they are. Wait until they're looking at me, then run past. The fence won't stop you."

"Wait! What do I do when I get over there?" She whispered it as loudly as she dared, but he was already running for the middle of the street. He slipped a knife from his belt and slashed his arm. Blood welled around the cut, and he dangled his fingers over the street, letting the blood drip down.

The pack gathered around the fence turned as one and shuffled toward him. Cressida looked from Adonis to the fence. He locked eyes with her and mouthed, "Go," but what were the zombies going to do to him? Wouldn't he need her help fighting them off?

If he was going to fight. He backed away from their shuddering advance, and she realized he couldn't run unless she did. With one final look, she sprinted for the fence, ready to jump and climb it.

Several of the zombies looked her way, a few taking steps toward her, their smears of eyes widening as if sensing she was alive. Maybe she was as alluring as Adonis's blood, maybe even more so, if the way they picked up their feet was any indication. She twisted away from their grasping hands and kept running. She sprang for the fence, bracing for the impact and telling herself she had to grab on and climb even if pain rattled through her.

She soared straight through the fence, breaking it apart into twinkling bits of light. With a yelp, she put her hands up to cover her face as green grass rushed toward her.

The air *oomphed* from her lungs as she landed, and shockwaves traveled up her arms. Her backpack smacked against her, something metal in it digging into her ribs. She eased up, favoring her arms but remembering the zombie hoard that was probably coming for her now that she'd destroyed the fence.

She glanced over her shoulder. The fence was gone, but so was the horde, the streets. A canyon wall rose up behind her, a clear stream flowing in front of it. A bridge of ivory spanned the stream and led to a gate in the wall, one that sparkled like gold. Birds chirped from nearby trees, and the bright green grass had a silky feel, like the finest golf course. She pushed up, wondered what the hell she was supposed to do now, and wandered toward the trees.

❖

At the fence to the Elysian Fields, Medusa guessed what Adonis was up to. He wanted ambrosia, and with a mortal on his side, he'd found a way to go around the regular channels, undercut the gangs in the Fields, maybe even corner the market depending on how much Cressida could bring back.

It was a good plan if dealing in ambrosia didn't turn her stomach. She raced to catch up, but she'd had to take another elevator, Stheno and Euryale leading her as they watched through the shade network. And they weren't the only ones watching, Medusa was certain.

Her conversation with Medea had been short, Medea cackling with glee as Medusa outlined her plan. She was always a good one for a cackle, no matter the circumstances. She was one of the greatest villains in Greek myth, after all, though the murder of her children had been a trick she'd played on her cheating husband. A sorceress could make someone see whatever she wanted him to see, including the bloodless bodies of his offspring. And he'd suffered for the rest of his days while she'd run away with their sons.

Even now, long after she'd died, Medea enjoyed the odd trick of making someone see what she wanted them to see. She'd get a nice illusion ready, and all Medusa had to do was lead Cressida into the middle of it.

But when Adonis cut himself in front of the pack of hungry dead, and Cressida leapt into the Elysian Fields, Medusa almost cried out. She'd meant to act before Cressida had a chance to enter the Fields, but as usual, she was a step behind. Now, what if Cressida got herself into more trouble than she could handle? Medusa couldn't rescue her. No one could. Maybe they'd get lucky, and she'd find some unassuming hero who would help her if she got into a jam.

Like Perseus.

Medusa snarled and hoped Cressida wouldn't run into him, not yet. It was vital that he have no idea who Cressida was; when Medusa was ready to spring the trap, she needed him completely off guard.

Though she'd never been to paradise, she knew the rules. Everyone who dwelled in the Fields was given the choice to be resurrected twice, keeping in mind only vague understandings of the lives they'd lived before. And if they accomplished enough heroic deeds in all three lives that the gods judged them worthy of the Fields, they would move on to the Isles of the Blessed, as close to godhood as they could come, and unreachable by anyone in the Underworld or the mortal world. Perseus would live on for eternity, untouchable and shrouded in the most exquisite bliss while Medusa's sisters faded into shades, with her one day to follow.

She gritted her teeth, and her power washed over her. One of the shuffling dead met her gaze and hardened into stone.

"Shit."

Adonis was still leading the dead on a chase, but if he saw this statue, he'd know she'd come. She crept from her hiding place, wrapped her arms around the statue, and pulled. It lurched forward with a horrid grinding sound. "Shh," she whispered, looking to Adonis again, but he didn't seem to notice. He'd never been one for realizing what was going on around him. She tugged harder, grunting with the effort and trying to tell herself she was strong enough, willing herself to believe it so it might have the possibility of being true.

The statue wobbled, toppling, and she leapt out of the way, grunting as she hit the pavement. Several pieces broke off as the statue fell, and after she tugged the hem of her robe loose from one of its elbows, she scattered a bit of refuse over it, making it into just one more broken bit of landscape.

❖

In the grassy meadow, the breeze smelled like fresh laundry with a hint of cookies.

"This is more like it," Cressida said.

Gentle laughter and the strains of music came from a group of trees nearby. She looked around for ambrosia the plant, but somehow, she didn't think Adonis had been talking about ragweed. She took a few steps toward the voices. Where better to find ambrosia than at a picnic of divine people hanging out in the afterlife?

She crept forward, alert for any threat that might leap at her from the woods, but she didn't see anything, didn't even know if she could sense anything. She was tempted to stroll, to whistle a happy tune, and knew it was because of the air around her, the scenery itself like a heaping helping of mood enhancers. She had to fight to keep on high alert, leaving her half on the edge of caution and half in bliss. It felt like an itch between her shoulder blades that wouldn't be alleviated by any twitching or scratching or squirming under the backpack.

A group of people lounged in a clearing ahead, dappled in sparkling sunlight and dressed in the draped dresses and chitons she'd been expecting from the first time she'd set foot in the Underworld. If these people could control their culture as the others could, they were ignoring any new fashion in favor of their past.

And everyone was spectacular looking, unearthly beautiful; it was hard not to stare at the women, even those that weren't completely human. Several ladies sported feathers or scales, and she tried not to dwell on who they might be; she didn't want to gawk. She focused on the cups they passed back and forth, those filled with golden, glowing liquid. That was either nectar or ambrosia, depending on what ancient text you consulted. She didn't see any food, just ewers full of the glowing stuff that never seemed to run out, passed back and forth as the drinkers laughed and spoke. She heard their words as if through a film, as if it was translated just as it got to her ears. Someone was telling a tale of an old battle, and while the others laughed, the occasional eye roll said most of them would rather be listening to anything else, but hey, at least there was ambrosia.

Cressida walked ahead slowly, wondering how close she could get before they noticed, but sure they *would* notice. A few glanced at her but didn't seem to sense anything strange. As Cressida joined the circle, a young woman with flowers strewn through her hair moved aside, making room.

Cressida sat and tried not to stare at anyone, though she guessed the flower woman and quite a few of the others were nymphs. Someone passed her a cup, and the closest nymph filled it with glowing liquid from one of the long-necked ewers. She smiled but didn't drink, knowing that would trap her here, though what a place to be trapped!

She mimed taking a drink and tried to put on a smile.

"And where do you come from?" the nymph asked. The flowers didn't seem woven through her hair but were part of it, green strands among the gold. She leaned forward invitingly.

Cressida blushed and told her eyes to stay on the nymph's face and away from the impressive décolletage now pointing her way. "Um. Nowhere special."

The nymph laughed and licked her full lips. "Have you come to play?"

And boy, that sounded like a fine idea. Cressida watched the nymph's tongue cross her lips a second time and turned away from temptation. She didn't know how strict the food and drink rules were. If the nymph had just drank ambrosia, and then they happened to kiss…

She told herself to shut up. "It sounded like a fun party, so I wandered over."

The ewer came back around; Cressida snagged it and filled the nymph's cup. The nymph laughed but took a long drink and let herself be drawn into conversation with the person on her other side.

Cressida held on to the ewer and scooted back a bit. When another ewer came around, she snagged it, too, all she could hope to carry. Adonis hadn't told her how much she needed. Bastard hadn't told her anything! Ambrosia had to be worth a lot; he wouldn't go through all this trouble just for a good drink, right? Of course, she'd met people who'd flown hundreds of miles for the same thing in the living world.

She scooted farther back. Around the circle, a few people began to frown, no doubt catching on to the fact that the ambrosia had disappeared. Before the frowns could deepen, winged creatures zipped through the trees bearing more ewers, and a hurrah went up from the company.

Well, all she had to do now was walk away. The nymph turned her way, and when their eyes met again, the nymph's head tilted. "There's something different about you."

"Nope, not me." Cressida stood, trying for nonchalant, but when the nymph squinted at her, she ran, heading for the border. Someone called out, but she didn't stop to answer. She headed straight for the stream and gate, wondering if it would fade away like the fence had or if she'd need to open it. No matter what, she'd have to keep moving when she reached the other side, or the zombies would be on her.

When she got to the stream, the trees beside it reached for her with their branches. She tripped to a halt. "What the shit?"

Something tugged on her shoulder, and she wrenched away, trying to keep the trees and whatever had grabbed her in sight.

The nymph's impossibly green eyes opened wide. "You're alive!"

Cressida gulped in a few deep breaths. "I have to go."

The nymph eyed the ewers. "You're alive, and you're an ambrosia runner?"

"Please, someone over there has my aunt, and if I give him this..." What? He would help her out of the kindness of his heart? She knew then that she should hold on to the ewers, maybe stash them somewhere until she saw June again.

The nymph's eyes narrowed. "Which gang do you work for? The next shipment's not due until next week." When Cressida shook her head, the nymph stalked forward, her perfect features settling into a disconcerting frown. "Someone thinks he can undercut us, does he? Kick us out of our own business?"

"Gang? What? I...thought people in the Elysian Fields didn't want to think of the people over...there."

"That's just for silly humans telling their silly stories." She reached out, and Cressida backed away. When the tree grabbed for her, Cressida ducked under its branches and ran. She hugged the ewers close, but the liquid didn't slosh out. Maybe in the Elysian Fields, no one ever spilled a drop. She pounded across the ivory bridge and ran full tilt for the gate, hoping she wasn't going to bounce off of it.

"We'll find your contact," the nymph called. "Tell them that no one crosses the Flowers and lives!"

The gate gave way as the fence had, and Cressida's foot came down on hard pavement. The moans of the zombies echoed around her, but she held the ewers close and put her head down, plowing ahead. She shouldered someone over and kept running. Someone else seemed to pass through her, and she shuddered, but she could only think to run as the city came into sharper focus with its boarded up warehouses and slick streets.

"Cressida!" Adonis waved. He'd lost his pack of zombies, and she streaked for him like a bullet, wondering if the nymph was just a step behind.

The zombies clawed at her, some of them dissolving like smoke into the shades they'd been. They pawed for the ewers, but she kept running, and Adonis waved her on, though he hadn't dived in to help. He even started running just as she got to him, gesturing for her to keep pace.

"Keep going," he said. "They'll weaken the farther we get from the barrier."

He reached for the ewers, but she snarled at him. When they ran up the block and around a corner, he finally slowed.

"I'll hold on to these until we get my aunt back," she said.

He put his hands on his hips. "And I'll refuse to help until I get my ambrosia."

She glared. "A nymph from the Flowers wanted me to tell you that they'll find you, that no one crosses them and lives."

He took a step back, just as she hoped. "You met one of the Flowers? What the hell were you thinking?"

"Well," she said after a deep breath. "They had a sign that said, 'Come meet us, and you can have a free slice of cake,' and I thought why not? Free cake."

He stared at her, and she felt like kicking him.

"*They* found *me*!" she said. "After your oh-so careful instructions and all the information you gave me about who to talk to and what to do, I had to improvise. I found some people. I grabbed this. I tried to sneak away, but a nymph caught me. All right?"

"Do they know who sent you?"

She shrugged, holding that information in reserve.

He ran a hand down his face, lingering at his mouth.

"Are you and Narcissus in a gang?" she asked. "And you all deal in this stuff?" She nodded at the ewers. "I'm guessing it's not just a cool and refreshing beverage?" When he didn't answer, she sighed. "How about I give you one and hold on to the other until I have my aunt back?" But she didn't hand either of them over, not yet, not until he agreed.

He rolled his eyes. "You'll never be able to hold it on your own."

"Why, is it going to grow legs?"

"No," a new voice said from the closest alley. "The denizens of the Underworld will tear it from your grasp."

CHAPTER FOUR

Cressida turned and then wobbled to a halt as if someone had yanked her around on a rug. Vaguely, she knew what she *should* be feeling: Alarm, fear, suspicion. Any of those would have been correct, even justified. But just like she knew her jaw was open and couldn't close it, she couldn't muster any thoughts besides, "Good God, look at *her*!"

Even without shoes, the stranger stood nearly as tall as Adonis, and Cressida had never been able to resist the tall ones. Her skin had a dusky, Mediterranean tint, and her hair shone like thick black ink, so dark it reflected the colors of the closest neon sign, giving her electric green highlights. Her eyes were green, too, though with slits like a snake's and streaks of yellow dancing through them.

And that figure! Curves on curves, she was the epitome of hourglass as she glided toward them. Even with mud flaking off her skin, spotting her white robe and jeans, she was beyond breathtaking. Breath-stealing, maybe. She locked up every breath and threw away the key.

Cressida tried to speak and ended up saying, "Who," and "How," more or less at the same time, leaving her with, "Whow?" Smooth, very smooth. She suddenly wished she was back in her undergrad classes, where any preface to asking someone out could start with innocuous questions like, "Excuse me, which chapter were we supposed to read?" or "Were we supposed to calculate just how big that stick up that prof's ass is?" Of course, Cressida had never had a class with anyone who looked like the embodiment of the word gorgeous. If this wasn't a goddess, who was?

Cressida licked her lips, tried to think of something that would cover her "whow," and ended up with, "How…how are you?"

The goddess lifted a thick black eyebrow. "I'm fine, thanks, and you can be, too, the sooner you get away from him."

"This isn't any of your business, Medusa," Adonis said.

Cressida burst out laughing, and they both stared at her. "No," she said, "you can't be." Though that would make her a demigoddess, half Titan, if the really old tales were to be believed, but Cressida had been ready to call her Persephone if not Aphrodite herself. Cressida tried to smooth her expression into something more suave and hoped like hell she succeeded. "I'm Cressida. Nice to meet." *You forgot a word! You forgot a word!* "You. It's nice to meet you. Nice that we're, um, meeting." She cleared her throat, and it came out far noisier than she intended.

Medusa took a step, and unlike her former glide, this was more predatory, putting Cressida in mind of Medusa's famous snake hair, which she currently wasn't sporting, though Cressida didn't think it would make her less beautiful, just more interesting. Snakes were very graceful, if she recalled correctly. And dangerous, at least for some.

Medusa's gaze flicked to the ewers. "Do you know what you have?"

"Ambrosia?" Cressida asked.

"The most powerful drug in the Underworld. In the Elysian Fields, it's just wine. Here, it's mixed with a special ingredient that gives anyone who drinks it more awareness."

"Making everyone happy," Adonis said.

"Not everyone," Medusa said, glancing at him. "Not the shades." She pinned Cressida with her gaze again. "When word gets out that you have this much ambrosia, you won't have a moment's peace, not from the gangs, not from anyone. Not even from the shades." She glanced up.

Cressida looked and took a step back as the fog billowed closer. She bumped into Adonis, who put his hands on her shoulders as if to protect her. She wriggled out of his grasp and stood so she could run from both of them if she had to, though her pelvis kept telling her to lean closer to Medusa. She told it to keep its mind on the problem at hand.

Cressida looked Medusa in the eye again and tried to keep her face serious; no longing allowed. "So, you want it instead?" She blushed at what could be the world's sloppiest double entendre and tried to look tough, afraid that with all her effort, she was landing somewhere just shy of sassy.

"I want you to dump it or throw it back where it came from."

"No!" Adonis took a threatening step, but Medusa didn't back up an inch. She gave him a glare famous for turning people into stone, though he remained flesh and blood, or spirit, or whatever. Maybe Medusa wasn't trying very hard. "Do you know how much that's worth?"

"Worth the destruction of souls who've never wronged you?"

"Better than becoming one of them." He jerked his chin toward the fence, the zombies.

"As long as people remember who you are, you won't end up like that," Medusa said.

"And how long can that be, really? Luck has to run out sometime."

Cressida shook her head. "Wait, if you drink the ambrosia, more people will remember you?"

"You gain more awareness." Medusa said. "Besides being remembered, drinking modified ambrosia is the only way to become more aware, but only after mixing the ambrosia with a shade."

Cressida frowned and tried to think through that. "*With* a shade?"

"Oh, he didn't tell you?" She glanced at Adonis, who sighed and crossed his arms. "The gangs in the Underworld mix the ambrosia with the souls of the weaker dead and consume them. It's a complicated, painful process."

"No one knows that it's *painful*," Adonis said.

"Undertaken by those desperate to remain aware, to remain powerful."

"This could save your sisters," Adonis said. "Look, we can both come out of this happy. You take one ewer; we'll take the other."

"I don't deal in soul eating."

"Then just stay out of my business, and we won't have a problem."

Cressida started edging away, wondering who was right, but they both agreed on one thing: what she was holding was dangerous. Maybe she should have never gotten involved with Adonis at all. Maybe she could find June on her own. She hugged the ewers tighter. She could trade them for help. Hell, that was what Adonis was offering, but if it was true that the drinker also had to eat the dead…

She wondered what Adonis meant by mentioning Medusa's sisters. Stheno and Euryale were part of Medusa's legend, though they were missing from the tales most people knew. According to older legends, the three sisters were powerful, part-snake demigods, and Medusa was targeted by the hero Perseus because she was the only mortal of the three. Newer legends dropped the sisters and claimed Medusa had fornicated—some tales said willingly, others not so much—with Poseidon in Athena's temple, so Athena turned her into a monster with a head of snakes whose gaze could turn someone to stone. In either tale, she'd been killed by Perseus, first to serve as a wedding present, then to help him petrify a horrific monster.

He'd murdered her while she slept, so legend claimed. Cressida had always thought of it as a sad story, but one that happened over and over in myth, one that cemented the notion that everyone was a plaything of the gods. Women often couldn't catch even the hint of a break, and Cressida's heart suddenly went out to the muddy demigoddess. Even with Adonis there, staring Medusa down, Cressida wanted to hug her for more reasons than one.

Medusa looked to Cressida again, and she blinked, seemingly surprised at the sympathy Cressida couldn't hide. Her head tilted as if Cressida was an interesting puzzle worth the time to figure out. "I'll help you find your aunt."

"In exchange for?" Cressida asked, glad that part of her mind was reacting on autopilot because her body wanted nothing more than to drape around Medusa and not let go.

Medusa smiled widely. "Nothing."

Cressida quirked an eyebrow and waited.

"I'll help you get your aunt, and then you decide whether or not you want to help me."

"To do…" Cressida said, getting pretty tired of everyone's reluctance to just say what they were thinking. But when Medusa licked her lips, Cressida changed her mind. She could watch Medusa think all day.

"Simple really. I need you to lure the hero Perseus over to this side of the fence so I can kill him, reduce him to a shade, and feed him to my weakened sisters with the small amount of ambrosia I have tucked away. One little murder for three lives? Not so bad, eh?"

Yeah, pretty bad, but Cressida was too stunned to speak. Even if Perseus deserved to be punished, Cressida had only ever sworn at another person in anger. She'd told herself she'd been prepared to hit Nero with the bat, but she wasn't certain she would have. "I thought you didn't deal in soul eating?"

"Don't fall for any of her bull," Adonis said. "You're halfway to your goal with me already. Just give me the ambrosia, and you'll have your aunt back in no time, and the two of you can be on your way."

Two people who were clearly in it for themselves, and she had no idea which might be the lesser of two evils. And whichever she chose, she'd wind up with at least one enemy. She looked to the ambrosia, trying to tell herself it didn't matter if the people of the Underworld destroyed themselves. The shades weren't her concern.

Even more than that, she tried to tell herself she wasn't swayed by the exquisite woman but by the offer to help before asking for a favor, rather than the other way around. She looked at the shades, at the way their formless eyes tried to focus on the ambrosia. They were hungry, too, for the power the ambrosia could give them even though they were the ones killed for it, the whole of the Underworld eating itself.

"Do you know how to get my aunt away from Hecate?" Cressida whispered.

Adonis started. "Well…" He waved vaguely. "There's, um…"

Medusa stepped forward. "As someone who's visited the goddess of magic many times, I know the ways in and out of her palace. All we need do is sneak in while she's distracted, grab your aunt, and sneak out before she notices. Even if she finds out, chances are, she'll be so taken with our moxie, she won't care to pursue us."

It wasn't much of a plan, but it was more than Adonis had.

"One small condition." Medusa nodded to the ewers. "Get rid of those."

Adonis squawked, but before Cressida could think better of it, she ran for the fence and chucked the ewers hard, sending them sailing over the head of the moaning zombies to disappear beyond the fence.

"No!" Adonis cried, but Medusa held him back. "We had a deal!"

Cressida shrugged, but she did feel a bit guilty. "And she has a plan."

He backed away, staring, and she knew she'd made an enemy, but she had to make a choice. He glared hard at Medusa, too, but if he had any parting words, he kept them to himself as he turned and strode toward the nearest elevator.

Medusa smiled, and Cressida hoped she hadn't been a fool by choosing the prettiest face.

"Well," Medusa said. "I'm honored you accepted my offer. Now, if you don't mind, I'd like to stop by my apartment and change before we continue." She held out the ends of her robe. "Believe it or not, this is not my usual style."

Cressida opened her mouth to say that Medusa would look fab dressed in a garbage bag, but she shut her teeth before the words could get out. "Sure." She gestured at the robe and felt as if something was needed. "I didn't know if you always wore…" Well, obviously not! "I mean…"

Medusa's lips quirked as if she wanted to laugh but was afraid of embarrassing Cressida further. "Well, a regular muddy robe is pretty much my go-to for hanging around the house, but I thought I might change into my more formal muddy robe for adventuring. I mean, it's just more rescue ready."

Cressida sighed a laugh before clearing her throat. "I'm sure. Lead the way." They walked together toward another elevator, and Cressida relaxed more than she had with Adonis, and she and Medusa had only met moments ago. It gave her bright hopes for the future. She'd found someone in the Underworld who seemed to have ethics, who'd offered to help June before asking for favors. Any way she approached it, things were looking up.

Apart from the whole murder thing.

Cressida was smitten; that much was very easy to see. She smiled every time Medusa glanced at her. Her cheeks had flamed red when they'd met, and Medusa caught the sweep of her roving blue eyes several times, muddy robe be damned.

Medusa couldn't help a few twinges of guilt, even past the ego boost of being desired by a very attractive woman. But she'd been upfront about what she wanted. It was just the implication that June would be rescued *before* Perseus was killed that had been the lie.

But June would get rescued. If she'd entered the Underworld as prepared as Cressida seemed to be, she had plenty of time. Time worked differently in the Underworld. From what she remembered of the old tales, the living didn't need to eat or drink as often as they did in the world above. It was only when they were tempted by the fruits of the Underworld that they felt the need to sate themselves. A strong-willed person could make very little stretch for a long time.

But how strong-willed was June? Medusa thought about asking, but she didn't want to put Cressida in mind of eating, either. And she didn't need Cressida worrying about June when it was going to be a while before they got around to rescuing her, if all went according to plan.

"So, how many people in the Underworld do the whole soul eating thing?" Cressida asked.

Medusa grimaced. She hated the practice of destroying the dead. That hadn't been a lie. Luckily, Perseus was far from innocent. "More than I care to think about. A few gangs deal in the stuff. Those who are less aware get hooked on it and have to keep coming back for more."

"Is that why you don't want it for your sisters? You're afraid they'll become..."

"Junkies? Yes. But the soul of someone as aware as Perseus should keep them going for a long time to come." She smiled brightly. "And he's as guilty as can be."

"How will you, um, turn him into a shade?"

"The same way he killed me. If he's beheaded with a similar weapon to the one he killed me with, that should have enough power to do it, or so say the sorceresses and oracles I've consulted." Like Medea. Medusa had to remember to contact her again as soon as Cressida was out of the room. It wasn't the most precise plan in the world, but never having killed someone from the Elysian Fields, imprecise plans were all she had. "Of course, that's only how you kill a hero. There are many ways for us regular dead folks to be reduced to shades, but a hero has to have something...poetic."

"I guess you've had a long time to think about it." Cressida flushed. "I'm sorry. That's very insensitive."

"Because you're calling me old?" When Cressida fumbled for an explanation, Medusa winked. "I know how long I've been around, thanks, alive and dead. There's a point where old passes to ancient and then becomes legend. That's when age becomes impressive. I was alive long before Perseus found me. My sisters and I were once goddesses in our own right, with our own worshipers, but gradually, our worship fell away, and my tale was changed."

"That's the story most people know, where you're cursed by Athena."

Medusa tossed her hair back, trying for nonchalant and certain the effect was spoiled when a shower of muddy flakes fell around her like dandruff. She tried to cover it with a confident smile. "I was always fearsome. I didn't need a curse."

"But you look so…"

"Ah, you were expecting the snake hair."

"And the gaze that can turn someone to stone."

"I still have my powers. They're just a little dampened. And I choose how I appear, both to the living and the dead."

"Oh." She seemed a little disappointed.

"You were hoping for more of a *Clash of the Titans* look, complete with a half-snake body?"

"I know that movie really bungled the myths, but it was my favorite as a kid."

"We love all the movies made about us, even if they're wrong. They increase our awareness, though the inconsistences do occasionally chap a few asses." When Cressida gave her a bright smile, she returned it. "Books and movies work differently down here than in the living world. We know about living culture and stories because minds in the living world are constantly thinking about the things around them, the world they live in, and those thoughts trickle down to us."

"Adonis said something similar. Trickle-down culture."

"If we concentrate on a particular notion, we can see it in all the minds that are thinking about it, so if we want a blockbuster movie—"

"You just think about it at the same time?"

"We screen them on the sides of buildings, and everyone shows up to have a good laugh at the myth-based films. I was looking pretty bad-assed in the newest one, metal bikini and all."

"But none of them mention your sisters, at least none that I've seen."

"They've been fading for a long time." Medusa sighed and let some of her real sadness show. "I think the only reason they're hanging around is because of the Internet. If we had to keep waiting for grad students to research them, they'd have become shades long ago."

Cressida glanced up at the drifting shades again. She didn't seem to notice, but a few had followed her, drawn to that shimmer of life she was probably unaware of. Medusa wondered if she knew they would descend on and consume her if they could, just to briefly share in what it was once like to be alive. Lucky for her, they didn't have enough form to accomplish such a thing.

"Do you mind if I ask you something intensely personal?" Cressida asked.

"Intriguing," Medusa said, unable to keep a bit of a purr out of her voice. "If it's about that metal bikini, I don't actually own one."

Cressida laughed a little breathlessly. "It's not anything, well…" She cleared her throat. "Your sisters are said to be immortal, and Perseus only came after you because he could kill you. But…"

Medusa nodded. "But why aren't they still alive? They were never immortal; nothing truly is, and they were murdered with me. But we are the children of a god and a Titan, older than some of the Olympians. Who knows how long we would have lived given the chance? There are still monsters walking the earth, old creatures from an old world, who have learned to hide. My sisters could have survived. I could have. Even if my sisters had perished, with my memories of them fresh and vibrant, they could have been ruling the Underworld."

"But you still would have been separated."

"There are ways to communicate with the living world. You just need someone there who can hear you. Now the best we can hope for is to kill the child of a god and consume his essence so we can stagger along a little longer." She didn't have to fake the wistfulness, the fear of eventual despair. Everyone in the Underworld shared it. The brave smile she put on did have a bit of fakeness, but she tried to tell herself that no matter what, she was doing the right thing. "Don't worry about it right now. I told you; we're getting your aunt first. And then you can help me if you choose. I want you to think it through, really consider it."

Cressida nodded, her face so downcast and thoughtful that Medusa wanted to both give her a hug and smile in satisfaction. She was very cute when deep in thought, with a little frown between her brows and part of her mouth turned down. Medusa had the strangest desire to pull on one of Cressida's silky red curls just to watch it bounce back into shape, but she kept her hands to herself.

The seed had been planted; now she could watch it grow. Cressida wasn't ready to commit to killing Perseus yet, but she would be, given time. She would see the injustice, would see Medusa's words backed up by everything in the Underworld, and Medusa had always been good at persuading people. She probably would have been able to persuade Perseus not to kill her if he hadn't snuck up on her while she was asleep. Sometimes, she'd wished it had happened like in the movies, that she'd gone out shooting arrows and trying to turn him into stone, but he'd found her napping in the garden, and it didn't matter *how* heroic deeds got carried out as long as they did.

She pushed thoughts of Perseus away, afraid she would rail against him too hard. She had to let the idea percolate in Cressida's brain. While they rode the elevator toward her apartment, she gave some thought about how to actually get June back. If Hecate did have her, that wasn't going to be easy. Medusa would have to set some things in motion while she was pretending to guide Cressida toward Hecate's palace. Maybe Medusa could arrange to have June rescued by someone else, to have her show up just in time to convince Cressida to kill Perseus. Adding obligation to the mix might push Cressida over the edge into actually doing the deed. And if not, well, Medusa could always hold June hostage until Perseus was dead, never mind that she would rather have the whole business seem like a free act on Cressida's part.

Medusa almost shivered. Soon she'd have her sisters back, they would unseat upstarts like Adonis and Narcissus, and the afterlife would be better than any life they'd ever known.

First things first, though. When they reached the apartment, Cressida stopped in wonder as Stheno and Euryale stepped into the large living room. They were caught, as they always were, between their human and winged snake forms. Scales covered half of Stheno's body, though her long black hair was as straight and human as ever. Her eyes were black pits like a shark's, something that once only happened when she was far too angry to control it.

Euryale's hair had transformed into snakes, but they were listless, hanging over her shoulders like dead things, their eyes staring at nothing. Wings sprouted from her shoulders, but they were crooked, half-finished and dangling down her back. Both were still beautiful; Medusa couldn't find them anything but beautiful, but the life had gone out of them. If they faded anymore, she'd be able to see right through them, and then nothing would hold their feet to the ground.

"My sisters," Medusa said. "Stheno and Euryale. They're not much for conversation."

Cressida's face held a look of such pity that Medusa wanted to hug her, but a twinge of guilt wouldn't allow it. After another look at her sisters, though, she frowned. What did she have to feel guilty for? Saving her family? She turned away before the warring feelings could show on her face. Maybe Cressida would understand even after Medusa tricked her into killing Perseus. Even if she didn't, it didn't matter. What needed to happen would happen.

"If you'll excuse me." Medusa hurried toward her bedroom. "Have a seat. I won't be long." She almost told Cressida to make herself at home, but she didn't want to put Cressida in mind of eating or drinking or using the bathroom; that would have her spending some of her precious resources.

Medusa walked into the bedroom and closed the door, trusting her sisters to call if Cressida decided to wander off, though Medusa didn't think she would. After all, if Hecate really had her aunt, what could she actually do without help?

Medusa stripped quickly and stepped in the shower to scrub off the flecks of mud. When she emerged again clean, she paused before her dresser. She was thinking of sensible underthings, something cotton, but thoughts of Cressida made her hands drift toward the red, lacy options. She wound up somewhere in between, a dark blue set, with just a little bit of lace to be interesting, though she told herself she wasn't going to need interesting. She couldn't let Cressida that close, not when she planned on tricking her.

She pulled on a clean pair of jeans, sneakers, and a long-sleeved tee. She didn't want Cressida to feel alone in her choice of outfit, and she didn't want to knock Cressida silly in one of her more slinky garments. Still, she paused as she perused her enormous closet. Showing her underwear might be out, but wouldn't knocking Cressida a little silly strengthen the chances of her plan succeeding? Would Cressida be more likely to help the more smitten she was?

"Now you're just playing games," Medusa muttered. Game playing was part and parcel of existing in the Underworld, but Medusa didn't want to play with Cressida more than she had to. "I must be getting soft."

She marched to her bedroom window and opened it, pulling a piece of shade fog toward her. She concentrated on Medea, her tall form, bright red hair and electric presence, the way her magic crackled through the air. "Medea."

"I was starting to wonder where you'd gone," Medea said, her voice vibrating through the fog, pitched so that it would carry only to Medusa's ears.

"She went to the Elysian Fields before I could stop her."

"Did she bring back ambrosia?"

Medea frowned at the eagerness in Medea's voice. She almost said that Cressida had brought back enough to make anyone rich, but she didn't want Medea getting ideas. "No, she wasn't able to."

"Shame. It would have made a great payment."

"As if me owing you a favor and making you the household name for magic again isn't payment enough?"

Medea chuckled, and it had the tinge of evil that made her so enticing. "I'm ready when you are. And if I may strum my own lyre, I've really outdone myself."

Medusa had to laugh. "Strum away. We should be headed your way momentarily. Are all the illusions to get us there in place?"

"Who in Hades do you think you're talking to?" The question had a playful tone, and Medusa could tell the famous sorceress was proud of what she'd accomplished.

"Fantastic. See you soon." Medusa let go of the shade, sending it to drift with the rest.

Cressida was sitting bolt upright on the couch, taking tiny sips from a bottle of water. Medusa didn't know what had put her in mind of it, probably the way Stheno and Euryale stared at her. It was clear she didn't know what to do with her hands as she watched them, too.

"Ready?" Medusa asked.

"Yes!" Cressida bolted to her feet, water dribbling over her hand. Clever girl that she was, she capped the rest and instead of shaking the excess off, lapped it off her knuckles.

Medusa drew in a sharp breath, struck at something so commonplace being so erotic, but she supposed it was the smarts combined with frugality. Endearing and entirely becoming. When Cressida caught her watching, tongue still out, she froze before straightening, an embarrassed look on her face.

"Sorry." She mumbled something else about wasting and wanting, but Medusa cleared her throat.

"Let's get going." She nodded to her sisters. They nodded back in sync.

Cressida gave them a vague wave. "It was, um, nice to meet you."

They nodded again, never speaking unless they had to. Cressida seemed as if she might back out of the apartment. In the old days, she wouldn't have faced them at all, fearing their power too much.

As they waited for the elevator, Cressida shuffled her feet. "I'm sorry. Even after what you said, I had no idea."

"They'll get better." She didn't add, "With your help," but she could feel the words between them and knew Cressida felt them, too. It was nearly enough to banish guilt as they hit the street and walked in the direction of Hecate's real palace. When they turned a corner instead of continuing straight toward the palace, Cressida didn't seem to notice. Medea's illusions had to be working, though Medusa couldn't see the ones she knew were there. Once she was inside Medea's place, she'd be as susceptible as Cressida, but she enjoyed the shows Medea put together. They were always quality.

As they walked, they chatted, and Cressida mentioned that she'd studied ancient Greek culture and myth. She said her aunt was a doctor of myth, and Medusa hoped that meant June could survive long enough for Cressida to find her after Perseus was dead. They paused several blocks from the palace in front of a low, long building, Medea's workshop, though Cressida wouldn't realize that, not as long as the illusions were working.

Cressida put her hands up, curling her fingers as if resting them on a fence that wasn't there. "Here we are again." She peered and craned as if trying to see the faraway palace, even though the wall of the workshop was only a few feet in front of her.

❖

Cressida stared at the fence, the acre of lawn. Sneaking in didn't seem possible; too much open space. And Hecate was sometimes called the goddess of keys, too. She guarded secret ways and paths. The goddess of locking things up wouldn't have an unbarred back door or a hole in her fence, not unless she wanted one.

Maybe Medusa planned to barter to get June back. Maybe Hecate would want ambrosia, too, and Cressida could fetch some more, soul eating be damned. Of course, now that she'd pissed off the Flowers gang, Cressida didn't know how easy that would be. They could have people guarding the entrance to the Elysian Fields, something they probably never had to do. Or they might be staring at two broken ewers of ambrosia and wondering what the hell her game was. Maybe she could slip them a note? Or maybe Hecate would give her something to trade, and then she'd be off on a string of favors across the Underworld, a never-ending quest. She and June could be long dead before it was over, but if they wound up in the Underworld, too, maybe they wouldn't even notice.

"Let's head around," Medusa said. As they walked around the fence, the lawn blurred and mutated into broken crags. Cressida watched, rapt, as the landscape reoriented itself into something that belonged in the depths of Tartarus, hell for those already dead.

The palace walls shuddered, sections sliding back into the whole, all of it moving and mixing like an enormous 3D puzzle. It made a harsh, grinding sound, stone sliding over stone with the occasional creak of moving wood. It morphed into a jumble of architecture, still with the odd column or two, but also borrowing from every type of construction Cressida had ever heard of: flying buttresses mixed with Persian motifs blended with Gothic gables. Parapets sprouted from random corners to fight with towers and balconies and renaissance cupolas. A huge, antebellum porch whirled out to circle the second floor, and stained glass windows sprouted between floors, with the occasional door, wood and steel, that opened to nowhere.

"Wow," Cressida said. "Adonis told me it would change, but I never expected anything like this!"

Medusa glanced away as if it held no interest for her. "Not fitting in with your expectations?"

"Nothing has so far, but that is really weird." She nodded, impressed. "Though I suppose it isn't weird for the goddess of magic. It takes collective consciousness to shape everything else, but I guess a goddess can do what she wants."

Medusa nodded. "She can do the palace, but sometimes she loses track of the fence."

That didn't sound like the goddess of keys Cressida had heard about, but she supposed Medusa would know better than her. Medusa led the way to a clump of scrubby bushes gathered near the fence but close to an alley. Cressida hadn't crossed this way before, couldn't say whether or not the bushes had always been there, but with the changing landscape, how would she know? The fence was the same wrought iron, though some of it blinked in and out of focus, appearing as stone or wooden slats before returning to its iron appearance. If Hecate was changing it, she wasn't paying a lot of attention. Medusa pulled the bushes aside, revealing a hole in the fence, though the edges of it faded in and out of focus, too.

Cressida gaped. "Was that here before?"

"For those of us who know it's here. For everyone else?" She shrugged. "I told you. Hecate likes the occasional surprise. She has a soft spot for those who sneak into her palace. Gives her something to do, I guess. Of course, if people manage to sneak in and she catches them, sometimes she doesn't let them leave."

Cressida swallowed hard. "What does she do with them?"

Another shrug. "Let's go if we're going."

They crept through the hole, sneaking from boulder to boulder and pausing near shrubs. Cressida watched the palace's numerous windows and never saw anyone looking out, though some windows had curtains or shutters. A few were just sparkling glass, darkened so she couldn't see inside. "How do we avoid getting caught? You said wait until she's distracted?"

"She has a lot to pay attention to. There are many magic users in the Underworld. Still, even with all that, no doubt she knows we're here."

Cressida stumbled. "But you said—"

"She's the goddess of magic. We're not going to get in her house without her knowing. Thing is, if we play our cards right, she'll forget we're here. She has a lot of irons in the fire, always. The trick is to not get caught. She admires that sort of thing."

"But if she knows we're here…"

"Not where we are or what we're doing. Trust me. I know her, and she likes a bit of hide-and-seek. Even if she catches us, she's not going to be that angry."

"*That* angry?"

"She'll probably just demand a tribute. Something easy. She might even offer up your aunt as the prize."

"Oh good." But Cressida's belly was tied up in knots. Medusa sounded confident, but she didn't look at Cressida as she talked, and even though they didn't know each other at all, Cressida had always thought avoidance of eye contact a sure sign that someone didn't trust her own words.

Hecate's front door had become the size of Hammurabi's gates, taking up most of the front of the palace, all thick wood and iron hinges, but Medusa passed them by, heading around the side of the palace and ducking to stay out of sight. She paused at a little door in the middle of a long wall, completely out of place just like everything else. It'd been painted robin's egg blue, setting it apart from the ominous black doors at the front. A chime hung next to it, a chain leading from inside an old copper bell. Medusa peered at it, examining it for a long while.

"Do we ring?" Cressida asked. "Or would that show too much bravado?"

"Why make it easy for her?" She disregarded the door after a moment and kept going, circling around the back of the building, staying in the shadows.

Cressida stayed right at her heels as they sneaked through a creepy topiary garden and so much statuary that Cressida thought they must be passing the same ones over and over again, but the house seemed to go on forever, far bigger than it looked from a distance. Medusa finally dug through a clump of bushes and uncovered an old cellar door straight out of a horror movie.

She looked at Cressida with a grin. "This is our way in."

"Were you waiting for the creepiest option?" Cressida whispered.

"I'm a fan of the odd horror movie or two. You?"

"Not enough to sneak into some cellar straight out of Wes Craven's nightmares!"

"He who dares..." Medusa lifted up one door by its old rusty handle. It creaked loudly and deeply, an ominous sound that would make any sound effects person shed a proud tear. An eerie wind gusted through the bushes right on cue, and if anyone was nearby—or below—they had to know someone was playing with the cellar door.

Before Medusa could throw the door open, Cressida caught her arm. "If it isn't locked, doesn't that mean it doesn't go anywhere important?"

"Or she likes people to come in this way. She wants a challenge."

"Or, *or* she really likes locking stupid people in her creepy basement dungeon straight out of every horror movie ever shown." Cressida shivered. "Any minute now, someone's going to shout, 'Don't go in there!'"

Medusa winked and headed downward with a crazy look on her face, and Cressida had to either stay with her or try things on her own. She stayed as close as she could without tripping both of them. With numb fingers, she dug a flashlight out of her backpack and hoped she wasn't walking into certain death.

CHAPTER FIVE

Cressida's stomach shrank into a hard knot. *God, it is a horror movie.* A dirt floor stretched ahead of the flashlight's circle, going on forever. The concrete walls held wooden shelves full of jars, and those were filled with all manner of colors and blobs that could have been fruits, jam, or various organs. Rusty tools hung from the ceiling, and an ancient metal bedframe rested between two rows of shelves, just waiting for someone to be strapped to it by a murderous hillbilly farmer.

Or a clown. Cressida shivered. A murderous hillbilly farmer clown. "Seriously," she whispered, "if this was a movie, I'd be screaming at the screen right now. 'You stupid kids get the hell out of there!'"

"Ah, but the stupid kids never had me," Medusa said.

A metallic noise came from the darkness. Cressida froze, pulling on Medusa's arm. The murderous hillbilly farmer clown would be dragging something toward them through the inky blackness. Maybe it was a hatchet or a cleaver or a length of chain, and the murderous hillbilly farmer clown was striking it deliberately along some metal surface, hunting the kids who should have never come down into the creepy basement.

But the kids never had a good reason for being there, except maybe one of them called the others chicken, or something equally stupid. But Cressida was searching for her aunt, who might be a prisoner, who might have walked this very route, and Cressida couldn't shame her by backing down now. June had never backed down from anything in her life.

Which was probably why she'd gotten killed by a murderous hillbilly farmer clown.

Shut up! Don't be a chicken.

Medusa kept walking but didn't shrug off Cressida's touch. Instead, she shifted a little in front, as if to shield Cressida from danger. When the creature they'd been hearing lurched out of the darkness—bloody dungarees, face paint, and all—Medusa lifted a hand. "Stay behind me."

Cressida couldn't have done anything else. She froze in horror, just like the stupid kids. If she'd been capable of shame in that moment, she would have been a puddle of embarrassment on the floor. She'd always been the one to say, "If that had been me, I would've run or moved or something!" Now all she could do was stare.

The creature lurched toward them, a boathook in one hand, and Cressida had enough time to think: *that doesn't even make sense.* Why would a basement so far from water even have a boathook on the premises? *And why* is *he a clown?* What use did a farmer have for the bright red nose, the blue wig? It made sense to her terror, but her logic cried foul. And why did he look like something she'd conjured in her imagination anyway?

Medusa's arm shuddered, and Cressida felt her biceps bulge. Her hair came alive, flowing in an invisible wind, the strands coalescing and developing heads with mouths and scales, and just as Cressida was gawking at the mass of snakes—some of which were staring at her—the boathook-wielding clown farmer stuttered to a halt, skin darkening to the gray of stone as he froze, a statue.

The snakes turned into hair again so quickly, Cressida didn't have time to blink. When Medusa turned, Cressida winced, shielding her eyes, but Medusa gently brought her hand down.

"You're safe." Her eyes were still those of a snake's, but surrounded by human flesh, they were compassionate, even amused. "Are you all right?"

Cressida looked to the statue, and even though it still made no sense, and they were still in the creepy basement, she'd never felt safer. "You're amazing."

Medusa gave a little shrug, though with a satisfied smile. "People in horror movies should invite me along more often."

Cressida took another look around. "This doesn't make sense. We were looking for a way in, and then we found one, and I was picturing how this place would look as if it was in a horror movie, and here it is, including him." She nodded at the statue. "I mean, I was thinking farmer clown, and there he stands, and why the hell does he have a boathook?"

Medusa tapped one fingernail dully against the stone maniac. Another noise came from the darkness, and she frowned. "What is it this time?"

Cressida's mind flashed with a picture of the murderous farmer clown's wife—also a clown—though with a paisley print dress that hadn't been in fashion for a hundred years. When it sprang from the dark, carrying a cleaver and wearing a bright pink wig, Cressida told her mind to shut the fuck up, please, if it knew what was good for it.

But her imagination was clearly on a roll. After Medusa dealt with the clown farmer's wife, a doll straight from the Museum of Horribly Creepy Shit came at them by racing over the ceiling, another tactic Cressida knew she was responsible for. Then a scarecrow lunged at them from a shadowy corner. They were all horrors Cressida had seen before, from one movie or another, or were at least based on movie characters, amalgamations of someone else's ideas. Strangely enough, Cressida's real fears didn't manifest: tests she hadn't prepared for or lovers who'd dumped her. She didn't see her parents or June riddled with cancer. It was all kiddie stuff that had been kicking around her hindbrain, and after several encounters, she tried to conjure the most bizarre things she could think of until fear faded to fascination.

"An alien," she whispered, "like, a big blobby purple thing with tentacles, and..." And nothing she was afraid of. The darkness stayed silent.

"If it's feeding off your thoughts," Medusa said, "try to think of a way out."

Right. A way out. People in horror movies always needed the hope of escape before they met the serial killer. *No, don't think about serial killers!*

The dusty shelves faded into a series of cells, rusty iron bars surrounding squares of clean cement flooring with dirty mattresses piled in the corner. A scream echoed off the walls as some demented killer tormented his latest victim.

Cressida swallowed hard, making her chest ache. "That's my fault. I'm sorry. You've been in Hecate's palace before, right? You never found anything like this?"

Medusa shook her head. "It's just like the rest of the Underworld, controlled by thought, but it seems more concentrated and volatile, and I think it's picking up on you more because you're alive." She cast a look over one shoulder. "Your aura is brighter."

"So this isn't real," Cressida said, touching one of the iron bars. "It feels real, but..." She shook her head and tried to tell the images to go away, but they kept seeping in, and now she doubted her power to banish them. Maybe she could only create. "Maybe it's a trap. You try to sneak into Hecate's house, and you wind up in here forever, meeting your nightmares." *Not true*, she tried to tell herself. *Don't let your imagination run wild!* "But I have you, and you can turn anyone into stone."

Medusa nodded, giving her a reassuring smile. "That's right."

Cressida kept repeating that in her head. Medusa could stop anything. This wasn't like a dream, where if she stopped believing in Medusa's abilities, they'd stop working.

Was it? *Stop it, stop it, stop it!* She took a deep breath as Medusa gave her a concerned look.

"So," Cressida said, "what is it that gives people in horror movies hope that they can escape?" She thought hard on it, focused, and when she turned, there it was: a rickety staircase leading up.

When they were almost there, Medusa turned. "But one of them always gets killed when they're running for the exit. Because while their backs are turned..." She peered into the darkness.

Cressida turned in time to see the serial killer rush from the darkness, but Medusa stepped in front of Cressida like a guardian angel, and Cressida's confidence in her bloomed. The killer turned to stone before he took two steps, powerless against Medusa's gaze.

Medusa snapped her fingers and laughed, and Cressida had to chuckle, too. She never should have doubted. With Medusa on her side, what could possibly get in her way?

❖

It was hard not to be proud, even though Medusa knew it was all fake. She'd never met Hecate, not in the flesh, and she wondered if the real palace was anything like this. Medea would know, being Hecate's daughter and all, so if Cressida told anyone of her experiences, and they knew what the real palace was like, they could confirm her story.

And oh, Medea had really outdone herself this time. The fabric of her illusions shaped by the minds of the people going through them, like a condensed version of the Underworld itself? Genius. And she was clever enough to have it shaped more by Cressida than Medusa, so that Cressida would feel as if she was at the heart of their little adventure. She would be the one guiding their path, responsible if they succeeded or failed, and Medusa would be her weapon. It was perfect, and Medusa was reminded that she owed Medea big, would probably owe her for some time to come, but with Medusa's sisters restored, they would be capable of some very big favors.

Still, she wanted to get a move on. Her sisters weren't getting better the longer they tarried here. "Try to clear your mind," she said as they mounted the stairs. "If we don't have any preconceptions, maybe we'll see the rest of the palace for what it truly is."

"The jumble that it looks like from outside?"

"Perhaps, though try to clear your mind of that, too." She fought to take her own advice, though curiosity kept trying to get the better of her. If the whole illusion looked like pieces of some dilapidated farmhouse from a horror movie, she thought she might scream. She didn't know if she could influence the illusion like Cressida could, but she tried all the same, picturing "Hecate" waiting for them at the top of the staircase.

But it stretched forever upward toward a wooden door that stood beneath a single yellowed bulb. The door's chipped white paint was streaked with dirt and a few smears of red rust, maybe blood. As well as she could see it, though, it never got any closer. Maybe Cressida thought it should always be just out of reach.

"Can you bring the door closer?" Medusa asked.

Cressida muttered something, and the door stopped moving away, letting them gain on it. Medusa gave Cressida another fond, supportive smile. She had a formidable mind. At last Medusa turned the rusty metal knob. The door opened with a creak as loud as someone shaking a sheet of tin, and Medusa fought down images of the cracked and stained Formica floor that would go with the dirt basement. Instead, she thought only of blank space, waiting for whatever Cressida came up with.

A black abyss opened up before her, and she sighed. "Are you thinking of nothing, too?"

"I'm trying to," Cressida said quietly.

Medusa chuckled, though her temper was beginning to flare. "Well, if we picture nothing, that's what the palace gives us."

"It was a nice try, though?" Cressida asked.

"Let's focus on a simple room, modern. How about an apartment with concrete walls and floor, minimal furniture, an open floor plan, stainless steel appliances in the kitchen, and Hecate waiting for us?"

It swam hazily into view until a voice chuckled from the blackness. "I never went in for all that modern stuff."

The modern room melted like candlewax and reshaped into a large space, the walls and floor covered in pale blond bricks instead of concrete. Huge painted columns supported a ceiling covered in frescos and friezes. Braziers lined a path to a massive dais that sported three thrones made of carved gemstones.

Three identical women sat there, all smiling at Cressida and Medusa where they stood at the end of the brazier path. The door and the staircase had vanished, and even though Medusa knew it was an illusion, it was hard not to quake in awe before the triple goddess. She had to summon every drop of confidence and remember that once upon a time, she and her sisters had been called divine.

Medusa stuck her shoulders back and marched forward; Cressida was looking at her to lead the way. The three goddesses smiled in sync. The one in the middle had a lamp set in the throne above her head, the one to the right had a key, and the one on the left had a hound, all part of her portfolio. Trust Medea to depict Hecate in her most impressive, three-bodied form. Their faces were mostly in shadow, hidden under a cowl, and a deepness around their eyes seemed like a well leading to unfathomable depths. Each wore a black robe blended with purple highlights, and a brooch near each figure's right shoulder glowed like a faraway star.

"You should have known better than to try to sneak past me," Hecate said with three voices, one normal, one a whisper, and the other a shout, though Medusa heard them all as clearly as if they spoke in her mind. A doubting voice said that maybe this wasn't an illusion. Maybe Medea had made her *think* she was sneaking into some illusory place, but it had really been Hecate's palace all along.

Medusa ducked her head and tried to banish the thought. She bowed low, signaling for Cressida to do the same. "O Night Wandering Hecate, Friend to Persephone, Queen of the Night, we thought you enjoyed finding those who sought unexpected entrance to your home."

"A game I appreciate from time to time." The triple goddess stood and descended the dais, her three forms flowing into one as she reached the floor. "Now, Daughter of Snakes, why did you bring me a living woman when I already have one?"

"Aunt June!" Cressida said. "Please, Queen of Magic, tell me where she is!"

Hecate's eyes widened, but at least Cressida had remembered an epithet. If it had been the real Hecate, she might have been punished for speaking out of turn, but...

Medusa stared at the illusion, looking for a flaw. She tried to pull Cressida back into a bow, but Cressida shrugged out of her grasp. Medusa stepped up with her, wanting to protect her. She couldn't have her revenge without Cressida's help, but it was more than that, as if the little time they'd spent together meant they owed each other something.

Hecate smiled softly. "She speaks highly of you."

"Please let me see her, Queen of the Night. You must—"

Hecate lifted a hand, and Cressida fell silent, but whether it was out of reverence or if she'd been robbed of her voice, Medusa didn't know. One meant it was really Medea playing a part, but the other...

Hecate shimmered, her form growing until she towered over them, the room darkening. "You do not order me, mortal," she said, her voice twisting as her two other faces appeared on either side of her head.

Cressida fell to her knees like a supplicant, laying out her arms as she should have done from the beginning if it was the real Hecate. Medusa started to sweat, uneasiness growing when Hecate returned to her one-woman shape and fixed her gaze on Medusa.

Medusa tried another bow, wanting to hurry this up. "Please, O Wandering Hecate, will you tell us of June's fate, though we be unworthy?" She hoped she wasn't laying it on too thick. She doubted anyone talked that way anymore, even Hecate herself.

"She is here, but she does not wish to go." Hecate returned to the central throne. "I have not had a mortal lover in a god's age."

Cressida's head tilted up, and she gawked. Medusa gawked a little herself, though a god having a mortal lover was not uncommon in the old days. The Olympians had done it all the time, all of them had, even Medusa. There was something about non-deity lovers, some spark that made them irresistible, and their emotions changed so quickly, almost with no warning and often for no reason. It was like living with a burning brand.

Still, Medusa was surprised Medea had gone with that excuse. She was part god herself and had only coupled with other god children, or so Medusa had heard. Maybe she knew something about Hecate that Medusa didn't, a mother and daughter secret.

"May we see her?" Medusa asked, knowing Cressida would have to see something to give her hope.

"Of course."

She waved, and a doorway appeared in midair behind the thrones, showing a woman about twenty years older than Cressida. She was dressed in a white chiton and seemed surprised to find herself facing the throne room. Her hand was raised as if she'd been fixing her hair before being spirited into Hecate's presence. It was a nice touch.

June spotted her niece and rushed forward. "Cressida? Is that you?"

Cressida launched to her feet and threw her arms around the false June. She was crying and wiping away the tears as if surprised to find them and in a hurry to be rid of them.

Before Cressida could speak, June pulled back and said, "I can't leave, Cressida."

"Wha...what?" Cressida frowned. "Did you eat something?"

"No." With a laugh, she gestured at the splendor around them. Her voice had an echoing quality that might have been because of the space or the fact that she was pure illusion. "I love it here."

"But, June, your family, your friends?"

Medusa heard the heartbreak in her voice, and it plucked at an echoing sadness inside her.

Hecate waved, and June disappeared. Cressida, to her credit, didn't babble or shout or burst into tears. Her eyes widened, and she cast about as if this might be some trick. Medusa was tempted to confess right then. Nothing got to her like family angst, but the image of her sisters wouldn't leave her. She put her hands on Cressida's shoulders and gave them a squeeze, but she kept her mouth shut.

❖

Cressida couldn't believe her eyes. Had it really been June, or had it been a dream? Maybe this was all a dream, but no, she'd had that thought too many times since she'd come here. Dreams were never this clear, this linear. Well, kind of linear.

At least they'd gotten to touch each other before June disappeared. She'd been so *cold*.

"I am not in the habit of giving my playthings away," Hecate said.

Cressida took a deep breath and summoned every shred of finesse she'd ever had or ever thought she'd had. She couldn't yell or make demands. She couldn't threaten a creature like this. It was like facing down an army. She had to do it just so, had to project the right air of obsequiousness and confidence. "What is your will, O Hecate?"

"Perhaps a tribute, Queen of the Night?" Medusa asked.

Hecate leaned her chin on one fist. "A tribute? Would you slaughter a calf for me, living girl?"

Cressida thought quickly on where she would get a cow and came up empty. Did calf spirits wind up in the Underworld? People ate here. She'd seen restaurants and bars. Maybe if someone thought hard enough about one, it simply appeared. "Goddess, I would find a way."

Hecate laughed. Medusa touched Cressida's wrist, and they both bowed again. Cressida couldn't stop thinking of June, how distant she'd seemed. She hadn't smelled like anything. Maybe she'd recently bathed, or she'd already been here too long. If she didn't want to leave, that had to mean something had been done to her; Hecate had changed her in some way.

Unless June was just that much in love. As far as Cressida knew, June had never fallen so hard, but if anyone could inspire such feelings, it was a goddess. Cressida peeked at Hecate, who didn't seem as smitten if she was willing to trade June away. If the love didn't go both ways that might make it easier to convince June to leave once Cressida had her back. She hated the idea of breaking June's heart, but better to spirit her away rather than leave her here until Hecate eventually tired of her. Gods and goddesses weren't known for their loyalty.

"I think we can do better than a simple sacrifice," Hecate said. "Let's have an old-fashioned quest." She paused, and the silence lingered long enough that an ache developed in Cressida's bowed back.

Medusa sighed, a tiny sound, but Cressida glanced at her, wondering if it was smart to show impatience. In the old tales, gods were always asking for something, and whether or not they honored their half of any deal depended on the god, but it wasn't wise to push, ever. People did so at their peril.

"What must we do?" Medusa asked.

Hecate appeared at her side at an instant, lifting her with one finger under the chin. "You have too much irreverence, Daughter of Snakes. Your sharp tongue may serve you well on the streets, but in my domain you will obey, and you will do it gladly!"

Medusa cast her eyes to the ground. "Yes, O Wandering Hecate."

Cressida noted her stiffening spine, though, and recalled the tales of Medusa and her sisters as demigoddesses, the gorgons with their famous tempers.

"We will do whatever you command, Night Queen," Cressida said, trying to get Hecate's attention back on her. June had come to the Underworld first, but Cressida couldn't help feeling as if the current situation was her fault. She'd been the one who'd agreed to do something for Adonis and then went back on her word. She'd drawn Medusa into this, never mind that Medusa wanted something from her. If she'd stuck with Adonis, this might not be happening. Maybe he would have offered Hecate some of the ambrosia, and that would have convinced her to hand June over.

"Rise and look upon me," Hecate said. "You will go to Tartarus and retrieve an item I want."

Cressida exchanged a look with Medusa as a pit opened up in her stomach. Tartarus, fantastic. Home to those who'd committed crimes against the gods, prison of the Titans and a horde of monsters. By the way Hecate stared at both of them, Cressida knew Medusa had to come, too. She hoped a quick look of contrition conveyed how sorry she was.

Hecate was watching when Cressida looked to her, and it felt as if the whole room was holding its breath. "And what is it you require, Keeper of Keys?" Cressida whispered.

"A weapon, the harpe of Cronos."

The air left Cressida like a popped balloon, and she knew she made a little sound; the others would hear, but they were lucky it wasn't a shriek. Cronos, the father of Zeus and several other Olympians, who'd eaten his own children rather than have his power usurped. His worship was from a time before Zeus, much like Medusa's worship, and as older gods, they were often cast as villains in the newer tales. But looking at Hecate, who was herself rumored to be one of the old gods, Cressida didn't doubt that Cronos would be as terrible as myth painted him to be, especially if he was truly locked in Tartarus for daring to challenge his son in battle.

And she had to go and steal his harpe, a sword with a hook on one end, a fearsome weapon, one that had nearly defeated the gods themselves. Somehow, she doubted he'd hand it over.

To mask her dread, Cressida dropped her gaze and focused on Hecate's shoes. They were covered in gold and jewels, very impractical, and Cressida made herself wonder how they would pinch the toes, anything to get away from this ball of dread in her stomach.

"It's simple, Cressida," Hecate said. "You can retrieve the harpe, or you can go home and leave your aunt with me. And if you're thinking of a way to steal her, remember this: unless I release her, my spells upon her will last forever, and she will pine for me until her dying day. Which would be all too soon." She sighed dramatically. "After all, what is food and drink compared to love?"

Anger burned through Cressida, baking dread into something more manageable. She closed her teeth on a comeback. Something about Hecate's silence told her that a plucky heroine wouldn't go down well at the moment. "Yes, O Night Queen."

"Good. And besides Medusa, you'll have three other helpers."

Medusa jerked, and Cressida looked up. Hecate had turned, and Medusa was glaring at her back as if they weren't in enough trouble already. Three people marched out of the darkness behind the throne. Cressida squinted at them, trying to make out who they might be.

The first looked as if someone had put a Goth and a cheerleader in a blender and set it to shred. Blond ponytails with black ends hung around a pale neck, and the face set above had the heaviest eye makeup Cressida had ever seen, and she went through a bit of a Goth phase herself in high school. The newcomer wore black lace stockings, artfully torn, underneath ripped denim shorts, with a black letter jacket all chained and covered in patches. Like Cressida, she carried a backpack that fitted tight to her back as if sewn to her jacket.

The second woman seemed incredibly normal in comparison, even bookish. She wore jeans and a brown sweater, very unobtrusive. Her long brown hair was held back in a simple clip, and brown eyes squinted out from behind large glasses.

The third was a man dressed in the armor of the Greek military, with a breastplate and a kilt of leather strips over a chiton that ended at his knees. He wore a red cloak over it all, secured at both shoulders of his breastplate. Older than the other two by several decades, he had gray hair mixed with the brown at his temples, and lines gathered at the corners of his brown eyes. Cressida wondered if he'd gotten the memo on how everyone could dress how they wanted and appear as any age they wished. Maybe he just liked appearing older. Maybe he thought it gave him gravitas.

"Arachne, Pandora, and Agamemnon," Hecate said.

Cressida's mouth fell open after the first name, and she couldn't close it again. She had to stop being so easily shocked. They were all famous names, and she nearly squealed like a schoolgirl. The first had challenged Athena to a weaving contest and was supposedly turned into a spider for her insolence, but apparently, the punishment hadn't stuck.

The second was the first woman created by the gods and was responsible for unleashing every evil in the world while making sure people retained hope. Cressida would have expected to find her in Tartarus, but the myth claimed she'd unleashed evil out of curiosity rather than malice. She certainly didn't seem old enough to be the first woman, but maybe this was how she'd always seen herself.

The last was the commander of the Greek army who'd laid siege to Troy in order to recover his brother's wife Helen. Cressida had to wonder what his special skills were, what any of their special skills were. At least the first two had their own myths. Agamemnon had always had to share with larger figures.

He bowed deeply before Hecate. "Most gracious goddess, O Night Queen, whatever your bidding might be will be both an honor and a pleasure." He bent over her hand, giving her a look that said a great many things would be his pleasure, especially if she wanted it in private.

Cressida recalled how he'd died: killed by his wife at the dinner table because he'd sacrificed their daughter to appease the gods before leaving for Troy. Cressida thought his wife had served him right. She wondered where his children were, each the stars of their own tragedies. Maybe they wanted nothing to do with him. Watching his oily smile, Cressida kind of hoped Hecate would turn him into a newt. Arachne rolled her eyes behind his back. Pandora just tilted her head and stared at him curiously.

Hecate took her hand back with a patronizing smile and gestured for him to join the others. "While assisting you in your task," she said to Medusa, "they'll also be seeing to another of my commands."

Cressida bowed her head along with the others.

"Good," Hecate said. "Everyone but Medusa may wait outside. I have a few more words for the daughter of snakes."

Cressida gave Medusa a look of apology, but Medusa waved her out with a resigned look. Whatever was about to happen, perhaps she was used to it since she and Hecate knew each other. Cressida hurried from the room, not stopping to speak with the others, though she was dying to. When Tartarus had first been mentioned, she hadn't been able to breathe through her dread, but now, even though June was still a captive, Cressida couldn't help a jot of hope. They were on the track to getting her back, and they had plenty of legends to help them along.

❖

"Well, slave," Hecate said. "What have you to say for yourself besides"—she struck a pose, one hand behind her hood—"give that woman an Oscar!"

"Cut the crap." Medusa put her hands on her hips and glared until the face of Hecate dissolved into the still beautiful but far less majestic face of Medea.

"I put a lot of energy into this," Medea said as she smiled. "You owe me big."

Medusa gestured around her. "Who asked for the whole throne room, and those weird guards, and whatever the hell that was downstairs?"

"A very nice, very thorough touch was what that was." She stuck her lower lip out. "I thought you'd appreciate it."

"All I asked for was a passable facsimile of Hecate and an illusion of the aunt."

"I had to make it look real!"

"Cressida doesn't know what looks real!"

Medea sniffed. "I have a reputation to maintain."

Medusa gestured around them at the empty room. "With whom? Arachne, Pandora, and Agamemnon? What the hell are they doing here?"

Medea laughed. "After that girl is gone, and you've gotten what you came for, I want word to spread. I'm going to be hip deep in jobs after this. And don't you worry about the others. They're as fooled as your girl is. I just thought I'd get something from Tartarus since you were already going down there."

"That wasn't our deal!"

"It doesn't change our deal. You should be happy for the help! Going to Tartarus is always dangerous."

Medusa sighed, not bothering to argue. "I suppose it doesn't matter. How did you find out what the aunt looks like?"

"Through the shade fog, darling. Any number of people have seen her. Does the human girl know what you're really up to?"

"She thinks I only need her to lure Perseus to Asphodel."

Medea sidled close. "Can you get her to do something for me? After you're done with her, of course?"

Medusa eyed her up and down, a protective urge rearing inside her. "Sorry, you'll have to bargain with her on your own."

"You couldn't ask for me after all the trouble I went to?"

Medusa felt anger slipping over her, sliding under her skin, the serpent threatening to break through. "I didn't ask for all this!"

"All right, all right. No reason to get angry." She smiled. "My snaky friend."

"I should petrify you just for that."

Chapter Six

Cressida fought the urge to gawk at the legends around her. Arachne was examining her fingernails, while Pandora stared with the unabashed innocence of someone who'd never understood the concept of rudeness and wasn't about to start. Cressida considered saying something about how staring was rude but didn't know a way to censure the first woman. Maybe, "If anyone has had the time to learn how to act, it should be you." Of course, rudeness hadn't been a thing until she'd let it out.

Before Cressida could say anything, Agamemnon captured her hand and kissed it, something he'd probably picked up since he'd died. He gave her a wink, and before she could pull away politely, he stared at her with wide eyes. "You're alive!"

Arachne sidled closer, looking her up and down. Pandora reached up as if to touch Cressida's hair, but Cressida slid away from all of them. "Um, sorry. I don't like to be pawed until we've been introduced."

Arachne laughed, and Pandora nodded as if she could relate.

Agamemnon put a hand on his chest. "Agamemnon, of the house of Atreus, commander of the Greek armies at Troy, at your service."

"She didn't say that pawing was *definitely* on even after the introductions, Pops," Arachne said. He puffed up as if to rebuke her, but she held a hand in his face and turned to Cressida. "What's a living person doing down here? Haven't seen one of you in ages." They watched her closely, Pandora with her head cocked as if Cressida was a novelty.

"I'm searching for my missing aunt. She's, um, a guest of Hecate's." Cressida didn't want to say prisoner, didn't want to get into it. She felt a further twinge of guilt for trying to force her aunt from the Underworld, but June couldn't be thinking clearly. She'd never abandon her family. It had to be Hecate's magical influence. "Hecate wants a sword to…pay for her staying here. Like a bill." She tried a smile and hoped it looked convincing.

"Tough break." Arachne jabbed a thumb at her own chest. "Well, with me around, you don't have to worry about not getting your sword. I'm what you might call a retrieval expert."

"You're a thief," Pandora said.

Arachne snorted. "Why are you even here? Does Hecate need someone to do this?" She mimed opening a box and then looking surprised and horrified at what she'd done.

Pandora turned away. "You're an idiot as well as a thief."

Before they could fall to bickering, Agamemnon tried something that started with, "Ladies, ladies—"

Arachne spun to face him. "We don't need any advice from the fat calf."

His face screwed up as if he knew he should be insulted but wasn't exactly sure why. "A…what?"

"You've got no skills to speak of, so you must be the bait," Pandora said.

Agamemnon turned several shades of purple. "How dare—"

"Didn't he lead an army?" Cressida asked.

Agamemnon pointed at her. "I certainly did, and Troy *fell*, if you'll recall."

"How much history do you know?" Pandora asked Cressida. "Just Homer? Were any of the good ideas ever Agamemnon's?"

While he sputtered after an answer, Cressida thought about it and couldn't come up with anything. He'd fought at Troy, but Achilles was mentioned more in the battles, and Agamemnon had nearly caused him to back out of the war. The wooden horse had been Odysseus's idea. Even during *The Odyssey*, Agamemnon had already been in Asphodel because he'd died such an inglorious death at the hand of his wife and his wife's lover.

Medusa came down the steps into the craggy yard, and Cressida ran to meet her. "What happened? She didn't punish you, did she?"

Medusa tilted her head, smiling. "Were you worried for me?"

"Well, you didn't ask for any of this."

"Not for them, at least." She stared at the others, mouth twisted. She had a roll of leather in her hand, a belt, Cressida realized, with a scabbard hanging from it.

Cressida leaned close. "Do you think they'll make trouble?"

"Well, Hecate was right about Tartarus being safer with allies. If things go sideways, at least the horrors trapped down there will have more to focus on than just the two of us."

"Are we doing this or what?" Arachne called.

"Let's go." Medusa glared at the three newcomers as they walked, keeping Cressida by her side. "If we keep our minds on the job, we should get out all right."

"Why doesn't Hecate get the harpe herself?" Cressida asked softly. "Is it a matter of pride? A goddess can't run her own errands?"

"It's more than that," Medusa said softly. "Cronos knew that his sword was one of the few weapons that could actually kill him, so he had it enchanted so it couldn't be wielded by a god or a Titan. Little did he know that Zeus would create humans."

Another thing that couldn't possibly be true if a person was going to believe in science. "So, Zeus created humans in order to have someone around who could kill his father?"

Medusa gave her a grin. "I guess you have Cronos to thank for putting ideas in his son's head."

"Does the human who wields the harpe have to be alive?"

"Oh yes. Any spirit would be rendered into a shade by that sword." Her voice got a bit wistful, and Cressida wondered if she was thinking of her sisters.

Still, if a dead person couldn't wield it and neither could a god... "But doesn't that mean that whatever Hecate wants the harpe for, I'll have to do it for her?" Or maybe she was going to get poor, lovestruck June to do her dirty work.

Medusa shook her head. "She gave me a scabbard and said to tell you to keep the harpe sheathed. I guess even she doesn't know what it might do." She handed over the belt, and Cressida strapped it around her waist, though she felt a bit silly carrying around an empty scabbard.

"What are you two mumbling about?" Arachne called. "If there's more to the plan, we kind of need to know."

"Just contemplating the future," Medusa said. "Have any of you ever been to Tartarus?"

"I have," Pandora said, "long ago." She didn't elaborate, and Cressida wondered if she'd gone there because she'd been punished and had since been released, or if she'd just visited. Maybe there was some kind of release program, only it didn't let anyone proceed higher than Asphodel.

"Care to elaborate?" Arachne said.

Pandora shrugged. "It's dangerous. Hecate was right to send a group."

Agamemnon frowned as if he wasn't so sure he wanted to be at Hecate's service anymore.

Medusa smiled wider. "Safety in numbers." She winked at Cressida, who tried to smile back, but her imagination was running loose with all the things they would find in Tartarus, guards or traps. She glanced at the others and couldn't help the nasty little thought that she didn't have to be the fastest in the group, just the second slowest. It was probably what the others were thinking, too, though if she was the only one who could wield the harpe, they'd have to make sure she got out alive.

It still wasn't very comforting. She didn't want to see anyone die. *No worries*, her inner jerk said. *They're already dead!*

Everyone fell quiet as they trooped to the nearest elevator, Medusa staring down any passersby who paid them too much mind. Sometimes, all she had to do was return one curious look with another, an air of quiet menace by the queen of staring contests. Other times, she hissed softly, as if mimicking a cat or a snake, but it did the job. No one gave them any trouble, and quite a few curious onlookers hurried away as if suddenly remembering they'd left the oven on.

In the quiet elevator, Agamemnon cleared his throat. "So, unless I've lost my ability to interpret faces, you haven't been alive long, have you?" He looked Cressida up and down. "Twenty years or so?"

"Too young for you, Pops," Arachne said.

Agamemnon ignored her. "Don't you hate it when people can't seem to butt out of others' conversations?"

Arachne snorted. Cressida tried to give Agamemnon a kindly, yet off-putting smile. "I'm twenty-four. I'm also a lesbian, in case you were wondering."

"Ah." He turned to regard the wall.

Arachne quirked an eyebrow, mouth twisted in a wry grin. Pandora pushed her glasses up her nose. "Many of the people in the Underworld are bi or pansexual," she said.

"Good to know," Cressida said. "But I'm firmly on my side of the fence."

Agamemnon shrugged as if there were other fish in the sea. "I expect you're in a rush to get home to a special lady?"

She fought the urge to sigh. It was like having a conversation with an over-inquisitive yet well-meaning uncle. "I would like to get my aunt and go, yes." She snuck a peek at Medusa. Well, maybe not right away. It had been a long time since she'd had a special lady, lover or good friend. Her studies had always been more important, and besides, June never seemed to need anyone. Until now.

"Did your aunt come here searching for anyone or anything in particular?" Pandora asked.

"No, she..." But Cressida wasn't entirely sure. "She's an explorer. She, um, she likes a challenge."

Agamemnon sniffed. "Exploration doesn't get anyone anything but trouble. Ask Odysseus."

"Because *you* can't," Arachne said. "Because he's in the Elysian Fields, and you're stuck with us."

"I heard Odysseus moved on." Pandora stared wistfully into the middle distance. "Got reincarnated, managed to attain the Elysian Fields three times, and moved on to the Isles of the Blessed."

Agamemnon sighed and shared in her wistful stare at nothing. Arachne rolled her eyes as if she couldn't be bothered, but Medusa stiffened as if someone had pulled her strings taut.

"They're the only newcomers we ever get down here anymore," Pandora said.

After a slow look at all of them, Cressida asked, "Newcomers?"

"Well, there's the occasional pagan who still practices the old ways, but other than them, the only new souls are those who are reincarnated from the Elysian Fields. Then when they die, they come back to the Underworld, but we don't get any others." Her head tilted. "And I suppose the reincarnated ones aren't really new."

"I remember reading that," Cressida said. "When a soul goes to the Elysian Fields, it can choose reincarnation or to spend eternity there."

"Oh yes," Agamemnon said. "Everyone knows about the Elysian Fields, and all the wonderful things they get to do there." His voice took on a high-pitched, mocking tinge. "The sun is always shining, and it's teatime all day long. Bastards."

Arachne elbowed Cressida in the ribs. "In case you hadn't noticed by the clothing, he thinks about the past a lot. It makes some people bitter."

"Shut up," Agamemnon said over his shoulder.

Pandora cleared her throat. "Those who are reincarnated have some of their old soul intact, enough to realize what they have to do to make it into the Elysian Fields, and if they do it three times…"

"The Isles of the Blessed, right," Cressida said. "Right next door to the Olympians."

"And then they're untouchable." Medusa leaned against the side of the car and stared hard at the wall as if she could petrify it.

"Couldn't they move down to the Fields again if they wanted to?" Cressida asked.

"Nope," Arachne said. "And they wouldn't want to even if they could." She took out a knife and started cutting her fingernails like random foolish badasses occasionally did in movies. "People in the Elysian Fields, they know there are other layers to the Underworld, but people in the Isles of the Blessed?" She shrugged. "They don't even realize there is anywhere else. At least, that's the rumor."

"The living can't go there," Medusa said. "No one can unless they're sent by the gods."

"But the gods can go there, right?" There were gods, she realized as she spoke the words. The Greek gods were real. She'd just met one. She had to lean on the wall as the thought reached her knees.

"Well, the gods are Blessed adjacent," Pandora said. "I've heard most people who live in the Isles are allowed to move back and forth to Mount Olympus freely."

"Mount Olympus?" Cressida laughed and heard the crazy tinge in it. She covered her mouth, trying to make the sound into a cough, but it kept bubbling, wanting to turn her into a madwoman, and why not? The whole place was crazy. She might as well join in.

"It's not a physical place that the living can go," Agamemnon said. "Never was, really. It exists outside of time, like here."

"How do you know all this?" Cressida asked. "If you've never been, and no one ever comes back, how do you know? How..." She'd been about to ask how any of it was real, but how could they answer that when they were part of it?

"Everyone knows," Agamemnon said.

Cressida sputtered a laugh again and tried to contain it before she spat on everyone. "Oh, everyone knows? It could be a terrible place, absolutely bonkers. No one who knows anything about the Underworld would ever expect this."

As if on cue, the elevator halted, and the doors slid open to reveal a satyr walking by wearing a plastic suit, neon green, with transparent patches that moved across it as he walked.

"So," Cressida said, "what if the Isles of the Blessed have taken on their own life, too, apart from beliefs? What if it's absolutely dreadful there, and all the gods who lived adjacent to it are dead?"

They stared at her far too long, taking her past the squirming stage to the point where she was ready to walk away, right over the edge of the platform if necessary. The elevator doors started to close, but Medusa stuck her hand out, keeping them open.

Finally, Arachne burst out laughing, making everyone jump. "Oh, that would be fab!"

Pandora shook her head, mouth turned down in distaste. Medusa wore a little smile.

"Take that back," Agamemnon said. He pointed a shaky finger in Cressida's direction. "Dead gods? Heroes left to wander somewhere dreadful? Take it back, young lady, take it back now!"

"Easy, Pops," Arachne said.

He took a menacing step in Cressida's direction.

Medusa stepped in front of him with one smooth motion. "Calm down."

"I will if she takes it back."

Behind them, the door started to shut again, and Arachne wedged her foot inside. "Come on, Pops!"

"I was only saying—" Cressida started.

He slashed a hand through the air. "What is said can never be unsaid."

"Then why would it matter if I took it back?"

"Don't you dare use logic on me, young lady!"

Medusa lifted her hands. "Let's agree that anyone can be wrong here. None of us knows for certain what goes on in the Isles or on Mount Olympus. Okay?"

"Fine," Cressida said. Agamemnon was nearly shaking, and she supposed she should have known that someone who still dressed in a military uniform thousands of years old wouldn't appreciate having his worldviews challenged. Or maybe he was the only one who got to talk shit about the heroes in the Elysian Fields or the Isles of the Blessed, and he wouldn't stand it from anyone else. "I'm probably wrong."

He lifted an eyebrow. "Probably?"

"What do you care, anyway?" Arachne asked. "You can't make it there, Pops; none of us can. There are no second chances here."

"That doesn't matter one jot." He huffed away, stomping down the platform to street level, moodily staring anywhere but back at them.

They followed slowly, Cressida keeping Medusa in front of her. Pandora leaned close to Cressida again. "Most of his friends are either in the Elysian Fields or the Isles of the Blessed. They were his comrades in arms." She shook her head sadly. "Can you imagine being the general of an army, a name of legend, but most of your troops went to paradise while you're stuck here? He probably wishes he'd died in battle. Even Hector, the greatest warrior of Troy, got to go to the Elysian Fields, and his side lost."

Yeah, that would rankle. And people like Arachne probably gave him no end of shit. Cressida sighed. There was nothing she could do for Agamemnon, but at least his problems gave her something to think about besides the fact that gods and goddesses existed and that she would soon be going to Tartarus on an errand for one of them.

They'd traveled to another edge of the city, though there was no fence, no group of hungry ghosts. Instead, a massive cliff loomed in front of them, similar to the one Cerberus had poked his snouts out of. Cressida wondered if the Meadows of Asphodel were surrounded by cliffs, but when she turned to look behind them, the shade fog was too dense to see through. Skyscrapers jutted into it like knives, flashing neon lights breaking through in bursts of pink, blue, and green lightning. The elevator cables crisscrossed it like spider webs, and the occasional car would race through gaps in the fog before disappearing again. Even near the cliffs, the fog stretched high above, disguising the sky, if there even was one, but the ambient gray light had to be coming from somewhere. Maybe the shades gave off light when they were all packed together.

The cliff wall continued well into the fog, and Cressida wondered if it ended, if there was a top somewhere up there, or if someone could climb up forever. Maybe like Hecate's palace, it would depend on what the climber expected to find.

A massive dark spot marred the wall like the eye of Jupiter, a giant cave, the entrance to Tartarus. At least it was big. She'd feared crawling through dark spaces or worse, that she'd be stuck in an elevator for hours as it traveled down and down, with nothing to do but pick random fights with her companions.

As she looked from the cave to the land before it, she spotted a lone train car sitting on a track that led into the well of blackness. Her spirits perked up a little. Maybe they could catch a ride.

"We might have to do some finessing," Medusa said.

Agamemnon felt around his belt as if looking for a purse. "I don't think I have any change."

Not a train car, Cressida noticed as they came closer. It looked more like a trolley or a cable car, but it lacked the electrical wires. A green roof hung over rows of wooden benches, and the breeze whistled through glassless windows. No one waited for a ride. No restless shades floated down to twine about the car. Cressida supposed Tartarus wasn't very popular as a family fun spot.

A man sat at the front, ankles crossed over the control box. He held a newspaper in front of his face, but as Cressida watched, it mutated, looking like a magazine for an instant before shifting into a book in an eye-watering shimmer that made her look away, blinking, to study the man instead.

He'd dressed like something out of the San Francisco tourism guide: blue trousers with a gold stripe, a white shirt, and a blue vest. He wore a dark blue cap and had a gold watch hanging from his pocket. Then as the light shifted, he was suddenly wearing denim coveralls and then a crisp white uniform. For a second he wore all of them at once, and she could see each through the other. A headache pinged through her temples, and she had to focus on the trolley car instead, only letting her gaze pass around the driver.

"Charon?" Medusa called sweetly.

Cressida tried not to stumble. She'd have to get used to people throwing around famous names. Now here was the ferryman of the Underworld, who was supposed to guide the dead to their rightful places. When she got home, she'd have to make a scrapbook devoted just to the people she'd met. She could see it now: the Charon page with its skull and bones motif and Medusa's page covered in snakes.

Or not covered in anything at all. Her gaze slid to Medusa without her permission, and she told it to pay attention.

A young, mustachioed face peered at them over his newspaper, but when he lowered it, the shadowed half of his face shimmered, looking for a second like a bleached skull. Cressida mewled and then coughed, clearing her throat loudly and masking a sound that a terrified person might make when confronted with half a face.

"No rides to Tartarus today, love," Charon said.

Pandora pushed her glasses up. "There haven't been any rides to Tartarus since people stopped committing crimes against the gods."

He tilted his head and ran through his faces and costumes, adding a very old man to the mix along with the young man and the skull. Cressida focused on his boots and clamped her teeth shut to stop dry heaving as her head swam.

"No fares anywhere of late," he said. "No river crossings, no rides from one part of the Underworld to another." He sighed. "Still, leaves me lots of time to catch up on my reading."

The magazine turned newspaper turned book shifted as he went back to it.

Cressida looked away and tried to breathe shallowly. "I wish he'd stop doing that," she muttered into her chest.

"Temporal displacement," Pandora said near Cressida's ear. "Charon is in charge of transportation across the Underworld, so he's in lots of places at lots of times."

Arachne rested one combat boot on the trolley's cow catcher. "Look, we need to get into Tartarus, all right? Surely we can make some kind of deal?"

Charon coughed a laugh and kept reading. "I've heard every bribe and plea and threat in the books. Go on; surprise me."

Agamemnon started some speech beginning with, "Look here, fellow—"

"Next," Charon said.

Arachne sniggered. Agamemnon puffed up, but Medusa pulled him back. Cressida took a step away from them, bumping into Pandora, who steadied her, but as she regained her feet, she turned and looked toward Charon.

He'd lowered the book enough to watch them, the corners of his eyes creased in a smile that said he didn't get much entertainment and enjoyed watching people stumble and argue. Their eyes met, and he shifted again, making Cressida wince as her insides roiled.

Charon stood, and everyone fell silent. "Are you alive?" he asked.

Cressida stared at a point to the left of his ear. "Um hmm."

"How did you get past the dog? How did you get past me?"

"Charon—" Medusa started.

He leaned forward, over the controls, peering at Cressida. At least, she thought he was peering. She was studying the space over his head. "Well," she said to it, "Cerberus was in the mortal world, trying to stop Nero. He's the last hierophant, you see, and—"

They gasped and muttered, Arachne whistling softly. "All the hierophants are dead!" Pandora said.

Cressida shrugged, fighting so hard not to look at Charon that her eyes were beginning to water. "And yet, here I am. I came through a tunnel. I didn't even see you, Charon, and I'm sorry you missed out on your fare." She didn't want to pat her pockets. She knew she didn't have any change.

She couldn't tell if he narrowed his eyes, but his stare continued. "And why would a living person want to go to Tartarus?"

Everyone else went silent so quickly, it felt like a shout. They didn't even fidget, and that was more telling than if they'd coughed and given Cressida significant looks that said, "Mind what you say."

Cressida tried to keep her face neutral and said the first thing that popped into her head. "Scrapbook fodder?"

For a few seconds, Charon didn't speak, and she felt the urge to pull at her collar or play with her hair, anything to break the nonmoving silence. She continued to stare to the left of him and wondered if their entire party seemed frozen in time.

Finally, Charon sputtered a laugh that turned into a guffaw. "Scrapbooking. Did not expect that." He sighed deeply and gestured to the trolley car. "Well, you might as well climb on board. A laugh isn't much of a fare, but I haven't had a good one in a long time."

Cressida hesitated, remembering Adonis and how she should have asked more questions. "Um, you don't want us to do anything for you, right? Like, fetch anything?"

"Nope, the laugh is enough." As everyone else piled into the car, he leaned closer, and Cressida resisted the urge to leap away. "I think you're in deep enough as it is."

"What do you mean?" Still suspicious, she took the bench across the aisle from Medusa.

He didn't answer, only sat back down at the controls, and the trolley hummed to life and began to roll gently forward.

When Medusa touched her knee, Cressida jumped then laughed a little breathlessly. "Sorry. I'm on edge."

"It's all right." Her hand lingered, and Cressida tried to breathe through the little fire the slight contact started within her. "Don't worry. He freaks everybody out, and he often says things no one understands. Part of the ambiance."

Cressida smiled, but even to her it felt strained.

"I won't let anything bad happen to you, Cressida."

And that did make her feel better, but she wondered how long Medusa had been following her and Adonis. Had she been wandering by the fence in front of the Elysian Fields, or had she been with them for some time? Cressida supposed it didn't matter in the end. What was done was done. She had to focus on getting June back, which meant a mission for the goddess of magic to retrieve not one but two artifacts from Tartarus, a place that, if their motley crew was to be believed, was even more dangerous than Asphodel.

Cressida poked her head out the empty window, watching the cave mouth come closer. The upper lip of the tunnel had large, jagged stalactites. The cliff face itself was a mass of rough shapes, the shifting shadows creating depth where there couldn't be any. Like, that outcrop above the tunnel couldn't be a huge nose, with two littler caverns for nostrils, and those sunken bits to the sides weren't dimples. Couldn't be. But now that she peered, the stalactites and stalagmites inside the cavern did look an awful lot like teeth, and holy shit, it was a giant open mouth.

Massive, the lower jaw was buried in the rock to make a flat track, and as more shapes swam out of the dimness, Cressida realized the jaws were held open by a series of giant chains, each as thick as the cables that held up the Golden Gate Bridge. They wound up into the shade fog, heading for the top of the head, and she was so glad she couldn't see if it had eyes.

It couldn't actually be a person, could it? She breathed deeply and tried to tell herself it was just a carving, but in the myths, Tartarus sometimes referred to the place and also to a Titan. But that was like saying the Underworld was sometimes called Hades after its ruler. She stared at the teeth again, the massive cheeks. He'd been buried in rock, body secured under the Underworld. A faint, warm wind passed over the car like a shallow breath.

Or a breeze, she screamed at her inner self. Nothing unusual about a breeze in a cave. But now the idea was in her head. She pictured those huge jaws snapping closed, doing away with the trolley as easily as a normal-sized person would treat a crumb. If he moved, he would shake the entire Underworld loose from its moorings, and if they were actually inside the Earth, the whole planet would swing out of balance.

Unless they were someplace outside of time and space, just as Pandora said. Then Tartarus would just eat the people here and be done with it. Cressida was thrown back to thoughts of Cerberus and wondered how many times she'd have to worry about someone eating her in the Underworld. She'd have to keep a tally.

The thought made her chuckle, and she knew it was because she was getting lightheaded, giddy from the enormity of her own thoughts, the enormity of the jaws around her. But the mouth stayed open, and they passed through, traveling into darkness and away from the bright lights of the city. The trolley's dirty yellow headlight winked on, barely penetrating the infinite blackness and only illuminating the track a few yards ahead.

And then, as big as she knew the mouth was, it didn't seem big enough. Cressida had never thought of herself as claustrophobic, but she couldn't help picturing the mouth giving way to a throat, a throat that could swallow, closing on her, crushing her. She squinted into the dark, trying to see whether the "walls" were slick with saliva, though the air wasn't as humid as she would expect. The trolley kept up a sedate pace, and the track in front of them seemed clear.

"Tell us about the last hierophant," Pandora said.

Cressida jumped, heart fluttering at the sudden noise. She turned and tried not to recoil at the shadowy faces. A weak bulb overhead made all of them look like the specters they really were, with only black pits where their eyes should be. Cressida tried not to latch on to the thought that these were in fact dead people. Famous dead people, dead people who didn't seem in the habit of eating brains, but dead people nonetheless: walking, talking corpses.

She closed her eyes and counted, trying to calm her pounding heart, the screaming parts of her brain that wanted to go running back to the city. "Okay." Talking was better than thinking, anyway. She blurted out what had happened with Nero, and Pandora listened eagerly. Even Arachne took a break from crossing her arms and staring at nothing to listen.

"A practicing hierophant means we might get other living chumps down here," Arachne said. "Especially if your guy seems to have gotten the hang of it now."

"I don't think so," Cressida said. "He only sent me to get my aunt back. Once Cerberus showed up, I think he knew he'd done something wrong. He's supposed to induct people into the Mysteries, not send them to the Underworld, especially if it's just my aunt being curious." And sticking her nose in where it didn't belong.

Still, they looked thoughtful, all but Medusa, who glared at everyone but Cressida as if she didn't like them asking after details and would petrify them if they put a foot wrong. Cressida wondered if she was still angry for the dressing down Hecate had given her, but living in the Underworld, she was probably used to gods and goddesses pushing people around.

"Think what an influx of living people would do," Pandora said. "The trade in ambrosia alone—"

Agamemnon cleared his throat. "Not our business, really."

"Screw that, Pops," Arachne said. "If we do this job right, we could climb up the food chain in any number of organizations, and if we know more chumps are coming, we can get our hands on them before anyone else." She glanced at Cressida. "No offense."

"So much taken," Cressida mumbled.

"So what about you, Snakes?" Arachne asked Medusa. "What are you in this for?"

Medusa shrugged.

"She's helping me," Cressida said.

"In exchange for what?" Pandora asked.

Medusa gave Cressida a warning look, so Cressida shut her mouth. The other three looked back and forth between them, clearly waiting.

After a moment, Arachne sat back with a satisfied look. "It's all right. You don't have to say. It's no secret. She's been nursing the same grudge for millennia."

Medusa gave her another dark look, and to Arachne's credit, she lost a little of her smugness and scooted back in her seat.

"Revenge," Pandora said with a sigh.

They all sighed, and Cressida realized the Underworld was probably full of people who'd been done wrong, the kind of people blues songs were written for. The air turned thick with nostalgia as they all wandered into their own little worlds. If living people did begin trickling into the Underworld again, the dead wouldn't be the only people who could profit. Cressida pictured living people offering courier services or handing out discounts on revenge packages. Of course, she also wondered what a living person could take back to the mortal realm besides their life.

The ride rambled on and on, heading steadily down, and Cressida remembered reading that Tartarus was supposed to be as far below the rest of the Underworld as the gods were above it. She dug into her backpack for a granola bar, feeling a nagging in her stomach that might be hunger or boredom. She didn't feel tired, nor did any of her companions seem to feel the need to sleep. Maybe that just wasn't something they did.

As the journey stretched on, someone stirred behind her back. Agamemnon leaned over her bench, and she could almost see herself as one of those ghosts selling favors to the dead. Still, she waited to hear what he had to say.

"My wife…"

Cressida sighed and wondered if he'd ask her to kill his wife or just lure his wife close so he could kill her. Well, he could forget it. She could only entertain thoughts of one death at a time. "What about her?"

"I haven't seen her since I died. If she's in Asphodel, I don't know where, and no one seems to want to tell me."

Cressida tried to remember if his wife had done anything heroic but came up empty. "The Elysian Fields?"

"I don't know. She could be in Tartarus, though I don't think so. If she is in the Elysian Fields, well…"

"You want me to lure her out so you can kill her?"

He was silent a moment. "Is that what Medusa wants you to do?"

She turned to look him in the eye. "What's it to you?"

He shook his head and leaned closer as if he feared the others would hear him. "If you do see her, my wife…"

"Yes?"

"Can…can you find out how she is?"

Cressida waited for more, but he just stared hopefully. "That's it?"

"I'd like to know that she's happy." He sighed deeply. "I never made her very happy. I never made any of them very happy."

In the near dark, she couldn't read his expression, but he sounded like someone with regrets. By the way he acted, she didn't think he thought himself deserving of the death he got, but maybe all his years had made him realize he was partly to blame for what happened to him. She wondered if he'd ever spoken to the daughter he sacrificed, though some tales claimed she was saved by the goddess Artemis and whisked away to another land, though her mother still thought her dead. Maybe she was in the Elysian Fields, too.

"I'm sorry for yelling at you earlier," he said softly.

He'd paid the ultimate price for his crimes, getting murdered and all, but he still went to Asphodel instead of the Fields. Fair treatment didn't seem to exist in the Underworld, even if a person never got it in life. They could only have whatever kind of life they managed to build, and if people forgot them, they became shades. Cressida wondered then if Agamemnon's wife was living it up somewhere, or if she had regrets like her husband and just couldn't face him.

"If I see her," she said softly, "I'll ask."

He gave her a kindly smile. "Thank you." He put on a smarmy grin again, and she thought he was going to say something that would sweep all her sympathy back under the rug, but he seemed to think better of it and sat back.

CHAPTER SEVEN

The tunnel opened into a room of infinite black except for a large wall that stretched across it, cutting the darkness in half. The ground was featureless gray, and if there was a ceiling or a sky it was hidden in black; the wall continued until it too stood shrouded. Torches burned white hot on either side of the wall's wooden gate, but they barely held back the suffocating darkness that seemed to push against them, wanting to snuff them out so Tartarus could finally swallow them.

Cressida pushed that thought away as quickly as it could go, remembering Hecate's basement of horrors. She didn't know if any other parts of the Underworld could be shaped by her thoughts, but she wasn't about to risk it here in the belly of a Titan.

The trolley came to a stop at another dimly lit platform at the end of the track. Charon set the brake handle, and the car wheezed and shuddered before going dead. Without looking at them, Charon resumed his former position: legs up on the controls, newspaper or book or magazine perched in front of his nose. "I'll wait for you," he said, "because that's the kind of guy I am."

The others mumbled assent as they peered around interestedly.

Cressida caught Pandora's eye. "Is this like you remembered?"

"The gates are the same. As for the rest, we'll see."

No more than large tree trunks banded with copper, the gate sported geometric shapes carved in the wood and filled with metal that glinted in the light so they seemed to move with every flicker. Cressida wondered how many people had stood before them since

Zeus had ceased chucking people into the enormous Titan. As she came closer, she picked out scenes like those on the sides of ancient vases: Sisyphus doomed to roll his rock uphill for eternity and Prometheus having his liver eaten each day by an eagle only to heal overnight and start again the next morning. Cressida swallowed hard at scene after scene of torture, beginning with the Titans imprisoned inside another of their kind.

She swallowed several times to keep her granola bar from making a run for it. "Anyone know how to get inside?"

"Getting in is the easy part." Pandora pulled one of the enormous brass handles, and the gate swung open easily, no ominous creak, no heavy burden they would have to share in. It wanted them to come in, and Cressida imagined the whole place thinking, "Oh thank goodness! I haven't had someone new to play with in a god's age!"

And now, she commanded her brain, *you will shut the fuck up.*

The gates swung open, and she craned her neck to see a long, featureless hallway. She thought maybe it had morphed into a modern prison with bars and gates, but then she noted the second hallway next to the first and another leading along both sides of the outer wall, each of them the same, featureless stone under the black sky, each with the same white hot torches lining the walls.

She opened her mouth to ask what this was, but the excitement building inside her knew the answer before she did. "It's a labyrinth."

"Yes," Pandora said with a sigh.

The others groaned, and Cressida wanted to ask what the hell was wrong with them. This was a labyrinth! Maybe even *the* labyrinth, the same one built by Daedalus and eventually defeated by Theseus.

Home of the Minotaur.

Her excitement banked a little, and she took a deep breath. "So, who knows the way through?"

"We don't want the center," Pandora said. "We need to find the items we're after."

"And you know where they are?" Cressida asked.

They all looked to one another. "Vaguely," Medusa said.

Well, it wouldn't be a quest if it wasn't challenging, but still, she wondered if she would have been relieved or disappointed if one of them had pulled out a map with everything clearly marked. "I never expected a labyrinth in Tartarus. I thought there'd be like, fire or something."

Pandora nodded. "Me, too, the first time I saw it. I wanted a little lava."

"Lots of crags," Arachne said. "Huge caverns full of suffering people. I mean, we may have done some bad shit in our lives—"

"Speak for yourself," Agamemnon said.

"But down here is where they put the worst of the worst," Arachne continued, ignoring him.

"Worst?" Cressida shook her head. "Humanity doesn't see Prometheus as a bad guy."

"Oh, he was pardoned ages ago," Pandora said. "But you're right. The people or…things caught down here aren't really humanity's enemies. They were born of nightmares, the creatures who wanted to send the world back to chaos. But they were also the creatures who challenged the will of the gods. A lot of the struggles that went on in the early days had nothing to do with humans at all, but that doesn't mean that humans wouldn't have been destroyed if the gods hadn't taken action."

Cressida shivered, both at the idea of world-shaking mythological events going on around an unsuspecting humanity, and also at the fact that without the intervention of the gods, humans might have been a footnote in the wars between monsters. She wondered what other bullets humanity had dodged, how many other religions had their own warring deities. And how many of those deities actually cared about humans and didn't see them as something outside of what was really important? Humans had been ambling on, evolving, minding their own business while an invisible world pulsed around them, occasionally touching their lives. Then the gods had come to need human thought, to be powered by human belief as the chaotic nothingness they were formed of came further to order.

"When did they realize that human belief had started…powering them?" Cressida asked.

"They didn't want to believe," Medusa said. "That turned out to be their ultimate punishment. They thought humans didn't really matter, so as belief waned, so did they." She looked around them. "Maybe that's always how gods get replaced."

"Ah," Arachne said with a grin, "but doing the odd terrible thing is guaranteed to get you thought about. Belief isn't only powered by pleasant thought. The really nasty stories are how gods hang around. Now, let's get moving."

She took one end of a length of string from the back pocket of her backpack and tied it to a bar on the trolley platform. It sparkled in the meager light, fragile looking, as if Cressida could snap it with a flick of her fingers. It trailed behind Arachne as she moved, the other end lost in her pack. When Cressida twanged on it, it held, vibrating and giving off a low hum. She thought of the invisible thread hooked to her lifeline and shuddered.

Arachne shivered, too. "Don't twang my string until we get to know each other better, baby." She winked and followed as Pandora led them down the rightmost hallway. Pandora muttered to herself as they walked, and Cressida tried to recall everything she could about the original labyrinth. Theseus had been warned to go straight, but that was to seek out the center of the labyrinth, and as Pandora had said, they didn't want that. Was the Minotaur here as it was in the myth? Maybe something even more dangerous?

Medusa and Pandora had their heads together, occasionally arguing about the way. They took turn after turn down blank hallways, and Cressida began to wonder where the prisoners were. Maybe they'd all been released like Prometheus. Legend told of Zeus pardoning many of the Titans. Well, the female ones anyway. But some tales told of Cronos making it out and later guarding the Elysian Fields. And there were supposed to be guards here, but the only deterrent she'd seen was a long trip and a slightly grumpy conductor.

As the labyrinth stretched on, everyone fell to silence except for the occasional disagreement between Medusa and Pandora. They had the same intense looks on their faces that said they were expecting danger. Tension had replaced Cressida's excitement, and pain sang in her shoulders, but that might be from carrying her pack for so long.

At her side, Agamemnon walked with his hand on his sword, craning his neck to see down each hallway, but the stone and the torches stayed the same, with no sound except for their footfalls and a gentle hiss as Arachne's string played out of her pack. Time seemed to have even less meaning here than it did in Asphodel, and Cressida had to fight to keep her mind from wandering. Maybe the real hell was just eternal boredom.

At last, Arachne sighed, and the sound was so loud, everyone started. Arachne threw her hands into the air. "What gives?"

"I haven't the foggiest notion." Agamemnon dropped his hand away from his sword, but it crept up again. He rubbed the back of his neck with his other hand, and Cressida knew how he felt. She wanted to shrug out of the pack and rest a while.

Pandora was frowning at the way ahead but still walking at a sedate pace, Medusa just behind her. "It has to be around here." She glanced at Medusa. "Right? It *has* to be."

Medusa frowned before she gasped, her eyes widening. "We're close."

"Demigod senses." Pandora gave them all a knowing nod. "I knew they'd kick in when we were close enough."

"Wait," Cressida said. "Does that mean you didn't really know where we were going?"

Neither Pandora nor Medusa answered. Arachne prodded Pandora a few more times, finally reaching out, but before she could grab Pandora's arm, the way branched off to the side, to a round cul-de-sac with an enormous black box nestled in the middle.

"Yes!" Medusa rushed forward and reached toward the box but then drew back quickly, as if she didn't know how to proceed. The box stood high above their heads, as large as a school bus, and it gleamed like obsidian in the torchlight. Cressida walked around it, but it only reflected her distorted image in the chipped and pitted surface.

"Is the weapon inside?" Arachne asked.

Pandora studied the box and smiled. "Now can you see why Hecate hired me?"

Arachne stared for a moment before she laughed. "Hot damn! If anyone knows how to open a box, I guess it's you."

"Stand back." Pandora ran her hands over the obsidian, and Cressida watched as closely as she dared. Medusa leaned forward, and Cressida knew she was straining to get a look at the harpe of Cronus, a sword so like the one Perseus had used to kill her.

Pandora tapped the box along one edge, head close as if listening. She did this several times, stopping now and again for a little smack, a pat, a smoothing of fingers down its sides.

"What's taking so long?" Arachne asked at last.

Pandora glared at her and gave the box a final tap. One of the sides fell over with a resounding crash.

Everyone jumped back, and Pandora turned her chin up, a smug smile in place. "There hasn't been a box crafted that I can't open."

Cressida stared into the box at a wall of blackness as impenetrable as the darkness that surrounded the labyrinth.

As she peered, though, it seemed as if this darkness had depth, a feeling of space, like the one time she'd gone spelunking, and her group had turned their lights off. It was utter, absolute blackness, but there was still the feeling of air, of space around them. This darkness went on into the box, though the torchlight couldn't penetrate it, and when Cressida shined her flashlight in, the light bounced back at her.

"Is it empty?" Agamemnon asked.

Medusa reached but pulled back quickly. "It burns."

Cressida put her own hand down before it could inch forward. She noted a slight vibration and thought it might be from the box or maybe her pounding heart, but it didn't relent, and she realized it was coming from the labyrinth.

Agamemnon drew his sword. "What is that?"

Medusa's eyes widened. "Scatter!"

Without waiting for an explanation, Cressida darted for the rounded edges of the cul-de-sac. Footsteps, she realized, running footsteps. "Oh God, the Minotaur!" They'd been wandering around his prison, and now he was running to find them, using his preternatural senses to come kill them. She hoped Medusa's gaze worked against him or that Agamemnon was as good with a sword as the tales made him out to be.

A giant rounded the corner, and Cressida's brain reset. Three or four times her height, it didn't sport the bull's head she expected, but it more than made up for it with the fifty or so human-looking heads it did have. They sprouted as if barnacles from its many necks and chest and back. And as hard as it was to tear her gaze away from the heads, it was the arms that really drew the eye. Fifty lined each side of the giant, but she knew that more from memory than from counting them. There'd be a hundred in all.

"Hecatonchires," she whispered. Myth called him one of the Titans but disagreed on his fate, though as he reached for Arachne with his many hands, it seemed he was a guardian of Tartarus. He stood taller than the walls around them. How could they possibly fight him? *And also*, her brain reminded her with an insane little giggle, *there are supposed to be three of them.*

Cressida ran into the labyrinth proper and felt a *whoosh* of air behind her. She flattened. Another of the giants rumbled through where she'd been standing. In the cul-de-sac, Arachne threw one of her gossamer strings, catching the Hecatonchires in the back and swinging around it. The string that led into the labyrinth was plastered to the wall, and Cressida ran to stay away from it, not wanting to snap it.

The third Hecatonchires came around the corner to join the fight, and Cressida slid as she tried to change direction. Her feet came out from under her just as the Hecatonchires kicked. It roared in pain as Agamemnon clipped its departing foot with his sword. He caught hold of Cressida's backpack and hauled her to her feet.

"How in the world do you fight something like that?" he asked.

When the Hecatonchires turned for them, Agamemnon leapt to the side, pulling Cressida with him. Bellowing made them turn. Medusa's back was to Cressida as she stared down the first Hecatonchires. Her long, lustrous black hair had become a snarl of snakes. Her body seemed to shimmer. Wings sprouted from her shoulders and scales covered her skin, though she still had arms and legs instead of the half-snake body she sported in the movies.

The first Hecatonchires faltered, trying to cover its eyes with its multitude of hands. It shuddered as if fighting the urge to turn to stone, and it let off another bellow that Cressida felt deep in her body as well as her ears. The other two Hecatonchires ran to help their brother.

"Come on!" Pandora waved everyone toward the box, and they had no choice but to run that way or be torn apart by the many-handed Titans. Medusa backed toward the box, but the other two Hecatonchires were headed toward her.

Pandora plunged into the darkness, crying out as she went, and Cressida hoped she didn't meet her death in some inferno. Agamemnon hurried after her, but Cressida stepped toward Medusa, wanting to help if she could, though a greedy little voice said she didn't need Medusa anymore. If Medusa was left behind, Cressida wouldn't have to lure Perseus out of the Elysian Fields. Cressida faltered, but she couldn't let Medusa die, not like this, not like anything. It would be like a light going out of the world.

"Hurry up!" Arachne cried.

Cressida risked a look over her shoulder. "But Medusa—"

With a swear, Arachne threw another of those gossamer strands and caught Medusa around the middle.

"Pull!" Arachne cried.

Cressida hauled on it with all her strength, but it was the surprising strength of Arachne that made Medusa fly toward them, knocking all of them into the box together.

Darkness surrounded Cressida, and she braced herself for heat, but burning cold engulfed her, stealing her air as if someone had stuffed her insides with icepacks. She cried out and heard an echo from Arachne. It felt like the world's most epic polar bear dive, and when they landed hip deep in snow, she wasn't surprised.

However, the lack of surprise did nothing to help the shivering that drove all other thought away. She was the coldest a person had ever been, ever would be. Emperor penguins would give up on this cold. Killer whales would rate it too much to handle. Ice itself would declare, "Too cold for my blood." It was the cold of deep space and black holes.

Pandora pulled her upright while Arachne shrugged off Agamemnon's help. Medusa stood from a snowdrift, fully human again. Cressida wrapped her arms around herself, but nothing would stop her teeth from chattering, and her muscles jumped and bunched to keep from freezing solid.

Pandora grinned and gestured to the frozen landscape that surrounded them. "I guess it's larger inside."

How in the world could she smile? But Cressida did look around, and bigger was right. They stood inside a glacier, all shifting spears of blue and white ice covered in layers of snow, a huge cave or crevasse, the edges hemmed in by cliffs of white ice, and all of it lit by a soft glow. It was as if they'd passed to a different world, but like the labyrinth, it was absolutely silent except for the sounds of their breathing and a gentle hum coming from a wall of blackness behind them, the doorway through which they'd entered.

Pandora leaned close to Cressida's ear again. "I once heard Zeus say his father hated the cold. It reminded him of empty space."

Cressida could only shiver. She worked her jaw enough to unfreeze it and tried to say, "I'm just glad Zeus didn't put him somewhere where he's constantly being eaten." It came out in fits and starts, but she didn't care if anyone heard. She knew what she meant. She tried to ask how Pandora and Medusa weren't shivering like the rest of them, but her jaw wouldn't obey again.

Medusa caught her look and moved closer. "Don't be cold, Cressida. It's an illusion. You can think it away." She gently took Cressida's shoulders, and her touch burned like hot brands. Cressida couldn't help leaning into her.

Medusa stiffened, then her arms eased around Cressida's shoulders, her soft T-shirt so warm against Cressida's cheek. "I figured it out when I touched the darkness," Medusa said softly. "There was nothing there to be cold. It's just the idea of cold, a spell to put you in the right mood, and then you do its work for it. Like…Hecate's basement."

Cressida snuggled deeper into her embrace, resting against her shoulder and watching as Pandora tried to explain the same thing to Arachne and Agamemnon. They looked as baffled as she felt, though they didn't hug one another. Cressida never wanted to step away from Medusa's warmth, her strong arms. Their bodies fit so well together, curves to curves, softness to softness, and heat of a different kind bloomed through Cressida's insides, even though the cold fought to seep through her backpack and into her bones.

"Hold me tighter," she mumbled.

Medusa took her chin and made her look up. "This isn't your punishment. It only looks cold, but it's not really, and neither are you. It's *not your punishment*, see?" She had two bright spots of color in her cheeks as if she was feeling something more than normal warmth, too. "Though I will admit, it would be nice to let you believe it so I could hold you a little longer."

Cressida couldn't stop staring at her lips. There was something they were supposed to be doing, not just cuddling in the snow, but her brain felt frozen, too. She wanted to lie down, to get some sleep, and maybe when she woke up it would be warmer, especially if Medusa lay down with her, and there weren't these pesky clothes in their way.

Medusa put her warm cheek to Cressida's and breathed in her ear. "Look around, Cressi. It's not meant for you. It's like a picture in a book."

Cressida told her overactive imagination that she knew she'd asked it to shut up many times, but it could go to work now. It could convince her she wasn't freezing to death. She tried hard to think, to notice that the snow wasn't melting where it touched her. The ice wasn't shifting and cracking. She thought of movie sets, all the "winter scenes" where the snow hadn't melted as it rested on people's hair or touched their faces. She'd wondered what it had been made out of, thinking of all those beautiful actors and actresses covered in asbestos.

The cold faded as if someone shut off a switch, but Medusa's arms were still warm on her shoulders, her cheek hot on Cressida's own.

She was hugging Medusa in Tartarus. She'd thought of kissing her, and Medusa had seen her all dopey and fooled by illusion and needy with lust.

Cressida stepped away quickly, her cheeks burning so hard, she expected even the illusion of ice to melt. "Sorry about that. Sorry." She straightened clothes that didn't need straightening. "Right, illusion. Everyone got that? Good."

Arachne and Agamemnon were peering at the landscape as if figuring it out, and she hoped they hadn't been watching as she and Medusa almost made out. Or more likely, *she'd* almost made out while Medusa stood there awkwardly, and Cressida drunkenly pawed at her. But Medusa was watching from the side of her eye with a little smile playing about her lips that said she was at least amused, which was better than hurt or offended, though not by much.

"Sorry," Cressida mumbled again.

"It's all right," Medusa said. "Everyone needs a hug now and again."

"Right." Cressida nodded hurriedly. Everyone needed a *friendly* hug now and again, but she could still feel Medusa's warmth clinging to her, though she no longer needed it for that. She could smell Medusa's sandalwood soap, feel the way their bodies had pressed together.

Yes, all right, she told her imagination. *You can go back to sleep now. We've figured it out, thanks.*

As she looked around the frozen landscape, Cressida breathed deeply, fighting the images of cold that wanted back in, making her want to rub her arms and legs. The imagery didn't disappear, but it was hard not to buy into it. Arachne and Agamemnon seemed to have the same trouble, reaching for their shoulders or rubbing their fingers together.

"I don't get it," Arachne said, "is the harpe buried here somewhere?"

"Maybe in the sides of the glacier?" Pandora asked.

Agamemnon studied the glacier walls. At one in particular, he squinted and tilted his head far to the side. "That's no glacier. It's the father of the gods."

Cressida peered at the wall of unassuming ice. It wasn't nearly as big as the mouth of Tartarus, but it stood large enough to hold a giant. Through the ice, she could pick out hints of his limbs, his head far above them, taller than any dinosaur that had ever walked the earth. How had he existed? *Where* had he existed? Had he ever run around free, or was his entire existence powered by belief, and he'd always been down here, frozen into a mountain because people believed that was what had happened to him?

She grabbed Medusa's hand, suddenly very sorry for all the denizens of the Underworld. Had any of them done what their legends said they'd done? Maybe all their tales were in their heads, and they were walking the Underworld because people put them there in their stories. She swayed a bit, lightheaded.

"What's wrong?" Medusa asked.

"I'm just a bit overwhelmed."

Medusa squeezed her hand and gave her a sympathetic smile. Cressida's gaze brushed Medusa's lips again, and she told herself to bottle those feelings. This was the woman who'd asked for Cressida's help in killing someone, someone who was already dead, but still. Would it be easier to think of him as someone who'd never existed? As Medusa's lips curved in a smile, Cressida knew it would. If she decided to help, she would have to think of Perseus as someone who existed only to fill his role in this tale.

"Tartarus is a terrible place," Medusa said.

"It's not just that." Cressida looked at the frozen Cronos. From his feet, she could barely make out the mask of rage that was his face; the ice broke his features into many pieces, the perspective slanted. "It's all of you trapped here forever. I mean, you're alive-ish, but you can't go anywhere. No wonder some of you get stuck on..." She shut her mouth quickly.

"On revenge?" Medusa's fingers tightened slightly, but whether it was a warning or simply a reaction, Cressida didn't know. "Killing Perseus isn't just about revenge."

Cressida nodded, knowing it was about Medusa's sisters, too, but the passion that flared in Medusa's eyes when she spoke said there was even more to it than that. "It's your reason for being."

Medusa took her hand back, her expression unreadable as she looked away. Cressida wished she'd kept those words inside, but they'd come rushing out, and she didn't know how to apologize. She told herself it was this place getting to her, and even though she felt bad for what she'd said, without Medusa's hand in hers, she could breathe a little easier, and her thoughts fell into more orderly rows.

CHAPTER EIGHT

Medusa felt a pang of guilt and risked another look at Cressida. More than just a pang. They'd shared a moment, cuddling in Cronos's prison, as silly as that sounded in hindsight. The way Cressida had stared at her lips had set off an avalanche of naughty thoughts, ones she'd pulled back quickly as she realized Cressida wasn't completely sane in that moment. And now that Cressida's thoughts had taken a different track, Medusa knew she'd made the right decision.

She was tempted to argue that revenge *wasn't* her reason for living. Killing Perseus was about her sisters, about justice. She wanted to ask what choice she had if she wanted to save her family. Was she supposed to obliterate an innocent shade instead? Should she hunt down others she deemed guilty, who'd never done anything to her personally, so she could sacrifice them on the altar of saving her sisters? No, that should be reserved for someone who deserved it, a so-called hero who slaughtered others in the name of greatness and was rewarded for it by a system that valued great deeds over a simple life well-lived.

But she didn't want to drag up that pain and lay it out in front of the others. For a moment, she'd been having fun on their little jaunt, even with the danger. She supposed it was good that Cressida was thinking about helping her, weighing the options. Even though her words had dredged all these thoughts up, they were kind, sympathetic words, but they only served to remind Medusa this was all a sham. There was no quest from Hecate, no dangerous journey that Medusa had been pulled into because she was in the wrong place at the wrong time. They were on a task cooked up by Medusa herself to secure the harpe of Cronos so Cressida could kill Perseus.

And it was working, Medusa reminded herself. She should be happy, but instead she was edging on misery made worse because Cressida was clearly attracted to her, and she was feeling the same way.

This was going to get worse before it got better if she didn't nip this guilt in the bud.

As the others peered around Cronos's prison, searching for clues to the harpe's whereabouts, Medusa made herself relive the past, painful as it was. She'd heard the various stories of how she'd supposedly died and the perils that Perseus had faced in order to claim her head, but she remembered things differently. She remembered baking bread.

"A house is never small if the hearts within are full." She'd heard that somewhere. Long after they were tired of ruling kingdoms with their fearsome powers, she and her sisters had retired to share a house, split up the housework, tend the garden with its few olive trees, and fetch water from the river nearby. People had thought Medusa was the only mortal among the three mighty gorgons, but their godhood had long slipped from them, and they hadn't used their powers in ages. She and her sisters had faded from the minds of men, but that didn't matter because they were alive, and they lived in peace.

Stheno had been in the garden that day, Euryale at the river. Medusa had stepped out into the sun and stretched before dusting the flour from her hands. She'd flicked some Stheno's way. Stheno had said something about not risking a fight with a woman who had her hands buried in dirt, and Medusa had backed away, chuckling. She'd laid down on a wooden bench in the shade, looking up into sun-dappled leaves. Euryale had come through the gate with a basketful of wet washing, and when Medusa had offered to help, Euryale had kissed her forehead and told her to relax because she was going to do all the cooking that night. She'd groaned theatrically but smiled all the same. Stheno's soft singing had lulled her to sleep.

She'd often wondered what had woken her: Stheno's song falling silent, or the soft sound her head made when it hit the grass.

Stheno's staring eyes had been the first thing Medusa had seen upon waking. Her sleepy brain hadn't been able to make sense of it right away, nor had she known what to make of the legs coming toward her backward. She followed them up a young man's body, to another pair of wide eyes, these looking at her in the reflection of a shield.

The hiss of his sword cutting through the air had been the last thing she'd heard, and then she'd been standing on the shore of a river with a host of other souls. Not understanding what was happening, she pushed through the others, searching for her sisters, not wanting to find them, but she found Stheno quickly.

"Where is Euryale?" they said at the same time.

Medusa choked down her own tears. "Not here, not here. Maybe she hid."

"What happened? Where is this place?" Stheno wept, grabbing Medusa's shoulders. "We were in the garden. We were just in the garden."

As they watched, some of those around them lost form, floating up to join a fog that drifted over them, over the river. Some among the crowd reached for the drifting others and caught them as one might catch a cobweb. With cries of horror, they let them go.

When the robed figure poled a long, flat boat over to meet them, they all cried out, wailing for children or parents, and their cries were echoed by the half-formed faces in the drifting fog.

"That's Charon," Medusa whispered. "We're dead. That man killed us."

"What man?" Stheno clutched at Medusa's hands. "Where is Euryale?"

Maybe he meant to rob them? No. He'd been walking backward, so he knew what she could do. He'd been after the gorgons, but if Euryale was around the side of the house, he might have missed her, might have thought there were only two instead of three. Legends could be so, so wrong.

Then she pictured Euryale finding their bodies and having to live out the rest of her long life alone. Maybe she would become a monster of legend again and track down their murderer. Maybe she would find the nearest village and turn everyone to stone. More likely, she'd find the quickest way to end her own life out of heartbreak.

"Medusa? Stheno?"

Stheno leapt at their sister gladly, but Medusa shut her eyes in quiet horror. She knew by Euryale's confused look that she'd been murdered, too.

"We're dead," she said. "A man killed us, and now we're dead."

Charon had carried them to the Meadows of Asphodel, where all the souls lived who hadn't done enough deeds that the gods deemed great. Even there, she and her sisters had found a way to be happy through the long years, but now her sisters had faded almost to the point of shades, and they would be easy pickings for those who harvested souls for their ambrosia.

Medusa made a fist. She wouldn't let that happen. And before she saw Perseus obliterated, she would tell him she would have helped him in his quest had he asked. If it would have saved her sisters, she would have done it. If it would have saved *anyone*, she would have done it.

But that was one of the things that made a hero great. They never asked. They took what they wanted, and the gods rewarded them by giving them even more. Well, now it was her turn. If any of the gods remained, she'd see what they thought of that. Such a ballsy deed might please some of them; they might even move her and her sisters to the Elysian Fields. Oh, how she'd laugh then. Maybe she'd have revenge on more of the heroes: throw Jason to Medea, give Hercules to the many he'd killed. Those would be great deeds indeed.

Medusa stared up at Cronus's face. Under the layers of frosted ice, his eyes were white pits, his mouth open in a primal scream. He would have appreciated her plan.

"Legends say Zeus released him," Cressida said softly.

Thinking of her own stories, Medusa smiled. "Legends say a lot of things."

"But if this place is shaped by belief..."

"Well, there's what really happened and what people believed happened. Belief from the mortal world keeps us sentient, yes, but the reality of our existence can be quite different from what people expect, as you've seen."

Cressida frowned as if she either couldn't accept what she'd seen with her own eyes, or she didn't like that the Underworld was the way it was.

Medusa chuckled. "Well, if you truly believe we're all shaped by human belief, you might want to stop thinking of Cronos as free. Unless you want him to be."

Cressida shook her head rapidly, and Medusa had to smile. Unless he'd also been maligned by myth, he was famous for eating his own children; not someone she wanted to meet. Medusa sighed. Maybe Cressida was right. Who knew what to believe anymore?

"Anything?" Pandora called.

Arachne was suspended above them, clinging to the ice wall from one of her gossamer strands. She had climbing spikes attached to both feet, and as they watched, she put her hands to the ice and looked inside. "The harpe's not sheathed at his waist." She flung another strand upward and pulled herself that way.

"How much rope does she have?" Cressida asked.

Medusa bit her lip. "It's not really my story to tell."

Cressida turned her head slowly. "Oh?"

"You know a lot about myth, yes? You said you had studied it?"

"I'm getting my master's in classical literature. It's my aunt that has a doctorate." She pointed upward at Arachne, mouth open as if she might say something, but she put her finger down and shut her mouth, as if she didn't really want to know what was in that backpack, whether it was full of string or if Arachne was spinning it herself, and the pack was hiding a spider's abdomen.

"It's up by his head," Arachne called. "As if he was trying to swing it when he was frozen. We're going to have to chip it out."

"Help me up," Pandora said.

Arachne sent down a loop of string and passed it through a piton. She lowered the string, and Agamemnon hauled Pandora up as she sat in the loop.

"It's got to be huge," Cressida said. "Since he's so big. Forget wielding it. How are we even going to get it out of here?"

"Magic weapons," Agamemnon said with a shrug. "They find a way."

Cressida didn't seem convinced, but Medusa had heard the same. Still, she pictured all of them dragging the harpe through Tartarus while being chased by the Hecatonchires, not to mention also carrying whatever Medea wanted for herself.

Above them, Pandora nodded as she touched the slick surface. "I think I can open a way, but if we crack the ice…"

"We might release him," Agamemnon said. Icy wind gusted through the glacier as if to punctuate the words, and everyone shivered, though Medusa knew it was more from fear than any illusion of cold.

"Are we sure this is a good idea?" Agamemnon asked.

"Hecate commanded it," Medusa said. They were so close; she wasn't going to let them back out now.

Agamemnon's mouth set as if he might argue, but he didn't say anything. Arachne and Pandora exchanged a glance but also stayed quiet. They couldn't argue with Hecate. A goddess would not be pleased if they came back empty-handed, never mind that they'd never been dealing with a goddess in the first place.

Arachne handed something to Pandora, a stethoscope. She put it against the ice. Maybe they'd be able to hear Cronos's giant heartbeat. Arachne tapped over the ice with little tools. Medusa backed away enough to see Cronos's face again. The Hecatonchires had resisted her power. She had no doubt that Cronos would be able to do the same. Cressida backed up to join her, the worry lines between her brows speaking the same fears.

A pattern of cracks appeared around the harpe as Pandora and Arachne sought to get it out. At last, the ice cracked in one long splintery line, jagged around the edges, the sound grumbling through the landscape.

They all froze, and Medusa grabbed Cressida's arm, ready to drag her from this place. She was the important element, not the harpe, though it was the surest way to kill Perseus and preserve his essence. If Medusa had to, she could find another weapon, though that would require distracting Cressida for a little longer.

Cressida held on to her as if grateful for the protection, and Medusa saw something else besides gratitude, besides the bit of attraction they'd been throwing back and forth. She was touched by Medusa's protection. That was beyond attraction to affection, and even though Medusa was prepared for that, it still caused her a further shiver of guilt. She couldn't let Cressida love her. It couldn't get that far.

Even if that was what she needed to succeed?

She tried to push the thought away. All that mattered was that the crack stopped when it exposed the pommel of the harpe.

"You're up," Medusa whispered.

Cressida gawked at her. "There's no way I can lift that. It's huge!"

"It's all a matter of perspective." Medusa led her to where Agamemnon was lowering Pandora. "The weapon will conform to the needs of the wielder." At least, she hoped so. She tried to put on a confident smile.

Cressida grumbled something about people asking her again and again to touch strange things, but she took Pandora's place. She looked a little green as Agamemnon hauled her upward, but she didn't complain as she reached Arachne's side. She put her hand in the ice and strained forward, grunting.

Inside the ice, the harpe flickered blue, and Cressida pulled her hand out slowly, the grip of the sword resting neatly in her palm. She stared at it with wide eyes.

"Titans aren't always huge," Pandora called. "They're whatever they want to be, so their weapons have to fit that."

As Agamemnon lowered her to the ground, Cressida stared in wonder at the sword, turning it to and fro. It wasn't a magnificent piece, wasn't covered in acid etchings. It didn't gleam. The pommel wasn't ornate or topped with jewels. It was simple, brutal, the grip well worn, and the metal heavy and nicked. Something about it screamed sharpness, as if it would cut you for looking at it wrong.

"Let's get going," Agamemnon said. "We've got one more stop to make, and we have to get past the Hecatonchires."

"Not a problem," Cressida said, her voice dreamy.

"Maybe you should put it away," Medusa said. When she gestured to the sheath, Cressida growled at her like a wild animal, and Medusa pulled her hand back. "Cressida?"

A tiny sound came from behind them, as if someone had dropped a champagne flute. Medusa turned as she walked, all of them did, though they seemed to be moving in slow motion. The crack Pandora had made inched downward as they watched, making another of those little, delicate sounds.

"We have to run." Arachne's voice had a strangled quality, and the last syllable was lost as the tinkle grew to a crack, and then to a great grinding sound as huge chunks of ice dropped from Cronos's prison, exposing one blue-veined hand.

They all froze as that hand flexed, fingers reaching.

Medusa grabbed Cressida's arm and ran for the wall of black, the way back to Tartarus. Cressida lifted the harpe as if she might take on the father of the gods with his own weapon, but Medusa didn't know if he could call the harpe back to his hand, send it reeling from Cressida's foolish mortal grip and into his so he could reap them like wheat.

They streaked for the entrance, and Medusa readied her power, knowing they would have company as soon as they emerged.

Cressida didn't know why they were running. She had the key to victory in her hand, a weapon as inevitable as a bolt of lightning. No one could defeat her while she wielded such a weapon, not Cronos, not the Hecatonchires, not mighty Zeus himself. A nagging thought tried to tell her that it was exactly that kind of thinking that had gotten Cronos imprisoned in the first place, but she promptly told her brain that it didn't know what the hell it was talking about.

Still, she ran with the others; she supposed it was bad form to kill a Titan with his own weapon, even if it would have been a piece of cake. But when they careened through the blackness and heard the roars of the Hecatonchires, she knew she wouldn't be dissuaded again. She'd put the harpe to good use.

Everyone was shouting and rushing around. Arachne was throwing her webs, and Agamemnon had his sword out. Medusa took a wide stance as if she could defeat the Hecatonchires with sheer moxie. Cressida knew she should have been terrified, at least a little worried, but all she felt was a slow simmer of anger. For the first time in her life she was keenly aware of the play of muscles under her skin, the potential for power in her shoulders, and the way a blade felt in her hand, with just enough weight to remind her of the damage it could do.

Glee wrapped around the anger, bolstering it. She would show these upstart creatures, oh yes. She'd been pushed around enough, pulled from one crisis to the next because everyone wanted something from her and instead of trying to win her over, they threatened or promised or implied that they alone could change the fate of everyone involved. Well, not anymore.

Her hindbrain kept up a steady refrain of, *Oh shit, oh shit, oh shit*, but she laughed past it. That logical part of her tried to say that she didn't know how to fight, but the set of her knees seemed to argue. And when the first Hecatonchires ambled toward her, she leapt straight into the air as if the gods themselves were lifting her and sheered through three reaching arms with the ease of a lawnmower cutting through a grasshopper.

"Yeah, mutha fucka!" she yelled as the blood washed over her in a spray so warm and soothing it was like a hot shower after a long day. "How do ya like me now?"

Gross, her brain said. That was disgusting, and she should have acknowledged that, but her brain wasn't really in charge anymore, at least not the parts that didn't want to bathe in blood. Before, she would have said that was every part of it, but now she wasn't so sure. Now she saw what she'd been missing by talking to people instead of killing them.

The Hecatonchires howled from his fifty heads, trying to cradle his wounded arms. He backed toward the other Hecatonchires, and they stared at her in fear. *Damn straight they should be afraid.* That was only right. It was just. She'd take care of them, and then she'd go after the rest of her no-good, backstabbing turncoat family.

Her what?

Someone spun her around and shook her, yelling and pointing toward the black box. It was shaking, shuddering as if something was trying to come through, and Cressida backed away from the arms restraining her, a face she couldn't even recall. A haze of wind and cold flashed in front of her face, and she staggered. She was still stuck in the blasted ice, just when she'd thought she'd gotten free enough to slaughter these Titans, she was still stuck in prison.

Was it a dream? No, someone was shaking her again and trying to tell her something, and she blinked away enough fog to ask, "When did I get this short? I didn't say I wanted to be so small!"

"Cressida!"

Another flash, but it wasn't of the ice or her ungrateful family. She saw a woman older than her, one who was depending on her, but no one depended on her. They were afraid of her, and they were right to be because fear was the only thing you could count on to keep everyone in line.

"Cressida!"

"No!" And it wasn't the right voice, only it was, and she felt like two people, maybe three. She looked to the harpe and the Hecatonchires, and it wasn't her they were afraid of. It was the sword and the box and what seemed to be struggling to get out of the box. "This isn't me."

The hands in front of her pointed to something at her waist, a sheath, and she tried to slide the harpe home, but those parts of her that had gotten a taste for killing were still hooked into the rest of her, and they weren't letting go easily. They howled as she moved her hand toward the sheath, gibbered at her to keep the sword drawn. She would need it when she finally got free, and the killing could begin in earnest.

With a groan of mortal effort, she sheathed the harpe sideways, letting the hook stick out the back, and the strength went out of her legs. She slid to her knees, only Medusa's steadying arm keeping her from sliding all the way to the ground.

"Medusa?"

"It's all right, Cressida. It's all right now." She reached past Cressida and tied the leather straps hanging from the sheath, keeping the blade inside.

But it wasn't all right. She was covered in gore, and her legs felt as if she'd done a thousand squats. She turned to see how the others were faring against the Hecatonchires, but the monsters had fled, and the others were staring at her wide-eyed.

The black box had stopped shaking as if the call of the harpe had deadened Cronos's ability to come forth. Still, Cressida didn't want to stay near it in case he tried again. Just a brief touch with his mind had been enough to know that he didn't have an ounce of pity or compassion. He was anger and fear, maybe the source of it for all the world.

Agamemnon sniffed. "Well, if I had known you had such skill with a blade, this trip wouldn't have seemed so ominous."

Cressida let out a breath, feeling lighter, as if his words had sucked some of the horror out of the room.

"We shouldn't stay here," Medusa said.

Arachne nodded. "Right. You've got what Hecate sent you after; now we have to get the item she wants from us."

The farther they walked into the twisting labyrinth, the more of those horrid boxes they saw, and Cressida knew they all held complete hell for whoever was trapped inside, a custom-made punishment. It was terribly efficient, and Cressida couldn't help picturing Hades sitting behind an enormous desk, filling out paperwork and designing specialized hellscapes for new arrivals. Of course, there hadn't been any arrivals worthy of their own personal hells in a long time. Maybe he dreamed them up anyway, manufacturing crimes just so he could think of a way to punish those who might commit them. It gave her shivers just thinking about it.

The presence of the harpe, even sheathed, was enough to keep the Hecatonchires away, though Cressida wasn't in a hurry to draw it again. She wondered about the one whose arms she'd lopped off, if the others would take pity on him or cast him out even though he still had ninety-seven arms to operate with. Maybe they had elaborate dinners where exactly one-hundred arms were needed to dine properly, and the one she'd maimed would have to eat by himself in the kitchen.

She tried not to think such pitying thoughts about a monster that had seemed determined to squash her, but she couldn't help it. It felt as if the dark, bloodthirsty thoughts of Cronos had to be tempered by charitable thoughts, and nothing else would cleanse her of the taint of his mind. Nothing she had in her pack would cleanse her of the taint of the blood, either, though she'd done the best she could with wet wipes. Nero had given her some side eye when she'd first packed them; she'd have to tell him to make them a part of every Underworld explorer's kit from now on.

They finally stopped at another black box, though Cressida couldn't tell it from any of the others. Pandora examined it and nodded before she felt around it, searching for a way in. Eventually, she tapped it, and one side fell away. They lined up, ready to walk in, though when Cressida tried to tell her feet to take her inside, they ardently refused.

Medusa started forward, but when Cressida didn't follow, she looked back over her shoulder. "What's wrong?"

Cressida nodded toward the box. "What's in there?"

"I don't know," Medusa said with a sigh. "I don't know what Hecate wants." She took Cressida's hand. "But I've got you, don't worry." Her normally sexy smile slipped into one that was soothing, one Cressida could fall asleep looking at.

It seemed a better thing to focus on than going into one of the horrid boxes again, so her imagination took a brief leap, thinking on all the things she could do with Medusa besides fall asleep. She shook her head, telling herself yet again that she had a job to do, but she'd started on a track, and visions of Medusa in bed wouldn't leave her so easily. Out of desperation, her brain replayed Nero talking about dental dams, and that dried any desire she had right up.

"Come on," Medusa said. "Let's do it together."

Oh, the entendres, but it got Cressida's feet back under her. They stepped into the box together, and Cressida told herself that whatever environment they encountered would be an illusion, but heat still hit her like an open furnace, and she sagged, wilting among the onslaught of a lava-dotted landscape. Well, she had been looking for lava since she came to the Underworld. It was about time it stopped disappointing her.

Rivers of lava ran across mountains of volcanic glass and oozing patches of slowly melting rock. The air glowed and shimmered, and the landscape extended into obscurity, unlike Cronos's hemmed in glacier.

"I guess 'watch your step' goes without saying," Cressida said. The others seemed too hot to laugh, all of them wiping their foreheads and cursing. Cressida tried to tell herself it was an illusion, but the feeling was hard to overcome when the visuals were leeching sweat out of her every pore.

"Where's the prisoner?" she asked.

Arachne grinned back at her. "Tartarus isn't just used as a prison. It's also a vault for things the gods would rather not fall into our hot little hands."

"Why not keep them wherever the gods are, then?"

Agamemnon smiled condescendingly at her. "Because they'd rather the items not be in one another's hands, too. No, best to hide them down here. Best to hide all the dangerous weapons." He pulled at his collar, and she wondered if he was envisioning the axe coming for him.

"Okay, so where's the vault?" Medusa asked.

"This is it." Pandora took off her sweater to reveal a modest tank top. "That's why we're actually feeling the heat. Now we just have to find what we're looking for and not be reduced to shades in the process."

Arachne slung them from solid ground to solid ground using her string, an unending supply, and Cressida began to think of them as webs and wondered again if she was hiding her spider bits in that backpack. If she could exist as part spider and part woman, it could mean that all that was under that canvas was a swollen black abdomen and spinnerets. It made it hard not to peer, and she forced herself to look away before she was caught.

They walked for what seemed like forever, and Cressida lost the ability to think, having to focus on her feet and try to ignore the oppressive heat.

After too much walking and not enough changes in scenery, Medusa pulled Cressida to a halt, making everyone stop. She didn't think Cressida had noticed, but there'd been a few looks shared between the other three as they marched across this hot wasteland, and when Cressida had asked what they were here for, they'd stumbled for an answer before Arachne finally said, "We'll know it when we see it."

Cressida seemed to accept that as no more bizarre than anything else she'd heard, but Medusa's hackles had been inching up. Something about the heat of this place pulled at her, sparking half-buried memories of her childhood.

"I can't help but notice you march as if you know where you're going," Medusa said, "yet by my calculations, we've been traveling in a circle."

"What calculations?" Pandora asked. "I haven't seen you making any. Can you do trigonometry in your head?"

Medusa ignored her. "You're waiting for something to happen, but what?"

Arachne looked at the rest of them. "We're waiting for the guardian to attack so we can get the item we're looking for."

Medusa looked at the landscape again and ran through the creatures she knew that preferred the hottest climes. Another Titan? But which one? If there was a guardian, it should have attacked by now. A Titan would be able to step over the rivers of lava, unless it was one that lived in lava and could leap through it.

Or swim.

A tickle started at the back of her head, sparking memories again: Eyes, watching her from a pool of boiling water. Green-gold eyes with slits like Medusa's, they'd belonged to someone who would have loved to live in the lava, but who knew her daughters couldn't stand that much heat. So they'd only lived near it, close enough that the water boiled in the ground.

Here, with no daughters to worry about, she could slip from lava pool to lava pool with ease. Even with the heat, the thoughts were enough to freeze Medusa's insides. "Oh, please no. It can't be."

Cressida took her hand. "Are you all right?"

Pandora's expression stayed impassive, but Agamemnon looked a little guilty, and Arachne turned away.

"What do you want with her?" Medusa asked.

Cressida looked around them. "Who?"

Medusa's power began to flow over her, but she kept it in check, barely. "Daughter of Helios, slain by Zeus in the old legends, but not until after she'd birthed her daughters from Phorcys, Cronos's brother, ancient god of the primordial deep."

Cressida's brow furrowed. "Aix? Wasn't she a…" Her mouth fell open, and she stared over Medusa's shoulder.

Medusa's heart sank further, and she turned slowly. A giant, frilled snake reared from one of the closest lava pools. She gleamed gold in the light, green eyes shining, not with a human's intelligence but with enough to recognize her offspring. They locked gazes, and Aix made some noise deep in her throat, a happy, welcoming purr. Her body rippled downward, coiling until she could look her daughter in the eye.

"Mom," Medusa whispered. "I'm sorry I haven't thought of you in so long."

"Your…mother?" Cressida asked.

Medusa didn't turn. Cressida would never understand, and Medusa didn't care to see her try. She'd call having a giant snake for a mother gross or weird, and that would kill any charitable thoughts between them. But maybe that was best. Maybe she should turn to confront the disgust that was no doubt infusing Cressida's expression, and then she could get on with her plan, lead Cressida by the nose, do away with Perseus, and then Cressida would be free to do as she would, and Medusa wouldn't have to care about her any longer.

But her feet wouldn't obey her. Instead, she rested a hand against her mother's golden snout, the scales slick under her fingers. "What are we here for?"

Even as she said the words, her belly went colder. They wouldn't. The gods couldn't have made Aix guard the very thing they'd made from her skin, could they? The world couldn't be so cruel!

But there, tied to Aix's back halfway along her length was the aegis of Zeus, his shield, made from Aix's golden scales, loaned to his daughter Athena, who'd given it to Perseus, and in return for its use, he'd adorned it with Medusa's own head. She'd heard it said that her head retained the full power she'd had in life rather than the diminished power she had now. The cold reflection of his eyes in its gleaming surface had been the last thing she'd ever seen.

She whirled to face the others, but only Agamemnon stood there, covering his eyes. She marched forward, feeling her hair coming alive to hiss and spit. "Averting your eyes won't do you any good when I shove you into the lava."

"Now, now," he said. "No need for theatrics!"

"You brought *me* to recover the aegis of Zeus? The one with my head, made from the skin of my dead mother?" She stabbed a finger in Aix's direction. "And now Zeus has her guarding it in the afterlife when she doesn't know any better?"

He continued to stumble away, and her only thought was to get her hands around his throat because Medea wasn't here, and Zeus wasn't here. She expected him to try to explain, but all he did was jog away, and she remembered Pandora's words about why they'd brought him.

He was the bait.

She turned as Aix cried out in outrage. Arachne had snagged the aegis while Aix had been fixated on Medusa. It gleamed as it spun through the air, her own head fixed to the front, turned from flesh into gold. Medusa ran for Aix, looking for Cressida and Pandora, but she couldn't spot them in the shimmering air.

She ran for Arachne, but Aix was already darting in that direction, striking with teeth longer than Medusa's arm. Arachne blocked with the aegis. Medusa looked for Cressida again and spotted her in the distance, being led by Pandora. Cressida's steps seemed wooden and unnatural, as if Pandora had done something to her.

"Bastards!" Medusa cried. As she was about to leap a narrow channel of lava, something heavy crashed into her back. She cried out as she flew through the air, twisting to see that Agamemnon had hurtled into her, but Arachne jerked him to safety. Medusa rushed toward the lava, the heat reaching up to claim her, and powerful as she was, she knew she'd be reduced to a shade, trapped either in Tartarus or up among the others, with Stheno and Euryale to join her soon.

A flash of gold whipped beneath her, and she tried to grab on to Aix's slippery scales, but she went flying again. Aix's jaws caught her gently and lowered her to one of the obsidian islands. Aix purred softly as she looked Medusa over.

"No, Aix, stop them!" Medusa pointed toward where the three were disappearing into the black box. "Mom, please!"

Aix looked that way, clearly confused, and then turned back to her daughter as if saying, "No, I want to stay with you."

"There, take me there!" Medusa shouted. "Quick before they shut us in!"

Confused as she was, Aix eventually obeyed, but by the time she ferried her to the black doorway, the others had disappeared, and when Medusa tried to follow, she bounced off darkness that had become as solid as a wall.

CHAPTER NINE

One minute, Cressida had been following Medusa through a lava filled hell in Tartarus, and the next she was sitting up in bed, nine years old, awakened by strange noises in the middle of the night while staying with June at a dig site in Turkey.

And Tartarus...had been a nightmare? Must have been. It'd felt so real, but that was impossible. And then she'd dreamed she was being chased by the Furies—one too many tales around the campfire—even though June had assured her that the Furies only pursued those who'd committed very specific crimes.

Sitting alone in a dark tent, Cressida didn't want to think about the kind of people the Furies went after. She wanted to hear that they were made-up stories. She wanted the kind of reassurance her parents provided, even though she'd often rolled her eyes when they took all the magic out of the world. With shadows stretching long fingers across the tent walls, though, she wanted their sensible presence instead of June's, who would rather there be monsters if the monsters had to play by certain rules.

Cressida crept from her tent and tiptoed to June's. She curled into the blankets at her aunt's side, but June slept too soundly to stir. Cressida didn't want to wake her; she'd already called herself a big baby for seeking the bed of a grown-up, but the unfamiliar night sounds kept creeping in, every rustle like the scratch of the Furies' claws.

She sobbed, curled her arms around herself, and June awoke with a start. "Cressi? What's wrong?"

"I had a bad dream."

"Oh, well, that's all over now," June said sleepily. Her voice banished a bit of the darkness but not nearly enough. "Let's get you back to bed."

She led Cressida back to her own tent, the night quiet around them, but it would be too hot to sleep. How had she ever fallen asleep in this heat?

Cressida blinked, overwhelmed with déjà vu. This had all happened before, just like this, only it wasn't so hot then. It had been fall, the night air so crisp it had given her goose bumps. Why was she sweating in her pajamas?

Inside the tent, coolness engulfed her, and she sighed. The air conditioner must have kicked on. Except tents didn't have air conditioners. She'd tried not to complain about the lack of climate control when she was little, didn't want anyone to think of her as spoiled.

"No one thinks you're spoiled," Pandora said.

Cressida staggered away from her, blinking away memory in favor of the cool, uniform walls of the labyrinth. "What?" She whirled around, spotting Arachne and Agamemnon. "Where?"

Memories rushed back: the golden serpent, Medusa whispering, "Mom," and Cressida knew it was Aix, though some legends put other people as Medusa's parents…

Then everything had gone blank, and she'd been in Turkey again. "What did you do to me?"

Pandora had the grace to look sheepish. She slipped something into her pocket. "A little loan from Hypnos, god of sleep. I must remember to return it to him right when we get back." She shrugged. "Sorry."

"You…hypnotized me?" She glanced at the box and all of them again. "Where's Medusa?" She saw the shield in Arachne's hands and did a double take. "Is that…that's not…the aegis of Zeus?" A familiar, snake-headed face stared at her from the middle, though it was covered in gold instead of flesh, but the details were so precise. Even the eyes were the same as Medusa's, though creased in anger as if even death couldn't quench her emotions.

Because it wasn't just the cast of a head. Cressida put a hand over her mouth. "You killed her!"

"Again, you mean?" Arachne said. "No, her spirit's still in there." She jabbed a thumb at the box. "And she's probably pissed as hell, so we'd better go before she and her mom find a way to bust out." All three of them began to march away.

Cressida didn't move, trying to figure out what the hell had happened. "You knew she'd fight you for the aegis? Is that why you didn't tell her what you were after?"

"She distracted her mother," Agamemnon said over his shoulder, "and now we have what we came for. Step lively, or you'll get left behind."

She took a few steps before stopping again. "Hecate said you needed me."

Pandora shook her head. "We've got what we were paid to get. If you're late delivering your own prize, that's on you." She tried a smile that was probably supposed to be kindly. "Cheer up. You have the harpe of Cronos. Now you can finish your deal."

"We didn't have to get you out," Arachne said. "We could have left you with Medusa, but that would be a waste of a living person." She smiled and shrugged. "And technically, we could take the harpe as long as we only touched the sheath. We just can't wield it. Now, come on."

Cressida looked to the box again. They were right. She couldn't stay here, and she didn't know how to open the box. The fact that she'd been tricked ate at her, but that seemed secondary to the fact that her guides were leaving and taking the helpful string with them as they went. Would Charon leave without her? What did he care? If she managed to find her way to the tracks and he was gone, she'd have to wait the eternity it took him to go and come back, if he came back at all.

She still had to free June, too. She did wonder what Hecate needed both the harpe of Cronos and the aegis of Zeus for, but that wasn't really her business. And Hecate might not need her to wield the harpe. If anyone could figure out a way around Cronos's rules, it was the goddess of magic.

Could she walk out of here without the woman who'd asked nothing of her save that she consider helping Stheno and Euryale? Cressida hadn't decided if she would or not. She didn't relish the idea of luring Perseus to his death, but Medusa had never pressured her. She'd left the choice up to Cressida, something no one else in the Underworld had done so far.

The others were already down the hallway. Soon they'd turn the corner and be out of sight. Pandora cast several regretful glances over her shoulder, but she didn't stop. None of them did. Looking out for number one was probably the only way to behave in the Underworld if a person wanted to survive.

But there was more to living than just survival.

Cressida stalked after them. "Now I know why you're all stuck in the Meadows of Asphodel. It's not because of what you did or didn't do. It's because of who you are!"

"Oh for gods' sakes," Arachne said. "No one cares what kind of person you are. Deeds are all that matter to the gods. Do you think Hercules is a nice person?"

No, she never had, but she didn't mention that. She pointed over her shoulder. "And leaving Medusa here is a good deed, is it?"

"Don't you think we tried to be the heroes of the Underworld when we first came here?" Agamemnon asked. "There is no law. There is no justice. You have what you have because you're powerful enough to take and keep it. The only people who get second chances to move up the Underworld ladder are those already inside the Elysian Fields."

"The rich get richer," Pandora mumbled.

Cressida thought of the heroes being resurrected when they were bored enough of paradise to try for something greater. She wondered what constituted great deeds in the modern age. As long as the heroes lived up to their full potential, even if they failed at their chosen tasks, she supposed that might be enough to return them to the Elysian Fields or the Isles of the Blessed.

"The gods don't bother to look at us," Agamemnon said. "So it doesn't matter what we do."

Cressida stared at him for a few seconds. "Fuck that." She turned and strode toward the box. "It doesn't matter if anyone's watching or not. I choose *not* to be a douchebag."

"What are you going to do?" Pandora called.

Arachne said, "Who cares?"

Cressida cast one glance over her shoulder, and they'd all stopped to watch her. "I'm going to do the right thing because it's the right thing, and if I wind up in the Fields someday because of it, so be it." She grinned. "I'll do my best to put in a good word for you." Unless they kept walking away. Then they could go screw themselves.

She drew the harpe and prepared herself for the onslaught of Cronos's mind. It felt muffled farther from his prison, but the gist was still there: slice, murder, kill.

"Yeah, yeah," she said. "But we're killing a box this time, okay?" She raised the harpe and swung just as the footsteps of the others came closer.

She'd prepared herself for the ting of metal hitting metal or the dull shockwaves she'd get if striking stone, but the sword sank fast and halted, as if she'd buried it in an enormous block of gelatin. The grip slipped out of her fingers, and momentum pitched her forward. She smacked into the box. Against the sword, it was gelatin, but to her face, it felt like a rock. Just her luck.

The others hurried back toward her. Maybe she was getting through to them because she wouldn't leave a friend behind, or maybe it was because she'd offered to try to help them attain the Elysian Fields. Whichever it was, she'd take it.

"Stop," Pandora said with a sigh. "You don't know what you're doing."

"Then help me!" After rubbing her face, Cressida grabbed the harpe, put a foot on the box, and pulled the sword free with a little pop. She felt over the place she'd cut, looking for a dent or a slice, but it seemed whole, and to her touch felt solid as marble. Maybe in a different spot? She raised her arms to strike again.

Pandora caught her wrist. "That isn't going to work. You can't open it if you don't know what you're doing."

"I haven't known what I was doing since I got here!"

Pandora stared as if Cressida was a mystical creature she'd like to study.

"Medusa wouldn't come back for you if she didn't need you," Agamemnon said. "You must know she's only helping you so that you'll help her."

"But she left it up to me! And when Hecate commanded I come down here and get this sword in order to free my aunt, Medusa came with me. She could have left me out to dry."

He exchanged a glance with Arachne. "Maybe, maybe not," Arachne said.

"You're her last chance to kill Perseus," Pandora said softly.

"Rumor has it that he's already lived two lives," Agamemnon said. "If he decides to be resurrected again…"

"She won't be able to touch him." Cressida put a hand to her forehead. "And yet she still offered to help me first, letting me choose whether or not I would help her."

Arachne frowned. "If you believe that, you'll believe anything."

Cressida waited for more, but Arachne just shrugged. Pandora was watching the box as if having second thoughts.

Agamemnon sighed. "If we let her out, she'll try to kill us, not to mention what her mother will do since we've stolen the aegis."

"I'll open the box for you," Pandora said. They all stared at her, but she only looked at Cressida. "Then the three of us are running, and you two can figure out how to get out of Tartarus on your own."

"Unless Charon decides to wait for us," Cressida said.

Arachne snorted. "He won't."

As she and Agamemnon started away, Cressida called, "Hecate wants the harpe, too."

"You'll find your way," Arachne said. "If you die, Medusa can drag your corpse up with her. She's got time." She smirked over her shoulder. "For some things, at least."

Pandora touched the box and then faced Cressida with what seemed like a genuine smile. "You seem like a nice person. Good luck." She put her hands on Cressida's shoulders, then one of Arachne's webs flew from down the corridor, caught her around the waist, and pulled her away.

As they rounded the corner, one side of the box dropped open with a slam.

Medusa stared at the wall of darkness. Her hair ruffled gently as Aix breathed in and out behind her. Memories of childhood rose again, and she clung to them, clung to anything besides the fact that she was trapped in Tartarus.

Her sisters had cared for her when she was very little; their mother couldn't do much more than hunt for them and protect them. It wasn't until long after Aix had died that Medusa had wondered who'd cared for her sisters as infants. She supposed that Aix had always done the best she'd could, even against Zeus himself.

She remembered being carried in her mother's mouth, grasping her mother's teeth. One day, after being carried far enough that Aix's mouth dried out, Medusa had tumbled into a sandy hole with Stheno and Euryale, and Aix had covered them with dirt. As Zeus rampaged through the desert, hunting them, they'd cried out for their mother to hide with them, but she was far too large to fit in the hole. Euryale begged Aix to flee and hide in the nearby mountain that was always belching smoke and lava, but she never ventured far from her young, and they couldn't stand the same great temperatures she could.

Aix had faced Zeus and lost, and she'd probably never understood what he wanted or why he'd come. She hadn't thought to run because she couldn't carry her daughters far in her mouth, and she hadn't thought to have them cling to her back. She'd never been smart, but she loved her children and died for them. After Zeus had skinned her, he'd let her daughters be.

Medusa slid her fingertips across Aix's snout. "I didn't know you were here, Mom. I looked for you in Asphodel. I hoped Zeus had sent you to the Elysian Fields, but why would he do that for a monster?"

And he wasn't even the one she was really mad at. She'd let her mother become just Aix in her mind, just another Titan, and she hadn't come to Tartarus because she didn't want these memories again. Tears started down her cheeks, and she couldn't stop them any more than she could stop breathing. "Well, we'll have plenty of time to get to know each other again."

Aix gently rubbed her head up and down Medusa's side and purred, a sound that dredged up deep memories of being lulled to sleep in her mother's warm coils. She supposed she'd come to enjoy it again.

If she couldn't figure a way out of here.

"Right." She wiped the tears away and thought of Euryale's words when they'd realized their mother was never coming back: "We always have to get back up."

She turned to the square of blackness and wiped her hands on her jeans. Cressida was counting on her. She didn't know what the other three were planning. They were probably leading Cressida away, and each second Medusa spent lost in the past feeling sorry for herself was a second the villains got farther ahead. She wasn't surprised at the anger inside her, the sting of betrayal, but the jot of fear was new and sharp. She recognized the familiar fear for her sisters, a lingering dread she'd gotten used to, made sharper by the fact that if Cressida slipped through her fingers, it was possible her sisters would as well.

This new fear, though, was all for Cressida's safety. If those bastards harmed her...

She had to figure out how to open the box first. She reached for it, ready to feel along it for weak spots, but her arm plunged inside, and she cried out as she slipped forward, the solidness evaporating. She felt a rush of air as her mother followed her, no doubt spurred on by her cry.

But she didn't have time to be surprised. She had to be ready to face whatever waited in the labyrinth. Power trembled through her, and she was ready to unleash it on the three turncoats, but when she saw Cressida, Medusa swallowed her power again.

Still, Cressida's wide eyes said she'd glimpsed Medusa's transformation. Luckily, their gazes hadn't met, and she didn't seem afraid by what she'd seen. She rushed forward, arms out, and crushed Medusa in a hug.

With a laugh of relief, Medusa started to hug her back, but Cressida pushed away slowly and stared as Aix's massive shape oozed from the box, curling around them until she blocked off the cul-de-sac.

"Cressida, this is my mother. Aix, this is Cressida."

Aix's large head dipped forward, her tongue flicking in and out.

"How do you do?" Cressida asked hurriedly, the words almost on top of one another, inflectionless in her obvious terror.

Medusa tried her best to ignore it. She couldn't afford to let Cressida's feelings for Aix affect her now. "Did they hurt you?"

"I'm fine, thanks." Cressida blinked and shook her head, giving Aix a tentative smile before turning to Medusa. "They used some kind of hypnotism, but I…couldn't leave without you."

Even as gratitude and affection washed over her, Medusa felt guilty as hell. "Thank you, Cressida. Where did the others go?"

"Toward the entrance. And if they get Charon to drive them back, I don't know how we're going to follow. It seems like a really long walk. I don't know if I have enough supplies or if June has enough to wait for me. And they took the string that leads out of the labyrinth."

Medusa glowered at the hallway beyond. "Don't worry about that. Aix, can you see the way out?" Her mother stared blankly, and Medusa gestured wildly, saying, "Out, we need to get out," several times before her mother seemed to get the gist. She reared up and then started through the tunnels.

Medusa seethed as they hurried toward the entrance. The others had to have been planning on dumping her from the beginning, which meant Medea had told them to do it, maybe under the guise of Hecate, but who knew.

But how had Medea known the way to the vault for the aegis? Medusa had been feeling her way through when she was looking for the harpe, but Pandora always seemed to have some inkling of where she was. Maybe they had someone else on their side who knew all the ways of the labyrinth? Someone who knew where the aegis was? A god? A goddess?

But Pandora had seemed to be playing it by ear, too. She'd even made a few false turns. Maybe she hadn't really known the way. Maybe there was no map.

Medusa put the heel of her hand to her forehead. "I've been such an idiot!" Even her mother swung around to look at her. "Perception. This whole place is built on perception. It creates what the prisoners think their hell should be like. It creates the guardian's ideal lair. Even this labyrinth. It's only here because we think it is. Pandora wasn't finding her way through it; she was opening it."

"With her superpower?" Cressida asked.

Medusa snorted a laugh. "She was unlocking it by not believing in it. If you think you're lost in the labyrinth, you'll stay lost."

"Like Hecate's palace? So, all we have to do is think about the way out?"

"Having something tangible like the string probably helps. And Aix can see over the walls, which will make us believe we're headed toward the entrance, especially if she believes it, too." She grinned at her mother. "As for making it out before you go through all your supplies, Aix can help us there. My mother is very fast when she wants to be."

Medusa began to walk again with purpose, confident her mother would find them the way out and hoping that confidence imprinted on the labyrinth around them. Cressida stayed by her side, eyes still pinned on Aix, and Medusa hoped she was believing, too.

"Your mother..." Cressida said.

"What about her?"

"She's a giant snake."

"Look, I know what you're doing. You're trying to picture what's possible and what isn't as far as breeding and genetics goes, but don't. If you try to match mythology and science, you're going to go insane."

"Well..." She drew the word out, and Medusa could almost see her logical brain stretched to the point of snapping. "Your mom is clearly a giant snake. Unless she doesn't exist, and I'm just picturing her there because you're seeing her."

Medusa gave her a look of mock horror. "Maybe I'm not here and neither are you. Maybe you're locked up in an insane asylum."

"Stuck in a cliché? That is terrifying."

Medusa waggled her fingers. "Spooky."

Cressida looked as if she was going to smile, but her mouth twisted as if trying to swallow any mirth. "You're just trying to distract me from the fact that your mom is a giant snake, and you're not."

"I'm not going to explain, but while you were distracted..." She gestured ahead to where the gates of the labyrinth stood wide open. "My giant snake mother and I have found the way out."

Cressida whooped, and Medusa couldn't help a laugh. Even Aix seemed amused, though a stranger wouldn't have been able to tell. When Aix turned to look at them, purring, Cressida pulled up short. "Is she growling?"

"It's a good noise. She likes you."

"How can you tell?"

Medusa shrugged. "She's my mom."

Cressida nodded, but it had a resigned air, as if she'd get used to that fact only under duress. The platform for the trolley stood empty, just as Medusa expected.

"Give us a hand, Mom." Medusa gestured upward until Aix lowered her head. Medusa put a foot behind one of her frills and pulled up to sit with her feet just in front of them, right behind her mother's head. "Riding on her back will be a little stomach turning, but it beats walking. Who knows? We might even catch up to them." She held a hand down.

After another look down Aix's length, Cressida grabbed Medusa's hand and let herself be pulled aboard. "If we do catch them, what do you plan to do? We can't keep the aegis from Hecate, can we?"

As Aix slithered up the tunnel, heading for Asphodel, Medusa frowned hard, wondering how she could explain taking the aegis and keeping it. It held *her* head, after all. Maybe if she made up some excuse about how Hecate didn't really want the aegis? But any excuse she concocted might unravel the lies she'd told. She sighed. Lying wasn't any fun unless she was the only one telling them, and that certainly hadn't been the case this time.

"I don't know," Medusa said. After lying, stalling was the best tactic.

"I wonder why Hecate wants the aegis. Maybe she thought you were going to betray her, and she wanted a way to turn your gaze back on you? But she's the goddess of magic. Surely she doesn't need your power in order to fight you."

Medusa's gaze wouldn't work on the real goddess of magic, no. And Medusa would have a hard time petrifying someone as aware as Medea, who had her own magical arsenal. Maybe the aegis was insurance of some sort. Unless Pandora, Agamemnon, and Arachne had truly struck out on their own and were double-crossing everyone. But they couldn't be stupid enough to risk having Medusa *and* Medea or Hecate as their enemies.

No, Medea's hand was at the heart of this. She needed the aegis for something more than just fighting Medusa, and Medusa had to find out what it was.

It was her *head*.

No, she told herself. She had Cressida, and she had the harpe. Now was the time to make directly for the Elysian Fields, invent a story about why Hecate wasn't getting the harpe and convince Cressida to lead Perseus out. Her plan had been to have Medea send them to the Fields in her guise as Hecate, but Medusa would have to think of something else now.

And while she was doing that, Medea would be free to do whatever she wanted with the aegis. She'd use Medusa's head and Aix's skin for whatever nefarious purpose she wanted. It was an outrage.

One that could be dealt with after Stheno and Euryale were restored.

Medusa curled both hands into fists. She *had* to find out what Medea planned to do with the aegis. She'd find out first, before she did anything else.

A very deeply ashamed part of her knew it was more than just the aegis that made her hesitate to bring Cressida to the Elysian Fields. Their time together was drawing to a close, and when it finally did, Cressida would end up hating her. With the lies Medusa had told, there was no other ending. Cressida would have to be the one to destroy Perseus, and she'd probably think of it as murder. And when Medusa really offered to help find June, Cressida might reject that offer. She might run into the Underworld, get herself in all kinds of trouble.

It made her stomach hurt just thinking about it, and she knew what she should do. She had to direct Cressida to the real Hecate. If June was there, Cressida could probably bargain for her, maybe even with the harpe. Medusa could always go to Hecate later and see if the goddess could be persuaded to help her kill Perseus. Maybe she'd be grateful for something new to do. Medusa didn't know anyone in the Underworld who wasn't bored.

First things first, though. She was going to find out what Medea wanted with the aegis. It was a quest that wouldn't wait.

It was her *head*.

❖

And now I'm riding a giant snake through Tartarus.

No, it was even stranger than that. Cressida was sitting on a giant frilled snake who was also a Titan with the Titan's daughter, Medusa, herself a demigod who could turn people into stone and occasionally had wings and snake hair. In Tartarus. With the harpe of Cronos strapped to her hip. Yeah, that was one collection of experiences she wasn't going to top anytime soon. If ever. If she lived a thousand lifetimes.

But if she returned here when she died, it could happen all the time. She wondered what that would be like. If Medusa had her revenge and her sisters were returned to themselves, the three of them could be happy. And if Cressida came back—and June, too—they could all be happy together. June could date the goddess of magic but as a proper dead person—if Hecate was interested in regular dead people—and she and Medusa could...

What? Be lovers? Girlfriends?

Well, as for lovers, Cressida thought, *yes, please*. Just thinking about it made her hyper aware of Medusa sitting in front of her. They had to ride in front of the frills to keep them from sliding along Aix's back, and that meant that with every slither, Medusa's lusciously curvy backside rubbed against Cressida's thighs, driving them open a bit wider. She closed her eyes and tried not to think too hard about that. It was difficult enough to keep hold of the frills rather than wrap her arms around Medusa's waist, maybe lean forward and bury her face in Medusa's neck and have a bit of a nibble.

Get a grip. Even if she did come back to the Underworld upon her death, who on earth would be left to remember her? She supposed if she had children or grandchildren by the time she died, they'd remember her for a little while, but even if there were pictures, how well would her great-grandchildren recall her? She might be remembered a while longer through her academic writing, if her work gained any success; a few students would carry her memory, but if everything she'd witnessed so far in the Underworld was true, she'd need a hell of a lot more belief to remain aware. Every shade might have once been remembered by someone, but after those people had died, too, shadehood had probably come on pretty quickly. After all, two people as well known as Stheno and Euryale were fading away.

And even if Medusa wanted Cressida now, she wouldn't want a shade later. After Cressida left, Medusa would probably move on pretty quickly. She wouldn't pine for the rest of Cressida's life. In fact, she might be angry because Cressida had angered Adonis, and he could pull Medusa into the whole gang-culture of the Underworld if he wanted revenge for the loss of his ambrosia.

It was a big tangled mess, but Cressida told herself she shouldn't be worried about it at all. She should have been thinking about getting June back and getting the hell out of the Underworld and living her life, no matter where she might wind up in the afterlife.

But what was there to focus on besides the Underworld's problems? The beautiful woman in front of her? The undulating, slightly sickening feel of the snake, the *mother* of the beautiful woman in front of her? Focusing on the hope for some hot loving was so much nicer.

Cressida grinned since Medusa couldn't see her. That did sound wonderful, but Cressida usually didn't let her mind wander to such things outside the privacy of her own home. She'd have been lying if she said she hadn't ever fantasized about the women of myth. Medusa had even been one of her fantasies, snake-headed and all. Letting herself fall in love with characters was so much easier than interacting with real people. Cressida's last date had been months in the past, and it hadn't progressed past heavy petting. And that had been in the real world with plenty of time to spare, not in the Underworld while running from one impossible task to the other.

Cressida's inner voice reminded her of what Medusa would appreciate much more than hot loving. Perseus's death would *guarantee* her further happiness once Cressida had gone.

And it might make her more receptive to any hot-loving-adjacent ideas.

Cressida frowned, telling herself that potential sex was secondary to Medusa's happiness, *thank you very much*. She would not let herself turn into some sleaze who only did nice things in exchange for sex.

Even if the sex would be very, very good.

With a firm command to her inner sleaze to shut the hell up, she nodded to herself, letting her hand rest briefly on the harpe. She'd cut the arms off a Hecatonchires. She could lure a hero of legend to his doom. After all, she didn't have to kill him, though she didn't know what comfort that would be in the middle of the night when she was staring at the lonely walls in her apartment. She wondered if Medusa would sneak up on him to do the deed or if she'd call him out like a gunslinger in a western.

Whatever she decided, Cressida didn't have to stick around to watch. She'd get June, she'd help Medusa, and then she'd hightail it toward Cerberus's cave. With any luck, Cerberus would be out chasing Nero and wouldn't be waiting for her. She touched over her heart where the oil connected to her lifeline and hoped Nero was okay, hoped she might have felt it if something happened to him.

When her eyelids began to droop, she went with it. The feeling of the snake was hypnotic, and she felt as if she needed a nap. Before she knew it, someone nudged her forehead, and she sat bolt upright, realizing she'd nodded off against Medusa's shoulder.

"I'm sorry," she muttered, wiping a bit of drool off her chin.

"We're here."

The streetcar sat where they'd first seen it, Charon's booted feet propped up on the panel in front of him, but he peeked around his newspaper-book-magazine as the giant snake glided toward him.

Cressida leaned close to Medusa. "Are you going to say anything?"

"What would be the point? I'm not going to change the ferryman of the Underworld, and I don't want to make an enemy of him. I want to save all my ire for…" She swallowed.

"Hecate? Or did you mean Perseus?"

"Hecate's three lackeys for certain, maybe her."

"Medusa…" But what could she say? The goddess tried to trap Medusa in Tartarus, but Cressida couldn't risk losing the chance to get June back. "Can you…"

"Wait until after you've traded your aunt for the harpe?"

Cressida breathed a nervous laugh. "Well, since you suggested it!"

"I think that deal is probably off."

"What? Why?"

When she didn't answer, Cressida's mind raced. What the hell was she supposed to do now? She supposed she could stand up to Hecate with Medusa, use the harpe and Cronos's battle knowledge to fight to get June back, but against a goddess who could warp her surroundings at will? And who knew what else she could do? Probably anything she wanted!

The snake slowed, halting as Medusa leaned far forward and whispered something. She slid down, and Cressida followed.

"What's the plan?" Cressida asked.

"We can't go riding Aix through town. Everyone would know we were coming." She rolled her lips under and stared at nothing, or she might have been following the lines of buildings and flashing lights, trying to think of a plan of attack. After a moment, she turned and caught Cressida staring. "Don't worry. I'm not suicidal." She sighed hugely. "But maybe we should part company."

"You're going to go up against Hecate alone?"

Another sigh. "I'm going to go after one of our three friends first, find out what they know." She stared at Cressida for nearly a minute, long enough for Cressida to fidget under her gaze. "Maybe you should go see Hecate by yourself. Plead your case. Hide the harpe somewhere so you can get it later." She chuckled, though it sounded more hopeless than humorous. "You might find she doesn't even ask you for it."

"You think this whole expedition was a trick to get rid of you? That she never wanted this sword in the first place?"

"Sounds as plausible as anything I've thought of. You should go straight to her temple, perform a prayer ritual, something she probably hasn't seen in a long time, and that might appease her enough to get your aunt back if your aunt is really there, if that wasn't another lie." She winced.

Cressida frowned. "But I saw her. We both did."

"Even if she isn't there, Hecate can help you find her if your supplication is sincere." She nodded. "And then..." She lifted her arm, halfheartedly gesturing in what could have been the direction of Cerberus's cave.

Deeply touched, Cressida shook her head rapidly. "No, I'm going to help you and your sisters. I've decided. I'm going to lure Perseus over."

She expected surprise, maybe gratitude, but Medusa gave her such a guilt-stricken look that Cressida had to lay a hand on her arm.

"Don't look like that," Cressida said. "None of this Tartarus stuff is your fault. You've only tried to help me, and people keep getting in the way."

"Gods, Cressida!" Medusa walked a few feet away, rubbed her forehead, and walked back again. "How can you be so..." Her smile had a strained quality as she breathed hard. "Good?"

"It's the only way to help your sisters, right? How can I ignore that?"

After another deep breath, Medusa shut her eyes tightly. "Go and plead your case to Hecate. Aix and I will be all right."

Cressida hesitated, looking toward the elevators that would take her to Hecate's palace if she could remember the way. Medusa might be right. Hecate might take the harpe in exchange for June if Cressida didn't have Medusa by her side, but she couldn't help thinking of them as a team.

"No," Cressida said, "we stay together."

Medusa turned wide eyes on her. "Go, Cressida. I'm not telling you again."

"Or what? You'll turn me to stone?"

Medusa took a threatening step forward, and fear crept through Cressida's entrails. This was a demigod standing in front of her, a creature of immense, terrible, ancient power. Who was she to defy that?

A woman who's been pushed around by mythological bullshit for too long, that's who. Cressida lifted her chin. "If we stay together, we can get everything we want."

Medusa sighed, and some of the fight went out of her eyes. "You don't know what you're offering, but if you're just going to follow me anyway..."

"I'm not sure I could find Hecate's palace on my own. Do you think you can find Pandora, Arachne, or Agamemnon?"

"With my sisters searching. They can hook directly into the shade network far easier than anyone else."

Cressida nodded, though the idea made her sad; it no doubt meant they were closer to shades than thinking beings. "Pandora seemed the most sympathetic. She's the one that let you out, though I got the impression that Agamemnon thought I was noble for staying behind."

"Well, let's start with the weakest link." She pulled upward and hooked a floating shade. "Stheno, Euryale, find Agamemnon." At Cressida's questioning look, she shrugged. "He has the greatest tendency to babble."

And of the three, he was the least powerful. Even if his awareness wouldn't allow Medusa to turn him to stone, Cressida bet Medusa could pin him in under eight seconds. And if not… Cressida patted her hip, though she didn't know if she should unleash the battle hunger of Cronos on anyone she wasn't prepared to kill, or at least chop a few bits off of.

"So, where do we stash your mom?" Cressida asked. "I doubt she'll fit in your apartment."

"I know a few places."

Aix had been watching them closely, head swiveling between them. When Medusa had stepped forward threateningly, her tongue had flicked out, but Cressida had no idea how to read a snake's expression. At the mention of her other two daughters, her eyes had fixed on Medusa for a few seconds, but if that was recognition, Cressida also couldn't tell.

Now she went where they led her, to a large warehouse sitting near the tracks, and as such, it had the same abandoned look as the places near the entrance to the Elysian Fields. "Aix, stay here," Medusa said, pointing to the floor. When they started to leave, though, Aix began to follow. "No, Mom, stay here. You have to wait here. I'll come and get you."

Aix's huge head moved back and forth. Medusa dragged in a shade from the cloud of them and hooked it under one of her mother's frills. "I will call you if I need you, but you have to wait here. Guard this warehouse."

Aix seemed to understand that better. She coiled in the middle of the floor and rested her head on the top loop, the better to watch the door. She watched them go, tongue flicking in and out, and her nictitating membrane covering her eye like a blink.

Outside, Medusa looked back inside the warehouse with an expression full of regret. Cressida knew the story of Aix's death, and she guessed it had taken place when Medusa had been a child, maybe an infant, if any of the timelines were remotely factual.

Cressida laid a hand on her arm. "I'm sure she would have been a good mom if she'd gotten the chance. She seems nice." But she had to stop herself from adding, "For a giant snake."

Medusa stared at her, expression transformed into wonder. Her gaze softened and drifted over Cressida's face, lingering on Cressida's lips. Cressida's insides bunched as the rest of her went rigid, waiting, so many emotions flicking through her brain it felt as if someone had switched it to hyper-drive. Her inner voice babbled, but as Medusa leaned across the small distance between them, she thought, *please, please shut up. Let's just enjoy this.*

Cressida's focus narrowed at the first touch of Medusa's soft lips, the lower one slightly fuller, pressing in and moving, the downward motion opening Cressida's mouth. Then their lips were between each other, their heads tilting. They pressed together, and Cressida savored each spot of contact, breasts and arms and shoulders. Medusa slid Cressida's backpack free, and her hands wandered across Cressida's back. Cressida wrapped her arms around Medusa's shoulders, sliding over the soft cotton of her tee and hooking around her neck. Medusa's hands shamelessly slipped downward to cup Cressida's ass, making her moan as Medusa's tongue snaked into her mouth and lured her own tongue out.

There really should have been fireworks. There should not have been a centaur passing on the other side of the street calling, "Get a room!"

Spell momentarily broken, they parted, limbs creeping back toward their owners. Medusa glared. "That street corner can have a new centaur-shaped art installation. Just say the word."

Cressida laughed, thinking that if someone hadn't shouted, they might now be writhing on top of a pile of hastily discarded clothing. With a centaur standing over them. She shivered and backed up a step, putting her backpack on again.

"That was…" She didn't have words, wished she hadn't started saying anything at all. "We should go." Medusa turned away, and Cressida realized how stopping before saying how the kiss had been could be considered a criticism. "Good. It was really, really good."

Medusa smiled over her shoulder, a look of pure confidence, and Cressida knew she shouldn't have been worried. "To be continued?"

"Abso-fucking-lutely."

Medusa laughed but faced forward again, and Cressida was a little sad she didn't offer an arm or a hand, something to cement the promise of the future.

CHAPTER TEN

Medusa called herself a stupid, selfish idiot even as she tried to maintain a calm façade. That kiss, though! Even if she could travel back to the moment it happened and try to stop herself, she didn't think she could. She'd have to stand and watch it happen.

And it wasn't just that Cressida was beautiful; she was also loyal and brave and sympathetic enough to compliment Medusa's mother in a way no one had before. She felt sorry for a creature everyone else viewed as a monster. Aix and her kind were usually fodder in heroic tales; no one pitied them.

Medusa fought the urge to sigh. For fuck's sake, she couldn't be falling in love. Their entire relationship was built on a pack of lies, and soon the whole thing would come unraveling. But Cressida wouldn't leave even when told to; it had become pretty clear she was the kind of person who stayed.

Medusa again considered coming clean, but then Cressida would march off on her own. She could get into serious trouble, but going it alone might be less dangerous than picking a fight with Medea. No, as Cressida walked happily at her side, Medusa thought they might be safer together no matter what, and she was *pretty* sure it wasn't just her hormones talking. Harpies wouldn't be the only things looking to make a meal of Cressida, and anyone else she met would be seeking a way to manipulate her just as Medusa had done. And June couldn't wait forever. No matter what supplies June had brought with her, they couldn't last through hundreds of quests.

"Cressida, give me a moment," Medusa said. "I want to check in with my sisters."

"Sure." She wandered a few steps away, lingering at the corner; her shimmer of life made her seem like the only true color in a colorized movie.

She pulled a bit of shade fog. "Stheno, Euryale."

"Sister?"

Medusa pictured them waiting for her call, always standing by the window because what else did they have to do but stand around waiting for her to help them?

Her fist tightened. Maybe she should just give in, mix up a few innocent souls with her small stash of ambrosia, feed it to them, and make them exist off the lives of others like many in the Underworld did. They could become the monsters that myth wanted them to be.

"Have you found Cressida's aunt?"

"Hidden from our sight."

Medusa rolled her lips under and resisted the urge to shout a curse. If they couldn't find June, that meant the shade fog couldn't penetrate wherever she was, and the stuff got everywhere. It was the fount of rumor in the Underworld. You could try to keep it out, but it always seeped in enough for someone to glean an idea of what you were up to.

June could very well be in Hecate's hands if the shade fog couldn't see her. Rumor had her there, and that meant someone had seen her heading in that direction. "Who in the Underworld is close to Hecate?"

"Persephone."

Medusa chuckled hopelessly. "Yes, and we've got as much chance getting in to see one as we do the other."

"Medea."

"Tried that one. Can you find her?"

They fell silent, and she knew they were sifting through the shade fog far faster than anyone else could. "No one can recall seeing her leave her factory today."

"Please tell me you've found Agamemnon. Or Pandora and Arachne?"

"Agamemnon is at a bar." Another silence followed, lengthier this time. Cressida glanced at her, and Medusa waved. She wondered if Cressida was curious about what she and her sisters were talking about, what was so important that no one else was allowed to overhear it.

"Pandora has returned to her home," Stheno and Euryale said. "Arachne is near there, too. Agamemnon is closest, down the street from you."

Medusa grinned and knew it had a tinge of wickedness to it. "What's the name of the bar?"

❖

Cressida almost felt sorry for Agamemnon. He clearly wasn't expecting anyone to sidle up behind him, meet his eyes in the mirror backing the bar, and say, "Do you think all these mirrors will protect you?"

He froze, meeting Medusa's gaze, his stare not bothering to flick to Cressida. Medusa's image seemed to shimmer, and hissing snakes flickered to life around her beautiful face. Her eyes flashed, but it happened quickly and was gone just as fast; it could have been a shadow.

"I'm immune to my own gaze," she said. "And the mirror might save you, but if you turn your head just a little…"

He swallowed hard. "How did you get here so quickly?"

Medusa eased onto a stool at his side. "I'm curious: How long did you think it would take?"

Cressida took a stool on his other side, and he glanced at her at last. She gave him a look that she hoped conveyed the sentiment that he'd made this bed, him and the others.

"I mean," Medusa said, "you know Cressida doesn't have much time. And Perseus will soon be out of my reach. Did you think I would be *less* angry if when I emerged, Perseus had moved on, and Cressida was dead?"

"We…" He cleared his throat, sipped his drink, and seemed to decide it was better not to speak.

"Who is the aegis for? Someone who has a bone to pick with me?"

"You think this is about you?" he asked. "You think we went with you to Tartarus, used you to get the aegis, all because we wanted to defeat you? No offense, my dear, but there are easier ways."

"Then why?"

He shrugged.

"Tell us what we want to know—"

"Or what?"

"Look," Cressida said loudly. Several of the patrons glanced at her, and she leaned in, pitching her voice lower. "I'm loving getting a peek into Underworld politics, really I am, but I want my aunt back, and I'm tired of being dicked around."

They both blinked at her.

"I know you've all got your problems," Cressida said, "some more than others, but I don't see what the hell, if you'll pardon the expression, any of your problems have to do with me. I want to help you," she said to Medusa, avoiding adding, *if only for the chance of another kiss.* She looked to Agamemnon. "And if I see your wife, I will ask her how she is, but my goal is to get June." She rested a hand on the harpe. "And I'm getting the impression that whatever Hecate wants this sword for, she's going to need my help there, too, and I'm getting really goddamned tired of being told what to do and where to go and whom to talk to. How come no one here just *asks* for help?"

She resisted the urge to order her own drink, knowing that would condemn her to stay, but the scent of alcohol filled her nostrils with its enticing promise of mellowness. She pulled a soda from her bag and cracked it open. She needed to stay sharp. "Now, I don't know how to fight with a regular sword, much less this hooked thing hanging from my hip, but Cronos does, and every time I pull the harpe, I feel him in my mind giving me instructions. So, how's about you answer my friend's questions, and help get me back on track to finding my aunt, or I'm going to lay waste to this bar with you being the first target in my metaphorical crosshairs."

They'd frozen, staring, and the barkeep—a black-haired satyr—had come close enough to hear and was now walking away with a practiced air of skillful retreat. A few other bar patrons seemed to sense a shift in the tone of the room; they put on hats or coats and said things in loud voices like, "Well, it's an early one for me," or "I've got a big day tomorrow."

"Well," Agamemnon said, drawing the word out. "Quite a speech."

Medusa flushed, frowned, and stared at Cressida's lips as if torn between the desire to make out with her or censure her.

"What's it going to be?" Cressida asked.

"One magic sword and you think you can push everyone around?" Agamemnon took another sip, but she saw the slight twitch in his hands, the way his eyes kept slipping toward where her hand rested on the harpe's grip.

She drew it slightly, wishing it had a metallic ring like swords in the movies, but the scabbard was oiled leather, and the sword slid through it like a razor through shaving cream. She didn't free it, but she began to feel Cronos behind her eyes, telling her to cut where certain arteries pumped close to the skin or where the tendons stretched taut, and the pain would hum through Agamemnon like the most perfect symphony.

He grabbed her wrist faster than she could move, but on the heels of that, Medusa put her hand on the back of his head, nails dimpling his skin. They all froze except for Medusa, who moved close to his shoulder, her canines stretching so long she couldn't close her mouth. She paused just above his cloak, and Cressida could see the light through her teeth; they'd be hollow to let the poison course through.

Agamemnon's gaze dug into Cressida's. "I don't know the whole story. I'm a hired hand."

"For whom?" Medusa asked as her teeth slid back to normal.

"Medea."

Cressida stiffened and noticed Medusa doing the same. A powerful sorceress rumored to have killed her own children to spite her cheating husband. Some legends also painted her as the daughter of Hecate, though as with all myths, no one could ever agree on someone's parentage. But now, with Hecate being the one who'd sent them to Tartarus in the first place?

"I can take you to Pandora," he said. "She knows things I don't."

Cressida nodded and let the harpe sink back into its scabbard. Agamemnon let her go, and everyone sat back a bit. "I trust I can finish my drink first?" he asked.

Cressida sipped her soda and nodded. "I think we're all going to need a drink."

"Seconded," Medusa said, and she looked more worried than Cressida had ever seen, more worried than when they'd first sneaked into Hecate's palace or were ordered to Tartarus. But what could Medea do to them that Hecate couldn't?

❖

Well, if throwing Medea's real name into the mix didn't let the cat out of the freaking bag, Medusa didn't know what would. But Cressida still seemed to think Hecate was at the start of their quest. How long could that last? Had Agamemnon known he was working for Medea all along or was he just as fooled as Cressida? Not knowing made Medusa want to pull her hair out. Such a convoluted scheme was so very Medea; she constructed plots so muddy no one knew which way to look. If Medusa now found out someone else had set Agamemnon into finding the aegis disguised as Medea, that would just take the cake.

But what could Medea want with the aegis, whomever she was currently pretending to be?

It made Medusa's head hurt, and she sipped her drink slowly, but they couldn't stay in the bar for very long. Cressida's living shimmer garnered a lot of looks. Even the least aware people in the room had to be sensing her by now. And some dark creatures in the corner, all bat wings and sharp teeth, were giving her hungry, harpy-like stares.

"We should go," Medusa said.

Agamemnon lifted his drink and sloshed the bit that remained.

"Slam it or lose it."

He glared but did as commanded. She wished she could get a few minutes alone with him, maybe wring some more info out of him away from Cressida, but just as they were leaving, Cressida spoke up.

"So, since Hecate commanded you to get the aegis, was that so she could give it to Medea, or did you give it to Medea without Hecate knowing?"

Medusa held her breath. Now for the moment of truth.

As they reached the street, Agamemnon cleared his throat. "Medea...always works on her own, except when she can wrangle more out of a deal than she's putting in. She might not have murdered her children, but that doesn't mean she's *not* a selfish asshole."

"She didn't murder her children?" Cressida asked.

"No," Medusa said. "She made Jason think she had."

"That's...but she had to live in infamy from then on!"

"The world's a big place," Agamemnon said. "Bigger than we ever dreamed when we were alive. Some myths had her marry another king, but the way she tells it, she left to live on her own. It used to be very easy to go somewhere where no one knew you. I expect it still is in some ways."

Cressida seemed to mull that over. Medusa tried to parse his answer for any indication about how much he knew. "What does Medea want with the aegis?"

He gave her a look, but if she was supposed to glean anything from it, she missed the point. "Still afraid she'll come after you?"

"There are plenty of other mirrors if she wanted to feel safe from me. Besides, Medea doesn't need the aegis to protect her. She'd use a magical deterrent before a weapon or shield."

"True enough," he said.

She frowned. "Then you don't know why she wants it?"

"I'm a hired sword." He laughed without humor. "I commanded armies once. I was a prince."

"Yes, yes, how the mighty have fallen," Medusa said. "Everyone in Asphodel has a sad story to tell."

"Do the others know?" Cressida asked. "You said Pandora knew more than you."

"I think she does. I don't think Arachne cares as long as she gets paid."

Cressida tilted her head back and forth. "Then maybe we can pay her to tell us what she knows. Or do you think Pandora will just offer up the information?"

He shrugged. "For a favor? Maybe."

"Here we go," Medusa said. "They'll have you running all over the Underworld, Cressida." *Look who's talking*, she said to herself, but it wasn't the same thing. She wasn't after trinkets or trifles. She'd lied to save her family, the noblest cause there was.

"I don't think she wants any*thing*," Agamemnon said. "She'd be more interested in firsthand knowledge of what it's like to be alive in the day and age you live in."

"Oh, that's no trouble," Cressida said. "As long as she doesn't keep me talking forever, I don't mind."

He shrugged again, and they kept walking. Medusa's heart sank with every step. Agamemnon might be covering for Medea's illusions, but Pandora might tell. What reason would she have for keeping it a secret, unless Medea had told her to? Maybe Medusa could pretend she'd been as caught up in the illusions as Cressida was.

Another headache was piling on top of the first one; she hadn't felt such dread since she'd been alive. Funny how she hadn't missed it one little bit.

Pandora lived in an enormous library as big as an apartment building. The books were gleaned from the consciousness of those populating the Underworld, so like everything else, they were spotty and uneven, the stories starting or stopping depending on what the people remembered or what filtered down from the minds of those in the living world. Bestsellers slumped down to the Underworld and overwhelmed many books at once, giving everyone only a few titles to read. Medusa remembered the bondage craze that had rocketed through a few years ago and given everyone who'd never considered it a few new ideas. Quite a few old flames had come calling at her doorstep, and she'd sent all of them packing. It didn't matter if they had new ideas; *they* were old ideas to her. The past was dead and gone except for one specific point which she could never get over no matter how hard she tried.

Pandora didn't seem surprised to see them, but she never seemed surprised at anything. She welcomed them in and led them to the third story, to an oak-paneled parlor, the walls and floors gleaming with polish, slender wooden columns holding up a second story balcony covered with rows and rows of books, varying sizes and colors, paperbacks warring with hardcovers fighting with heavy reference tomes and atlases and dictionaries.

"I knew you'd come here eventually," Pandora said.

"But not so soon, right?" Agamemnon plopped down in a leather loveseat and crossed his ankles on top of a mahogany coffee table.

Pandora lifted his feet and put a coaster under them. "No, indeed. I expect you found a mount. Aix?"

Agamemnon rummaged in a candy dish of sour balls and popped one in his mouth. "The giant snake is here?"

Medusa ignored him. "Medea. Aegis. Talk." Though the dread knotting her belly still worried what she'd say. Maybe if she started unraveling the lies, Medusa could leap over the table and throttle her.

Pandora sat in a plush, wingback chair. "Formidable as you may be, there are always stronger opponents."

Medusa wondered if she was a bit of a mind reader but decided probably not. "Someone will punish you for speaking to us?"

"Who?" Cressida asked.

Pandora turned to her with a look that seemed slightly more excited than her usual. "I've got some questions for you."

Cressida glanced at Medusa, who gestured for her to continue. "And if I answer them, you'll tell us what we want to know?"

Pandora nodded. "At least then I'd be risking my safety for something I want."

Perfect. If Pandora could keep Cressida busy…

"I'm just going to pop into the other room, Cressida, while you two talk," Medusa said. Cressida nodded, and Medusa slipped out of the room. She didn't think the others would hurt Cressida. They'd already had that chance, and Cressida had the harpe on her side if they tried now. She found an open window and the first shade she could grab. "Medea."

For a moment, there was nothing, and she wondered if Medea would refuse her call. The nearest shade to her factory would be hovering near her windows, smacking against them gently under the force of Medusa's will. "Medea?" She put a little more command behind it until she could almost hear the noise as the shade knocked against Medea's special effects department of a house.

"I was wondering when you were going to get out," Medea's voice finally said. "Faster than I expected!"

"That's what I keep hearing."

A pause. "Oh, so you've gone to my little helpers. Well, I didn't know I had to tell them to hide just yet."

"What the hell are you playing at?"

"Just a favor for someone with a bit more clout than you."

"You left me in Tartarus to die!"

"Well, technically, you're already dead. I never guessed the girl would have elected to stay with you. You really do have her twisted around your snaky little finger, don't you?"

"Leave her out of this. What do you want with the aegis?"

"Me, darling? Nothing. But I knew you would have objected, so I neglected to mention it to you. Tell you what! Just for the pain and suffering I caused, you don't owe me a favor anymore."

Anger burned through Medusa's temples, and she didn't even bother to keep it out of her voice. "Who wants the aegis?"

"Now that would be telling. And don't think you can wring it out of my little helpers because I never told them. It was your plan to impersonate my mother that gave me the idea for my own scheme! I do worry what Hecate would do if she knew we were throwing her name around so liberally."

"Is that a threat? Either I leave you alone or you run tattling to Mommy?"

Medea chuckled. "Well, she would forgive her own daughter far faster than anyone else."

Shouting from the other room drew her attention. She let go of the shade and hurried back to see Cressida standing with her hand on the harpe, though Pandora had stepped in front of her, seemingly shielding her from everyone else.

Agamemnon stood in the middle of the room, trying to shout down Arachne who crouched near the door, a web in hand, pointing at Cressida and demanding to know what she was doing there and who was double-crossing whom.

Medusa let her power flow over her and shoved a vase off a small stand, sending it crashing to a corner.

Arachne whirled and met Medusa's gaze. She was a strong spirit, very aware, and Medusa couldn't petrify her immediately. If they'd still been living, it wouldn't even have been a contest. Medusa's living gaze could turn Titans to stone.

Now, Arachne shuddered, backing up a step and trying to blink. Medusa could feel Arachne's skin and muscles hardening as Medusa's power tried to take her over.

"If I push, I'll win," Medusa said. "But I don't want that, not yet." The room had gone quiet—her real aim—and she bottled her power. "Now, let's all just settle down, shall we?"

Arachne took a deep breath and glowered, but she looped her web around her fist and shoved it into the pocket of her jacket. "How in the hell did you get back here so fast?"

"Yes, yes. We're back, and no one expected Cressida to get out alive, and yet there she is, and you're very lucky she kept the harpe sheathed." Medusa took a seat in an armchair, gesturing for everyone else to sit, but only Cressida and Pandora obeyed. Cressida sat as close to Medusa as she could, showing that they were still allies. Medusa almost snapped at her to move away, to not trust anyone.

"So, what are you going to do?" Arachne said. "If you haven't answered that question already?"

"Well, Medea won't give me any answers, so unless you three happen to know who wants the aegis, you're of no use to me."

"Someone's looking to shake up the whole structure of the Underworld," Pandora said.

"Hecate?" Cressida asked. "She's the one who wanted the aegis and the harpe in the first place. She's known as a companion and friend to Persephone in the legends, but is she trying to take over? Or is someone trying to unseat Hades?" She paused as if trying to work things out in her head. "Where are the rest of the Olympians?"

Arachne frowned at Agamemnon when Cressida mentioned Hecate, and Medusa thought, *she knows.* They all knew that Hecate hadn't been in this from the beginning. Question was, did they know that she knew? Or did they think Medea had been fooling Medusa along with Cressida?

When Arachne glanced at her, Medusa knew something had to have shown on her face, if Arachne's look of satisfaction was any indication. So, now the little wretch thought she had something hanging over Medusa's head. Well, they'd see about that.

"No one's seen the Olympians down here in ages," Pandora said. "Persephone and Hades keep to their palace in a restricted part of Asphodel known as the Terrace."

"I bet they're easy to pick out of a crowd," Cressida said.

Pandora shrugged. "They can appear however they want, but you're right. It's hard for them to hide their godhood."

"But what—" Cressida's words cut off as the building shook, booming and creaking. Plaster rained down over their heads, and Agamemnon was thrown to the floor. Near the wall Arachne clung to a bookshelf.

"What the hell?" Cressida yelled as she grabbed on to Medusa. Pandora ran for a window, throwing the heavy curtain to the side just in time for a Molotov cocktail to break through the glass and burst into flames upon the carpet.

CHAPTER ELEVEN

Cressida leapt for the door, but Medusa was faster. Her wings popped out in a flash, and she latched on to Cressida and sprang upward, one downbeat carrying them across the room. Pandora screeched, beating at the flames while the others told her to leave it. Agamemnon tried to pull her out the door, and Arachne was already through it.

More explosions rocked the building, and Medusa ran to another window in the hallway, but instead of pulling the curtain wide, she peeked out and cursed. "It's Adonis and Narcissus's gang."

Well, Cressida had known that particular sleeping dog wouldn't stay down. "What do they want?"

"If I had to guess, they think we're aligned with this crew, possibly with Medea, and they're declaring war."

"Tell them it was Hecate!" Cressida said. "Then they'll go away!"

"Don't count on it." Arachne threw the window open, and when a flaming bottle arced toward her, she lassoed it and sent it down at the thrower, sending several people diving for cover.

The building shook again, and Arachne looked straight down. "Holy shit! That's not all Molotovs, Snakes."

Cressida leaned over her shoulder and gawped. A monster banged on the bottom of the building, its tentacle legs knocking loose chunks of brick while its six serpentine heads gnawed at the woodwork and the façade.

"Oh, for fuck's sake!" Medusa cried. "How in Tartarus did they convince Scylla to work for them?"

Even through the fear, Cressida managed awe and disbelief, fascination and a strange sort of joy. Some stories painted Scylla as a born monster, a child of the Titans like Aix, but others said she was once a beautiful nymph, either cursed by a jealous goddess or poisoned by the sorceress Circe to turn into a monster. It was an early tale versus a later one again, and no matter which was true, she was still tearing pieces out of the building in the here and now.

Adonis swaggered into the street, several others guarding him with shields. Arachne attempted to whisk one away, but her webs slid off the shields as if they were greased. Adonis had changed from a white sweater to a black one, probably his action sweater, and she wondered how many he had.

He lifted a bullhorn to his mouth. "You can surrender now or when the building collapses. Your choice."

"Go to hell!" Arachne called before anyone else had the chance. She pulled her head inside. "We need a plan."

"Are you going to ditch us at the first opportunity?" Cressida asked. "Because that's been your plan so far."

"We don't have time to argue. We—"

With Agamemnon on her heels, Pandora ran from her library shrieking like a banshee. She shoved Arachne and Cressida out of the way and leaned far out the window. "You burned my books, you bastard!"

Everyone seemed taken aback by her ferocity, her blazing eyes and flushed cheeks. Power crackled around her, so much that her hair stood out from her body. She ran from the window and hurried to the stairs. After another glance at one another, everyone followed. Cressida wondered how many of them wanted to back her up in whatever she was doing and how many just wanted to see what she was going to do.

Pandora took the stairs in leaping bounds. With Scylla's banging and crashing, it was amazing she didn't trip. Cressida had to catch herself on the bannister several times as her feet slid out from under her. From the skidding and swearing around her, the others were struggling, too. She caught Agamemnon's elbow, and he had

Medusa's, and then the three of them had to catch one another again. The only one who didn't need their help was Arachne, who stuck to every surface. Any minute, Cressida expected to see her rappelling down the middle of the stairwell.

Pandora burst through the front door, still screeching. The tentacles of Scylla flared around the street, but Pandora paid them no mind. Cressida ran out behind her and had to stop and gawk at the bulk of the monster. It lowered its six heads and stared at Pandora, several of them moving as if to devour her.

Cressida scampered to the side of the street, Medusa with her, and Agamemnon and Arachne following hard. Agamemnon had his sword out, and Arachne readied her webs, probably to streak off through the city like Spiderman, but none of them did more than gawk.

Pandora held her hands a foot apart and grabbed empty air as if holding the edges of a book. She drew her hands apart slowly, and bright, blinding light shone between them. Cressida had to look away, everyone did, even Scylla, but as Pandora drew her hands farther apart, Cressida glimpsed something within the light. Dense blackness waited there, with tiny pinpoints of light, as if Pandora held the night sky between her hands.

A rushing sound like whitewater filled the street, and fabric began to flap around bodies while awnings lifted off the front of storefronts. Random bits of trash shuddered and rolled, smaller items skipping toward the hole and disappearing through it. Everyone was shouting, trying to be heard over the rush that was quickly edging toward a keen. Cressida's hair whipped around her face, and on the other side of the street, a small satyr slid sideways, hooves grating on the pavement.

"Grab hold of something!" Medusa shouted.

Cressida grabbed a streetlight, the others hanging on with her, but the pressure kept building. Cressida's feet began to lift from the pavement. Even Scylla lurched toward the hole, heading for that awful widening gap that seemed to lead into the heart of space itself.

The streetlamp groaned, but Cressida wrapped her legs around it. Medusa shouted something, her tone angry, and a length of web slipped around Cressida from behind. Arachne passed more strands around, and Cressida twirled them around her arms, trying to pass them to everyone else, though that bound all their fates to the streetlamp; at least it was stuck to the pavement.

Someone from Adonis's gang screamed as he toppled into the hole, but everyone else seemed to have secured themselves. Bystanders who had nothing to do with the confrontation were rolling down the sidewalk, and one tumbled by, getting sucked into space without even a scream. A green-skinned little man came close enough to grab, and Cressida held on to him. He clung to her backpack, and though pain wrenched through her shoulders, she hoped he was strong enough to hold on.

Scylla tried to scurry backward, massive tentacles backpedaling, but her heads were pulled taut toward the nothingness. She flailed, but nothing was strong enough to hold her, and the hole was now a yawning chasm, air shrieking toward it. Scylla flew upward with a roar, and then collapsed in on herself and disappeared into darkness. Cressida hoped that might be an end of it, but Pandora's face was still a mask of anger; she might not stop until she'd doomed them all.

"We have to do something," Cressida tried to say, but the words got lost. They couldn't throw anything. Adonis had tied himself and his gang to a storefront pillar, so he wouldn't pull loose until the rest of them did.

Arachne had coated herself in webs, and as Cressida watched, she dropped to the ground and clung to the pavement, though the ends of the webs streamed toward the hole, threatening to pull her loose. She left the ends of several strands stuck to the streetlamp, and like everyone else, Cressida grabbed on to one, ready to try to reel her in if she looked doomed. With painful slowness, Arachne crept toward Pandora in a belly crawl, sticking to the sidewalk. Her ponytails stood straight out from her head. When she reached Pandora's ankles, she yanked, pulling Pandora's legs out from under her.

Cressida thought Pandora might be thrown through her own tear in reality, but the pressure dropped as her hands fell. When Cressida's feet hit the ground, she struggled out of the web. Agamemnon cut it with his sword, letting everyone out quickly. As soon as she was free, Cressida ran for Pandora and piled on top of her just as the hole into space closed with a little pop of displaced air.

Cressida tried to remember any wrestling moves she'd heard of, any way to pin someone, but Pandora struggled like mad, and all Cressida could do was keep her hands covered while Arachne held her legs. The air huffed out of them as someone fell on top of Cressida, making the backpack grind into her ribs. They were all trying to grab Pandora, including the green-skinned man Cressida had saved. As she took another look at his mottled skin, she knew he must be a naiad, a water sprite, but she didn't have time to ask.

By equal turns wrestling Pandora and sitting on her, they had her subdued in moments. Arachne bound her hands with webs, and she lay in the street, muttering curses.

Adonis and his gang had cut themselves free, and Agamemnon pointed a shaky finger their way. "Stay back, or we'll let her up again."

Adonis seemed too dumbstruck to do anything but stare. "What the hell was that?"

"She can open anything," Arachne said, "so I guess she opened a portal to…" She stared at the air. "Gods know where."

Adonis stood up straighter. "Do you have any idea what Scylla costs per hour? Or what it will cost me when I tell Triton that I let his offspring, his moneymaker, be sucked into…whatever? How in fuck do I get her back?"

Pandora bared her teeth. "You don't. Serves you right. You burned my books, you asshole!"

He pointed at her but seemed at a loss for words. "No," he said at last. "Serves *you* right for throwing your hat in with people who go back on their word." He nodded, seeming to gain steam from the argument he'd just come up with. "That's right. You align yourself with dishonest people and look what happens."

Agamemnon drew his sword, and several of Adonis's gang drew weapons as well. "You attacked her home," Agamemnon said, "attacked all of us, and it wasn't even us you wanted?"

Adonis held his arms out. "Like I said, old man, you chose your side." He waved vaguely at Cressida. "Choosing liars. How is that a way to behave?" As if sensing his argument crumbling, he shuffled his feet, and those in his gang exchanged looks, all of them probably wondering where this was going, if they'd made a horrible mistake.

Adonis rallied, though, stabbing his finger in Cressida's direction again. "This is what you get for not following through. *You* burned her books, Cressida. *You* cast Scylla into space or whatever." He snapped his fingers. "Yes, you're responsible for that, too. I shall inform Triton."

Her mouth fell open, and it was all she could do not to march forward and punch him in the gut. "If you didn't want burnt books and missing monsters," she said, "you should have stayed at home!"

"Yeah," Arachne said. "Go home, pretty boy."

He bristled then paused as if searching for the insult in that statement. Finally, his face seemed to settle on affronted. "No."

Was this how they usually fought? Hurling insults like children or knocking monsters into each other's buildings and throwing Molotov cocktails? She wondered if the whole city would burn down, if it even could. And now they were having a standoff in the middle of the street; at least the bystanders had either ran off or been obliterated, so they didn't have to worry about more innocents getting hurt. Except for the naiad, who seemed to want to see how the whole thing turned out.

"You want to settle this, fine," Adonis said. "Cressida, come with us, get the ambrosia you owe me, and we'll call it even."

"I don't owe you anything!" she said. "You never found my aunt."

"It was ambrosia first, aunt second, and I notice that Medusa hasn't found your aunt, either."

"She's a hell of a lot closer than you are!"

"Whatever the two of you are fighting about didn't involve us," Agamemnon said, "but it does now. You attacked us, and we're not going to let you get away with it."

Everyone fell to shouting again, Cressida joining in, but the naiad touched her arm as if seeking sanctuary, and she couldn't help moving in front of him, small and slender as he was. First he'd almost been sucked into a void, then he'd helped tackle the person who'd made the void, and now he was getting pulled into a street fight between rival gangs and mercenaries.

"Cressida," he said in her ear, his voice a gentle hiss. It put her in mind of soft foam spreading over seashells and warm, wet sand between her toes, of the surf's gentle glide as the tide went out.

She turned and looked into eyes with such depth they were measured in fathoms, swirls of blue and green fading to impenetrable black. There was peace in those eyes, so much more of it than the shouting that had already faded to a gentle murmur.

"Cressida," he said again, but it wasn't him calling. It was the deep, all the majesty of the sea calling her to swim into eternity. It knew her, knew what was best, and as the deep began to move away, she moved with it, confident it knew where it was taking her.

❖

Medusa stood almost nose to nose with Adonis. After he'd called her out about Cressida's aunt, never mind that it was true, he'd kept pushing, his insults getting more personal until she'd had to stalk toward him. She was so tempted to use her power. It probably wouldn't work, but it would make him stutter for a moment.

When his gaze flicked over her shoulder the first time, she thought he was checking to see if any of his buddies were close enough to help him. When he looked again, she glanced around, too, and noted that everyone had squared off against an opponent who seemed to be making his or her insults very personal, all but Pandora, who was still tied up on the pavement.

And Cressida, who'd disappeared.

"You giant fuckhead!" she shouted to Adonis. "What have you done with her?" His face screwed up in a mockery of surprise, but it was the fakest reaction she'd ever seen. She grabbed his shirtfront. "Don't even try it. Where is Cressida?"

He swept his hands down and dislodged one of hers, but the other stayed wadded near his collar, sending his sweater skewing across his shoulders. When he tried to move away, the sweater gaped, the weave pulling, and his face darkened in real anger. He took a swing. She ducked, keeping hold of him so she could drag him forward when she straightened and bury her fist in his sculpted abs.

Her fist didn't sink in as much as she'd hoped, but she heard his *oomph* and knew it'd done some good. Yelling had turned to fighting around them, but no one was throwing fire again, not yet.

Adonis brought his elbow down on her scapula, and she let go as shockwaves traveled from her shoulder to her core. She went with the motion, falling down and balancing on her hands while she kicked for his knee.

He leapt back, croaked, "Run!" and dashed for an alley.

"No you don't!" Medusa pushed after him, her power roiling over her. One of the henchman ran in front of her and shuddered into stone, face locked in fear. She darted past him, following Adonis, but he outdistanced her quickly and knew enough to keep his people behind him. Arachne's webs grabbed one, and Agamemnon cut another down, but Adonis stayed ahead. He dove into an elevator that seemed to be waiting for him, his henchmen arrayed around him. He kept his eyes averted but still managed to give her the finger before the elevator doors slipped closed.

She skidded to a halt and banged on the doors, but they wouldn't open, and as the elevator car sped away, she had to stagger back so she wouldn't be dragged along. Her snakes writhed and curled around her ears, hissing, snapping at air.

"Um," someone behind her said.

She whirled, but Agamemnon had his face buried in his sleeve. "Are you still...you know?"

She bottled her power but barely, still gripped by rage. "You're safe."

"What happened?" he asked. "We were arguing and then—"

"They've got Cressida."

He sighed deeply. "Great. Now word will spread, and everyone will think we've joined forces." He gave her a look that hinted it was as much her problem as his.

She shook her head. "Well, you can try and fend them off if they come after you again, or you can come with me."

With another sigh, he gestured back the way they'd come. "Let's spread out and look for her."

She marched toward the others. "Did anyone see where Cressida went? We have to find her."

"We don't work for you," Arachne said, but Agamemnon peeked into the windows of buildings on one side of the street while Medusa tried doors.

"Untie me," Pandora said. "I'll help."

Arachne stood over her. "Fat chance."

"I'm quite sane again, I assure you. And now that there's no one to fight, I'm no threat." She sounded very reasonable, and she was another pair of eyes.

"Cut her loose," Medusa said. When Arachne didn't move, she added, "If you make me go looking for a knife, I'll want to use it for more than just untying someone. Want to be my target?"

Arachne rolled her eyes, but she cut Pandora loose.

The crazed look had gone from Pandora's eyes as she picked up her glasses. She bent the frames slightly and put them on before dusting off her sensible sweater and slacks. "Thank you. I saw Cressida talking to a naiad."

"The one she saved?" Medusa sighed and rubbed her forehead. "And here I was hoping she'd learned *not* to help random people."

"He called her by name, but I didn't hear anything else," Pandora said. "Nor did I see where they went, but if she didn't pass any of you, then by process of elimination, she had to go either this way"—she pointed behind them toward her house—"or that way." She gestured down the street to the left, the path that would have taken her past Medusa's back without crossing Agamemnon or Arachne. "And I doubt they went in the house."

Medusa started to the left, Agamemnon and Pandora staying with her while Arachne dogged their steps like an errant child. Medusa wondered why she didn't leave, but maybe something about a kidnapping intrigued her, or maybe she'd come to the same conclusion Agamemnon had: they were safer as a team than they were alone.

If the naiad had said nothing more than Cressida's name, it could still be powerful, especially from the lips of a creature with hypnotic powers.

"Hey, instead of opening random doors and scaring the populace," Arachne said, "why don't we ask this guy?" She'd gone back and returned with one of Adonis's henchmen, a satyr, webs holding his arms tight to his body.

"Oh, well remembered and well caught!" Medusa grabbed the satyr and beamed into his face. "Arachne, I could kiss you."

To Medusa's complete surprise, Arachne blushed, hints of red showing around her pale make-up. "Shut up." She shuffled her feet.

"Oh, my lovely," Medusa said to the satyr. "The things we will do to you if you don't start talking."

He rolled his lips under as if that could keep him safe or quiet. Medusa sighed and put a hand to her forehead as if tired. The other hand she drummed against the satyr, fingernails making a slight scratch against the logo on his T-shirt. She wanted to grab his horns and wrench his head until he told her where Adonis had taken Cressida, but she kept her voice calm.

"What do you think?" she said to the others. "I mean, we can turn him over to the powerful people we know."

They glanced at one another, and evil smiles started on their faces as they seemed to catch her gist. They wouldn't have to do a thing to him if they convinced him that they could.

"Let's give him to Medea," Arachne said. "She can make a person think his guts are slowly spilling out or his limbs are dropping off just by staring at him." She chuckled. "You know, once she made this guy think he was being cooked alive in an oven. I never heard anyone scream so loud, and the whole time, he was just sitting in a comfortable chair." She wrapped an arm around the satyr's shoulders. "We had to burn that chair, not just because of the random fluids he leaked, but because halfway through the session, his skin actually started to blister and flake."

The satyr trembled and stared at her with wide eyes.

"Oh," Agamemnon said, "there's no need to bring in other people. I have a sword. You have a knife. Pandora has no end of tools in her house. We can get creative." He thumbed the edge of his sword, making the metal ring dully. "You find out quite a *bit* about a person when they're losing *bits* of themselves." He grinned as if that was the cleverest thing he'd ever heard, and that was almost as frightening as his threat.

"Messy," Pandora said. "I can open him up without tools." She held her hands a few inches apart in front of the satyr's chest. "I focus on where the seams are and pull them aside. I can clamp off the arteries so there's hardly any blood, but we'll need a drop-cloth to catch the organs."

"Okay!" the satyr screamed. "Look, no one told me anything about ovens or swords or my chest opening and my freaking organs spilling out." He breathed hard, slightly green under his fur. "I just took this job the other day. This chimera was giving me a hard time, and my cousin told me to join a gang, but I didn't think I'd be rumbling my first day out, and I definitely didn't sign up for any of this shit!"

Medusa shrugged. "So, start talking."

"Do you think they told me anything useful?" His breath came in shorter and shorter pants. Any minute now, he'd pass out. "I mean, I knew we were after the living woman, and I knew her name was Cressida, and we were either supposed to incapacitate or distract you so the naiad could sneak off with her, but you've already figured that out." He stared pleadingly at Medusa. "You notice I said incapacitate or distract. Our orders were very clear. We weren't to kill you." He looked to Pandora. "And I am so sorry about your books, ma'am. You know, I'm quite the reader myself." He put on a sickly smile. "And if I can help you replace or repair any damages, just let me know. I have a cousin who's a carpenter, and I don't know if that will help—"

"Where are they taking Cressida?" Medusa asked.

"I don't know! Back to Adonis and Narcissus's place would be my guess, but the gang has a few hideouts, which I would be more than happy to show you." He grinned like a helpful realtor.

"You really think they'll take her anyplace a toadie like this knows about?" Arachne asked.

"A very helpful, very polite toadie," the satyr said.

Medusa didn't know for certain. It seemed unlikely they'd put someone as valuable as Cressida anywhere a low-level member of the gang would know about. This one was clearly cannon fodder, and they had to suspect someone like him might be caught.

"It's worth a shot," Medusa said. "We can't storm Narcissus and Adonis's house. It'll be too well guarded. But maybe one of their other properties will yield us a prisoner with more information."

The satyr nodded. "That is a very good plan, ma'am, very well thought out, if I may say so."

"Shut up."

"Yes, ma'am."

She looked to the other three. "So, are you coming with me, or is this where you give me a speech about this not being any of your concern, etc."

Arachne and Agamemnon exchanged a glance. Pandora said, "They burned my books," and Medusa knew she was in, at least until her books had been avenged.

Agamemnon sighed. "I do like that girl. She has courage. It's been a long time since I've met someone so willing to stick her neck out for other people." He smiled softly. "And I do love a good rescue operation. I'm in."

Arachne rolled her eyes. "Well, if you three freaks are going, we might as well make it four." She rested an arm on the satyr's head. "What do we do with him?"

"Why not make it five?" the satyr asked loudly. "One gang is as good as another, and I would really like to be on your side."

Medusa gave him a genuine smile. "And there's no way I'm trusting you, but I don't want to kill you either. You'll be here, tied up in Pandora's house until we come back."

He nodded hurriedly. "That is also a fantastic plan, ma'am. First rate and beautifully articulated." When she stared at him, wondering just where he went to toadie school, he beamed nervously. "And your hair looks fantastic. I like it." She had to keep staring, just to see what he would do, and his eyes took on a pinched, panicked look, his smile turning sickly. "Do you use a moisturizer?"

Arachne barked a laugh. "Let's park him and go already."

Cressida drifted with the fish and the waves, spiraling from one current to another, lost in endless blue. She'd forgotten what she was, air or water, fish or mammal. She was relaxation given form.

"How much longer?" someone said.

That wasn't right. No one could speak under the waves, at least not in a language she understood. Fish had their own language, and their sounds had surrounded her, but she couldn't understand them.

Because she was a person, not a fish.

And people couldn't breathe underwater.

She bent double and coughed, hands on her knees, and she expected water to come rushing out as she gasped and heaved, but there was nothing. She wasn't in the water at all but in a lushly appointed sitting room, all plush couches and armchairs and a carpet with such deep pile, she might have been able to lie down in it and disappear.

"I thought you said you could keep her under all day if necessary!" someone yelled, and she knew that voice. Adonis.

"I said the exact opposite, if you'll recall, which you won't because you never listen!"

"Well, maybe if you had something useful to say…"

"How long I can keep a person under is a very useful fact, I should think!"

Adonis mumbled something, and Cressida turned to where he stood talking to the naiad in the hall outside the room. They were ignoring her, though blocking the way out, and Cressida had already deduced that they'd done something to her to bring her here, though the past few moments were a bit hazy.

She stamped a foot as quietly as she could and nearly swore for all she was worth. This was the third time someone had taken over her mind since she'd come here! Definitely something to warn tourists about if she ever published her own Guide to the Underworld.

Adonis mumbled something else, his face turned toward the hall's marble floor.

"What was that?" the naiad asked.

"Nothing."

"Don't think I don't know what you and Narcissus think of me. I know you only like the pretty ones! Well, if I'm not pretty enough to be paid attention to—" He made as if to storm out but only took a few steps before Adonis caught his arm, reassuring him of his attractiveness and asking him what the gang could do to make apologies to Triton.

Cressida took a step toward a window, lifting the sheer curtain and peeking through the blinds beneath. They were on a third, maybe a fourth story. She'd brought a length of rope in her pack, but she didn't see it in the room. She didn't see the harpe, either. She pictured them carrying it carefully by the sheath or belt since they couldn't touch any part of the weapon itself. And there wasn't anything else she could use as a quick weapon unless she started throwing furniture. She walked the room, looking for another way out, some hint as to what she could do. She was about to yell at Adonis or the naiad when another man came from an intersecting hallway, stepped into the room, and smiled at her.

"Looking for the way out?" His hair was the color of spun gold, and though he wore it short, it was so artfully arranged and slightly tousled that it seemed begging for a hand to run through it. Like Adonis, he was so perfect looking she doubted he could be real, but he had an amalgamation of the traits said to make men attractive with just enough of a feminine slant that he seemed as if he could be a beautiful woman as well as a handsome man.

"Narcissus, I presume." She coughed, the words coming out partly as a croak. The water might not have been real, but the coughing fit had turned her throat raw.

"At your service." He leaned into the hallway. "Echo, bring our visitor's bag, please."

"Please," came a soft voice from the hallway, and then the barely there sound of footsteps faded away.

"Echo?" Cressida asked. Legend said she was a nymph who'd fallen in love with Narcissus, but as she could only repeat the words of others, she couldn't express it to him. She'd hidden in a pool of water, and when he'd seen his own reflection above her, he'd fallen in love with it, proclaiming his feelings, which Echo said back to him. He'd lunged for himself, fallen in, and drowned. Cressida had always thought it a stupid story.

He gestured for her to sit. At first glance, he didn't appear to be the dumbass his story suggested. His eyes seemed intelligent, even cunning, and the graceful way he moved, the care he seemed to take with his gestures, hinted that he knew about the effect his appearance had on people and used it to his advantage.

"What do you want?" Cressida asked.

"That ambrosia you wasted was promised to someone very powerful, someone who'd already been told it was going to be delivered."

She thought of the amount of time between when Adonis had greeted her and when she'd thrown the ambrosia into the Elysian Fields: a short time in which to make promises. "You must have been very confident that I'd succeed."

"And we were right."

"Wrong, actually."

He smiled, and it was dazzling enough to knock anyone off their feet. "And now we need to be right again."

She sighed. "I don't want to get involved."

"That doesn't really matter," Adonis said as he stepped into the room. The naiad had gone, leaving the hallway empty until a small, dark haired woman came in, lugging Cressida's backpack. She didn't look at anyone but put the pack at Narcissus's side and then hurried away.

"Thank you, darling," Narcissus called.

"Darling," she said from the hall before her footsteps faded again.

Cressida reached for the backpack, but Narcissus pulled it toward him. She sat back with a frown. "Oh, I see how it is."

"Good," Adonis said. "That saves us from having to say it."

"You're going to starve me out."

Narcissus flinched, but Adonis smiled, patting his hand. "Just do what you did before, Cressida, and you'll be on your way. I won't even charge you extra for Scylla."

"And if I'd rather die?"

"Then you're a fool. Also, we won't let you. We'll hypnotize you again if we have to. And if that still doesn't work and you won't do what we ask, we'll feed you the food of the Underworld and trap you here." He tilted his head and smiled. "After all, why should we be the only ones stuck as we are?"

Cressida tried her very best glower and said nothing. Narcissus turned away as if he found the entire discussion distasteful. Still, he didn't argue.

"And then there's auntie to worry about," Adonis said. "Who's going to rescue her if you're trapped here?"

"Wow," Cressida said. "You two must really be up shit creek."

Adonis leaned back. "Don't think our trouble can't become your trouble, too. The person expecting the ambrosia *is* very powerful, and if you're stuck down here, you're going to be at her mercy."

"Her" wasn't much of a clue, but it was more than she'd had before. She wondered if it was Hecate or Medea, the two names most bandied around when people were talking about who was supposedly in charge of what, but neither of them had mentioned ambrosia. Another powerful woman, then? One powerful enough to pull the strings of these two? Well, if they were afraid of powerful women, she had a few names to throw around.

"Medusa and I went to Hecate," she said, leaning into the sofa. "Maybe after I've finished my task for her, I can look into yours. Unless you want to give her a call? Ask if your ambrosia can move to the top of her list?"

They glanced at each other, Adonis without expression, but Narcissus seemed a bit worried. Time to push it, see how far she could bluff.

"No doubt that's what Medusa is doing right now," Cressida said, "beseeching the goddess to get me back. Or maybe Hecate will send Medea."

Now Adonis looked worried, too, and she thought hard for another push, another name she could drop that would really scare them.

Narcissus cracked the tiniest hint of a smile, and Adonis burst out laughing. "I knew you couldn't hold it!" Adonis said.

Narcissus chuckled along with him. "I tried looking scared, but when you started doing it, too, I couldn't bear it!"

"You are a terrible actor!"

"But you love me anyway?" Narcissus asked with a pout.

"How could I not?" They leaned in for a kiss so sweet it would've given marzipan a stomachache.

"What the hell?" Cressida said.

They blinked at her as if they'd forgotten she was there. "Oh, sorry, dear," Adonis said. "Didn't mean to pull the wind out of your sails, but we couldn't resist. It's so funny that you don't know."

"Don't know what?"

Narcissus leaned forward slightly. "That you're even farther up shit creek than we are."

She looked between them but didn't get the joke. Maybe they knew that her task for Hecate was complete except for delivery of the harpe, which they currently had. Or maybe they knew Medea had tried to leave Medusa high and dry.

"Should we tell her?" Narcissus asked.

"I think it would be cruel not to," Adonis said.

Narcissus looked to her and frowned sympathetically. "Oh, but her face, darling. She's going to be crushed!"

"Call it a goodwill down payment." Adonis scooted to the front of the divan. "Cressida, my sweet, Medusa has been playing you for a fool."

CHAPTER TWELVE

They'd checked two safe houses, sent Stheno and Euryale searching via the shade fog, but so far, Medusa and the others had come up empty. Cressida seemed to have disappeared underground or into some kind of illusion that Stheno and Euryale couldn't see through.

Underground was unlikely. The fabled rivers of the Underworld coursed under the Meadows of Asphodel, and some more enterprising gangs used them to pass unnoticed, but the rivers carried their own dangers. One dip into the Lethe could rob a person of their memories, and the rivers crossed one another so many times it was difficult to tell which was which and where they mingled. Only on the outskirts of town where the dead entered the Underworld was it possible to point out the River Styx. Medusa didn't think they'd risk taking Cressida down there, and even if they had, they would have emerged by now.

It didn't help that Adonis and Narcissus had love nests scattered through the city. Theirs wasn't the largest gang in the Underworld, but they were wealthy. She'd been in one of their houses and seen the opulence. They didn't keep a large force on hand but rented help when they needed it, like the naiad that had sneaked Cressida away. That and Scylla spoke of more money than they usually threw around. They might have a backer this time, someone who wanted their gang to rise through the Underworld's ranks.

She could tell the others were getting tired of going from place to place. They'd made casual inquiries after Adonis at each safe house, taking turns pretending to be someone who had business with the gang or with Adonis personally. Each time they'd been told he wasn't in, and if he wasn't there, neither was Cressida.

Not that the gang would necessarily tell them the truth, but each time they were close to one of the houses, Medusa felt for Cressida's living essence and came up empty, nor did they see the gang members they remembered from the Scylla fight. Arachne suggested setting fire to the houses just to make sure they weren't hiding anyone inside, but Medusa wanted to remain a bit inconspicuous.

After a time, even Pandora's ire seemed to cool, as if she could afford to wait for vengeance, but Cressida couldn't. Medusa didn't think Adonis and Narcissus would torture her—that wasn't their usual *modus operandi*—but they would find some way to manipulate her eventually, and they had the time she didn't.

As her worry for Cressida grew, Medusa realized she hadn't thought about her sisters in hours. Before Tartarus, any feelings for Cressida had been tempered by what ultimately had to happen between them: Medusa would have to manipulate or force Cressida to kill Perseus, and then Cressida would know that all of Medusa's "help" had been, if not quite a sham, then at least secondary to Medusa's plans to save her sisters.

Now she thought first of Cressida's safety and worried about what Adonis and Narcissus would force her to do. Their schemes might cost June's life or Cressida's own. By the time they checked the fourth safe house, she just wanted Cressida back safely, no matter what it cost. After that, she'd have to let Cressida leave.

Medusa clenched her fist, calling herself a coward and a betrayer. If she really loved her sisters, why would she abandon them when salvation was so close? Her lies and schemes were bound to come out anyway. Could she change plans midstream, help Cressida find June, and keep what she'd done a secret forever? Even then, Cressida could still volunteer to lure Perseus out of the Elysian Fields. Then what? Cressida had to be the one to kill him unless June volunteered. Medusa supposed she could capture Perseus and then say good-bye to Cressida, promising to kill him later.

Well, maybe tying him up and keeping him in her apartment for a while wouldn't be a bad idea. Until some other way to kill him presented itself, she could kick the shit out of him whenever she chose. Or maybe Cressida would want to see the killing done, and Medusa would have to come clean. Cressida would be so angry, she'd probably come after Medusa with the harpe. Medusa could say good-bye to her head, then.

Again.

No, she couldn't let that happen, and she wracked her brain to think of a way to have everything she wanted with the least amount of lying. Step one, get Cressida back.

"This is taking too long," Arachne said. "We can't search the whole city."

Medusa sighed. "What do you suggest?"

"Giving up," Arachne said. "Have our revenge later."

"We need more information," Pandora said. "We should get another captive, like we talked about before."

Medusa rubbed her chin. It was worth a shot. She hooked a bit of shade fog and called to her sisters, asking them to find someone at the next house, the largest on their list. When they found someone leaving and walking by himself, Medusa would pounce.

❖

It isn't true.

Cressida rubbed her hands over each other until the skin pulled painfully. She watched the floor while Adonis laid out a plan of systematic betrayal. Every time she glanced at them, Narcissus looked more and more sympathetic. He seemed as if he might reach for her a couple of times but always pulled back as if afraid to intrude.

Hecate's palace was an illusion, they said. Hecate herself had been Medea, hired by Medusa, who needed the harpe to kill Perseus. Cressida's stomach shrunk to a black pit. *I went back for her. I felt sorry for her.*

It isn't true.

But she'd wondered why the goddess of magic wanted a weapon only a living person or Cronos himself could wield. She'd thought that a goddess could find a way, but if that were possible, why not go to Tartarus herself?

You suspected something like this.

No, she hadn't, but she would have felt less like an idiot if she had. She'd lost her head over a pretty face, a sad story, and what she'd thought was an offer of help that hoped for but demanded nothing in return.

Or it isn't true. After all, these two wanted something from her, too.

"Her sisters are going to fade if she doesn't do something to stop it," Adonis said. "That part is true."

"And her plan for Perseus is sound," Narcissus said, "and I always thought it was romantic and heroic. Reduce her murderer to a shade and feed him to her sisters? Wonderful. But according to our research, the only weapon that can do it is in the other room, and the only hand that can currently wield it is either Cronos's, yours, or your aunt's."

"And rumor has Perseus very near to taking the final resurrection," Adonis said, "putting him out of Medusa's reach unless he somehow fails to attain the Elysian Fields again and winds up in Asphodel with the rest of us, but what are the chances of that?"

Of course some of the story would be true. That made it easier to wrap a lie around it. "And I have to be the one to kill him? Perseus?" Blood on her hands for all eternity. "How was she going to get me to do it?"

"We don't know." Narcissus moved to sit beside her, but she barely saw him through the tears that hovered like film over her eyes. "But Medea's been telling people the rest."

Medea, the person who wanted the aegis, who trapped Medusa in Tartarus. Why expose her partner now? Did she want something from Cressida, too? The tears kept hovering, but they wouldn't fall.

Because it's not true.

Adonis sighed. "The point is, you don't owe Medusa anything. She's been lying to you the entire time, so you don't have to think of working for us as working against her."

Narcissus took her hand at last, making her stop fidgeting. "We're not going to pretend that we three are friends, though I do feel sorry for you being tricked like that. We're offering the same trade that Adonis initially offered, only with a few threats thrown in to make sure everyone understands the stakes." He gave her a kindly smile despite his words.

Cressida pictured Medusa scouring the Underworld for her. She thought on every look they'd shared, every moment from their first meeting to their kiss. Either Medusa was the best actor in the world, or part of her had cared for Cressida even as she'd used her. Somehow, that seemed worse than if she didn't care at all.

And the voice telling her it wasn't true was getting weaker.

"Do you know where my aunt is? Is she really with Hecate?"

"It's a little worse than that, I'm afraid," Adonis said. "I thought it was Hecate, but it's…another goddess."

Cressida didn't think her headache could get any worse, but once again, she was wrong about everything. Only one other goddess made her home in the Underworld. "Persephone?"

"The same person the ambrosia was destined for," Adonis said with a smile that seemed a little sad. They'd had a thing once. Adonis had been torn between Persephone and Aphrodite, a feud that had ultimately caused his death if legend was to be believed. She supposed it was only fitting that they'd keep up their acquaintance after he died. "Persephone told me that June was with Hecate, but I think she said that so I wouldn't know she had June. When I asked her if she could get June away from Hecate in order to get some ambrosia, she…" He chuckled.

"She threw a fit," Narcissus said in clipped tones. "Because she didn't want to explain why she wanted to keep a mortal for herself."

"Caused me no end of problems," Adonis said. "That's what I was talking about when we first met. It's all sorted now though. You get the ambrosia, you get your aunt back. Simple."

Narcissus sniffed and looked away.

"Where's your proof?" she asked. "Why would Persephone want to give June back now when she didn't want to give her up then?"

They glanced at each other. "She's fickle," Adonis said quietly. Narcissus rolled his eyes, and Cressida wondered if Persephone had always been a sore spot between them.

"As for the proof," Adonis said, "Medea swore on the River Styx, and we're willing to do the same."

Cressida shut her eyes slowly. The punishment for breaking an oath sworn on Styx was to sleep for a year and then be banished for nine. And there was only one place worse than Asphodel to be banished to. It was a magical bond that no one would take lightly. She squeezed her eyes until they hurt. Now was not the time for tears.

"I want a real plan," she said softly, gaining steam as she went. "No more leading me around without any information. I want a plan in case I meet the Flowers gang again. I want to hear from someone who knows the layout of the Elysian Fields, and I want an oath that when I hand you the ambrosia, you give me June!"

She should have asked for an oath in the first place, but she'd been so much at sea when she'd first come here. She hadn't been thinking clearly. Maybe this place had messed with her head as much as Medusa's beauty did. "And I want to witness the oath where you declare that everything you've told me about Medusa is the truth."

Before they could speak, she added, "And not just an oath from you. I want one from Persephone. We'll all swear by the River Styx." They shared a small gasp. She sat back and crossed her arms.

"I'm not sure that's possible," Adonis said. "Persephone is…"

"Crazy," Narcissus muttered.

Adonis glared at him. "She's just lonely, I told you. Even if she did have some kind of breakdown—"

"If?"

"I will not let you vilify her!"

"Interesting as this is," Cressida said. "Until we swear together, my ass is parking right here."

They stared at her, but she was tired of taking everyone's shit. She kept replaying the kiss with Medusa, and it made her angrier each time. She'd been stupid, so blind, so naive. She felt like a schoolgirl led on by an upperclassman until that fateful day when she thought her crush was going to ask her out and instead asked to copy her homework.

A nasty little voice inside her sniggered that she should have known someone like Medusa couldn't have been interested in her, not *really*.

She gritted her teeth, and the room seemed to grow darker. Even Adonis seemed to notice. The shine of the Underworld dulled. Mystery and awe had uplifted her, even when it had frightened her, too. She'd had this thrill of excitement akin to a kid in an amusement park, a feeling that said no matter what happened, this was a good time, a magical dream. She'd been the hero who just needed confidence to keep her going.

Now, though, this was business. She should have been thinking like that since the beginning.

Adonis and Narcissus were giving each other meaningful looks. Narcissus picked up the cup of tea Echo had brought him and swirled it around before taking a sip.

Adonis sighed. He stared at Cressida and touched the top of her backpack as if giving her a not-so-subtle reminder that he held her future in his hands. Once Narcissus set his cup down, she grabbed it. He reached out but didn't touch her, and she brought the tea up to her face. It smelled lovely, like chamomile and honey.

"Go on," she said. "Dare me. Threaten me."

Narcissus shook his head. "You'll be trapped here. You won't be able to move between the layers of the Underworld anymore."

She swirled the tea gently. "Isn't this what you just threatened me with? Didn't expect me to call your bluff? If I'm trapped here, all your plans will be ruined. Unless Persephone can move between the layers, but she probably can't either. Eating the food of the Underworld is how she trapped herself here, too, right?"

"Shh," Adonis said softly. "Comparing yourself to a goddess is never a good idea."

"Especially not a crazy one," Narcissus said, "who makes crazy demands from the comfort of her crazy house."

Laughing without humor, Adonis said, "Stop calling her that."

"I'm not going to be jerked around anymore," Cressida said, getting pretty damn tired of them forgetting she was there, but from what they were saying, Cressida didn't know if she really wanted to meet Persephone anymore. She just wanted to leave. "The three of us will swear by the river, then I'll take my aunt, and get the hell out of here. No more games."

With a sigh, Adonis scooted her backpack toward her. She set the cup down with a little clink of porcelain. She didn't put it on the saucer, hoping it would leave a ring on the mahogany table.

"I'll be right back," Adonis said.

As soon as he was gone, Narcissus shifted over to the other sofa. "Are you going to take revenge on Medusa?"

Cressida winced, not knowing what kind of revenge she could get, if she even wanted any. "Her sisters will fade. Isn't that revenge enough?"

"It might be for some." He fidgeted with a pillow. "But you could always make things harder for her."

"How?"

"Well, you're going to the Elysian Fields again. It wouldn't be too hard to find Perseus and warn him. That way, even if some other poor, living sap winds up down here, Medusa will never be able to carry out her plan."

Could she do that? It hurt her chest even to think about it. But Medusa deserved it. Her sisters deserved it. If Adonis and Narcissus had told her the truth, then Medusa had been tricking her from the beginning, no matter that it was for a good cause. Medusa could have just *asked* for help.

Now everything between them was built on lies and illusions and promises that no one ever intended on keeping. Cressida pulled out a notebook and started working on the wording of the oath they would take, making sure getting June back occupied the prime spot.

❖

It took twenty minutes of hanging from a rafter before their captive told them everything. They'd tried the same tactics they used on the satyr, but this one had been with the organization a little longer and had needed a tad more convincing, but just a tad. Medusa was afraid things were going to get messy, but all it took to get this one's lips moving was being strung upside down in a warehouse and gently spun like a tetherball.

Shame he'd had nothing good to tell them. He knew Cressida was being held in a heavily guarded house. Well, they'd expected that. Adonis and Narcissus were both with her. They'd expected that, too. What they didn't expect was that the house was in the Terrace, the most exclusive place in Asphodel, rumored to be like an extension of the Elysian Fields, but that was just something the residents said to make themselves feel more special, according to those who weren't invited to live there. And it meant that Cressida was being held close to the palace where Hades and Persephone lived.

Like Hecate, the rulers of the dead had chosen to make their home among the shades and those who supposedly hadn't lived their lives to the fullest. Hades did it to be closer to the bulk of his charges, and Hecate said Asphodel suited her better, whatever that meant. But Persephone was trapped in the layer of the Underworld where she'd eaten the famous pomegranate. Rumor said she created the Terrace because she wanted a taste of what her life on Mount Olympus had been like. She no longer returned to the surface world, not since belief in her had waned, and since then, the Terrace had become even more closed off and elitist than before.

Medusa looked to the distance and imagined she could see the Terrace through the shade fog. Gates surrounded the whole area, which was built on a succession of ledges. The elevators that crisscrossed Asphodel didn't go there. Everyone had to go through the gates. Behind the Terrace stood a ring of mountains that marked the edge of the Underworld, though they were an illusion, and rumor had it that if you tried to cross them, you'd run smack into a wall like a movie set painting.

As for who lived in the Terrace, it was a mystery why some were chosen and others were not. Some were people who'd gained favor with Hades or Persephone in life. Well, mostly Hades, and those were few and far between. The people who'd gained favor with Persephone were often young men like Adonis, and they weren't allowed to *live* in the Terrace, though it seemed they were allowed to visit.

With others, though, who knew? Maybe the lord and lady of the Underworld just liked some stories better than others. And it was possible to be kicked out and new people brought in, though that would earn the newcomers the ire of the rest of Asphodel. Living in relative luxury, though, one could afford a lot of ire.

And now they had to find a way to sneak Cressida out of a heavily guarded, heavily watched section of the Underworld, out of a house that probably belonged to Persephone. The whole place was guarded by chimeras and dragons and all sorts of things that would be pulling guard duty in Tartarus if Hades didn't need them for his own little community of snobs.

"Well, that's it," Arachne said as they sat outside the warehouse, their captive still swinging gently inside. "We'll never get into the Terrace."

"Never is a big word," Medusa said.

"Sorry, Snakes, all the webs in the world won't get you past the guards at the gate, and neither will his sword." Arachne pointed at Agamemnon and then at Pandora. "And opening a door to space would probably just get us killed."

"I shall have to apologize to Scylla's family," Pandora said quietly. "I'm quite embarrassed. I wonder if they'll accept a fruit basket."

Agamemnon frowned. "I suppose there's always deception. Sneak into the Terrace and sneak out."

"We could wait until they move her," Arachne said. "Whatever they want her for, it can't be to hang around in there."

"It'll be ambrosia again," Medusa said.

"So we wait until they take her to the Fields, and then we grab her," Arachne said.

"No doubt she'll be highly guarded then as well," Agamemnon said.

"Then what's your idea, Pops?"

He glared at her. "You're far more ancient than I am, even though you've chosen to look like Undead Barbie."

"Shut up," Medusa said. Both fell quiet, seeming to sense she wasn't willing to listen to their nonsense.

They could try to take Cressida as she was moved, though that would be when Adonis would expect them. No doubt they'd act accordingly with guards and traps and blinds. She was mulling the possibilities of finding a way into the Terrace when she felt a tickle in the air, her sisters whispering her name.

"I'll be right back." She walked a short distance from the others and pulled a piece of fog. "What is it?"

"We have found the living woman."

"Me, too. She's in the Terrace."

"She has finally come out where we can see her."

Medusa gnawed on her bottom lip. "They must be taking her to the Fields. We'll have to hurry and put together an ambush. Can you track them? Keep me informed?"

"She is not moving."

Medusa paused. If they were foolish enough to have her walking around where anyone combing through the shade fog could see her, maybe there was hope for sneaking her out after all. "Which house?"

"The palace, in the garden, wandering. She seems thoughtful, sad."

"What?" Hades wouldn't let Adonis into the palace, which meant Persephone had sneaked him in, but why sneak in Cressida at the same time and risk the chances of exposing Persephone's lover and a living human? Hades probably didn't mind the lovers as long as he could pretend they weren't real, but under his own roof? And what would he think of a living mortal in his midst?

Unless... "It's not Cressida, is it? You've found June."

"Wandering the palace garden."

Medusa covered her mouth, but that didn't stop her smile. If Persephone was cooking up some scheme with Adonis and Cressida, that meant she'd taken her godly eye off June. They were probably planning to either dangle June in front of Cressida or threaten her to get what they wanted. Medusa ground her teeth; she'd thought of doing the same.

Well, now she had the opportunity to right some of her wrongs. She hurried back to the others. "Change of plans."

Cressida couldn't help feeling a little sad when Persephone didn't show up for the swearing. Since she hadn't actually met a goddess, she thought it would be another thing to check off her list. Then she reminded herself that expectation and wonder were stupid, and that she'd abandoned them for sheer, unadulterated fury.

Adonis and Narcissus swore by the River Styx that everything they'd told her was true to the best of their knowledge, and Cressida was surprised by the lurching feeling inside her. To the last, she'd been hoping Medusa hadn't lied about everything, but too good to be true was more than just a phrase people occasionally trotted out. It was a mantra she should have learned long before then.

Still, part of her clung to the idea that they could believe it all they wanted, and it still might not be true. It could be gossip. Medea could be spreading lies. If she wanted to hurt Medusa, what better way than to turn Cressida against her? But every time she clung to those thoughts, she kept coming back to a moment she and Medusa had shared, right after they'd come back from Tartarus, and she'd told Medusa she wanted to lure Perseus out of the Elysian Fields. She'd expected to see joy on Medusa's face, but Medusa's expression had been unmistakably guilty. Cressida had been surprised but hadn't questioned it. Now it seemed like the red flag it should have been, like so many other things were.

And Medea had sworn on the river, too.

Adonis and Narcissus swore that they would produce June once they had the ambrosia. Cressida swore that she would retrieve the ambrosia. As she did, she felt the air coalesce around her, as if the very stones of the Underworld were listening. A shimmer in the air seemed to seep into her skin, and she felt it humming within her, along with a subtle tickle in her mind like when she knew she was forgetting something but couldn't recall exactly what.

Except now she knew what it was. She *needed* to get the ambrosia more than anything she'd needed to do before. She wondered if this was how addicts felt. "I'm ready when you are," she said.

If she failed to get the ambrosia, she wondered if she'd be banished to the living world after her year unconscious, or if she'd be lost in either Asphodel or Tartarus, left to the devices of whoever found her. She wondered if she'd eventually fall for Medusa again, if she'd someday be as ready to forget the rest of her life had ever existed in exchange for another kiss.

Cressida snarled and turned away so Narcissus and Adonis wouldn't see. She tried to tell herself it wasn't her fault she'd been so trusting. It wasn't wrong to trust people; most people weren't looking to dick everyone over. But even though her logical mind told her this, she couldn't help seeing all the times she might have spotted it, all the times Medusa talked around questions rather than answered them, the little clues that said no one could be as altruistic as Medusa pretended to be. But Cressida had stubbornly believed in integrity. She'd known people who always helped others before they helped themselves, but she felt as if she shouldn't have expected everyone she met to be the same.

Maybe that was the worst thing Medusa would ever do to her: make her suspicious of everyone from now on.

Adonis handed her back the harpe of Cronos inside its sheath, and she buckled it around her waist. "I don't know if you'll need it," he said, "but better safe than sorry."

"I notice you waited until after the oath to give it to me."

He grinned. "Like I said, better safe than sorry."

"No doubt Medusa will try to snatch you back," Narcissus said, "probably while we're in route."

"I wouldn't go with her even if she begged."

They glanced at each other, and Adonis shrugged. He walked toward the door, but Narcissus lingered. "I wonder, is one of the reasons you agreed to help us because you know we're at cross purposes with Medusa, and you want to hurt her?"

She sneered so she didn't have to sputter that it wasn't true. It wasn't any of his business. "Now you don't want my help?"

He lifted his hands in surrender. "Just a friendly question. The desire for revenge can eat you up fast. Don't let it follow you into the world of the living when your task here is done."

She stalked past him to where a few of their gang waited at the doors. Someone draped a cloak over her, and she pulled the hood up. Someone else was chanting, calling an illusion into being.

"Think you'd forgive her in my place?" Cressida asked as Narcissus regained her side.

"Do what you like. I'm just warning you that if you hold on to revenge and mistrust, you'll make yourself sick."

It was so like something her aunt would have said that she nearly sobbed a laugh. "I just want this to be over." Frantic energy had carried her along so far, but it wasn't fun anymore, not the danger or the awe. She barely glanced at the palatial homes around them, barely looked at the view of the whole of the Underworld lying before her, elevator lines crossing and crisscrossing it. She could see mountains in the distance, past the shimmer of shade fog, and if she squinted, she imagined she could see the hole where she'd outrun Cerberus and began this whole adventure.

She realized she hadn't done more than nap since she'd gotten here, and that made her think of food, which made her stomach grumble. She dug into her snacks as they strode through the Terrace, out the gate, and onto one of the elevators that traversed the rest of Asphodel. The doors opened and closed multiple times, but any other passengers were put off by the car full of gang members.

She suddenly wanted her bed more than anything. She'd wind up in the covers and have a good cry. *Pathetic!* One woman lied to her, tried to use her, and she was reduced to tears? The thought stiffened her spine. People had been trying to use each other since time immemorial; she couldn't go to pieces when it happened to her.

But she kept reliving the looks they'd exchanged, the kiss, the way she'd gone back to Aix's prison to get Medusa out. How Medusa must have been laughing at her then. She'd probably kissed Cressida just to avoid laughing in her face.

When Cressida looked up, Narcissus was staring at her, and she gave him a dark look. What did he know? Just because he'd been sentient for thousands of years he thought he was an expert on everything. His tale wasn't even a revenge story. He'd died because he was stupid. Who drowned in a puddle trying to make out with his own reflection? It was a blessing he'd never had children.

But she would take his advice to heart, stupid as he was. When she returned to the land of the living, she wouldn't give a single thought to Medusa. If any student or professor brought her up, Cressida's only response would be that someone as odious as Medusa had probably deserved to be killed. If she'd even existed. Which she hadn't. Because she was a monster. And an asshole.

Cressida's silly, rational mind told her she didn't really believe that, but she told it to shut up, take a break for a while, and let anger rule for once. It helped a bit, carrying her all the way to the gate of the Elysian Fields without the elevator car stopping again. That suited her fine even as it seemed to confuse the gang, who muttered something about how it must be a slow day out on the streets. Whatever. She wanted to get this over with.

"Right," Adonis said as they walked through the terrible, hopeless part of town. "We've gotten word to one of our contacts. The Flowers gang is watching the gate pretty hard. We haven't been able to get our regular shipments."

"Why doesn't Persephone just command the Flowers to give the stuff to you? Why doesn't she ask Hades to fetch it for her?"

There was a shuffling of feet, and a long glance between Narcissus and Adonis. "Never mind that," Adonis said as Narcissus rolled his eyes.

She looked from one to the other. "Hades doesn't know she's in on this with you, does he?"

"Then he'd have to acknowledge that she screws around on him," Narcissus said, his face turned away.

Adonis had the grace to look sheepish. "Can you blame her for keeping secrets? You know how they met!"

"And he must know one of those secrets is you, unless you're too lowly for him to care," Cressida said. It was twisting an unnecessary knife, but she couldn't help it. Someone needed to be hurting besides her.

If the comment pained Adonis, though, he didn't show it. "As I was saying, you'll meet my contact, and she'll help you blend in."

"And your contact isn't carrying the ambrosia here because..."

"Because the Flowers aren't letting any of the Field's lesser denizens out. My contact's only been able to send messages across by way of chucking the odd one through the gate."

"Then how am I supposed to get back once I'm through?"

"You're going to look like a hero!" He grinned. "With the glamor we're slapping on you, you'll appear just like someone who's been resurrected and has returned to the Fields. And the Flowers won't try to stop a hero from coming and going; they'll assume that like everyone else, you won't want to visit Asphodel. After all, who would?"

"That's where things get a little tricky," Narcissus said. "When you get ready to leave, you're going to have to do it quickly; run for the gate before the Flowers realize what you're up to."

"So get in, meet my contact, get the ambrosia quick as you can, and get out," Adonis said. "If you have to talk to anyone but the contact, make yourself sound as impressive as possible. Make up a bunch of stuff that would qualify you for the Fields; say something about how you always knew you were destined for greatness, that sort of thing. Brag. Overstate. The lesser beings have learned to ignore most of the heroes and will wander off, bored."

"I'd wander off, too, if someone called me and my family lesser beings," she said.

"Oh, fine. Be as PC as you want out here." Adonis stabbed a finger around them. "But once you're in there, everyone is a lesser being unless he knows how to swing a sword or suck a god's—"

Narcissus cleared his throat. "I think she gets the point."

Cressida nodded. "Right, who's the contact?"

They described a dryad, and she expected a name like Mossoak or Honeyflower, but it was something with a lot of vowels that she couldn't pronounce. They told her not to worry. She wouldn't need to call the dryad by name. She'd be on the lookout for Cressida. There would be significant eye contact under a clump of trees not far from the gate.

Cressida hefted her backpack and turned to the gate, wondering when Medusa was going to put in an appearance. Maybe she'd decided to cut her losses and wait for the next live person to come floundering into the Underworld. Maybe she'd forgotten Cressida already.

Why in the hell did that thought hurt more than anything? She should have been thinking, good riddance, but the idea of Medusa forgetting her without a second thought felt like a knife in the heart. Well, no one liked being forgotten, but a small, very weak part of her admitted that she was hoping they'd eventually have it out. Maybe there'd be some explanation Cressida could live with, a way they could reconcile, or proof that Adonis and Narcissus were lying despite the oaths they'd taken. Maybe there'd be an epic blowout of a fight where passion would eventually overrule anger, and then...

You just want an excuse to try to get into her pants again!

Cressida called herself a stupid idiot as the fence came closer, and no Medusa appeared. Cressida was a romantic fool after all, just like June had been, just like her parents had been afraid she'd become. She had a vision of her and her aunt back in the living world, reminiscing over a bottle of wine about the time they visited the

Underworld and lost their heads over goddesses who ultimately broke their hearts. They'd be sadder but wiser.

A hard lesson to learn, and as the gang distracted the zombies, and Cressida walked through the fence, she wondered if any of it had been worth it. When she got home, she was going to tell Nero to burn his sacred objects and let the Eleusinian Mysteries die like they should have done thousands of years ago. This place deserved to fade away and rot, and one day, after mythology was buried under time, it would wink out of existence, and no one would have their heart broken by it again.

CHAPTER THIRTEEN

Hiking through the rivers of the Underworld would have been impossible. There was simply nowhere to put their feet. Medusa supposed she could have bribed any of the myriad sea dwelling beings to ferry her if they would have risked going in the river.

But why would she bother when she had a giant snake?

Medusa rode at the head in front of her mother's frills. Arachne's webs bound the others tightly to Aix's hide like whiny saddlebags. Aix glided effortlessly along the surface, pushing toward the Terrace. The water flowed placidly around them, and Aix cruised without a splash, keeping her face far above the water. This wasn't the Lethe, not exactly, but the rivers mingled constantly, and Medusa thought it would be just her luck to take a giant wave of forgetfulness full in the face.

The river wouldn't take them all the way to the palace, but as long as they got inside the Terrace, they could sneak the rest of the way. Hopefully. Medusa didn't relish the thought of fighting all the way to her target.

A bright glow shone from just ahead. "Slow down, Aix." The caverns housing the rivers were suffused with the same gray glow as the one that permeated the rest of the Underworld, but this was different: flickering orange torchlight mixed with the steady glow of electric light.

"What's going on?" Agamemnon whispered, a sound that managed to echo off the rock that hemmed in the river.

"Keep quiet." Medusa leaned forward along her mother's head and peered into the gloom. A grid of iron bars stretched across the tunnel, blocking the way forward. Water flowed through the gaps, and a strand of electric lights looped across the top while flaming sconces burned at the sides. "There's a gate. No guards."

Aix glided gently forward. Slime trailed through the water, curling around the gate; the bars had probably been there since the Terrace's invention. A small ledge poked out above the river on the Terrace side, and iron rungs followed the wall above, making a ladder to a manhole in the ceiling.

Medusa cut the others free, and they perched on Aix's back, staring at the bars.

"What now?" Arachne asked.

"There's no door," Pandora said. "Given enough time, I could find a weak spot, but metal is the hardest for me to open."

People with powers like hers were probably why the builders used metal in the first place. Something about it was harder to magic. Medusa yanked on the bars, but they had a sense of solidness that went beyond touch.

Agamemnon pointed into the shadows. "There. We can squeeze through."

The rock had eroded away from the wall, leaving a slight gap. Slime coated its pebbled surface. They could wriggle through, but Aix would have to wait there.

"I'll be back, Mom, Aix." Medusa climbed onto the slippery bars, then pointed to the manhole. "We'll come through there."

Aix bumped the bars gently, and Medusa gave her nose a reassuring pat. "We'll be back."

With the help of Arachne's webs, they eased through the gap, faces turned away from the water that flowed inches below, slurping past the gate and the slime ready to suck them into possible oblivion. Medusa held her breath as she eased through. If she fell, she had to remember to keep her eyes closed, her mouth closed. The water oozed past slowly. As dangerous as it was, it should have been rushing, snarling whitewater. She didn't think anything so sinister had ever flowed so placidly.

"Move it," Arachne said, and Medusa helped the others until they all stood on the Terrace side. After a final pat on her mother's nose, she climbed.

They sneaked above ground one by one, just inside the Terrace wall. Unlike the hodgepodge that made up the rest of Asphodel, the Terrace resembled a quaint, medieval village, though how they'd agreed on the décor, Medusa had no idea. Probably Hades or Persephone had told them what they'd like, and they'd had to agree. The streets were paved with cobblestones, and the houses were a mix of dark wood and white plaster with the occasional larger building made out of sandy colored brick. In the rest of Asphodel, houses changed as easily as minds, though it took collective consciousness to do it. Here, everything seemed stuck. The shade fog still covered the sky, but the residents of the Terrace couldn't change that if they wanted to.

Medusa and the others kept to the shadows. Wet and covered in slime, they didn't fit in with the stylish, modern dress of the Terrace, all suits and well-tailored clothes. They had to be thankful the medieval theme didn't extend to the clothing. Corsets were just too hard to get in and out of.

They headed upward, making for the huge walls that stretched across the Terrace's upper level. Medusa contacted her sisters again, who found June still in the garden, though sitting closer to the doors, as if she might soon go inside.

The wall rose far overhead, imposing and seemingly as impenetrable as the walls of ancient Troy. Stheno and Euryale told her that the guards walking the top seemed bored; a few had fallen asleep in various nooks and murder holes. They couldn't see much action. Who would break into a palace of the gods, after all? Medusa bit her lip and regarded the wall again. Very stupid, desperate people, that was who.

With Arachne's webs, they were over the wall in a moment, dropping into a world-spanning jungle, a dense collection of plants from every place on earth. Narrow pathways led between huge ferns and giant pink flowers, winding among apple trees warring with palm trees. At a tiny patch of wheat glowing gold amongst the greenery, Medusa thought of Demeter, Persephone's mother, the source of Persephone's love of growing things. Trapped in the Underworld, she had to miss the sun and air. Was this fantastic garden a gift from her mother or something Hades had given her to try to make up for the awful place he'd stuck a child of the harvest? Maybe Persephone had given the garden to herself to make eternity in the Underworld a little more bearable. Medusa imagined she'd shed buckets of tears before accepting her role as Dread Persephone and immersing herself in the schemes of the Underworld. Or maybe she still cried for everything she'd lost.

Medusa heard a sigh and held up a hand, signaling the others to stop. When she peeked around the corner, she saw a woman dressed in khaki cargo pants and a blue cotton button-up. Her graying red hair was pinned in a tidy bun, and a handkerchief hung around her neck. Her face was so familiar, it nearly made Medusa sigh. Throw in an enormous backpack and take twenty years off her, and she could have been Cressida.

They could snatch her up in a web and haul her over the wall, but Medusa didn't want to have to fight her. After knowing Cressida, Medusa didn't think June would take kindly to being manhandled.

"Stay here," Medusa whispered to the others. Before they could protest, she stepped into the open and cleared her throat. June started and stood slowly, peering into the shadows just like Cressida might have. Medusa shook off the eerie feeling that they already knew each other, that they had a rapport. The resemblance was so striking, she would have pegged June as Cressida's mother rather than her aunt.

June stared at her, too, as if trying to figure out who she was. Cressida had mentioned her aunt was a historian and a doctor of myth. Something about Medusa had to be ringing a few bells.

"Have we met?" June asked.

Medusa held out her hand. "My name is Medusa. Perhaps you've heard of me?"

When June's mouth fell open, she looked even more like Cressida, though Medusa hadn't thought that possible. It made her laugh, and June pulled up short of shaking her hand.

"I'm sorry," Medusa said, dropping her arm. "You just reminded me so much of your niece."

"My niece?" Panic infused her voice, taking it up several octaves. "Cressida is here?"

"Looking for you, and I promised to help her find you."

She looked around. "Is she here?"

Medusa bit her lip, knowing she had to tread carefully and hating herself for it. "I'm afraid she's fallen in with a bad crowd. They've promised to trade you to her in exchange for a dangerous task, but I plan to rescue you and head them off before she gets in any deeper."

"Rescue me?" June nodded slowly, no doubt thinking fast, but unlike her niece, her expression was unreadable. "I always felt bad for you in your myth, but I've learned something since I came here: not everyone is who they seem in their stories. I need a reason to trust you."

"You're more cautious than your niece."

Her stare sharpened. "What happened?"

Medusa told the same lies she'd spun for Cressida, adding that Cressida was in the clutches of Adonis and Narcissus, that Persephone was almost certainly involved, and that they were probably going to trade June for ambrosia.

June nodded as she listened, her thumb caressing her chin. "I've been...a guest of the dread goddess for..." She frowned and whispered as if trying to count the days. "I can't get a handle on the time here."

"No one can. They'd go mad."

"And Arachne, Pandora, and Agamemnon are hiding around that corner?"

"And they're getting impatient," Arachne called. There were shushing sounds, and Agamemnon poked his head out.

"Apologies, madam," he said with an oily smile. "We await your pleasure."

"Well, well," June said with a look of wonder.

"If you don't mind," Medusa said, "what have you and Persephone been doing all this time?"

June sighed loudly and sat. "We've laughed; we've loved. We met in a shop. She got between me and some thugs and whisked me away to the palace. She said she and Hades don't see each other anymore. She said she liked the 'flame of my life.' The first few days were the most glorious I've ever spent, but then..."

"She lost interest?"

June arched an eyebrow. "She's unstable."

"How so?"

"She changes moods faster than a chameleon changes colors. She lashes out at people for no reason. She had three different people reduced to shades and then wept about it for hours before laughing her head off and taking a bath in whipped cream. Even the most eccentric people would label her…disturbed. Frankly, I think she's lost her mind."

June shook her head and looked to the sky. "I tried to help her, tried to talk to her, but I'm not a regular psychiatrist, let alone someone qualified to diagnose a god. She's stopped speaking to me."

Medusa shrugged, not really caring what was wrong with Persephone as long as she didn't come looking for them. "I know it's a cliché, but it's not you. It's her. Take it from someone who knows, gods can't be anything but fickle. It's in the genes. Her whole involvement in the ambrosia trade is probably just to try to alleviate her boredom. Now, your niece awaits."

June barked a laugh. "She should never have come looking for me, but I suppose I have myself to blame for that." She smiled fondly. "Cressi always did want to follow in my footsteps, no matter what her parents thought. It used to make me proud."

Medusa smiled. "It still does. I can tell."

June's lips flattened, and she gave Medusa a strange look. "We don't know each other."

"I got to know your niece a little, and you seem a lot alike. So, how about it?" Medusa nodded in the direction of the wall. "Want to thwart the plans of a goddess? Get your niece back?"

"And if this has nothing to do with Cressida, and you're kidnapping me for some plan of your own?"

"If you're close to Persephone, can't you call for her, and she'll come running?"

"Not running," June said, frowning, "but she'll come once she finds out I'm missing. She…doesn't like to lose things she considers hers." After a shudder, she stood, nodding. "All right, but if we don't see Cressida soon, or if you've hurt her and this is a trick, I will hunt you to the ends of the Underworld."

The light seemed to coalesce around her as if the very air was listening, making her proclamation into prophecy. Medusa swallowed, shuddering as she realized that she feared this woman. She tried to shake the feeling as they started walking toward the wall. After all, what could a mortal actually do to her?

Well, besides summon a goddess who could stomp the shit out of everyone in their little rescue party. And Medusa *had* hurt Cressida already and would probably hurt her more before their adventure was done, at least emotionally. Maybe June would only count physical wounds, thinking them harder to heal than emotional scars. But Medusa knew that the only physical pain a person couldn't come back from was death. Betrayal lived on and on forever.

Medusa shook her head as June and the others introduced themselves. June *couldn't* hurt her. She simply wasn't strong enough. "We'll see Cressida soon, I promise."

They shared a slight smile, and Medusa couldn't shake the feeling of familiarity, but she couldn't let herself be fooled into thinking this was Cressida. She couldn't trust this woman, even if Cressida wouldn't betray anyone.

That thought brought an avalanche of guilt, but with it came an idea. June was mortal. She was older and wilier, and she could wield the harpe. Maybe killing wouldn't make her squeamish. Maybe she'd even done it before. And if she couldn't be convinced to help, maybe her help could be bought.

"All right, up and over," Arachne said as they reached the wall. "We've got a snake to catch."

When the first guard cried out from somewhere on the grounds, Medusa thought they must be back in Medea's illusion; it was only right to be spotted just as they were leaving. But Arachne was quick with her webs, and the guards were still running toward them along the wall as Medusa reached the top with June and Arachne. Everyone would be over long before they were caught.

Arachne leaned over the wall, ready to cast a web for Agamemnon and Pandora, when a harpy barreled out of the shade fog and knocked into her, sending her tumbling over the other side. Medusa ran for her, but more harpies dove from the fog, their rank wings open to slow their descent, all of them crying out in alarm.

Medusa grabbed June and threw her flat. The harpies skimmed over the wall, and Medusa's power flowed over her, but the harpies flew too fast to lock gazes. The guards slowed and covered their eyes, still advancing. Maybe someone had warned them she might be coming.

June wriggled out from under her and ran for the edge. "Arachne's dangling, but she's alive!"

"We have bigger problems." The guards held shields and spears. Maybe they planned to stab wildly until they hit something, or maybe they were going to herd them along the wall until the harpies could pick them off.

June waved her arms. "Here, here! Come and get me!"

"June, get down!" Medusa said.

Two of the harpies wheeled for June; she ran toward the guards, dropping at the last moment. The harpies shrieked, and one managed to launch herself to the side, but the other slammed into the guards. The tangle of them fell in a heap, crying out in pain.

Medusa barked a laugh as June ran back, but there was no time to crow. She looked for Arachne, but someone slammed into her back, all wet feathers and bloody breath. Claws dug into her side, and she tried to turn, her power roiling within her, but the harpy's face turned away, and Medusa tried to dislodge the claws tangled in her T-shirt.

"Get off her, asshole!" June said, and the harpy wrenched backward but didn't let go. The three of them teetered toward the edge.

"The wall, the wall!" the harpy cried. "I cannot carry us—"

They plunged over the side, and the harpy shrieked, spreading her wings. Medusa twisted, wrapping her arms around the harpy with June clinging to the harpy's back. The wind rushed around them, and the harpy beat her wings, but they were too heavy. Maybe if June landed on top she could survive. Medusa squeezed her eyes shut, but that wouldn't stop the end from coming. She wondered if Cressida would eventually figure out how sorry she was.

A sound like a twanging rubber band echoed off the wall, followed by another and another. They slowed, caught in Arachne's webs, though these seemed more elastic than usual. They slowed more, the webs pinging and popping like bungee cords.

And if these webs truly acted like rubber bands, they were all three about to go shooting up into the sky.

Medusa yanked the harpy's head around. "Sorry about this." She turned the creature to stone, and the extra weight snapped the webs like paper. The ground rushed up from only a few feet away, and the air left her in a whoosh as the statue bounced off her side.

Agamemnon hauled her to her feet, cutting the webs.

"How did you get out here?" Medusa asked.

He gestured to a neat hole in the wall, as if someone had tunneled through the bricks. Pandora was helping steady June.

"Right," Medusa said. "She can open anything."

"We're not out of danger yet." When the harpies dove at them, Agamemnon faced them with a practiced stance, and they pulled away to avoid him. "Let's go."

They hurried through the streets, the well-heeled residents of the Terrace staying out of their way and screaming in fear as if Medusa and company were a pack of hooligans. Word spread, and soon guards were coming out of the woodwork, the harpies still crying out and tracking them from the sky.

Medusa could see the manhole that led to the river, but more guards streamed from the outer wall, probably so happy to finally be useful that they weren't going to let anyone escape.

"Mom!" Medusa cried. "Everyone, help me call!"

"For our mothers?" June asked.

"They know what I mean. On the count of three," Medusa said. "One, two, three, Mom!"

They shouted as one, and the street began to tremble. Some of the guards wobbled and fell. Others kept running. Medusa kept her power bottled, not wanting to turn innocent bystanders, but the others readied their weapons. Pandora even had her hands up as if she might open another hole to somewhere else. The rumbling continued, but Aix didn't appear, and Medusa thought the street might be too strong. Just her rotten luck. As hope plummeted, Aix's head burst upward in a shower of cobblestones right below the Terrace wall. It leaned, bits of it collapsing into the hole as Aix steamed upward, mouth open in a roar that rattled every window.

Passersby dropped and curled into balls like pill bugs. Several guards abandoned their weapons and ran without ever turning to see what was behind them while still others shrieked and froze in fear. Some took a few steps toward Aix, but she rushed forward, lightning fast, moving like a scythe and flattening anyone in her path. Several guards tumbled into the gaping hole, crying out as they splashed into the river.

Aix streaked for Medusa, purring loudly. Medusa hugged her snout and kissed her between the eyes. "Well done, Mom!"

Medusa climbed aboard and kept June with her while everyone else tied on as best they could. Before the guards could regroup, Aix slid down into the river again.

The floating guards shouted at them, but instead of the expected, "Hey you," or "Get back here," one called, "How did I get down here?"

Another said, "Who are you?"

"I was hoping you knew," the first one said.

Medusa swallowed hard. "June, keep out of the water."

June put her hands on Medusa's shoulders. As they rode, she muttered happy things like, "Marvelous," and "fantastic" before saying, "I don't know how I'm ever going to be happy at home after this."

Medusa grinned and had to remind herself again that she didn't know this woman; she couldn't trust June, a woman who'd be a lot harder to trick than Cressida. The thought didn't do anything to ease the guilt. Gods, she hoped Cressida was all right. If not, she vowed to help June get revenge, but her inner voice suggested that after revenge was done, she could still convince June to help Stheno and Euryale. Cressida might want that.

Then she cursed herself for a conniver and thought of anything else.

❖

Cressida tried to imagine how a hero of legend might walk. She tried to recall everything she'd seen Agamemnon do. He'd never been in the Elysian Fields, but he had a big ego, so she supposed she could do worse, pompous role-model-wise.

She strode, a wide-legged walk, one hand swinging freely, the other resting on the pommel of the harpe. The whispers of Cronos were further from her mind now, as if he was having a hard time hearing the sword from all the way in Tartarus. She wondered if he'd ever really woken up past what they'd seen or if he was still stuck in the ice, mind searching for his lost property.

It didn't give her much hope for her fighting skills, if it came to that. She could fake it, she supposed, but better to not get in that situation at all. She tried to keep a confident air as she wandered, searching for the dryad.

There were nymphs everywhere, mostly clustered around the entrance; the Flowers gang was on high alert. When they looked at her, she gave them a bright smile, seeking to project the image Adonis had put in her head: a returning hero who wants to tell everyone about his heroic deeds from every life he's ever lived, and who doesn't care how boring he might be. And if he ran out of the "time he killed the Whatever of Wherever," he would happily regale everyone with the "time he loosened the really stuck lid," or the "time he slowed way down so some baby ducks could cross the road."

She hoped her smile conveyed the right mix of hope, ego, and immunity to the boredom of others. When several nymphs wouldn't meet her eyes and several more ran as she veered toward them, she thought she must be doing something right. She headed for a dense grove of oaks and saw a lone, bark-skinned figure standing in the shadows, her dark tones blending with her surroundings.

A cluster of nymphs stood nearby, whispering and casting dark looks toward the gate. The dryad looked to Cressida with eyes so blue they glowed like sapphires under a bright light. Her gaze flicked to the nymphs, then she looked down at her fingernails, expression screaming, "Play it cool."

Cressida strode up to the dryad and shouted, "You'll never guess at all the completely heroic things I've done!"

The dryad froze before smiling hesitantly, her teeth bright where they weren't covered in moss. "Um, really?"

The nymphs ceased muttering and stared.

"Yes!" Cressida said. "In the life I just finished, I held open myriad doors for people I didn't even know! I once unclogged the toilet of a neighbor! Even though I was very busy running my Fortune 500 Company that was featured in many top magazines"—she winked—"I once gave change to a homeless man! I braked for turtles! Would you like to hear about various monsters I might have slain in my former life?"

The nymphs were edging away, but at the mention of a former life, they ran. The dryad craned her neck and peered over Cressida's shoulder. "Okay, they're gone. Nice speech."

"Thanks. You got the stuff?" And now she really was in a bad movie.

"Ready to go." The dryad pulled a sack from a hole in a tree trunk. "Any idea when things are going to cool down? It's not easy being a woodland creature that's not part of the Flowers gang."

"You'll have to talk to your regulars about that. I'm more concerned about how I'm going to get out of here."

"Just keep going from one group to the other with your loud hero routine, make your way toward the gate, and when you're close enough, run. You have someone waiting on the other side to help you, right?"

Well, they'd probably help by shouting, "Throw me the ambrosia," but they'd have to pull her fat out of the fire first. "Sure."

The dryad hooked the ambrosia bag onto Cressida's backpack. She imagined it looked rather silly, a bag on top of a bag, but the nymphs wouldn't see it past the glamor. Cressida ambled back toward the gate, still putting on the air of someone desperately seeking eye contact so she could regale them with stories about that one time she'd found a small child crying in a grocery store and had done the right thing by finding the first woman who wasn't fast enough to get away and thrusting the child upon her.

She supposed heroes did actual heroic things, too. There must have been people in the Elysian Fields who'd saved others, who'd fought against invaders and whatnot. Maybe they were hiding, too, and the only people you could find if you went looking were blowhards who couldn't stop talking about themselves or the various children of the sea and forest who were doomed to listen to them.

She could see the bridge now, the nymphs clustered around it still. Her sense of impending danger wanted to avoid their eyes and slink or sidle, hands in pockets; it was hard to maintain the thought that to remain unobtrusive, she had to be as obtrusive as possible.

When a nymph not only met her eyes but approached her with a fond smile, Cressida fought the urge to wince or let her face freeze into a rictus of a grin rather than a smile. She put on what she hoped was a pleased look and not a desperate one.

"Hello," the nymph said. She bore a striking resemblance to the one Cressida had seen before, but they all had traits in common: perfect mouths and bright, intelligent eyes. They differed slightly in hair color, but she did recall that all nymphs were supposed to be sisters or something. Then again, none of the ancient myths featured much genetic drift.

"Hello, fair nymph," Cressida said, wondering what her glamor voice sounded like. "Have I told you about the time I slew a bat that got caught in my greenhouse? Not nearly as exciting as some of the things we got up to in the old days, but well worth a listen!"

Instead of fleeing, the nymph brightened. "How very interesting. Tell me more."

It's a test. "Um, yes." She told June's story about killing a bat with a hockey stick, adding a few embellishments that would have made June proud. Through it all, the nymph retained a look of curious fascination, but there was something else about her eyes, a certain glazed look that even her wide-eyed stare couldn't disguise, as if she was practiced in listening while tuning the speaker out. She even nodded at the right places and muttered things like, "How exciting!" and "That must have been a surprise!" but they sounded like autopilot.

As Cressida hoped, the nymph said, "Well, I better not keep you," at the end of the story and fled.

Cressida tried to look disappointed as she said good-bye, then she turned quickly and felt a jostling thump. She froze, her heart hammering. She turned slowly, but she knew what had happened. She'd hit the nymph with her backpack, invisible to everyone who didn't already know it was there. The nymph squinted at the air around Cressida's back, her brow furrowed.

Cressida ran. The nymph called out, and everyone began to turn. Cressida tried to run faster. As before, the same tree reached for her, and just as before, she ducked under its grasping branches. She reached for the harpe, but roots erupted from the ground and tangled around her knees, tripping her. She fought to rise, but they held her tightly.

"Unhand me!" she tried. "I wish to go…mock those who…were not brave enough to—"

"Save it." The nymphs clustered around her, petite women with flowers in their hair or along their garments, but their frowns said they were anything but twee and jolly.

"A glamor," one said. "We didn't expect that."

"Whoever's cutting us out has some powerful resources," another said.

"That's right," Cressida said. "This ambrosia is for Persephone, so you'd better keep your roots to yourself."

The nymphs looked to one another, and the tree stood Cressida upright, though it didn't let her go.

They smiled at one another. "Well, who else?" the original nymph said. "It figures that she'd try to go around us."

"She'll think better of it from now on," a small one said. "Once she sees what we're going to do to her messenger."

Well, that wasn't good. They should have been trembling in fear, but they sported evil little smiles. They didn't fear the dread goddess of the Underworld. Why should they? She couldn't walk among them.

"Who is we?" Cressida croaked out. "Who's in charge of the Flowers gang?"

"Poor, sweet, living girl," one of the nymphs said, and Cressida thought this might be the one she'd originally spoken to, though she still couldn't be sure. "You don't get to know that, but she is more than a match for Persephone."

Another goddess then. Cressida fought the urge to swear.

"Bind her arms," the nymph said.

The tree gave up its roots, breaking them off, and the nymphs tied Cressida's hands in front of her, binding her arms to her body. She didn't know if they could see the backpack or the sword yet or not, but she wasn't going to mention either.

More humans wandered close as the nymphs led her farther into the Elysian Fields. Heroes of legend. Had to be.

Cressida fell to her knees. "O spare me, children of the flowers! I have committed no wrong against your goddess!"

They looked at one another, then down at her. "Yes, you did, you stole—"

"Is it a crime to seek out heroes of legend, to seek someone to be my champion against foul monsters and evil gods?"

"What the hell are you—"

"Woe!" Cressida cried. "Is there not a hero who will aid me in my nearly impossible task for which there are great rewards? Is there no one handsome enough to rescue a frail woman who has wandered into the Underworld? Is there no time to maybe sign a few autographs?"

The heroes looked to each other, and quite a few brows were furrowing, and looks were getting cast back and forth. She saw something start in the eyes of one or two, something that said they hadn't had a new story to tell in thousands of years.

A nymph hauled on her arm. "Get up."

"Stop, forest children!" someone cried. "Unhand that maiden!"

Cressida nearly cried out in triumph, not even bothering to correct the maiden part. The less he knew, the better.

"Stay out of this," the nymph said.

"Yes," Cressida called, "do not risk your safety, hero. I would only ask to be rescued by the bravest of the brave, whose bravery is unsurpassed by any braver heroes in the old tales...of braveness!"

She was running out of ways to say brave, but the mumbling had grown, and now it was turning into calls of, "Yes, unhand her!" and "How dare you!"

The nymphs had converged in a circle, facing out, and the roots of the nearby trees cracked like whips around them. "Get back! Do you know who we work for?"

The heroes cried out various names of darker gods and monsters. One hero pleaded with the nymphs, but others shouted threats and warnings. When the first person in a soldier's chiton leapt from the fray and tackled a nymph to the ground, the fight was on, fists and roots flying. Cressida lunged to her feet and fled into the trees, arms still bound as she headed for the bridge and the gate.

An arm stopped her, and she nearly tripped. She skipped back as a handsome young man smiled at her. "Lady, let me loosen your bonds." He had a knife and slit the roots as easily as if they were paper.

"Thanks," she said, shrugging them off. "I'll be going, then."

"But this quest you spoke of?"

"I'd better get back to it." The fight was still raging, but she didn't know how long it would last. She headed for the bridge again.

He frowned but stayed with her. "I know what lies through that gate, or I did know and have forgotten." He had an open, honest face, with curly brown hair that fell into his dark eyes. He wore a simple chiton, light blue, with an unadorned brooch at one shoulder, and she couldn't help wondering who he was, if it was polite to ask. But just like that, she knew he had to be Perseus. That would be par for the course. And if he followed her, he'd wind up right where Medusa wanted him.

Well, he had murdered her, and he got to go to paradise because of it. Even though Medusa was a cheat and a liar, that didn't excuse what Perseus had done. Should she let him follow her, then? If Adonis was right, there was nothing Medusa could do to him without help, except capture him, maybe.

Cressida took a deep breath. "What's your name?"

"Pylades."

Her breath left her in a rush, a happy sigh. He had nothing to do with the Perseus myth. "Well, I can't promise you won't find someone over there who wants to kill you, but you're welcome to come along."

He gave her another bright smile, and she licked her lips as a question loomed large in her mind. "You don't know Perseus, do you?"

"Met him a few times."

Part of her wanted to say, "Don't let him out of here again," but another part of her, a far nastier part, wanted to find him and bring him over so she could say to Medusa, "Here he is! You can't kill him, and I'm not going to, and you're just going to have to stand there and like it."

She wondered what Perseus would think of that. Whether he'd apologize to Medusa or laugh in her face. He might not remember her. That would be far worse, and it made Cressida's heart lurch. She might actually kill him if he couldn't recall the people he'd slain.

"He's not here," Pylades said.

Cressida nearly stumbled. Maybe he was in Asphodel if he hadn't done so well during his resurrections. Medusa would be pissed that she'd missed him for so long. "Where is he?"

"On his third life." He smiled happily. "If he makes it to the Elysian Fields this time, he'll move on to the Isles of the Blessed. Lucky bastard. I'm still trying to pluck up the courage to go back for my second life."

"Oh." Emotions warred within Cressida, smug satisfaction and sadness and relief. Now her only question was, should she tell Medusa or not? If she left without saying anything, Medusa might go on hoping. Maybe that would be worst of all.

CHAPTER FOURTEEN

Instead of stopping when they drew closer to the Elysian Fields, Medusa prompted Aix to take them into the open, sacrificing secrecy for speed. Aix seemed happy to be let loose on the population. She opened her mouth wide and roared whenever anyone appeared in the distance. When people jumped for cover or took off as if fired from a cannon, Aix shivered, and Medusa knew she was laughing.

"Can we slow down?" June cried. "I'm going to be sick!"

"We're nearly there."

She heard mumbles thanking various deities. In the distance stood the fence and its ghosts, but standing well back from it was another group, some leading the hungry ghosts away, but more were watching the fence as if expecting someone to come through. Cressida had to have crossed over already. Medusa wondered if she'd thought about Perseus, if she'd run into him or asked after him.

She told herself it didn't matter. Well, she tried to, but the part of her that had been searching for a cure for her sisters for so long was screaming that there must be a way to get what she wanted. But then her thoughts drifted to that damned kiss, how she'd drank Cressida in like water. And it was more than lust. Cressida had come back for her. With everything to lose, she'd stayed. Now Medusa wanted to keep her for reasons that had nothing to do with her sisters.

"Fuck."

June leaned around her. "Everything all right?"

"No!" She thought of her earlier idea to ask June if Cressida couldn't be persuaded, but even that was too dangerous. Still, it was on the tip of her tongue to ask, but when she opened her mouth again, what came out was, "When we find Cressida...grab her and run for the exit. She's too good for this place."

June nodded and sat back, offering no comment.

They were close enough now that Medusa could tell Adonis from the others. "Plow right into them, Mom."

Some malicious edge to her voice must have conveyed what she wanted far better than her words could. Aix picked up speed, and as the henchman turned and cried out, Aix barreled into their midst. As Medusa leapt from her mother's back, she had one final thought: She and her sisters were dead, and Cressida was alive. It had been the truth since they'd met, but something in Medusa had refused to acknowledge it. Now, suddenly, it meant everything in the entire world.

She tackled Adonis to the ground. "What did you do with her?"

He rolled and tried to grab her, but she shifted into her snake form, and his hands slid over her scales as his eyes squeezed shut. "Get off me!"

As fighters, Medusa felt as if they were the worst in history. She'd never been good at hand-to-hand, but luckily, Adonis was just as shitty as she was. She'd been propelled by rage, mostly at herself, but that was calming. She and Adonis sort of slid over each other, neither having the upper hand. They grabbed at each other's wrists when they could and kicked when they couldn't.

Someone grabbed Medusa's shoulder and hauled her up. When she saw Narcissus's hand, she sank her teeth into it. He shrieked and fell backward.

Adonis heaved her upward. "Asshole!" he cried. Anger gave him enough strength to push her away.

She was tired of wrestling anyway, and at least she'd gotten to bite someone. Adonis rushed to Narcissus, but even with the poison, he'd be fine. "Where is Cressida?" Medusa asked.

"Where do you think?" Adonis said. "We need that ambrosia."

"She's leaving as soon as she gets back. I don't care whether you get your ambrosia or not."

"We swore by the Styx," Narcissus said. "She gives us the ambrosia, she walks away."

Swearing by the river. Cressida never admitted she knew about that. If she hadn't, no one was going to mention it to her. Medusa wondered why she hadn't insisted on it before, but she seemed to trust everyone. Why shouldn't she? She'd never lived anywhere like the Underworld. She probably thought everyone was good at heart.

"She really needs to get out of here," Medusa mumbled.

Adonis frowned but then sighed. "I agree with you. It sort of breaks your heart."

"If you've hurt her," Medusa said, "I'll break more than your heart."

"Lighten up," Adonis said as he pulled Narcissus away. "She's fine. Like I said, we swore by the river." He stared pointedly at Medusa. "She can leave as long as no one stops her."

Medusa wanted to say she wouldn't. It was her idea that Cressida should leave as quickly as possible, but she choked on the words. The specters of her sisters loomed in her mind. How could she face them if she let Cressida walk away? How could she face herself if she didn't?

"Cressida!" June ran for the fence where Cressida was emerging next to a man in a chiton. Medusa's heart sped, both at the sight of her and the young man. His features seemed to blur for a moment, and she thought, *Oh, she's done it*. Even after everything Medusa had put her through, Cressida had lured Perseus within reach.

She took a step closer, fists clenching and unclenching. Maybe it didn't have to be the harpe that killed him. Maybe the oracles were wrong, and she could squeeze the life out of him with her bare hands. As she stalked closer, though, she knew his features weren't blurring. She was trying to make them into someone else's. He looked a bit like Perseus, but it wasn't him.

Cressida hugged her aunt fiercely, and Medusa heard her asking over and over if June was real. Over June's shoulder, Cressida looked to Medusa, and her face transformed with rage. She knew she'd been lied to. Coldness spread through Medusa's guts even though she'd known this was coming. Maybe Cressida had asked a young hero to come with her so she could taunt Medusa with him somehow, a well-deserved revenge.

Medusa took a step, trying to think of a way to explain, but no words would come. June glanced her way and tugged Cressida in the direction of the exit. Cressida broke away from her, and Medusa's heart lifted. In spite of everything, perhaps they could say good-bye, maybe share a hug and throw their arms around each other for one last kiss?

Fat chance. Cressida ran to Adonis and shoved a pack into his hands. They exchanged a few words before Cressida gestured to her aunt, and they started toward Cerberus's cave, taking revenge with them. Medusa trailed after them for a few steps, unable to help herself. The vision of her sisters wouldn't leave her. "Wait," she whispered. "Please."

Cressida turned. "He's gone." She breathed so hard her shoulders moved up and down. "Perseus is living his third life." She lifted her arms, dropped them. "I'm...sorry. You'll have to find another way to help Stheno and Euryale."

The strength went out of Medusa's legs even as she told herself she couldn't fall.

It's just a setback.

You'll find another way.

There is... You can... We'll find...

Nothing. Medusa sagged to the ground. She tried to gulp in air as a shriek built inside her, a noise so loud that even the gods would hear it, but she couldn't take in any air at all. She doubled over until her forehead touched the cracked pavement. She was dead, petrified as she was, and doomed to stay that way forever.

It was too hard to watch. Cressida had wanted to hurl Perseus's news at Medusa and take glee in how much it hurt, but she hadn't wanted this picture of sorrow. She wouldn't have wished it on her worst enemy, let alone a woman she'd come to care for, no matter what else had happened between them. As Medusa shook with sobs, Cressida wanted to hold her close and yell at her later.

"Cressida, come on!" June said.

Cressida gripped June's hand, a real, warm hand, and not some fabrication. She should have known that Medea's illusion wasn't real. This one talked the right way, acted the right way. She smelled like hand cream and peppermints, June's smell. She was warm and alive, her presence too much for even the Underworld to dim. When she'd run toward the Elysian gate, she'd been a balm to Cressida's scattered nerves and runaway emotions. Everything had made sense again.

Until now. "June, I can't just leave her."

June looked to Medusa, her expression pitying, but she shook her head. "There's nothing we can do."

But Cressida and Medusa had shared something. For all the lies, there had been something real between them. She took a step toward Medusa, but June kept hold of her arm.

"We can ask Nero for advice," June said, "but for now, we're going." She looked into the distance. "You don't understand, Cressida; we have to go before she comes looking for me."

Cressida glanced at her, but she had one of those looks that promised to explain everything once danger was no longer imminent. "But—"

"Now!" June grabbed Cressida's other arm, too, as if to drag her away. Her hand brushed the harpe, and she froze, eyes drifting downward and staring at the sword as if caressing it. "What have you got there?"

"Ah, right. I should leave that behind." She didn't know if it was possible to bring back souvenirs from the Underworld, but even if it was, she didn't know if the world was ready again for a magical sword.

She unbuckled the belt and wondered where it would be safe, but since only living hands could wield it, she supposed it didn't matter. "I should give it to Medusa in case—"

June's grip locked around her wrist again, but this wasn't caring Aunt June leading Cressida away from danger. Her face had gone still, serious, the expression she used whenever someone tried to rob or cheat her, when anyone had the mistaken impression that female couldn't equal dangerous.

"I know that sword. I used to have something like it."

She frowned as if trying to remember, and Cressida thought of June's collection of antiques and all the pieces that had passed through her hands over the years. There had been a few swords, but not a harpe, not that Cressida remembered.

A roar from the sky made everyone look up. Cressida thought her mouth couldn't fall open in surprise ever again, but there it went, well trained by this point. A chariot roared overhead, flames coating the outside of the cart, leaving an afterimage in the gray shade fog. Two small dragons held it aloft, wings flapping, and a wild looking redhead drove them. She leaned far to the right as if searching the ground below.

Flaming chariot. Dragons. Red hair. "That's Medea, Aunt June. That's fucking Medea!"

But her awe at meeting yet another legendary name fled as she remembered that Medea had been the one to trick her at Medusa's request, no matter that they'd seemed to turn on each other later.

With such a powerful player entering the field, Cressida thought it best to take June's advice and sort everything out later, but June wouldn't budge. She frowned at Medea as if putting current events together.

Medea beamed at them. "Now, hero, fulfill your destiny!" She chucked something over the side of the car, sending it whirling toward them in a flash of gold.

"Look out!" Pylades yelled.

He pushed forward, and Cressida wondered how Medea had known he'd be there, if she'd set up their meeting somehow. Before she could ask, June shoved both him and Cressida out of the way. Her arm shot out and grabbed the golden thing out of the air. She looped it over her arm, a shield of golden scales with a gorgon's head, the aegis of Zeus.

June ran her hand over it lovingly. "I remember."

Cressida opened her mouth to ask, but June's other hand lashed out and drew the harpe in one smooth motion. She gave it a few experimental swings, and even to Cressida's unpracticed eye, it seemed as if she knew what she was doing.

"Aunt June?"

June beamed at her. "Now, in this life, but part of me always remembered who I used to be."

"In this life?" Like a reminder reel in a movie, it played in her head: the heroes from the Elysian Fields being resurrected, remembering just enough about themselves to try to earn another place in the Fields, all so they could eventually move on to the Isles of the Blessed. And June was so courageous. She never backed down, always one to run toward danger rather than away from it, and myths were always more real to her than they were to anyone else, so much so that her family worried for her safety.

Pylades looked at June more closely before smiling. "Hello, Perseus. Fancy meeting you here!"

❖

Medusa hadn't realized just how much the idea of revenge meant to her. Even if she never got help, and her sisters continued to fade, she would have kept plodding after revenge like a donkey heading for a mirage. Cressida had been right. It defined her.

And now revenge was dead, just like her. But Cressida was free from any lies Medusa had told her, free from any obligation she might have felt. She was alive, and she was free, and if Medusa could only get up, there could be truth between them.

Even curled up in the street, Medusa had felt Cressida's hesitation; the bright glow of her life burned steadily nearby. Medusa wanted to reach out and bathe in that light, something she hadn't even realized she would miss when it was gone. But she didn't move. Cressida would come to her if she called, even after everything. Medusa had seen enough pity in those eyes to know that her pain would be undeniable, so she made it her gift to stay tucked in her misery. June would lead Cressida to safety, and one day Cressida might realize that living her life well was the only thing that mattered, and that she should only give her love to someone who deserved it.

And no one could say that of the dead.

Then Medusa heard Medea's voice and felt a shudder in the air, a ripple of converging events. She raised her head to see what calamity was befalling them this time. The fight had paused; Adonis's gang were withdrawing. Aix, Arachne, Pandora, and Agamemnon stared into the sky. They gasped as the aegis winged through the air toward an arm that had once wielded it.

"I knew she looked familiar," Medusa whispered. She'd thought it was because June and Cressida were so alike, but she and June had met before. Perseus lurked behind the lines of June's face, behind the feminine slope of her chin, the smaller nose, the muscled curves. His spirit swam inside her, and it had been calling out ever since they'd laid eyes on each other. And now that June's soul realized who it had once been, it was so clear. Medusa didn't even need the words of the random hero to confirm it.

June faced Medusa with a shield adorned with her own head caught in its gorgon form, and this harpe was even more powerful than the one June had wielded as Perseus. She had all the power she'd ever need to reduce Medusa or anyone else to a shade.

June's eyes held a hint of callousness she'd lacked before, a trait every ancient hero had to possess in order to undertake the trials of the gods. Still, she didn't smirk, only blinked at Medusa calmly, neither ashamed nor proud. But of course, Perseus hadn't killed Medusa because he'd enjoyed it. It had been a task he'd been given, pushed on by the gods, and as a hero of legend, he was as unable to deny that as he was his own heartbeat.

"Stand away, Cressida," June said.

Cressida's mouth hung open again, but Medusa couldn't blame her. If she made it back to the mortal world, Medusa doubted anything would ever surprise her again. "Aunt June, please, don't kill her."

Medusa stood slowly. She didn't know if her powers could still turn a living person to stone, and June had the aegis to hide behind. Still, Medusa clenched her fists and promised every god still in existence that she would go down fighting this time.

A piece of shade fog drifted down to her, and she heard the voices of her sisters vibrating through it. "We are coming."

Medusa didn't tell them what to do. They had the right to choose their oblivion. But she wouldn't wait for them. Her snake form slid over her, and she circled June, looking for an opening.

June hid behind the shield. "Stand away, Daughter of Snakes. I seek entrance to the Fields again, and killing the dead won't get me there."

As if that mattered. Medusa leapt for her, but June swung the harpe in a wide arc, forcing Medusa back.

"Agamemnon," Medusa said, "give me your sword!"

"Um." He stood well back. "I don't think—"

"Now!" Something wrapped around her, sending her lurching to the side as several voices cried at her to look out.

A ball of flames splashed across the ground where she'd been standing. Arachne's webs were tangled around her.

Medea laughed as she landed her chariot. "Stay out of her way, Medusa."

Pandora and Arachne moved to flank Medusa, each grabbing on to an arm. "She's too powerful," Pandora said in Medusa's ear. "You'll be killed."

Medusa tried to squirm away from them. She had to get to Perseus, cleave him in half if she could, choke him if she couldn't.

"Forget it, Snakes!" Arachne said. "You won't get past Medea."

"Traitorous bastards, let me go!"

"This time it's for your own good," Pandora said. "Think of Cressida! This love story isn't going to be a very good one if you kill her aunt!"

Sappy as it was, it made Medusa's power slip back inside her. Cressida was staring between Medusa and June as if lost.

"So, that's it?" Medusa cried. "You get to kill me and walk away, Perseus? I thought your current incarnation felt sorry for my fate, for many of the women of myth."

June nodded. "It's easy to muster sympathy for events that stand at a distance. Now I see the necessity of the times." She moved past Cressida and circled the rest of them, wary but not attacking. Medusa frowned and looked at everyone else, wondering who June's target would be. Everyone but Cressida and June were already dead. June needed something monumental enough to get her to the Elysian Fields a third time. Maybe the living world no longer held any tasks the gods considered worthy. Maybe June had always felt driven to the Underworld, seeking that last deed that would propel her to the Isles of the Blessed.

"Look!" Adonis said, a crazed whisper that nevertheless cut through the silence.

In the distance, from the direction of the Terrace, a cloud billowed; lightning flashed in its depths as it rose into the sky, pushing through the shade fog.

"She's coming," Adonis said.

Narcissus grabbed his arm. He'd wound a bandage around the bite mark. "But she never leaves the Terrace."

"She's coming for me," June said, head cocked to the side. "She's coming because no one takes what's hers."

Cressida trailed her aunt, still frowning. "We have to go. We can make it. We can leave before…" She cast a glance at Medusa, a look full of both hurt and longing, and Medusa leaned toward her, wishing she could reach out.

"Kill her, June," Medea said. "Kill Persephone, and the Isles of the Blessed are yours! Hades himself sanctions it, I swear by the River Styx!"

Everyone gasped. June nodded slowly. "You go, Cressida. I'm going to secure my eternity."

"By killing Persephone?" Medusa muttered. "You're going to kill a lover, just like that?" She glanced at Medea. "Why would you want her dead?"

Medea winked. If she'd wanted Persephone dead this whole time, she'd had a convoluted plan indeed. She'd needed a mortal to wield the sword, and if she'd known Perseus was walking around in the world, she might have found some way to influence him, to prompt him toward the Underworld. Like Medusa's plan, this one had to have been percolating in Medea's mind a long time.

And then June had come, but Persephone had grabbed her first, and Medea must have been waiting, biding her time and trying to figure out a way to unlock Perseus from June's mind. And then Cressida had come like sweet ambrosia, and when she'd fallen into Medusa's hands, Medea must have danced with glee. She'd known Medusa would come to her for help; they'd talked of Medusa's need for revenge many times. Medea must have thought it was almost too easy. She knew Medusa needed to go to Tartarus, needed the harpe, and while they'd been there, she'd used Medusa to get the aegis, too, an object she needed to bring Perseus out and secure his victory over Persephone. She probably didn't even need the harpe. She could have found another weapon, and having Perseus armed with the sword of Cronos had to feel like cake at this point.

Even after Adonis had gotten hold of Cressida again, Medea must have known how closely she could manipulate the situation. She hadn't even needed to bring Persephone here. Medusa had done it for her.

But why? This felt as if it had another hand behind it.

Medea stepped from her chariot but was smart enough to stay out of reach. "You should see your faces, everyone trying to figure it out." She chuckled as the lightning cloud drew closer. "Persephone should have been expecting something like this, as brutal as she's become. She drove Hades out years ago, and he's gone wherever the rest of the gods disappeared to."

Everyone listened to her closely, faces half turned so they could watch the lightning cloud.

"And the other gods can't bring her to them. She's as caught here as the rest of us. And that's made her vengeful. And lonely, but who could blame her? That's a pretty toxic combination for a god. Powerful but too erratic. It's time for a new queen, one who thinks the dead and the living are ready for a bit of that old black magic."

Medusa had to bark a laugh, the sound making Pandora and Arachne jump. It was too much. The goddess whose name they'd all been dropping had been working through them from the beginning.

"Hecate," Cressida whispered. "Aunt June, you're going to kill Persephone for Hecate?" She paused as if remembering something. "Wait, Medusa said *lover*..." Her eyebrows climbed to her hair. "You and Persephone were lovers?"

June smiled over her shoulder. "I'll tell you when you're older. And I'm not doing this for anyone other than us."

"Hades promises it will get her into the Isles of the Blessed," Medea said, "and you, Cressida, as her heir, will have a legacy. It will be a deed felt through the Underworld and into the mortal realm, and the world will know both your names, and when you die, you'll be known and remembered even if you can't get to the Elysian Fields on your own." She faced the advancing cloud and breathed deep, smiling still. "You'll be a force to be reckoned with, kiddo."

Cressida's mouth worked as if she had no idea what to say. Medusa didn't know what to say, either. Here she'd been lamenting how things would never change, and now it seemed they would do so all too quickly. And all she had to do was watch the epic fight of June-Perseus versus Persephone; the thought nearly made her bark another inappropriate laugh. June was about to get splattered across the pavement.

"You can't fight a god," she whispered. But wasn't this what tales of heroes were all about? Impossible odds? No, people thought they were like that, but how often was the hero in real danger? He usually had gods looking out for him and magical weapons and helpful sorceresses making sure he was all right in the end. Was Hecate watching? Undoubtedly yes, through the shade fog and her daughter; she might even be among them in one guise or another, and who knew what powers she'd back June with?

And if Hades was on her side, too, that probably meant Zeus and the others were waiting for the outcome, though she couldn't imagine that Demeter was too happy about her daughter being killed. Maybe the others were distracting her. None of the male gods would be happy having a woman in charge of the Underworld. Had Hecate told them that Hades could be in charge again? From the way Medea was talking, it didn't sound as if she'd be keeping that promise.

"She's going to die," Cressida said. "I've got to stop her."

"Let me go!" Medusa said, her eyes locked on Cressida.

Pandora and Arachne released her, and she ran to Cressida's side. "June has the aegis of Zeus and the harpe of Cronos, the tools of the strongest gods of two different ages. She has the goodwill of a goddess older than Persephone. And she's a hero of legend, Cressida! The deeds she's done have already gotten her to the Elysian Fields twice!"

Cressida stepped away from her. "Even if she wins, why do you care? Are you going to sneak up on her while she's tired from battle and cut her head off so you can have her shade?"

Well, at least they were talking. "That…wouldn't work." Oh, but it would feel so nice. "If she dies, she'll move on to the Elysian Fields, and her body wouldn't do me any good. She's lost to me, Cressida.

Perseus is lost." *Hold it together*. She took a deep breath. "But this."
She pointed toward the cloud, close enough now to see the darkness at
the heart of it: Persephone's chariot. "This could change everything."

"You're not suggesting we help her?"

"Why not?" Narcissus said as he stepped up beside them. "Let's
have a change."

"It's barbaric!" Adonis cried. "We can't just stand here and
watch a murder."

"She won't go gently," Medea said. "It'll be a fair fight."

Narcissus sighed dramatically. "Adonis, how many times do I
have to tell you that someone who really loves you wouldn't hurt
you? She needs to go."

Adonis stepped back as if he'd been slapped. "She...she doesn't
mean..."

"I am so sick of hearing that," Narcissus said. "It's an excuse,
like all the others." He stabbed his finger at the cloud. "How many
times have you talked about leaving her? And then she either buys
your forgiveness or threatens you—"

"Are we seriously doing this?" Agamemnon asked, looking
between all of them. "That is the dread queen of the Underworld
coming, and we're standing here arguing? Except for most of your
gang, who have fled, I might point out."

"If we're going to leave, we'd better do it now," Arachne said.
"If this goes down, and we weren't backing the winning side, we're
next on the chopping block."

Pandora nodded. "It might be better to remain neutral."

"Too late," Medea said. "You're all in this hip deep." She made a
fist. "Think of the rewards if you cheer for the winning team!"

They fell to bickering, and Medusa tuned them out, turning for
Cressida. "We've been static for so long down here."

"I can't let my aunt die! Tell me this isn't a fight to the death. Tell
me that's not how epic fights end!"

Medusa wanted to, but she knew how stories like this went.
"Even if she dies—"

"I'm not ready to lose her!" Cressida turned to June. "June,
get over here this instant. We are leaving!" It was probably a good

approximation of her mother or maybe even June, and June's shoulders twitched as if it worked on some level. Medusa felt a tingling in her own feet as if they really wanted to obey, but she fought to stay where she was.

"Please," Cressida said, her voice filled with sorrow. "Aunt June, please!"

The person who looked over her shoulder was the same woman Medusa had briefly known, and yet it wasn't. Her concern for Cressida was plain but also secondary, as if she'd finally accepted that destiny trumped everything else, including love. "I'm sorry, Cressi. I have to."

Cressida's lip trembled as if her heart was breaking, and she didn't know how to stop it. It roused everything in Medusa that used to be alive, cutting through the obsession that had kept her going for thousands of years. But even with that obsession, there had been some things she wouldn't do, like have her sisters consume innocent souls. Some prices were just too high.

"We could grab her," Medusa said. "Maybe between us we can carry her to Cerberus's cavern and force her inside."

"Don't even think about it," Medea said.

Medusa sneered at her. "Hecate can do her own dirty work."

"Yeah," Adonis said. When Narcissus glared at him, he added, "Persephone isn't all bad. She doesn't deserve to die! She needs help."

"I'm serious," Medea said. "I don't want to fight you when I should be watching the most epic fight I'll probably ever see."

"She'll keep trying to come back." Agamemnon rested a hand on Cressida's shoulder. "Even if you knock her out and drag her from here, she knows her destiny now, and nothing she will ever do in the mortal world will top what she might have done here. You'll never get the hero out of her now."

A few tears slid down Cressida's cheeks, and she dashed them away as if embarrassed by them.

Medusa took a deep breath and reached hesitantly for Cressida's shoulder. "Whatever you want to do, that's what I'll do. I know I've been a real ass. I know that nothing can make up for the fact that nearly every word out of my mouth has been a lie, but I am truly sorry,

Cressida. My sisters are coming, and they'll help you, too. You just have to tell us what you want."

Cressida turned teary eyes Medusa's way. Bright pink spots bloomed in both cheeks, her strong emotions making the glow around her intensify. She made revenge seem almost trivial. Even visions of Stheno's and Euryale's murder, of her own, were nothing compared to the sight of Cressida's eyes swimming with tears, nothing compared to the fact that Cressida needed her help.

She was a fool, a dead, lovesick fool.

CHAPTER FIFTEEN

Cressida wanted everyone to live; that was the most important thing. But then it occurred to her as it had several times that Medusa wasn't really alive. None of the people in the Underworld were. No matter what happened, no matter how she felt, she would have to travel back to the living world eventually and leave the dead to their fate.

And now she was supposed to believe that June was actually Perseus, resurrected and meant for glorious deeds, including a glorious death. In a strange way, it made sense, but she wasn't ready to watch June die, even if it meant her soul would travel to the Isles of the Blessed. Even with the tools of the gods, she might kill Persephone, but it would kill her in the process. That was the way epic tales worked.

"What is Hecate going to do?" Cressida asked. "After Persephone is dead?"

"Anything is better than never changing," Narcissus said.

Medea smiled like the cat with the canary. "She's going to bring magic back to the mortal world and inspire belief in the gods again. Think of it! Your aunt will fulfill her ultimate purpose and go to the Isles of the Blessed, and you will get to return to a world where magic walks once more!"

But what did that mean? Heroes and quests and magical artifacts? And monsters? Who the hell wanted those? "What will she do for the people here?" Cressida asked. "Can she bring them back to life?"

Oh, how the ears perked up then! Everyone tore their eyes away from Persephone's approach in order to listen to Medea's answer, but her smile grew wider, and she shrugged.

Cressida heard the gasps, but that shrug could mean anything.

"Who?" Adonis asked. "Just sorcerers like you? Or anyone?"

Another shrug. Either she didn't know, she didn't want to answer, or the answer was no. Still, the very idea would get quite a few people onto her side.

Cressida could only picture the Minotaur or the Hecatonchires rampaging across the world. The gods and monsters and dead might return, but the living would be screwed.

"No," Medea said quietly.

Cressida turned to look at her and noticed two hazy forms wandering up behind her, her sisters frozen halfway between their snake and human forms, between thinking, reasoning beings and shades.

"We're dead," Medea said. "All of us. We had our time, and it's over."

Agamemnon clenched a fist and then regarded it as if he didn't know quite what to do with it. "Some of our lives were cut short. Yours, too."

"That doesn't make this right. The world belongs to the living."

"Living," her sisters echoed.

"We can fight all we want amongst ourselves, but the dead should stay buried." Medusa took her sisters' hands and seemed sadder than Cressida had ever seen her. Cressida wanted to put her arms around Medusa and hold her close, but she stayed where she was.

Medea shrugged. "It's not up to you, is it?"

And she was right. Persephone was almost upon them. Her hair was inky black, dark as night, and her skin was a deep purple, her eyes shining with white fire. She wore a crown of blazing embers, and midnight black horses pulled her chariot, the clouds gathered around them. She lifted a hand from the reins and threw a ball of shadowy darkness.

"Scatter!" someone cried.

Cressida lurched to the side as someone pulled her away, but they needn't have bothered. The ball of blackness streaked toward

June, who raised the aegis and knocked it to the side, sending it toward the fence to the Elysian Fields where it hit the ground with a splat and rolled along like a giant ball of tar, consuming hungry ghosts in its wake.

June lifted the aegis, and even from behind, Cressida felt power billow out from it. Medusa had said her powers were weaker in death—everyone's were—but Cressida had never expected her petrifying gaze would have such weight. It felt as if even the empty space was solidifying and gaining mass, and she felt a rush as the air escaped. Persephone flung a hand in front of her eyes, but one of her nightmare steeds whinnied once, a shrill, piercing call, before it dropped from the air as stone, taking the chariot with it.

The crowd cried out, but whether in joy, agony, or surprise, Cressida didn't know. Persephone leapt free and landed on the pavement, her dress billowing around her like the petals of a flower. The ground cracked around her sandaled feet, and she stood easily, face drawn in a scowl. She lifted a hand, and darkness curled around it like a living thing.

"Not too shabby, my little love," she said, almost a croon. But as swiftly as her face relaxed, it tightened into rage. "Why does everyone leave me in the end?" Her voice echoed through the streets like a rusty saw trying to cut metal, and everyone clapped their hands to their ears.

June didn't respond, and the two circled each other, one armed with the harpe, one with darkness itself. *This can't be happening*, Cressida thought. Her aunt was *not* Perseus reborn, and she did *not* at one time kill the woman Cressida had come to have feelings for. Cressida didn't know if she exactly loved Medusa, but the fact was that someone she *didn't* care about could never have hurt her so badly. And now she couldn't believe June was throwing her life away for the chance at eternal paradise by killing a god, an act sanctioned by some other gods who would rather do away with a problem than actually solve it.

Who was the villain here?

"Stop." Cressida needed time to breathe, time to think. Maybe June needed time, too, maybe then she'd see how fucked up this was. "Stop."

June swung the harpe, and Persephone shifted out of the way. As Persephone threw another ball of blackness, and June batted it aside, Cressida screamed, a sound that rang in her ears as the inky ball arced toward a group of bystanders who raised their arms to shield themselves, but it wouldn't be enough. They were going to die, just like June. Maybe just like everyone if June somehow failed, and Persephone turned her ire on the spectators.

But for now, the doomed bystanders needed to not be standing where they were anymore.

And so they weren't.

Cressida's scream died in her throat as the group of five goners appeared beside her, arms still raised, faces creased with the expectation of pain. When it didn't come, a few opened their eyes and peered around cautiously.

"What the fuck?" Medusa said. "Did you do that? Who did that?"

"I think…" Cressida looked back to the fight, but Persephone and June didn't seem to notice what had happened. Pressure built inside Cressida again as June dashed forward, swinging the harpe and cutting a line of fire across Persephone's arm. Persephone cried out in a voice that vibrated through Cressida's core and shook the buildings in their foundations. Persephone caught June and hurled her toward a streetlight that would surely break her back.

"No!" Cressida called, and the streetlight sagged, becoming transparent. When June crashed into it, it folded around her like a giant gummy candy, and she rolled unhurt to the street.

Cressida put a hand to her chest. She felt something similar to what swearing by the River Styx had done to her, a pressure that had vanished when she'd handed over the ambrosia. But this wasn't as if she was forgetting something. It felt more like remembering. The Underworld was built on belief, that's what everyone had told her, and some parts of her brain appeared to have been listening harder than others. The denizens of the Underworld shaped their surroundings, some more than others like Medea with her illusions. And just like in Medea's basement, Cressida's belief counted for more because she was alive, and that meant June's counted for more, too. June had wanted this to happen on some level, and so it had, everything lining up so she and Persephone could duke it out in front of an audience.

"Son of a bitch!" Anger churned like acid in Cressida's heart. She'd been a pawn so many times in this adventure, just like the women she'd pitied in myth, those who'd been unfortunate enough to be caught in the schemes of gods.

"Well, not anymore, you fuckers!" She shrugged out of her backpack and threw it to the ground. A few people sidled away, and everyone gave her a wary glance. "What the hell are you looking at?"

"Cressida?" Medusa asked as she stepped away from her sisters. "What's—"

"Just watch this!" Cressida concentrated, and the pavement between June and Persephone lifted in a tearing crunch and the squeal of metal as Cressida divided them. June stumbled back, eyeing the newly made wall.

"Are you...doing that?" Agamemnon asked.

Medusa smiled slowly. "You're using your belief."

"How is that possible?" Adonis asked with a frown.

Cressida gestured for them all to stay back. "Who's the big dick now?"

"Um, you?" Narcissus leaned toward Adonis. "Is that what she wants to hear?"

Agamemnon's face screwed up as if he might disagree, but Arachne jabbed him in the ribs and gave Cressida a slightly panicky smile. Pandora was watching her with open-mouthed wonder.

On the battlefield, June frowned as if working out what was happening. "Cressi, is that you? Don't interfere!"

"Like hell!"

A chunk of the pavement wall blew outward, and Persephone stepped through. Cressida concentrated and brought the street up, circling Persephone like a fence, looping it over and around itself, pulling at the pavement for miles across.

"Stop it!" Medea cried.

Medusa got in her way, her snake features flowing over her. "Stay back."

Cressida waved a hand, and Medea disappeared as Cressida sent her to the other side of the Underworld.

"Whatever you're doing," Adonis said, "keep it up. Maybe I can get in there and talk to Persephone, try to calm her."

Yes, if everyone could just talk, they could settle down, but she could hear Persephone beating on the walls of her prison. Maybe Cressida could move her to the Terrace, or imprison her somewhere it would take her a while to get out of, and Cressida could drag June back to the real world.

But when she tried, Persephone wouldn't budge. Cressida pushed harder, believing Persephone elsewhere with all her will, but the sounds from inside the asphalt continued. Well, she supposed the will of a god had to be pretty strong.

But she felt the rest of the Underworld trembling, awaiting her command. Even Tartarus was twitching in his prison, the whole place longing for someone to put it on the right track. It had been operating on the belief of its denizens for so long, changing at their whim, but maybe that wasn't enough for it. The rest of the gods were gone, and its queen seemed to have forgotten about most of it. Cressida felt it reaching for her, wanting her to say what it should do and when, and all she had to do was put her finger on the right button.

She felt another will pulling at hers and thought it might be June or Hecate or even Persephone trying to wrest control. She pushed against them, but the ground lurched, and the sounds of Asphodel snapped away. She turned and slid on a marble floor that gleamed so brightly she couldn't look directly at it. Glowing fog surrounded her, as if she stood in the middle of a cloud punctuated with lights so bright they could have been stars.

Shade fog? No, it was too bright, though hazy forms glided through it. She saw figures that might be people, but a feel of otherness surrounded them, as if they were simply a collection of parts put together for some purpose other than just living.

She squinted at them, seeing more than just limbs, torsos, and heads. She spotted the slope of a helmet and a spear carried by a figure in a dress, and her education saved her again as she thought of the attributes of various Greek gods. Helmet plus spear plus dress equaled Athena.

As she peered, she saw more objects standing out: the golden points of Hera's crown, the curve of Artemis's bow, and the arcs of Hermes's winged sandals. At the center of them, on a high dais, she saw the outline of a throne with the brightest light shining inside it.

That would be Zeus, and flanking him was a form holding a trident, and one wearing a helmet, his light containing swirls of darkness: Poseidon and Hades.

There were more, scores of them, too many to count, and she heard their whispers, but no loud booming voices. Like the rest of their brethren, they'd faded. She felt their words more than heard them, the Hades figure being angriest of all.

"Ah," Cressida said, her own anger still bright within her. "This is the *deus ex machina*, yes? The end of the Greek play where the gods sort everything out?"

And now the whispers flew fast, some voices furious, others intrigued. They really wanted to bring their worship back. They'd come to depend on belief, to be fueled by it as their creation, humanity, grew and began to change the world to suit humans instead of gods. Then as belief waned, so did the gods who'd come to feed on it. They'd created their own destruction.

But even here, in what she assumed was left of Mount Olympus, she could feel the fabric of the place waiting. Yes, they were powerful, but just like everything else, they were finished. And the very air around them was crying out for something new, something aware, something that had moved with the times or was at least a product of it.

As she focused on moving herself back to where she'd been, she felt the gods' surprise. The specters of Athena, Demeter, and Hermes moved closer. They agreed with her, with one twist: Yes, their time on earth was done, but the afterlife needn't be as bleak as what she'd seen. And Demeter didn't want her daughter to die. Persephone had been driven out of her mind by loneliness, but she didn't have to be lonely forever. She could be healed. There could be change without death.

The paths through the Underworld didn't have to remain shut.

Cressida grinned and focused, and with the help of the three gods, shifted back to Asphodel. Persephone had fought her way out of her pavement prison and was pursuing June again.

Medusa grabbed Cressida's arm. "You disappeared!"

"I know."

"Cressida, you have to leave now. It's too dangerous. My sisters and I will find a way to tackle June, and then we'll follow you to Cerberus's cave—"

Cressida laid a finger over her mouth. "I'm going to unstick you."

Medusa's eyebrows raised. Cressida laughed, and even though she hadn't forgiven Medusa, she understood the lies. And she hoped she understood why Medusa wanted her to leave. Even before their kiss, Medusa had wanted Cressida to go. Her conscience had been too loud; that had to mean her feelings for Cressida had grown as strong as Cressida's had for her.

"Help me." Cressida took one of Medusa's hands and then one of Adonis's. "If you don't want Persephone to die and the living world to fall under the sway of gods and monsters again, help me."

Before they could ask what she meant, she showed them, and they gasped at the presence of the three gods. They hadn't come with Cressida in what was left of their physical forms. She sensed they couldn't do that even if they wanted to, but they'd lent her some of their essence, and everyone that got close to her had to feel it.

Cressida felt along the paths that kept the dead locked where they were, everyone forbidden from moving to the layer above them. Then with the help of the gods and those around her, Cressida tore down the gates of paradise.

Cressida's arrival and the tasks they'd undertaken together would go down in history as the most memorable in Medusa's unlife. They would have made her living top ten as well. She'd gone to Tartarus and reunited with her mother; she'd witnessed a fight between a hero of legend and a god; discovered a deep attraction that was blossoming into something even deeper; she'd found the man who'd murdered her, only he was the aunt of the woman she was falling for; and now she was helping that same woman—with three *other* gods—to tear down the gates that separated the Underworld's eternal haves from its everlasting have-nots.

She sighed as the gates fell. Agamemnon, Pandora, and Arachne shouted as the fence to the Elysian Fields dissolved. Rolling hills of fresh green grass stretched into the distance, dotted with trees and sparkling streams. And sunlight! Artificial but worlds better than Asphodel's ghastly gray fog.

Heroes and nymphs paused in the middle of a huge brawl and turned to look at the Asphodel side with faces full of wonder and terror, and Medusa knew many of them had forgotten there was anything but paradise. The nymphs, dryads, and others of their kind sometimes crossed back and forth, but the heroes almost never did. They didn't want to remember, but now they wandered toward Asphodel, calling out names, searching for people they once knew.

June and Persephone had stopped fighting to look at the Fields with the same open-mouthed wonder as everyone else. Persephone took a step toward the light, bright eyes wide. "Mother?"

"Cressida, what are you doing?" June shouted. "Stop this!"

"Can't fight if you don't have anything to fight for," Cressida muttered.

Medusa gasped as something sparkled in the distance, in the middle of the Elysian Fields, a shimmering doorway. Through it, she glimpsed mountain peaks and a sparkling lake, and somehow, she knew that if she was standing right beside it, it would smell like the greatest things on earth.

"No!" June cried. "You can't offer paradise to the undeserving!"

"That's not you talking!" Cressida said. "Not you anymore!"

June stumbled, shaking her head and frowning as if wondering if that might be true. She launched herself at Persephone's back.

"Look out!" Adonis cried.

Persephone turned in time to catch the harpe full in the chest. She staggered and cried out, the sound rolling from her in waves, shattering glass and battering Medusa's eardrums so that she fell to the ground, everyone arrayed around her.

Cressida's hand clamped down on Medusa's. "I can't stop her! I can't move her or June!"

Medusa heard the shrieking of the gods, felt their support withdrawing as despair overwhelmed them. June left the harpe in Persephone's chest and lifted the aegis toward her wide-open eyes. Cressida sobbed as June's face wavered between what she used to be and who she was becoming again.

Medusa jumped to her feet, popped her wings out, and leapt, flapping them once to rocket forward. She couldn't let Cressida's aunt slip away forever, not when it would hurt Cressida so much. And if

June wanted to be Perseus right now, at least that would make her easier to hit.

June swung the aegis in Medusa's direction, and her power roiled from it, but she grinned into the force, reveling as it slid harmlessly around her. She tackled June to the ground.

June's face seemed to morph into his, and Medusa punched it without hesitation. June's head rocked back and thunked into the ground with a sound like a coconut falling on a board. Medusa punched twice more, and the part of her that still craved revenge wanted to rip out June's throat. June might move on to the Isles of the Blessed, but the way was open now. No one would be safe there anymore.

Medusa clamped her teeth together as they tried to grow longer. "Listen to me," she said, half to June, half to herself. "Listen!"

June stilled, her eyes squeezed shut.

Medusa's own head dug into her ribs where the aegis lay between them. "I won't kill you." *Do it, do it, do it!* Even if she couldn't get her hands on Perseus's shade, killing him would feel so good!

No! There was *more* to her than revenge. Hadn't she already proven that? But Perseus's throat had never been so close. With a deep breath, she reminded herself that this wasn't Perseus; it was June. Medusa focused on her face, on the hints of Cressida there. "I won't kill you. Cressida wouldn't want me to. Think on that. Think on your family, June, before you make your next move."

June slowed her breathing, and her face lost some of Perseus's lines, but she made no sound. Cressida and Adonis knelt on either side of Persephone. Her eyes rolled, and she groaned in agony.

"If I pull the harpe out, the gods think they can fix her body," Cressida said.

Adonis nodded. "Narcissus, help me."

Narcissus stayed back, rubbing his elbows.

Adonis looked to him, face stricken. "Please, my love, she needs our help!"

With a sigh that could have been disgust or resignation, Narcissus marched over and took Persephone's other arm.

Cressida looked to Medusa. "Have you got her?"

"For the moment." Medusa settled more squarely onto June in case she decided to try to get up again, but June had stilled.

Cressida smiled, a kindly look, but it lacked the openness Medusa had come to expect. "Everyone ready?"

"I'm sorry, Cressida," Medusa blurted. "I'm sorry for lying to you."

"I know. And I'm not doing this for you. I'm doing it for everyone else here. I don't forgive you. Not yet."

Harsh words but totally deserved, and she didn't say them with venom, but Medusa was smart enough to know that not everything could be cured with time. She had no reply, but none was needed.

Cressida yanked the harpe free, and Persephone shrieked again. The hole in her abdomen glowed white like a supernova, but Medusa didn't look away. Persephone's godly essence flooded into the air, but before it could escape, Cressida shoved at it with her hand, forcing it back inside.

Under her touch and the will of the gods, the hole closed, and Persephone sagged back into Adonis's and Narcissus's arms. She lifted one hand toward Adonis's face. "I remember you. We met once or twice." She sagged, eyes closing.

He smiled at her sadly, and the dead were gathering around their little tableau, heroes and denizens of Asphodel alike. Cressida's eyes remained closed, her lips bent in a smile.

❖

"Is she all right?" Adonis asked. "She's not moving."

"She's weak, but..." Cressida shook her head. The essences of the three gods hovered around her as Cressida leaned over Persephone's head. The wound was closed, and the other gods were trying to speak to Persephone, but she wasn't hearing them. Any moment she might get up and start fighting again, but Cressida didn't want to hurt her. Persephone had been kidnapped then abandoned, tricked and trapped. Cressida could understand why her mind might have broken, but she needed help, not punishment. There was no reason for her to die.

The other gods were trying to pull Persephone bodily to the place they'd retreated to, but her attachment to the Underworld felt as solid as stone. Cressida hadn't been able to move her, hadn't been able to compete with the belief of a god, but this was more than that.

Cressida thought along Persephone's story again, searching for answers. "When she ate the pomegranate, she was bonded to Asphodel by the Fates, so can't they let her go?"

"What are you—" Adonis said.

She waved him to be quiet, waiting for the gods to answer. They told her that the Fates weren't holding her anymore. She was holding herself. Her belief in her own prison was so strong, she wouldn't let herself be released. They said the only reason they could heal the harpe's damage was because Persephone also wanted it gone.

"When she ate the fruit of the Underworld," Cressida said slowly, "she got caught, and she's forever looping herself back to that moment, so she's trapped here."

Adonis and Narcissus glanced at each other. "Maybe if she ate some ambrosia?"

Adonis offered her some from the bag Cressida had given him, but she pushed it away. "Mother," she said. Demeter's comforting presence surrounded her, but only through Cressida. The gods were stuck where they were, too, left in the last home available to them, far even from the Isles of the Blessed, and they couldn't leave it anymore. They didn't have the power.

And Cressida couldn't give it to them. They were only speaking through her as if she was a version of the shade network, but it clearly wasn't enough. Persephone needed to go home, or she'd be stuck in this endless circle of loneliness and impotent power.

Persephone looked to Cressida with a stare so weighty it seemed to carry eternity. Cressida wanted to look away but couldn't. Her eyes were drawn to the crown of the Underworld: a tool, the gods whispered, that should have let Persephone shape the Underworld as Cressida was doing, but she'd fallen too far inside herself to really use it.

Adonis stroked her arm, tears dribbling down his cheeks. "She's caught herself here, and we're not helping. Everyone else believes she's caught, too, so she's doomed."

Persephone mumbled something about killing the ones you loved. She frowned hard before a few glowing white tears slipped down her cheeks.

Cressida shook her head. "There are rules, even when someone's doomed. The gods believe in deeds, and that means Persephone does, too. If someone makes a great enough sacrifice to free her, that should do it. She just has to be part of a different story."

June wriggled. "Cressi, what are you thinking?" More traces of Perseus left her face. "Let me up, Medusa, please!"

"A new myth," Cressida said. If June had the blood of gods inside her, that had to mean a bit of it floated in Cressida's veins. "Like, the woman who traded places with Dread Persephone?"

June's eyes widened. "No!"

"What?" Medusa asked.

Cressida bent over Persephone again. "Is that what you want?"

Persephone's mouth worked for a moment. "I want to go home, Mother." She trailed a touch as soft as flower petals down Cressida's arm. "Home in time for tea."

Like so many other women of myth, she'd been done wrong, and Cressida had the opportunity to stop it, really stop it instead of just offering revenge. Well, hadn't she been bashing heroes for their lack of nobility? This was a chance for real heroics, and if she didn't step up, she'd forever call herself a hypocrite.

June grabbed for her arm. "Stop! Medusa, stop her!"

Medusa was looking at her in horror and fascination and something that might be pride. "Are you sure about this?"

Cressida wanted to reassure them, but she didn't want Persephone to wait any longer. Her wrong could be righted so easily.

"Ye—"

The ground exploded upward, cutting off Cressida's air and her voice as she slammed into the pavement several yards away, everyone else scattered around her. The landscape twisted, making everyone cry out as buildings sprouted tentacles, and the streets became valleys of broken glass. Wild laughter echoed around them, and by the dread of the three visiting gods, Cressida knew two things: Medea had returned, and she'd brought Hecate with her.

CHAPTER SIXTEEN

As Medusa slammed into the ground, she felt she really should have seen this coming. Her team had seemed to gain the upper hand or at least stopped a big fight, and even though it sounded as if Cressida had been contemplating taking Persephone's place as dread queen of the Underworld, it sounded like they were winning. And now, before she'd even had a chance to think about the fact that Cressida was claiming godhood or that she'd be around forever or even if Medusa should encourage her to take the job or leave it, they'd all been blown up.

At least she could put off the decision a little longer.

She'd managed to keep hold of the aegis while June had fallen off the back of it. That was a checkmark on the positive side. Medusa dragged herself upright, proving she had all her limbs, and they worked. Another plus. A few yards away, Cressida was standing. Check. And she had the harpe. Check, check. Persephone didn't look to be getting up anytime soon, which could be a minus or a plus, depending on whether she turned her attention to them or if she focused on the sleek red Lamborghini Aventadore that had appeared in their midst.

No flaming chariot for Hecate. Medusa briefly wondered if she actually drove the Underworld's one car around its twisting streets or if it just appeared where she wanted it. Then all thought was driven away as Hecate stepped out in high-heeled sneakers that looked as if they'd been molded from solid gold. She wore a reimagined chiton, a one-shouldered number with an asymmetrical hem that hung past her knees on one side and stopped at mid-thigh on the other. Green silk, it fluttered behind her as she stepped forward and lifted mirrored sunglasses on top of her head, pushing back a mass of curls that fluttered through the color spectrum as she walked, matching the irises of her eyes.

Medusa was at a loss for words or anything else. If they'd met in a bar, she would have offered to buy the whole place just for the chance of a smile from that beautiful face. Hecate's figure made Medusa scroll through all her various pick-up lines and find all of them wanting. If Hecate had said, "I win this fight," Medusa feared the first words out of her own mouth would have been, "Okay."

Hecate smiled, and her eyeteeth shone like diamonds. "Looks as if I'm late to the party."

Medea swaggered to her side from the other car door, smug look firmly in place.

Hecate tsked as she surveyed the gathered people, the Elysian Fields bare for everyone to see, and Persephone laid out on the ground. "Someone's going to have a hell of a cleaning bill."

She strode toward Persephone. Medusa looked for Aix and found her hovering over her spectral daughters. Good, they were out of the way then. Medusa hurried to Cressida, ready to do whatever she wanted and was relieved to see that her mouth stayed closed this time, though Medusa didn't know how she managed it. Good that one of them had some decorum, she supposed.

"Did you finally find someone willing to give you the story you were looking for, darling?" Hecate nudged Persephone gently with one gold-plated toe. "Poor, sad, little thing."

Persephone frowned. "I didn't order this." Adonis struggled to her side and leaned over her as if to shield her. Narcissus held tightly to Adonis's shoulders as if he wanted to yank him away but couldn't move. Hecate ignored both of them.

Cressida took a step forward. "You were supposed to be her ally!"

Hecate lifted a silvery eyebrow. "I heard you kowtowed just to the image of me. Where's your worship now, mortal?"

Cressida lifted the harpe.

Hecate laughed, the sound as delightful as a tinkling bell. "Everyone's tired of having her in charge." She nodded to Persephone. "But a mortal will only take the throne...well, over my dead body."

Everyone moved at once. Medea hurled a ball of fire, but Aix shot forward and swallowed it. Cressida, lovely fool that she was, charged Hecate. Medusa, also a fool, charged with her.

Hecate turned her gaze Medusa's way. Medusa lifted the aegis, ready to channel her former power, but the street turned to gelatin, and she sank to her knees. Cressida slapped the ground, turning it back to normal. Hecate chuckled and stepped away when Cressida swung the harpe wildly; all the grace she'd shown with the Hecatonchires appeared to have vanished.

Medusa pulled herself out of the jelly and thought hard on what powers Hecate truly possessed. She could manipulate the fabric of the Underworld, but Cressida seemed to have tapped into that, too. She couldn't obliterate them, or she would have done it already, and Medusa wondered if that was why she wanted the crown of the Underworld, if her power had slipped so much that only a relic like the crown could bring it back. Hecate retained more power than the other gods because she lived smack in the middle of those who'd once worshipped her. The other gods removed themselves, and so their power waned, but Hecate seemed as vital as ever.

But appearances could be deceiving.

Medusa reached Cressida's side, and they advanced together, Medusa covering each of them with the shield.

Hecate laughed. "Come on! Think what fun it will be with magic back in the world."

"A world of Titans and gods?" Cressida asked. "No, thank you. I've read the old tales."

And if Hecate couldn't blink them out of existence, how the hell could she bring magic back to the mortal world? Did she really think ruling the Underworld would make her that powerful? It hadn't made Persephone or Hades that powerful, and it couldn't just be because Persephone was stuck as she was.

Hecate waved a hand, and the pavement erupted around them again, pulling itself into a monster of asphalt and manhole covers. Cressida fell back, Medusa with her.

"I can't hear Cronos!" Cressida said. "It's as if he doesn't want me to win."

"I guess he believes her," Medusa said.

"What the hell am I doing?" Cressida said. "I don't know how to fight like this."

June stepped up beside her, her shoulders squared. "I do." She grabbed the harpe from Cressida's hands and faced the asphalt monster. "Fight with your belief, Cressi. Let me take care of this."

Cressida eyed her warily for a moment, and Medusa made a fist, ready to punch her lights out if even a trace of Perseus shone through. June gave them a wink, and Cressida smiled. Without the need to win paradise, maybe Perseus had sunk back into her soul. But even as herself, June was still a hero. She charged the monster.

Hecate went for Persephone again. Cressida frowned, and a wall of sidewalk reared up to stop Hecate's progress. She stuttered to a halt, sighing, but before she could turn their way, the ground moved like a shaken sheet, and Cressida lashed a hand out. The pavement monster hurtled toward Hecate just after June cut a chunk out of it.

Hecate blinked out of its way, and her expression went from amused to annoyed. "Enough of this mortal bullshit. Cerberus!" The air shimmered and stretched, twisting itself into a long tunnel. Darkness reached from it, and a running shape appeared in the middle, small but growing larger by the second.

Medusa and Cressida dove to the side as Cerberus rocketed from the tunnel, his three heads slavering. "I didn't know she could summon Cerberus!" Cressida called.

"Me neither!" Medusa said.

Hecate laughed at them. "Dogs are part of my portfolio, darling. How did you think you got past him in the first place? Did you think you were just lucky? I've been waiting for a plucky mortal or a returning hero for a long time, but if you're not going to kill Persephone, you've outlived your usefulness. Now, Cerberus, my pet, do your duty and return this annoying mortal to the land of the living."

Cerberus darted forward, and Medusa lifted the aegis, but he closed his six eyes; he didn't need them to find his way around when he had three noses. He reached for Cressida with one mouth, but she ducked. Another head dipped for her, and Medusa batted it away with the aegis, but that left one more, and there was nothing to stop his jaws from closing over Cressida's body.

June leapt in front of her, uttering a war cry she probably hadn't used since her days as Perseus. Cerberus's mouth closed around her, but he didn't clamp down, and Medusa nearly cried out in relief that Cerberus was always a good one for following orders: Hecate had instructed him to *return* a mortal to the living world. Once he had June in his teeth, he disappeared, and the harpe clattered to the ground.

❖

Cressida cried out as June disappeared, worry for her aunt warring with pride and love, though she'd noticed that Cerberus hadn't bitten June in half. June had won in the struggle between who she'd been and who she was, but Cressida had always known June would be victorious, or that's what she'd tell her aunt if they ever saw each other again.

Which wouldn't be anytime soon if Hecate had her way. Cressida's power of belief couldn't rival Hecate's. Every change she made was unmade or redone in moments. Even with the help of the three spectral gods, Cressida wasn't as powerful. Persephone probably was, but she seemed content to lie in the street and mope. Her belief that she was stuck as she was had no doubt prevented Hecate from removing her before. And maybe Hecate volunteering to be the new dread queen wasn't a story Persephone could accept. Since it would have stuck Hecate in Asphodel, Hecate probably couldn't accept it either.

"This is impossible!" Medusa yelled as the street turned to butter.

Cressida agreed as Hecate laughed. She couldn't help feeling that the goddess was toying with them. As Cressida wasn't really part of the Underworld, Hecate didn't seem able to shift her, but Cressida felt a tingle as if Hecate was trying to move Medusa elsewhere, and only Cressida's need was keeping her there. Cressida hoped the rest of their allies stayed out of the fight, or Hecate would just believe them somewhere else, and there they'd go. Maybe they knew that. Or maybe they were smarter than her and had decided not to get involved.

She picked up the harpe again, but Cronos stayed silent, though she could feel his frustration. He wanted out, but he also really wanted to tell her where to slash. And even though Medusa wielded the power of the aegis, Hecate simply lowered her mirrored shades, and their reflective surface turned one hapless bystander to stone.

This is stupid, this is stupid, her brain repeated. How did heroes manage this? Maybe they had more faith in their swords than she did. She was pretty sure Hecate could keep her busy forever. Maybe she was drawing this conflict out because she had nothing better to do. Maybe it was another way to alleviate her boredom.

That made Cressida angrier than anything else. When a wall of cacti sprang up in front of her, she set it on fire.

"When I say," Medusa said, "run around the—"

"No!" Cressida nearly threw the harpe to the ground. "This is idiotic. I can't out-magic her, and you don't do the whole swords and shield thing."

"Giving up already?" Hecate called. "Everyone will be so disappointed."

Cressida resisted the urge to chuck the harpe at her, but then her words sank in. "Everyone, now there's an idea." There had to be some people who didn't want Hecate in charge of the Underworld and who also didn't want Persephone to die. Someone had to believe that she *couldn't* do what she promised, especially when Cressida had done more for the regular folk of the Underworld lately than any of their gods. Cressida looked at Persephone, who tapped the side of her head, just under the crown. Cressida didn't know if it was a random movement or a hint, but she knew what she had to do.

She sent a wave of glass at Hecate. "We need your sisters to tap into the shade network. Let's battle belief with belief."

Medusa grinned wickedly. "Don't die while I'm gone." She pushed the aegis into Cressida's hands. "Be careful where you aim this."

Oh yes, easy, not a tall order at all. Cressida faced Hecate again. She'd turned the glass into a shower of rose petals and watched the retreat of Medusa with a quirked eyebrow. Cressida brought the aegis up and tried to look as fierce as her aunt but couldn't help feeling like a child playing dress-up.

"So, now your friends and your aunt have abandoned you," Hecate said.

"My aunt will be safe in the living world."

"Leaving you all alone with me." She smiled brightly. "There's no reason we can't be friends. You opened the gates to paradise, but if no one remembers you when you die, it won't matter. I can remember you. I can keep you from becoming a shade. Worship me, and the rewards will be great."

"And all I have to do is kill Persephone?"

"She's weak, but she's still stubborn. It'll be easy for you, difficult for me. How's that for a start to your new life, a god owing you a favor?"

And it was tempting. Guaranteed power versus the slim chance of winning. She'd always imagined herself being one of the people who took the money on a game show rather than the ones who gave it all up for what was behind the mystery door.

But not for the price of murder. Everything seemed to come back to that here.

"Sorry," Cressida said, "I won't kill her for you. But if you want to leave now, no hard feelings."

Hecate laughed and lifted a hand then stopped, frowning. Cressida felt the air coalesce around her as if holding her tight. The shade fog drifted closer, and Cressida felt the landscape solidifying as Medusa's sisters spread the word through the Underworld that the mortal who'd allowed them into paradise needed their help. Cressida couldn't manage it alone, but the collective belief of the Underworld descended on Hecate and held her in place.

Many wills surrounded them, including the heroes from the Elysian Fields. Even if they didn't like defying the gods, they always seemed to appreciate moxie.

Hecate was held fast, and Cressida could feel Cronos stirring, mumbling that now would be a good time to strike. Seemed he couldn't ignore a helpless victim. The heroes around Cressida called to her to plunge the harpe into Hecate's chest, but Cressida hesitated. She'd never killed anyone; she didn't want to start with a god. If she was going to take Persephone's place she didn't want to start her reign with murder, no matter who thought it was justified.

She reached instead for the home of the gods. If the time hadn't been right for a full *deus ex machina* before, it was now. She willed them to police their own, and their essences responded to her call, surrounding Hecate, though they were still arguing: some saying they should let Hecate go, while others said she should be sentenced to join them where they'd fled.

"No!" Hecate screamed. "I can bring magic back. I can bring you back to life!"

They wanted to rejoice, but Athena, Demeter, and Hermes added their doubts. If she could do that, why had she never done it? What would the crown of the Underworld give her that she didn't have?

The gods looked into Hecate's mind, towing Cressida along with them. They wanted to see if there was any hope, and with the belief of the Underworld holding her still, they could manage.

They found nothing but lies, all lies, just like most things in the Underworld.

Hecate snarled. "Curse you all, listen to me! I don't know what the crown can do for us until I have it. It's worth a try!"

But inside her head, the gods discovered that she didn't really believe it was possible. And belief was everything here.

The anger of the gods burned like a white hot flame. Even Hades joined their cries of outrage, and killing his wife had been his idea. Hecate tried to use her belief to stay where she was, but she wasn't trapped like Persephone. She knew she could be moved; she just didn't want to go. Cressida felt her force of will clawing to stay put, but all the minds of the Underworld were against her now. Someone took Cressida's hand. Medusa. Her eyes were closed as if she was using every ounce of will. Her sisters stood behind her, and they marshalled the belief of the shades.

Slowly, the fog descended around Hecate until she was lost to view, and Cressida felt her shift to the place of the gods, a place they could never leave. She cried out one final time before she disappeared forever.

The power of the gods began to withdraw, but Cressida said, "Wait." She looked to Medusa, who opened her eyes, their gazes locking.

Medusa's head tilted, and her smile was soft and sweet, a little sad. "You did it."

"No one deserves to suffer forever."

Medusa frowned as if she didn't understand. Her gaze shifted to Persephone, but Cressida wasn't thinking of anyone but Medusa. Her belief in Cressida was so bright, Cressida could almost see it in the air.

Cressida tapped into the power of the gods and stretched it across the whole of the Underworld, through the shade fog, separating the shades into the people they used to be, the people they could be again. When she touched Stheno and Euryale, she flooded them with belief, with the certainty that their family could be happy if it were whole.

The shade fog glowed as it mingled with the artificial sunlight of the Elysian Fields. Shades dropped from it like rain, turning solid as their feet touched the ground, and they became men, women, and children, mostly human with a few other species mixed in. They ran to and fro, hugging each other, calling out for those they'd lost, and their cries spread through the Underworld for loved ones to come and find them, whole generations of the forgotten reunited.

"Medusa!" someone called.

Medusa stiffened, and Cressida glanced past her to see her sisters returned to their human forms, peering around, clasping their arms around each other and hugging their mother.

"Stheno?" Medusa whispered, but she didn't turn. "Euryale?"

"They're right there," Cressida said.

Medusa shook her head wildly. Tears trickled down her cheeks, and she shuddered as if holding back sobs. "I can't look. They're not real."

"Go on," Cressida said.

"I...can't. They'll disappear or..." Her breath shuddered in and out as she met Cressida's gaze. "You couldn't have done this! Why did you do this? No one ever does anything just because they're nice!"

Cressida kissed her cheek. "Moron. Go hug them already."

With a sob, Medusa whirled around as her sisters reached for her. They fumbled their way into one another's arms, weeping.

"Stop crying!" Stheno said. "If you don't stop, I can't stop!"

"I can cry if I want!" Medusa said.

"I hate crying in front of people."

"It's a moment. Just enjoy it!"

Euryale shook them both gently. "Both of you shut up." She pulled them closer, arms across their shoulders, a move that seemed as if it could easily turn into a headlock. "Mom! Mom! Come on!"

Aix hovered over them, purring, and Cressida could feel their joy shining brighter than the sun in the Elysian Fields, brighter even than the gentle warmth floating from the Isles of the Blessed.

Now there was only one thing left to do. As she strode toward Persephone, everyone she met asked if she was sure. Adonis and Agamemnon, Pandora, Arachne, and Narcissus. She felt Medusa's gaze. She could almost hear what her parents and June would say. She could leave the Underworld now. She'd done enough. The gates were down. The shades were people again. Hecate was gone. All that was left was poor lonely Persephone, but Cressida didn't owe her anything. They weren't friends. If she left, maybe Persephone would tear herself apart at the seams, and everything would slowly fade again, back to the way it was, and everyone in the Underworld could return to their static states and find whatever comfort they could wherever they could.

And she would go back to being a grad student and wonder what might have been.

She knelt at Persephone's side and wondered how hard this would be, what grand words she'd have to use, what rituals she'd have to perform.

"Can I see the ambrosia?" she asked.

Narcissus pressed it into her hands without a word, and she knew he was anxious for Persephone to be gone.

"Go on, then," she said to Persephone, "go and find your mom. I'll take your place." She dipped a finger into the bag and licked it. Warm honey coated her tongue before an alcohol-like burn tore down her throat. She tried not to cough, but it came out in huge, undignified gasps. She hope they left that part out of the official story.

Adonis grimaced. "You're not supposed to have it straight," he whispered.

She kept coughing, wishing someone had mentioned that.

With a sigh and a smile, Persephone faded like the afterimage of a really bright light. She'd been holding on for so long. One little push was all she'd been waiting for. As her presence withdrew, taking

Cressida's three helper gods with it, a tingle built around Cressida's forehead, but she didn't have to lift a hand to know she'd just been crowned dread queen of the Underworld.

Still sputtering and coughing, she turned to face the assembled masses, some of whom were staring at her expectantly. Most were ignoring her as they sought out loved ones and friends. A few were fighting, and she supposed that was to be expected.

Medusa took a step toward her. "Cressida, are you all right?"

Truthfully, she didn't feel that much different. "Party at the palace?"

EPILOGUE

Medusa had long ago given up on, "Sometimes, things just work out." She hadn't really believed it when she was alive, either when she was ruling cities and terrifying the populace or when she was retired. It seemed even less true after she'd been murdered and not at all true when she'd known she'd be spending eternity dead.

Now though, she had her sisters and her mother. She'd visited the Elysian Fields a few times and the Isles of the Blessed once. She'd punched the hero Jason right in the face, never mind that she was no longer on good terms with Medea, who'd been keeping a low profile without her mother's power to back her up.

It was a good time, and it looked to be a good eternity, but for one thing.

"Go and talk to her," Stheno said.

Medusa stared out her apartment windows at an Underworld still celebrating its freedom. Fireworks occasionally boomed in a sky that now looked distinctly sunnier. "I've tried! She keeps putting me off. First she was touring the Underworld, and then speaking with her aunt via the hierophant, and then she was doing every other goddamn thing. She doesn't want to see me."

"So, park yourself outside of the palace until she lets you in," Euryale said as she packed boxes in the kitchen. They were moving into one of the warehouses so Aix could live with them. "Serenade her under her window. You have to pull out all the stops."

Medusa rested her chin in one hand. "She says she needs time."

Stheno folded a sweater and packed it away. "Time and *effort*. If you just sit around waiting, she'll think you don't care."

"What do you know?"

They kept pestering, saying she needed to send gifts and notes and songs she'd written with her own tuneless hands. They talked about poetry and sacrifice and deeds done in Cressida's name. But this wasn't a foot put wrong or a word out of place; there was broken trust between them. Was there enough chocolate in the whole of the Underworld to mend such a gap?

And Cressida didn't need Medusa's help with anything. She could do whatever she liked with her powers. Medusa didn't have anything to offer her.

When her sisters kept badgering her, she left and tried to tell herself she was picking random directions and wandering aimlessly, but as they always did, her steps took her through the open gates of the Terrace and all the way to the palace. She found Agamemnon on guard duty, captain of the guard, really, and he blocked her way as he had before.

"She's busy," he said.

Medusa sighed. "Or that's what she told you if I came around?"

He had the grace to duck his head and clear his throat as she started to turn away. "But someone else has been waiting for you." He nodded down the wall. She frowned but started that direction, and he grabbed her arm. "But if she tells you to go, you go."

"Okay," she muttered, not having any idea who he was talking about. She went in the indicated direction and found Arachne leaning against the wall.

"Finally!" Arachne said. "I thought you'd given up!"

"What's going on?"

"Up and over, like before." She winked. "We've got it all figured out. You surprise her, say something witty, she falls into your arms, and neither of you moon around anymore!"

"Who's we?" She paused. "She's been mooning over me?"

Arachne rolled her eyes. "By we, I mean all us hopeless romantics." She winked again before her face went serious. "But if she tells you to go, you go."

"Yeah, I heard that from Agamemnon. I'm guessing you're talking about Cressida?"

"Who else?"

Medusa sighed and supposed it was worth a shot. "She's going to tell me to go from the start."

"Not if you talk fast enough."

Great. Arachne slung them up and over the wall, telling her to meet Pandora near the entrance to the garden, and Medusa did so.

"Wait right here," Pandora said, "and remember—"

"Yeah, yeah. I go if she tells me to go."

Pandora blinked. "I was going to say, remember to believe in yourself." After a shrug, she ran into the palace.

Cressida emerged a few moments later and stuttered to a halt when she saw Medusa. She was dressed in a different T-shirt and jeans, and now the crown of the Underworld circled her brow. For Persephone it had appeared as glowing embers, but on Cressida it was a silver circlet with one shining ruby in the center. "Pandora said it was an emergency."

"It is," Medusa said quickly. "Well, it kind of is." Her heart was hammering, and she was amazed a human could make her feel this way after so long, like the younger one in the relationship with less experience to draw on. "I…wanted to see you."

Cressida smiled kindly, but it had a removed, talking-to-the-peasants air. "I'm sorry. I've been busy."

"Right."

"So?"

"Ah." And even though she knew she had to talk quickly, all the words left her. What could she offer the queen of the Underworld, who had all the famous figures of Greek history and myth awaiting her every call? She blurted the first thing that came to mind: "I was wondering if you wanted a ride on my giant snake sometime."

Cressida's mouth twitched as if she was trying to keep that kindly smile in place, but then her lips wobbled, and she sputtered a laugh before getting herself under control. "I bet you say that to all the girls."

Medusa grinned. "Not anymore. Now it's just you."

Cressida's head tilted. "You want me to forgive you."

"No," Medusa said, and she was surprised to find she meant it. "I don't deserve forgiveness. What I'd like to do is start over, if you want. I'll prove myself so that one day, the good memories will outweigh the bad."

Cressida shoulders sagged, and she looked across the ground as if weighing her options. "Are you offering to quest for my favor?"

Medusa grinned. "If that's what you want."

"Well, that and the giant snake rides."

Medusa laughed softly and stepped forward, daring to take Cressida's hands. "I will be whatever you want me to be. And if you need someone to watch me, then have someone watch me. I will take every test you require."

"I have lots of helpers."

"Are any of them falling in love with you?"

Cressida breathed deeply, and her eyes drilled into Medusa's. "I don't think so, and I don't miss any of them like I miss you." Medusa moved forward to kiss her, but Cressida pressed a finger between their lips. "Trust has to be rebuilt, proven, you said so yourself."

And Medusa agreed, but she couldn't say it again, not with Cressida standing so close. "Well, I'm happy to prove that I'm still a good kisser."

❖

Cressida smiled and let her gaze linger on Medusa's lips. "Maybe just a little one. A promise of the future?" She dropped her hand.

Medusa moved so swiftly, Cressida nearly drew back, but Medusa grabbed her by the waist and pulled her close in a rush that left her breathless. That was okay; there wasn't really time to breathe as Medusa claimed her lips.

Cressida couldn't help leaning in and opening her mouth, matching Medusa's passion with her own, their lips pressing together so hard, she felt a few teeth. Cressida's hands wandered without telling her until she grabbed Medusa's ass as Medusa had once grabbed hers and was rewarded with a moan that made her knees weak.

She wanted to make a joke about how this wasn't exactly a little kiss, but her pent up desire had rolled a sheet over the rest of her brain, putting it to sleep. All she could think at that moment was that there were too many clothes between them.

Cressida stumbled to the side, taking Medusa with her into the bushes. They rolled on the grass, and Cressida tried to tug Medusa's shirt upward, but it got caught on a stray branch.

"Here, here," Medusa said, trying to pull it off.

Cressida concentrated, and the clothes between them vanished, as did the harpy who took that moment to call, "Get a room!"

Medusa laughed, but Cressida couldn't focus on anything but Medusa's skin. She tongued the line of Medusa's collarbone and the hollow between her breasts. Medusa's hands tangled in her hair, skating over the crown of the Underworld, but she couldn't take that off, ever. As Medusa brought Cressida's head up and kissed her, it seemed she didn't mind.

After their hair snagged in the bushes several times, and a rogue twig poked Medusa in the eye, Cressida took the harpy's advice and moved them into the palace, into the enormous bedroom she'd taken as her own. To her credit, Medusa didn't gawk as much as Cressida would have in her place. In fact, it wasn't long before Medusa had their lovemaking as well in hand as she seemed to have everything else. Her natural confidence always allowed her to adapt, it seemed, a trait Cressida would have envied if she'd had time to think beyond the pleasure cascading through her or the supple sweetness of Medusa's body. It wasn't long before Cressida was pulling at the sheets and moaning at the things Medusa could do with her fingers or tongue, all the clever places she found to kiss or stroke. She made all of Cressida's former lovers seem like the dead ones. Cressida might have felt a little embarrassed by her own efforts if she wasn't so lost in acres of pleasure.

"Enough," Cressida finally said. "I can't take it anymore. I love it, but I...just...can't."

"We stopped touching each other two minutes ago," Medusa said from beside her.

"Oh." The aftershocks were still fading. She was happy to see that Medusa looked a bit satisfied, too, though she didn't know if Medusa was as overcome with the urge to turn into a puddle. Why had she kept this fabulous woman away for so long?

The lies. Right. The calculating part of her wondered if she should get really angry again just so Medusa would have to make it up to her like this. Or maybe she was always so passionate. If Cressida let her stay, maybe they could have this sort of sex all the time.

I'll die. But what a way to go.

And now that the rest of her brain could function, it couldn't get off the past. Passion had carried her through—she paused, trying to count the orgasms and failing. Passion had carried her through a really, really good time, but there had to be more than passion between them if they were going to have a relationship.

To Hades with relationships. Think of the sex, woman!

"You're frowning," Medusa said. "Is it because of me?"

"If you're so good at reading people, how did you not know how shitty it was to lie to me?"

Medusa sighed. "I'll explain myself again if you want. I'll apologize forever. If you want to yell at me, I can take it, but I won't argue with you, Cressida. I know what I did was wrong."

They'd had plenty of arguments in Cressida's head the past few…weeks, she supposed she could call them. As she'd traveled the Underworld fixing it up, she'd spoken to Medusa many times in her head. And they'd ended up in bed in a few of those fantasies, and Cressida had ended up punching Medusa in a few of them, too.

But she didn't really want to hurt Medusa, not like that. What she wanted was to go back, to remake their relationship, but her power couldn't do that. And that would mean changing Medusa on some fundamental level anyway, and she didn't want that, either. That was a slippery slope even Persephone had never undertaken.

She'd thought a lot about how she might punish Medusa as she freed the prisoners in Tartarus. She'd told them to behave, or she'd lock them up again. Most of the Titans had stayed down below, taking over the place as their own. Cronos had given her a few looks as if thinking to challenge her, but she reminded him that she didn't need his sword. She could close Tartarus with her mind, imprisoning him there again. She'd kept the sword anyway, just in case, as a reminder about using caution when it came to trusting people.

June and Nero had talked with her about it after June had gotten over the initial shock that her niece had become queen of the

Underworld. There were already plans for everyone to visit during Christmas, though Cressida didn't envy June that talk with Cressida's parents. At least Nero could still feel her lifeline and could always reassure her family that she was all right. Nero had said to forgive Medusa; June had warned her to be cautious, but Cressida anticipated that. June probably wasn't looking forward to sharing a holiday table with the woman she'd killed in a former life. Talk about an awkward dinner party.

Cressida had ended up talking about her problems with Medusa to anyone who would listen, and the romantics usually said to go for it, and everyone else either shrugged or said it had to be her decision. Pandora had added, "Eternity is a long time to be lonely."

"Do you want me to go?" Medusa asked.

"No, and I think I should be mad at myself for that."

"Because you think I'll betray you?"

"Because now that you have your sisters back, I'll never know."

Medusa winced, but Cressida couldn't be sorry.

"I want to be happy," Cressida said. "This isn't what I imagined for my life, but for the most part..." She grinned. "It's been pretty awesome. But the idea of spending eternity alone—"

This time, Medusa put a finger to Cressida's lips. "Don't think in eternity. You might get tired of me after you've worn me out for a few centuries."

Cressida smiled. She took the finger between her teeth and gave it a lick before letting go. "Will I just stay alive down here forever? Or will I die and then pop right back up again?"

Medusa shrugged. "You're unprecedented." She traced the crown. "But I don't think this will just let you die, and neither will I, Cressida. If you need more time to think, I can suffer through your absence. Only just," she added when Cressida frowned. "And if you can stand my presence, whatever you want to give me, friendship or love, it will be enough. I will always come when you need me, and I will always be there for you, I swear by the River S—"

Cressida clapped a hand over Medusa's mouth. Her heart raced in her ears. "Don't say that. Something might prevent you from being there or coming when I need you, and you'd still suffer the consequences of that swear." She dropped her hand. "But I love that you were willing to try." She had a few tears hovering as she kissed Medusa deeply, and if there wasn't exactly forgiveness behind it, there was the start of a road.

When they came up for air, Cressida stretched and discovered she wasn't quite as melty as she'd thought. "Now that we've got a room, we might as well make the most of it."

Medusa grinned. "Sure you're done talking? I'm quite knowledgeable on a variety of subjects if you'd—"

"Shut up and kiss me."

Medusa nibbled her earlobe. "What happened to that harpy, anyway?"

"Is that shutting up and kissing me? I don't think so."

"Your will, Dread Cressida."

As Medusa kissed her, Cressida responded with all the passion she could muster, forcing her brain to stay on task and focus on something that mattered.

Really, really good sex.

With the one person in the Underworld she cared for more than any other.

It was a start.

About the Author

Barbara Ann Wright writes fantasy and science fiction novels and short stories when not ranting on her blog. *The Pyramid Waltz* was one of Tor.com's Reviewer's Choice books of 2012, was a *Foreword Review* Book of the Year Award Finalist, a Goldie finalist, and made Book Riot's 100 Must-Read Sci-Fi Fantasy Novels by Female Authors. It also won the 2013 Rainbow Award for Best Lesbian Fantasy. *A Kingdom Lost* was a Goldie finalist and won the 2014 Rainbow Award for Best Lesbian Fantasy Romance.

Books Available from Bold Strokes Books

Basic Training of the Heart by Jaycie Morrison. In 1944, socialite Elizabeth Carlton joins the Women's Army Corps to escape family expectations and love's disappointments. Can Sergeant Gale Rains get her through Basic Training with their hearts intact? (978-1-62639-818-4)

Before by KE Payne. When Tally falls in love with her band's new recruit, she has a tough decision to make. What does she want more—Alex or the band? (978-1-62639-677-7)

Believing in Blue by Maggie Morton. Growing up gay in a small town has been hard, but it can't compare to the next challenge Wren—with her new, sky-blue wings—faces: saving two entire worlds. (978-1-62639-691-3)

Coils by Barbara Ann Wright. A modern young woman follows her aunt into the Greek Underworld and makes a pact with Medusa to win her freedom by killing a hero of legend. (978-1-62639-598-5)

Courting the Countess by Jenny Frame. When relationship-phobic Lady Henrietta Knight starts to care about housekeeper Annie Brannigan and her daughter, can she overcome her fears and promise Annie the forever that she demands? (978-1-62639-785-9)

Dapper by Jenny Frame. Amelia Honey meets the mysterious Byron De Brek and is faced with her darkest fantasies, but will her strict moral upbringing stop her from exploring what she truly wants? (978-1-62639-898-6E)

Delayed Gratification: The Honeymoon by Meghan O'Brien. A dream European honeymoon turns into a winter storm nightmare involving a delayed flight, a ditched rental car, and eventually, a surprisingly happy ending. (978-1-62639-766-8E)

For Money or Love by Heather Blackmore. Jessica Spaulding must choose between ignoring the truth to keep everything she has, and doing the right thing only to lose it all—including the woman she loves. (978-1-62639-756-9)

Hooked by Jaime Maddox. With the help of sexy Detective Mac Calabrese, Dr. Jessica Benson is working hard to overcome her past, but they may not be enough to stop a murderer. (978-1-62639-689-0)

Lands End by Jackie D. Public relations superstar Amy Kline is dealing with a media nightmare, and the last thing she expects is for restaurateur Lena Michaels to change everything, but she will. (978-1-62639-739-2)

Lysistrata Cove by Dena Hankins. Jack and Eve navigate the maelstrom of their darkest desires and find love by transgressing gender, dominance, submission, and the law on the crystal blue Caribbean Sea. (978-1-62639-821-4)

Twisted Screams by Sheri Lewis Wohl. Reluctant psychic Lorna Dutton doesn't want to forgive, but if she doesn't do just that an innocent woman will die. (978-1-62639-647-0)

A Class Act by Tammy Hayes. Buttoned-up college professor Dr. Margaret Parks doesn't know what she's getting herself into when she agrees to one date with her student, Rory Morgan, who is 15 years her junior. (978-1-62639-701-9)

Bitter Root by Laydin Michaels. Small town chef Adi Bergeron is hiding something, and Griffith McNaulty is going to find out what it is even if it gets her killed. (978-1-62639-656-2)

Capturing Forever by Erin Dutton. When family pulls Jacqueline and Casey back together, will the lessons learned in eight years apart be enough to mend the mistakes of the past? (978-1-62639-631-9)

Deception by VK Powell. DEA Agent Colby Vincent and Attorney Adena Weber are embroiled in a drug investigation involving homeless veterans and an attraction that could destroy them both. (978-1-62639-596-1)

Dyre: A Knight of Spirit and Shadows by Rachel E. Bailey. With the abduction of her queen, werewolf-bodyguard Des must follow the kidnappers' trail to Europe, where her queen—and a battle unlike any Des has ever waged—awaits her. (978-1-62639-664-7)

First Position by Melissa Brayden. Love and rivalry take center stage for Anastasia Mikhelson and Natalie Frederico in one of the most prestigious ballet companies in the nation. (978-1-62639-602-9)

Best Laid Plans by Jan Gayle. Nicky and Lauren are meant for each other, but Nicky's haunting past and Lauren's societal fears threaten to derail all possibilities of a relationship. (987-1-62639-658-6)

Exchange by CF Frizzell. When Shay Maguire rode into rural Montana, she never expected to meet the woman of her dreams—or to learn Mel Baker was held hostage by legal agreement to her right-wing father. (987-1-62639-679-1)

Just Enough Light by AJ Quinn. Will a serial killer's return to Colorado destroy Kellen Ryan and Dana Kingston's chance at love, or can the search-and-rescue team save themselves? (987-1-62639-685-2)

Rise of the Rain Queen by Fiona Zedde. Nyandoro is nobody's princess. She fights, curses, fornicates, and gets into as much trouble as her brothers. But the path to a throne is not always the one we expect. (987-1-62639-592-3)

Tales from Sea Glass Inn by Karis Walsh. Over the course of a year at Cannon Beach, tourists and locals alike find solace and passion at the Sea Glass Inn. (987-1-62639-643-2)

The Color of Love by Radclyffe. Black sheep Derian Winfield needs to convince literary agent Emily May to marry her to save the Winfield Agency and solve Emily's green card problem, but Derian didn't count on falling in love. (987-1-62639-716-3)

A Reluctant Enterprise by Gun Brooke. When two women grow up learning nothing but distrust, unworthiness, and abandonment, it's no wonder they are apprehensive and fearful when an overwhelming love just won't be denied. (978-1-62639-500-8)

Above the Law by Carsen Taite. Love is the last thing on Agent Dale Nelson's mind, but reporter Lindsey Ryan's investigation could change the way she sees everything—her career, her past, and her future. (978-1-62639-558-9)

Actual Stop by Kara A. McLeod. When Special Agent Ryan O'Connor's present collides abruptly with her past, shots are fired, and the course of her life is irrevocably altered. (978-1-62639-675-3)

Embracing the Dawn by Jeannie Levig. When ex-con Jinx Tanner and business executive E. J. Bastien awaken after a one-night stand to find their lives inextricably entangled, love has its work cut out for it. (978-1-62639-576-3)

Jane's World: The Case of the Mail Order Bride by Paige Braddock. Jane's PayBuddy account gets hacked and she inadvertently purchases a mail order bride from the Eastern Bloc. (978-1-62639-494-0)

Love's Redemption by Donna K. Ford. For ex-convict Rhea Daniels and ex-priest Morgan Scott, redemption lies in the thin line between right and wrong. (978-1-62639-673-9)

The Shewstone by Jane Fletcher. The prophetic Shewstone is in Eawynn's care, but unfortunately for her, Matt is coming to steal it. (978-1-62639-554-1)

A Touch of Temptation by Julie Blair. Recent law school graduate Kate Dawson's ordained path to the perfect life gets thrown off course when handsome butch top Chris Brent initiates her to sexual pleasure. (978-1-62639-488-9)

Beneath the Waves by Ali Vali. Kai Merlin and Vivien Palmer love the water and the secrets trapped in the depths, but if Kai gives in to her feelings, it might come at a cost to her entire realm. (978-1-62639-609-8)

Girls on Campus edited by Sandy Lowe and Stacia Seaman. College: four years when rules are made to be broken. This collection is required reading for anyone looking to earn an A in sex ed. (978-1-62639-733-0)

Heart of the Pack by Jenny Frame. Human Selena Miller falls for the domineering Caden Wolfgang, but will their love survive Selena learning the Wolfgangs are werewolves? (978-1-62639-566-4)

Miss Match by Fiona Riley. Matchmaker Samantha Monteiro makes the impossible possible for everyone but herself. Is mysterious dancer Lucinda Moss her own perfect match? (978-1-62639-574-9)

Paladins of the Storm Lord by Barbara Ann Wright. Lieutenant Cordelia Ross must choose between duty and honor when a man with godlike powers forces her soldiers to provoke an alien threat. (978-1-62639-604-3)